THE HORROR HALL OF FAME

THE HORROR
HALL OF FAME

EDITED BY

Robert Silverberg AND
Martin H. Greenberg

Carroll & Graf Publishers, Inc.
New York

First Carroll & Graf edition 1991

Carroll & Graf Publishers, Inc.
260 Fifth Avenue
New York, NY 10001

Library of Congress Cataloging-in-Publication Data

The Horror hall of fame / edited by Robert Silverberg
    and Martin H. Greenberg. — 1st Carroll & Graf ed.
        p.   cm.
    ISBN 0-88184-692-9
    1. Horror tales, American. 2. Horror tales, English.
I. Silverberg, Robert. II. Greenberg, Martin Harry.
PS 648.H6H66   1991
813'.0873808—dc20   91-12569
                                                        CIP

Manufactured in the United States of America

Contents

6   Contents

Acknowledgments

For permission to reprint the stories in this anthology, grateful acknowledgment is made to:

"The Willows" by Algernon Blackwood—appears by arrangement with A. P. Watt, Ltd., London.

"Yours Truly, Jack the Ripper" by Robert Bloch—Copyright 1943 by Weird Tales, Inc.; copyright renewed © 1971 by Robert Bloch. Reprinted by permission of the Scott Meredith Literary Agency, Inc., 845 Third Avenue, New York, NY 10022.

"The Small Assassin" by Ray Bradbury—Copyright 1946 by Popular Publications, Inc.; copyright renewed © 1973 by Ray Bradbury. Reprinted by permission of Don Congdon Associates, Inc.

"Calling Card" by Ramsey Campbell—Copyright © 1981 by Ramsey Campbell. Reprinted by permission of Kirby McCauley, Ltd.

"The Whimper of Whipped Dogs" by Harlan Ellison—Copyright © 1973 by Harlan Ellison; and appears in the Author's collection *Deathbird Stories*. Reprinted by arrangement with, and permission of, the Author and the Author's agent, Richard Curtis Associates, Inc., New York. All rights reserved.

"Coin of the Realm" by Charles L. Grant—Copyright © 1981 by Charles L. Grant. First appeared in *Tales from the Darkside*, published by Arkham House. Reprinted by permission of the Author.

8   Acknowledgments

"Pigeons from Hell" by Robert E. Howard—Copyright 1938 by Weird Tales, Inc. for *Weird Tales,* May, 1938; copyright renewed © 1966 by Mrs. P. M. Kuykendall. Reprinted by permission of Glenn Lord.

"The Reach" by Stephen King—Copyright © 1981 by Stephen King (as "Do the Dead Sing?"). First appeared in *Yankee* magazine. Reprinted by permission of the Author, Arthur Greene, and New American Library. All rights reserved.

"The Graveyard Rats" by Henry Kuttner—Copyright 1936 by Weird Tales, Inc.; copyright renewed © 1964 by the Estate of Henry Kuttner. Reprinted by permission of Don Congdon Associates, Inc.

"Smoke Ghost" by Fritz Leiber—Copyright 1941 by Street and Smith Publications, Inc.; copyright renewed © 1969 by Fritz Leiber. Reprinted by permission of Richard Curtis Associates, Inc., New York.

"It" by Theodore Sturgeon—Copyright 1940 by Street and Smith Publications, Inc.; copyright renewed © 1968 by Theodore Sturgeon. Reprinted by permission of Kirby McCauley, Ltd.

Introduction

In 1967, Random House published Ira Levin's second novel, *Rosemary's Baby*. The theme of the novel was not particularly original: a modern young woman discovers that she has become the mother of the anti-Christ. Nevertheless, the book became a runaway best-seller, and its popularity increased with a scrupulous film adaptation by Roman Polanski the following year.

Like the innocent Rosemary Woodhouse, Levin and his readers could not appreciate at the time what they had just given birth to. In the wake of Levin's achievement, an increasing number of authors began producing books with horror themes. The modest success of Thomas Tryon's *The Other* and Richard Matheson's *Hell House* in 1971 helped pave the way for the cultural phenomenon of William Peter Blatty's *The Exorcist*. Three years later, the publication of Stephen King's novel *Carrie* officially inaugurated the modern horror explosion.

Almost twenty-five years after Ira Levin made horror fiction palatable for general tastes, one can walk into the local bookstore and choose from entire walls of horror titles or, in some cases, sift the most recent horror releases from the mainstream fiction racks. It is the rare week that one, or sometimes as many as two or three horror novels do not claim prominent positions on the hardcover and paperback best-seller lists. It's not always easy to recognize a horror book by its cover, since horror elements have managed to creep into mysteries, thrillers, science fiction, and just about every other popular fiction genre. But that doesn't stop read-

ers and critics alike from drawing attention to horror's perva-
siveness. Indeed, when mainstream writers like Joyce Carol
Oates, Marianne Wiggins, John Updike, and Brett Easton El-
lis incorporate elements of the gruesome and grotesque into
their fiction, it commands front-page book reviews and critical discussion of the cross-pollination between popular fiction
and literature.

It would take a room full of psychologists, sociologists, and
anthropologists to come up with a reasonable explanation
why so late in the twentieth century horror has become an
inextricable component of the popular mind-set and produced
in Stephen King one of the best-selling authors of all time.
Certainly a number of critics, both literary and social, have
put forth theories, but no matter how perceptive or inept
their conclusions, all fall short of the mark in their inability
to answer the same basic questions that were asked when
Gothic fiction enjoyed its heyday over two hundred years ago:
Why do we read horror fiction? Why do we find pleasure in a
literature consciously designed to upset us? How can we rec-
oncile with our supposedly rational faculties our delight in
being scared?

There are no simple answers to these questions, and if
there were, we probably wouldn't read horror fiction. For a
start, though, the curious reader could turn to the stories
collected in *The Horror Hall of Fame*. These eighteen tales of
horror, chosen by readers and writers of horror fiction, are
considered landmarks of their kind. They describe a tradition
of literary excellence that extends beyond the 138-year interval separating the oldest from the most recent and give a
good idea of why horror has become an enduring and popular
form of fiction.

The idea for *The Horror Hall of Fame* was first proposed at
the 1981 World Fantasy Convention, an annual gathering of
professionals and amateurs in the horror and fantasy fields to
discuss issues important to the genres and give awards for
the year's best fiction in novel, novella, and short-story
length. Although the fantasy field had enjoyed such honors as
far back as the International Fantasy Awards (1951–1957),
prior to the first World Fantasy Convention in 1975, there
had been no formal ceremony for recognizing and rewarding

literary achievement in horror fiction. *The Horror Hall of Fame* was conceived with the idea of paying tribute to the many writers and stories that predate the World Fantasy Convention and have helped make horror the rich and complex body of literature it is today.

Of course, to extend such honors to *every* pre-1981 horror story deserving of recognition is a task that would require a small library of books. *The Horror Hall of Fame* is selective by necessity, presenting the dozen and a half stories that received the highest number of votes when participants in the 1981 and 1982 World Fantasy Conventions were polled. Such limitations notwithstanding, the stories reprinted here cover a vast amount of territory. They extend chronologically from horror's Gothic origins to its current status as a fiction marketing category and they showcase the imaginative variety that has characterized horror fiction throughout its literary evolution in both the United States and Great Britain.

Establishing the beginning of anything so nebulous as a literary tradition is a difficult proposition, one that is likely to exclude an important work simply because it falls outside of some arbitrarily determined cut-off point. Yet the literature of horror—that is, fiction whose objective it is to induce a sense of fear in a reader—is generally considered to begin with Horace Walpole's *The Castle of Otranto* (1765), the first of the cavalcade of Gothic novels that dominated the literary landscape of the late eighteenth and early nineteenth century. The Gothic school of fiction arose in direct response to the rationalism of its time. Its writers produced a torrent of tales filled with incestuous villains, violated heroines, and bleeding apparitions, and the readers, to the dismay of critics, gobbled them up, a clear case of popular need prevailing over prescribed tastes.

The greatest works of Gothic horror—among them William Beckford's *Vathek* (1786), Ann Radcliffe's *The Mysteries of Udolpho* (1794), Matthew Gregory Lewis's *The Monk* (1796), and Mary Shelley's *Frankenstein* (1818)—ran to novel length and thus fall outside the criteria for this book. However, the Gothic novels originated most of the themes and motifs one finds in the stories selected for *The Horror Hall of Fame:* the spectral presence, the reanimated corpse, the pursuing demon, the haunted house, the terrifying transformation, the premature burial, the madman, etc. Gothic horror tales embedded these often excessive elements in narratives whose dark mood and atmospheric texture allowed readers to entertain the wildest speculations. The history of the horror story can be read as each age's reinterpretation of the lessons taught by the Gothic school.

Certainly, this can be seen in the work of Edgar Allan Poe. Although considered a late-Gothic writer, Poe wrought significant variations on the Gothic form that anticipated the concerns of modern horror. His corresponding fascinations with insanity and the psychopathology of evil produced tales such as "The Fall of the House of Usher," "Ligeia," and "The Tell-Tale Heart," in which the conflicts of Gothic horror are internalized and transformed into shadowplays of the diseased psyche. Unlike most of his predecessors, Poe rarely employed the machinery of the supernatural; his monsters of the mind were so powerful that they achieved a presence close to objective existence. The ambiguous relationship between the inner and outer world that deepens the mystery of so many stories in *The Horror Hall of Fame* first achieves full expression in Poe's work.

In the fifty-year gap that separated Poe's "The Fall of the House of Usher" from Ambrose Bierce's "The Damned Thing," few American writers distinguished themselves as writers of horror fiction. In Britain, it was another story altogether. Horror flourished, particularly in the form of the ghost tale. Poe's contemporary, Joseph Sheridan Le Fanu, liberated the ghost from its narrow role as the avenging specter of early Gothic fiction and imbued it with its own sinister nature. At the same time, Le Fanu used the supernatural to suggest more about his characters than could be tastefully described. The spectral monkey that appears to the protagonist in "Green Tea" represents that character's sublimated passions, as well as a supernatural being that preys upon such flaws in Man's moral armor. M. R. James thought Le Fanu the greatest writer of the ghost story and proved his most apt pupil. In his two collections, *Ghost Stories of an Antiquary* (1904) and *More Ghost Stories of an Antiquary* (1911), he distilled the quality that so distinguished Le Fanu's fiction from his forebears' and turned it into an aesthetic approach to horror fiction in general: restraint in the delineation of creatures of inhuman malevolence. As is evident from "Casting the Runes," James used the term "ghost" broadly to describe a host of supernatural beings. Though his ghosts are more than simply spectral and far from harmless, James rarely shows them directly, preferring instead to describe his characters' emotions when they confront or come into contact with them.

Jamesian reticence was, in fact, the hallmark of literary horror and certainly the preferred approach to horror fiction in the late nineteenth and early twentieth century. Rather than hindering horror writers, the demands of subtlety seems to have inspired them to seek out horrors that superseded those of the simple ghost tale and find new ways of suggesting them. W. W. Jacobs interposed an unopened door between the human and presumably unhuman in his masterpiece of implied horror, "The Monkey's Paw." Arthur Machen evoked horrors too terrible to tell in his revision of Welsh folklore, "The White People," and left the task of describing them to a naive child. In "The Willows," Algernon Blackwood conceived of elemental forces vastly more powerful than puny human beings and strove to express them through the perturbations of a windblown forest in the night. Even Robert W. Chambers, whose tale "The Yellow Sign" is seasoned with the decadence of *fin de siècle* bohemia, appropriated the hazy illogic of dreams to portray what might have been too terrible to stomach had it been presented directly as a tale of cause and supernatural effect.

With the short fiction of American writer Ambrose Bierce, however, one encounters a distinct backlash against the subtle approach to horror. Bierce was no Gothic atavist, but neither was he above resorting to graphic descriptions to jolt readers who had been numbed by the carnage of the American Civil War. "The Damned Thing" shows another side of Bierce's writing that was to become his trademark: a sardonic sense of humor that makes it seem as though the most grotesque human fates are a supreme jest of the supernatural world.

From Bierce it is a very short walk to the American pulp

fiction magazines and the bifurcation of horror into literary and popular fiction streams. The weird fiction pulps were the closest that America ever came to staging a Gothic revival. Although the influential *Weird Tales* published the fiction of H. P. Lovecraft, Poe's direct literary descendant and an advocate of the school of implied horror, more typical of what the magazine offered is Henry Kuttner's "Graveyard Rats" and Robert E. Howard's "Pigeons from Hell," stories that reshuffled the most gruesome props of the Gothic thriller in an American milieu and proved that they still provided excellent entertainment.

As a counterbalance to *Weird Tales,* John W. Campbell brought out *Unknown Worlds,* a fantasy magazine that attempted to rehabilitate the classic figures of horror and prepare them for life in contemporary urban America. Although *Unknown Worlds* stories were more likely to poke fun at traditional monsters and the incongruity of their existence into the modern era, tales like Fritz Leiber's "Smoke Ghost" and Theodore Sturgeon's "It" successfully adapted them and the horrors they evoked to the age of industrial waste, crowded housing, and job stress. The example of Campbell's magazine proved so infectious that even *Weird Tales* began to sound like it when it bought Robert Bloch's "Yours Truly, Jack the Ripper," an updating of the Jack the Ripper legend for the twentieth century.

The trail blazed by *Unknown Worlds* has proved to be the course horror has taken in the years since World War II. Horror fiction continues to address itself to the concerns of the modern age. In the last two decades, though, it has done so with a candor surpassing any preceding era. The Freudian anxieties symbolized by the murderous child in Ray Bradbury's "The Small Assassin" have been replaced by more transparent fears: the fear of the adverse influence of environment on character in Harlan Ellison's "The Whimper of Whipped Dogs"; the fear of alienation and lack of self-esteem in Charles Grant's "Coin of the Realm"; the fear of growing old and helpless in Ramsey Campbell's "Calling Card"; and in Stephen King's "The Reach," the ultimate fear which, in one guise or another, has sustained horror fiction for over two centuries: the fear of death. As these stories bring their anxieties closer and closer to the surface, so do they move closer and closer back toward a literary mainstream waiting to embrace them.

In looking over the stories in *The Horror Hall of Fame,* one notices some curious absences. There are no vampire or werewolf stories and, speaking realistically, there are no traditional ghost or haunted house stories, either. The reason for this is simple: although these are the themes by which horror has traditionally been identified, they are not necessarily the ones that have produced the most memorable stories. Horror *is* a tradition, but it is not static. Most of its best stories have come from its imaginative fringe, where it is forever seeking new forms of expression and new fears to express. The fearlessness with which horror addresses the fears of each brave new age awaits you in the stories ahead.

The Fall of the House of Usher

Edgar Allan Poe

The literature of Gothic horror abounds with ruined castles inhabited by supernatural menaces and only slightly less threatening human occupants. Edgar Allan Poe, however, viewed the human mind as its own haunted palace, teeming with the specters of guilt, obsession, and neurosis. Poe's 1839 tale "The Fall of the House of Usher" is a direct descendant of the British Gothic tradition in which the titular dwelling isolates its owners from the outside world and leaves them at the mercy of what lurks behind its claustrophobic walls. At the same time, the story is a modern psychological study of the morbid mind in solitude, collapsing into madness. Though it hints of supernatural machinations at its climax, its refusal to distinguish the paranormal and the psychologically aberrant was both a hallmark of Poe's fiction and a quantum leap in the evolution of the horror tale.

> *Son coeur est un luth sus-*
> *pendu;*
> *Sitôt qu'on le touche if*
> *résonne.*
>
> De Béranger

During the whole of a dull, dark, and soundless day in the autumn of the year, when the clouds hung oppressively low in the heavens, I had been passing alone, on horseback, through a singularly dreary tract of country; and at length found myself, as the shades of the evening drew on, within view of the melancholy House of Usher. I knew not how it was—but, with the first glimpse of the building, a sense of unsufferable gloom pervaded my spirit. I say insufferable; for the feeling was unrelieved by any of that half-pleasurable, because poetic, sentiment with which the mind usually receives even the sternest natural images of the desolate or terrible. I looked upon the scene before me—upon the mere house, and the simple landscape features of the domain, upon the bleak walls, upon the vacant eyelike windows, upon a few rank sedges, and upon a few white trunks of decayed trees— with an utter depression of soul which I can compare to no earthly sensation more properly than to the afterdream of the reveler upon opium; the bitter lapse into everyday life, the hideous dropping off of the veil. There was an iciness, a sinking, a sickening of the heart, an unredeemed dreariness of thought which no goading of the imagination could torture into aught of the sublime. What was it—I paused to think— what was it that so unnerved me in the contemplation of the House of Usher? It was a mystery all insoluble; nor could I grapple with the shadowy fancies that crowded upon me as I pondered. I was forced to fall back upon the unsatisfactory conclusion, that while, beyond doubt, there *are* combinations of very simple natural objects which have the power of thus affecting us, still the analysis of this power lies among considerations beyond our depth. It was possible, I reflected, that a mere different arrangement of the particulars of the scene, of the details of the picture, would be sufficient to modify, or perhaps to annihilate, its capacity for sorrowful impression; and, acting upon this idea, I reined my horse to the precipitous brink of a black and lurid tarn that lay in unruffled luster by the dwelling, and gazed down—but with a shudder even more thrilling than before—upon the remodeled and inverted images of the gray sedge, and the ghastly tree stems, and the vacant and eyelike windows.

Nevertheless, in this mansion of gloom I now proposed to myself a sojourn of some weeks. Its proprietor, Roderick Usher, had been one of my boon companions in boyhood; but many years had elapsed since our last meeting. A letter, however, had lately reached me in a distant part of the country—a letter from him—which in its wildly importunate nature had admitted of no other than a personal reply. The MS. gave evidence of nervous agitation. The writer spoke of acute bodily illness, of a mental disorder which oppressed him, and of an earnest desire to see me, as his best and indeed his only personal friend, with a view of attempting, by the cheerfulness of my society, some alleviation of his malady. It was the manner in which all this, and much more, was said—it was the apparent *heart* that went with his request—which allowed me no room for hesitation; and I accordingly obeyed forthwith what I still considered a very singular summons.

Although as boys we had been even intimate associates, yet I really knew little of my friend. His reserve had been always excessive and habitual. I was aware, however, that his very ancient family had been noted, time out of mind, for a peculiar sensibility of temperament, displaying itself, through long ages, in many works of exalted art, and manifested of late in repeated deeds of munificent yet unobtrusive charity, as well as in a passionate devotion of the intricacies, perhaps even more than to the orthodox and easily recognizable beauties, of musical science. I had learned, too, the very remarkable fact that the stem of the Usher race, all time-honored as it was, had put forth at no period any enduring branch; in other words, that the entire family lay in the direct line of descent, and had always, with very trifling and very temporary variation, so lain. It was this deficiency, I considered, while running over in thought the perfect keeping of the character of the premises with the accredited character of the people, and while speculating upon the possible influence which the one, in the long lapse of centuries, might have exercised upon the other—it was this deficiency, perhaps, of collateral issue, and the consequent undeviating transmission from sire to son of the patrimony with the name, which had, at length, so identified the two as to merge the original title of the estate in the quaint and equivocal appellation of the "House of Usher"—an appellation which seemed to include, in the minds of the peasantry who used it, both the family and the family mansion.

I have said that the sole effect of my somewhat childish experiment, that of looking down within the tarn, had been to deepen the first singular impression. There can be no doubt that the consciousness of the rapid increase of my superstition—for why should I not so term it?—served mainly to accelerate the increase itself. Such, I have long known, is the paradoxical law of all sentiments having terror as a basis. And it might have been for this reason only, that, when I again uplifted my eyes to the house itself, from its image in the pool, there grew in my mind a strange fancy—a fancy so ridiculous, indeed, that I but mention it to show the vivid force of the sensations which oppressed me. I had so worked upon my imagination as really to believe that about the whole mansion and domain there hung an atmosphere peculiar to themselves and their immediate vicinity: an atmosphere which had no affinity with the air of heaven, but which had reeked up from the decayed trees, and the gray wall, and the silent tarn: a pestilent and mystic vapor, dull, sluggish, faintly discernible, and leaden-hued.

Shaking off from my spirit what *must* have been a dream, I scanned more narrowly the real aspect of the building. Its principal feature seemed to be that of an excessive antiquity. The discoloration of ages had been great. Minute fungi overspread the whole exterior, hanging in a fine tangled webwork from the eaves. Yet all this was apart from any extraordinary dilapidation. No portion of the masonry had fallen; and there appeared to be a wild inconsistency between its still perfect adaptation of parts and the crumbling condition of the individual stones. In this there was much that reminded me of the specious totality of old woodwork which has rotted for long years in some neglected vault, with no disturbance from the breath of the external air. Beyond this indication of excessive decay, however, the fabric gave little token of instability. Perhaps the eye of a scrutinizing observer might have discovered a barely perceptible fissure, which, extending from the roof of the building in front, made its way down the wall in a zigzag direction, until it became lost in the sullen waters of the tarn.

Noticing these things, I rode over a short causeway to the house. A servant in waiting took my horse, and I entered the

Gothic archway of the hall. A valet, of stealthy step, thence conducted me, in silence, through many dark and intricate passages in my progress to the studio of his master. Much that I encountered on the way contributed, I know not how, to heighten the vague sentiments of which I have already spoken. While the objects around me—while the carvings of the ceilings, the somber tapestries of the walls, the ebon blackness of the floors, and the phantasmagoric armorial trophies which rattled as I strode, were but matters to which, or to such as which, I had been accustomed from my infancy— while I hesitated not to acknowledge how familiar was all this—I still wondered to find how unfamiliar were the fancies which ordinary images were stirring up. On one of the staircases, I met the physician of the family. His countenance, I thought, wore a mingled expression of low cunning and perplexity. He accosted me with trepidation and passed on. The valet now threw open a door and ushered me into the presence of his master.

The room in which I found myself was very large and lofty. The windows were long, narrow, and pointed, and at so vast a distance from the black oaken floor as to be altogether inaccessible from within. Feeble gleams of encrimsoned light made their way through the trellised panes, and served to render sufficiently distinct the more prominent objects around; the eye, however, struggled in vain to reach the remoter angles of the chamber, or the recesses of the vaulted and fretted ceiling. Dark draperies hung upon the walls. The general furniture was profuse, comfortless, antique, and tattered. Many books and musical instruments lay scattered about, but failed to give any vitality to the scene. I felt that I breathed an atmosphere of sorrow. An air of stern, deep, and irredeemable gloom hung over and pervaded all.

Upon my entrance, Usher arose from a sofa on which he had been lying at full length, and greeted me with a vivacious warmth which had much in it, I at first thought, of an overdone cordiality—of the constrained effort of the *ennuyé* man of the world. A glance, however, at his countenance, convinced me of his perfect sincerity. We sat down; and for some moments, while he spoke not, I gazed upon him with a feeling half of pity, half of awe. Surely man had never before so terribly altered in so brief a period as had Roderick Usher! It was with difficulty that I could bring myself to admit the identity of the wan being before me with the companion of my boyhood. Yet the character of his face had been at all times remarkable. A cadaverousness of complexion; an eye large, liquid, and luminous beyond comparison; lips somewhat thin and very pallid, but of a surpassingly beautiful curve; a nose of a delicate Hebrew model, but with a breadth of nostril unusual in similar formations; a finely molded chin, speaking, in its want of prominence, of a want of moral energy; hair of a more than weblike softness and tenuity; these features, with an inordinate expansion above the regions of the temple, made up altogether a countenance not easily to be forgotten. And now in the mere exaggeration of the prevailing character of these features, and of the expression they were wont to convey, lay so much of change that I doubted to whom I spoke. The now ghostly pallor of the skin, and the now miraculous luster of the eye, above all things startled and even awed me. The silken hair, too, had been suffered to grow all unheeded, and as, in its wild gossamer texture, it floated rather than fell about the face, I could not, even with effort, connect its arabesque expression with any idea of simple humanity.

In the manner of my friend I was at once struck with an incoherence, an inconsistency; and I soon found this to arise from a series of feeble and futile struggles to overcome an habitual trepidancy, an excessive nervous agitation. For something of this nature I had indeed been prepared, no less by his letter than by reminiscences of certain boyish traits, and by conclusions deduced from his peculiar physical conformation and temperament. His action was alternatively vivacious and sullen. His voice varied rapidly from a tremulous indecision (when the animal spirits seemed utterly in abeyance) to that species of energetic concision—that abrupt, weighty, unhurried, and hollow-sounding enunciation—that leaden, self-balanced and perfectly modulated guttural utterance—which may be observed in the lost drunkard, or the irreclaimable eater of opium, during the periods of his most intense excitement.

It was thus that he spoke of the object of my visit, of his

earnest desire to see me, and of the solace he expected me to afford him. He entered, at some length, into what he conceived to be the nature of his malady. It was, he said, a constitutional and a family evil, and one for which he despaired to find a remedy—a mere nervous affection, he immediately added, which would undoubtedly soon pass off. It displayed itself in a host of unnatural sensations. Some of these, as he detailed them, interested and bewildered me: although, perhaps, the terms and the general manner of the narration had their weight. He suffered much from a morbid acuteness of the senses; the most insipid food was alone endurable; he could wear only garments of a certain texture; the odors of all flowers were oppressive; his eyes were tortured by even a faint light; and there were but peculiar sounds, and these from stringed instruments, which did not inspire him with horror.

To an anomalous species of terror I found him a bounden slave. "I shall perish," said he, "I *must* perish in this deplorable folly. Thus, thus, and not otherwise, shall I be lost. I dread the events of the future, not in themselves, but in their results. I shudder at the thought of any, even the most trivial, incident, which may operate upon this intolerable agitation of soul. I have, indeed, no abhorrence of danger, except in its absolute effect—in terror. In this unnerved—in this pitiable condition—I feel that the period will sooner or later arrive when I must abandon life and reason together, in some struggle with the grim phantasm, FEAR. "

I learned moreover at intervals, and through broken and equivocal hints, another singular feature of his mental condition. He was enchained by certain superstitious impressions in regard to the dwelling which he tenanted, and whence, for many years, he had never ventured forth—in regard to an influence whose suppositious force was conveyed in terms too shadowy here to be restated—an influence which some peculiarities in the mere form and substance of his family mansion, had, by dint of long sufferance, he said, obtained over his spirit—an effect which the physique of the gray walls and turrets, and of the dim tarn into which they all looked down, had, at length, brought about upon the morale of his existence.

He admitted, however, although with hesitation, that much of the peculiar gloom which thus afflicted him could be traced to a more natural and far more palpable origin—to the severe and long-continued illness, indeed to the evidently approaching dissolution, of a tenderly beloved sister—his sole companion for long years, his last and only relative on earth. "Her decease," he said, with a bitterness which I can never forget, "would leave him (him the hopeless and the frail) the last of the ancient race of the Ushers." While he spoke, the lady Madeline (for so was she called) passed slowly through a remote portion of the apartment, and, without having noticed my presence, disappeared. I regarded her with an utter astonishment not unmingled with dread, and yet I found it impossible to account for such feelings. A sensation of stupor oppressed me, as my eyes followed her retreating steps. When a door, at length, closed upon her, my glance sought instinctively and eagerly the countenance of the brother, but he had buried his face in his hands, and I could only perceive that a far more than ordinary wanness had overspread the emaciated fingers through which trickled many passionate tears.

The disease of the lady Madeline had long baffled the skill of her physicians. A settled apathy, a gradual wasting away of the person, and frequent although transient affections of a partially cataleptical character, were the unusual diagnosis. Hitherto she had steadily borne up against the pressure of her malady, and had not betaken herself finally to bed; but, on the closing in of the evening of my arrival at the house, she succumbed (as her brother told me at night with inexpressible agitation) to the prostrating power of the destroyer; and I learned that the glimpse I had obtained of her person would thus probably be the last I should obtain—that the lady, at least while living, would be seen by me no more.

For several days ensuing, her name was unmentioned by either Usher or myself; and during this period I was busied in earnest endeavors to alleviate the melancholy of my friend. We painted and read together; or I listened, as if in a dream, to the wild improvisation of his speaking guitar. And thus, as a closer and still closer intimacy admitted me more unreservedly into the recesses of his spirit, the more bitterly did I perceive the futility of all attempt at cheering a mind from which darkness, as if an inherent positive quality, poured forth upon all objects of the moral and physical universe, in one unceasing radiation of gloom.

I shall ever bear about me a memory of the many solemn hours I thus spent alone with the master of the House of Usher. Yet I should fail in any attempt to convey an idea of the exact character of the studies, or of the occupations, in which he involved me, or led me the way. An excited and highly distempered ideality threw a sulphurous luster over all. His long improvised dirges will ring forever in my ears. Among other things, I hold painfully in mind a certain singular perversion and amplification of the wild air of the last waltz of Von Weber. From the paintings over which his elaborate fancy brooded, and which grew, touch by touch, into vagueness at which I shuddered the more thrillingly because I shuddered knowing not why;—from these paintings (vivid as their images now are before me) I would in vain endeavor to enduce more than a small portion which should lie within the compass of merely written words. By the utter simplicity, by the nakedness of his designs, he arrested and overawed attention. If ever mortal painted an idea, that mortal was Roderick Usher. For me at least, in the circumstances then surrounding me, there arose, out of the pure abstractions which the hypochondriac contrived to throw upon his canvas, an intensity of intolerable awe, no shadow of which felt I ever yet in the contemplation of the certainly glowing yet too concrete reveries of Fuseli.

One of the phantasmagoric conceptions of my friend, partaking not so rigidly of the spirit of abstraction, may be shadowed forth, although feebly, in words. A small picture presented the interior of an immensely long and rectangular vault or tunnel, with low walls, smooth, white, and without interruption or device. Certain accessory points of the design served well to convey the idea that this excavation lay at an exceeding depth below the surface of the earth. No outlet was observed in any portion of its vast extent, and no torch or other artificial source of light was discernible; yet a flood of intense rays rolled throughout, and bathed the whole in a ghastly and inappropriate splendor.

I have just spoken of that morbid condition of the auditory

nerve which rendered all music intolerable to the sufferer, with the exception of certain effects of stringed instruments. It was, perhaps, the narrow limits to which he thus confined himself upon the guitar, which gave birth, in great measure, to the fantastic character of his performances. But the fervid *facility* of his *impromptus* could not be so accounted for. They must have been, and were, in the notes, as well as in the words of his wild fantasias (for he not unfrequently accompanied himself with rhymed verbal improvisations), the result of that intense mental collectedness and concentration to which I have previously alluded as observable only in particular moments of the highest artificial excitement. The words of one of these rhapsodies I have easily remembered. I was, perhaps, the more forcibly impressed with it, as he gave it, because, in the under or mystic current of its meaning, I fancied that I perceived, and for the first time, a full consciousness, on the part of Usher, of the tottering of his lofty reason upon her throne. The verses, which were entitled "The Haunted Palace," ran very nearly, if not accurately, thus:

> In the greenest of our valleys,
> By good angels tenanted,
> Once a fair and stately palace—
> Radiant palace—reared its head.
> In the monarch Thought's dominion,
> It stood there!
> Never seraph spread a pinion
> Over fabric half so fair.
>
> Banners yellow, glorious, golden,
> On its roof did float and flow,
> (This—all this—was in the olden
> Time long ago)
> And every gentle air that dallied,
> In that sweet day,
> Along the ramparts plumed and pallid,
> A wingèd odor went away.
>
> Wanderers in that happy valley
> Through too luminous windows saw
> Spirits moving musically

To a lute's well-tuned law,
Round about a throne where, sitting,
(Porphyrogene!)
In state his glory well befitting,
The ruler of the realm was seen.

And all with pearl and ruby glowing
Was the fair palace door,
Through which came flowing, flowing, flowing,
And sparkling evermore,
A troop of Echoes whose sweet duty
Was but to sing
In voices of surpassing beauty,
The wit and wisdom of their king.

But evil things, in robes of sorrow,
Assailed the monarch's high estate;
(Ah, let us mourn, for never morrow
Shall dawn upon him, desolate!)
And round about his home the glory
That blushed and bloomed
Is but a dim-remembered story
Of the old time entombed.

And travellers now within that valley
Through the red-litten windows see
Vast forms that move fantastically
To a discordant melody;
While, like a rapid ghastly river,
Through the pale door,
A hideous throng rush out forever,
And laugh—but smile no more.

I well remember that suggestions arising from this ballad led us into a train of thought, wherein there became manifest an opinion of Usher's which I mention not so much on account of its novelty (for other men have thought thus) as on account of the pertinacity with which he maintained it. This opinion, in its general form, was that of the sentience of all vegetable things. But in his disordered fancy the idea had assumed a more daring character, and trespassed, under certain conditions, upon the kingdom of inorganization. I lack words to express the full extent, or the earnest *abandon* of his persuasion. The belief, however, was connected (as I have previously hinted) with the gray stones of the home of his forefathers. The conditions of the sentience had been here, he imagined, fulfilled in the method of collocation of these stones—in the order of their arrangement, as well as in that of the many fungi which overspread them, and of the decayed trees which stood around—above all, in the long undisturbed endurance of this arrangement, and in its reduplication in the still waters of the tarn. Its evidence—the evidence of the sentience—was to be seen, he said (and I here started as he spoke), in the gradual yet certain condensation of an atmosphere of their own about the waters and the walls. The result was discoverable, he added, in that silent, yet importunate and terrible influence which for centuries had molded the destinies of his family, and which made *him* what I now saw him—what he was. Such opinions need no comment, and I will make none.

Our books—the books which, for years, had formed no small portion of the mental existence of the invalid—were, as might be supposed, in strict keeping with this character of phantasm. We pored together over such works as the Ververt and Chartreuse of Gresset; the Belphegor of Machiavelli; the Heaven and Hell of Swedenborg; the Subterranean Voyage of Nicholas Klimm by Holberg; the Chiromancy of Robert Flud, of Jean D'Indaginé, and of De la Chambre; the Journey into the Blue Distance of Tieck; and the City of the Sun of Campanella. One favorite volume was a small octavo edition of the *Directorium Inquisitorium*, by the Dominican Eymeric de Gironne; and there were passages in Pomponius Mela, about the old African Satyrs and AEgipans, over which Usher would sit dreaming for hours. His chief delight, however, was found in the perusal of an exceedingly rare and curious book in quarto Gothic—the manual of a forgotten church—the *Vigiliae Mortuorum Secundum Chorum Ecclesiae Maguntinae.*

I could not help thinking of the wild ritual of this work, and of its probable influence upon the hypochondriac, when one evening, having informed me abruptly that the lady Madeline was no more, he stated his intention of preserving her corpse for a fortnight (previously to its final interment) in one of the numerous vaults within the main walls of the building. The worldly reason, however, assigned for this singular proceeding was one which I did not feel at liberty to dispute. The brother had been led to his resolution (so he told me) by consideration of the unusual character of the malady of the deceased, of certain obtrusive and eager inquiries on the part of her medical men, and of the remote and exposed situation of the burial ground of the family. I will not deny that when I called to mind the sinister countenance of the person whom I met upon the staircase, on the day of my arrival at the house, I had no desire to oppose what I regarded as at best but a harmless, and by no means an unnatural, precaution.

At the request of Usher, I personally aided him in the arrangements for the temporary entombment. The body having been encoffined, we two alone bore it to its rest. The vault in which we placed it (and which had been so long unopened that our torches, half smothered in its oppressive atmosphere, gave us little opportunity for investigation) was small, damp, and entirely without means of admission for light; lying, at great depth, immediately beneath that portion of the building in which was my own sleeping apartment. It had been used, apparently, in remote feudal times, for the worst purposes of a donjon-keep, and in later days as a place of deposit for powder, or some other highly combustible substance, as a portion of its floor, and the whole interior of a long archway through which we reached it, were carefully sheathed with copper. The door, of massive iron, had been also similarly protected. Its immense weight caused an unusually sharp grating sound, as it moved upon its hinges.

Having deposited our mournful burden upon trestles within this region of horror, we partially turned aside the yet unscrewed lid of the coffin, and looked upon the face of the tenant. A striking similitude between the brother and sister now first arrested my attention; and Usher divining, perhaps, my thoughts, murmured out some few words from which I learned that the deceased and himself had been twins, and that sympathies of a scarcely intelligible nature had always existed between them. Our glances, however, rested not long upon the dead—for we could not regard her unawed. The disease which had thus entombed the lady in the maturity of youth, had left, as usual in all maladies of a strictly cataleptical character, the mockery of a faint blush upon the bosom and the face, and that suspiciously lingering smile upon the lip which is so terrible in death. We replaced and screwed down the lid, and, having secured the door of iron, made our way, with toil, into the scarcely less gloomy apartments of the upper portion of the house.

And now, some days of bitter grief having elapsed, an observable change came over the features of the mental disorder of my friend. His ordinary manner had vanished. His ordinary occupations were neglected or forgotten. He roamed from chamber to chamber with hurried, unequal, and objectless step. The pallor of his countenance had assumed, if possible, a more ghastly hue—but the luminousness of his eye had utterly gone out. The once occasional huskiness of his tone was heard no more; and a tremulous quaver, as if of extreme terror, habitually characterized his utterance. There were times, indeed, when I thought his unceasingly agitated mind was laboring with some oppressive secret, to divulge which he struggled for the necessary courage. At times, again, I was obliged to resolve all into the mere inexplicable vagaries of madness, for I beheld him gazing upon vacancy for long hours, in an attitude of the profoundest attention, as if listening to some imaginary sound. It was no wonder that his condition terrified—that it infected me. I felt creeping upon me, by slow yet certain degrees, the wild influences of his own fantastic yet impressive superstitions.

It was, especially, upon retiring to bed late in the night of the seventh or eighth day after the placing of the lady Madeline within the donjon, that I experienced the full power of such feelings. Sleep came not near my couch, while the hours waned and waned away. I struggled to reason off the nervousness which had dominion over me. I endeavored to believe that much, if not all, of what I felt was due to the bewildering influence of the gloomy furniture of the room—of the dark and tattered draperies which, tortured into motion by the breath of a rising tempest, swayed fitfully to and fro upon the walls, and rustled uneasily about the decorations of the bed. But my efforts were fruitless. An irrepressible tremor gradually pervaded my frame; and at length there sat upon my very heart an incubus of utterly causeless alarm. Shaking this off with a gasp and a struggle, I uplifted myself upon the pillows, and, peering earnestly within the intense darkness of the chamber, hearkened—I know not why, except that an instinctive spirit prompted me—to certain low and indefinite sounds which came, through the pauses of the storm, at long intervals, I knew not whence. Overpowered by an intense sentiment of horror, unaccountable yet unendurable, I threw on my clothes with haste (for I felt that I should sleep no more during the night) and endeavored to arouse myself from the pitiable condition into which I had fallen, by pacing rapidly to and fro through the apartment.

I had taken but few turns in this manner, when a light step on an adjoining staircase arrested my attention. I presently recognized it as that of Usher. In an instant afterward he rapped with a gentle touch at my door, and entered, bearing a lamp. His countenance was, as usual, cadaverously wan— but, moreover, there was a species of mad hilarity in his eyes —an evidently restrained *hysteria* in his whole demeanor. His air appalled me—but anything was preferable to the solitude which I had so long endured, and I even welcomed his presence as a relief.

"And you have not seen it?" he said abruptly, after having stared about him for some moments in silence—"you have not then seen it?—but, stay! you shall." Thus speaking, and having carefully shaded his lamp, he hurried to one of the casements, and threw it freely open to the storm.

The impetuous fury of the entering gust nearly lifted us from our feet. It was, indeed, a tempestuous yet sternly beautiful night, and one wildly singular in its terror and its beauty. A whirlwind had apparently collected its force in our vicinity; for there were frequent and violent alterations in the direction of the wind; and the exceeding density of the clouds (which hung so low as to press upon the turrets of the house) did not prevent our perceiving the lifelike velocity with which they flew careening from all points against each other, without passing away into the distance. I say that even their exceeding density did not prevent our perceiving this; yet we had no glimpse of the moon or stars, nor was there any flashing forth of the lightning. But the under surfaces of the huge masses of agitated vapor, as well as all terrestrial objects immediately around us, were glowing in the unnatural light of a faintly luminous and distinctly visible gaseous exhalation which hung about and enshrouded the mansion.

"You must not—you shall not behold this!" said I, shudderingly, to Usher, as I led him with a gentle violence from the window to a seat. "These appearances, which bewilder you, are merely electrical phenomena not uncommon—or it may be that they have their ghastly origin in the rank miasma of the tarn. Let us close this casement; the air is chilling and dangerous to your frame. Here is one of your favorite romances. I will read, and you shall listen;—and so we will pass away this terrible night together."

The antique volume which I had taken up was the *Mad Trist* of Sir Launcelot Canning; but I had called it a favorite of Usher's more in sad jest than in earnest; for, in truth, there is little in its uncouth and unimaginative prolixity which could have had interest for the lofty and spiritual ideality of my friend. It was, however, the only book immediately at hand; and I indulged a vague hope that the excitement which now agitated the hypochondriac might find relief (for the history of mental disorder is full of similar anomalies) even in the extremeness of the folly which I should read. Could I have judged, indeed, by the wild overstrained air of vivacity with which he hearkened, or apparently hearkened, to the words of the tale, I might well have congratulated myself upon the success of my design.

I had arrived at that well-known portion of the story where Ethelred, the hero of the Trist, having sought in vain for peaceable admission into the dwelling of the hermit, proceeds to make good an entrance by force. Here, it will be remembered, the words of the narrative run thus:

And Ethelred, who was by nature of a doughty heart, and who was now mighty withal, on account of the powerfulness of the wine which he had drunken, waited no longer to hold parley with the hermit, who, in sooth, was of an obstinate and maliceful turn, but, feeling the rain upon his shoulders, and fearing the rising of the tempest, uplifted his mace outright, in this instance, I did actually hear (although from what direction it proceeded I found it impossible to say) a low and apparently distant, but harsh, protracted, and most unusual screaming or grating sound—the exact counterpart of what my fancy had already conjured up for the dragon's unnatural shriek as described by the romancer.

Oppressed, as I certainly was, upon the occurrence of this second and most extraordinary coincidence, by a thousand conflicting sensations, in which wonder and extreme terror were predominant, I still retained sufficient presence of mind to avoid exciting, by any observation, the sensitive nervousness of my companion. I was by no means certain that he had noticed the sounds in question; although, assuredly, a strange alteration had during the last few minutes taken place in his demeanor. From a position fronting my own, he had gradually brought round his chair, so as to sit with his face to the door of the chamber; and thus I could but partially perceive his features, although I saw that his lips trembled as if he were murmuring inaudibly. His head had dropped upon his breast—yet I knew that he was not asleep, from the wide and rigid opening of the eye as I caught a glance of it in profile. The motion of his body, too, was at variance with this idea—for he rocked from side to side with a gentle yet constant and uniform sway. Having rapidly taken notice of all this, I resumed the narrative of Sir Launcelot, which thus proceeded:

> And now, the champion having escaped from the terrible fury of the dragon, bethinking himself of the brazen shield, and of the breaking up of the enchantment which was upon it, removed the carcass from out of the way before him, and approached valorously over the silver pavement of the castle to where the shield was upon the wall; which in sooth tarried not for his full coming, but fell down at his feet upon the silver floor, with a mighty great and terrible ringing sound.

No sooner had these syllables passed my lips, than—as if a shield of brass had indeed, at the moment, fallen heavily upon a floor of silver—I became aware of a distinct, hollow, metallic and clangorous, yet apparently muffled reverberation. Completely unnerved, I leaped to my feet; but the mea-

and, with blows, made quickly room in the plankings of the door for his gauntleted hand; and now pulling therewith sturdily, he so cracked, and ripped, and tore all asunder, that the noise of the dry and hollow-sounding wood alarummed and reverberated throughout the forest.

At the termination of this sentence I started, and for a moment paused; for it appeared to me (although I at once concluded that my excited fancy had deceived me)—it appeared to me that from some very remote portion of the mansion there came, indistinctly, to my ears, what might have been, in its exact similarity of character, the echo (but a stifled and dull one certainly) of the very cracking and ripping sound which Sir Launcelot had so particularly described. It was, beyond doubt, the coincidence alone which had arrested my attention; for, amid the rattling of the sashes of the casements, and the ordinary commingled noises of the still increasing storm, the sound, in itself, had nothing, surely, which should have interested or disturbed me. I continued the story:

But the good champion Ethelred, now entering within the door, was sore enraged and amazed to perceive no signal of the maliceful hermit; but, in the stead thereof, a dragon of a scaly and prodigious demeanor, and of a fiery tongue, which sate in guard before a palace of gold, with a floor of silver; and upon the wall there hung a shield of shining brass with this legend enwritten—

Who entereth herein, a conqueror hath bin;
Who slayeth the dragon, the shield he shall win

And Ethelred uplifted his mace, and struck upon the head of the dragon, which fell before him, and gave up his pesty breath, with a shriek so horrid and harsh, and withal so piercing, that Ethelred had fain to close his ears with his hands against the dreadful noise of it, the like whereof was never before heard.

Here again I paused abruptly, and now with a feeling of wild amazement; for there could be no doubt whatever that,

sured rocking movement of Usher was undisturbed. I rushed
to the chair in which he sat. His eyes were bent fixedly before
him, and throughout his whole countenance there reigned a
stony rigidity. But, as I placed my hand upon his shoulder,
there came a strong shudder over his whole person; a sickly
smile quivered about his lips; and I saw that he spoke in a
low, hurried, and gibbering murmur, as if unconscious of my
presence. Bending closely over him, I at length drank in the
hideous import of his words.

"Not hear it?—yes, I hear it, and *have* heard it. Long—long
—long—many minutes, many hours, many days, have I
heard it—yet I dared not—oh, pity me, miserable wretch that
I am!—I dared not—*I dared not speak! We have put her living
in the tomb!* Said I not that my senses were acute? I *now* tell
you that I heard her first feeble movements in the hollow
coffin. I heard them—many, many days ago—yet I dared not
—*I dared not speak!* And now—tonight—Ethelred—ha! ha!—
the breaking of the hermit's door, and the death-cry of the
dragon, and the clangor of the shield!—say, rather, the rend-
ing of her coffin, and the grating of the iron hinges of her
prison, and her struggles within the coppered archway of the
vault! Oh, whither shall I fly? Will she not be here anon? Is
she not hurrying to upbraid me for my haste? Have I not
heard her footsteps on the stair? Do I not distinguish that
heavy and horrible beating of her heart? Madman!"—here he
sprang furiously to his feet, and shrieked out his syllables, as
if in the effort he were giving up his soul—*"Madman! I tell
you that she now stands without the door!"*

As if in the superhuman energy of his utterance there had
been found the potency of a spell, the huge antique panels to
which the speaker pointed drew slowly back, upon the instant, their ponderous and ebony jaws. It was the work of the
rushing gust—but then without the doors there *did* stand the
lofty and enshrouded figure of the lady Madeline of Usher.
There was blood upon her white robes, and the evidence of
some bitter struggle upon every portion of her emaciated
frame. For a moment she remained trembling and reeling to
and fro upon the threshold—then, with a low moaning cry,
fell heavily inward upon the person of her brother, and, in

her violent and now final death-agonies, bore him to the floor a corpse, and a victim to the terrors he had anticipated.

From that chamber, and from that mansion, I fled aghast. The storm was still abroad in all its wrath as I found myself crossing the old causeway. Suddenly there shot along the path a wild light, and I turned to see whence a gleam so unusual could have issued; for the vast house and its shadows were alone behind me. The radiance was that of the full, setting, and blood-red moon, which now shone vividly through that once barely discernible fissure, of which I have before spoken as extending from the roof of the building, in a zigzag direction, to the base. While I gazed, this fissure rapidly widened—there came a fierce breath of the whirlwind—the entire orb of the satellite burst at once upon my sight—my brain reeled as I saw the mighty walls rushing asunder—there was a long tumultuous shouting sound like the voice of a thousand waters—and the deep and dank tarn at my feet closed sullenly and silently over the fragments of the House of Usher.

Green Tea

Joseph Sheridan Le Fanu

Many horror stories document the mischief of supernatural agents, beings whose very existence is an affront to rational thinking. The monkeylike creature that terrorizes the Reverend Jennings in Joseph Sheridan Le Fanu's "Green Tea" (1869) stands apart from this supernatural cabal insofar as its objective existence never is confirmed. Is it a demonic being that has maliciously singled out Jennings for sport, or merely a projection of the doomed protagonist's buried psychological conflicts? Le Fanu's refusal to answer this question conclusively creates the ambiguity necessary to sustain the horror reader's willing suspension of disbelief in the story's events. Dr. Martin Hesselius, the voice of reason in "Green Tea," appeared in a number of Le Fanu's tales and is recognized today as the prototype for such later occult investigators as William Hope Hodgson's Carnacki, Algernon Balckwood's John Silence, Seabury Quinn's Jules de Grandin, and Margery Lawrence's Miles Pennoyer.

Prologue: Martin Hesselius, the German Physician

Though carefully educated in medicine and surgery, I have never practised either. The study of each continues, nevertheless, to interest me profoundly. Neither idleness nor caprice caused my secession from the honourable calling which I had just entered. The cause was a very trifling scratch inflicted by

a dissecting knife. This trifle cost me the loss of two fingers,
amputated promptly, and the more painful loss of my health,
for I have never been quite well since, and have seldom been
twelve months together in the same place.

In my wanderings I became acquainted with Dr Martin
Hesselius, a wanderer like myself, like me a physician, and
like me an enthusiast in his profession. Unlike me in this,
that his wanderings were voluntary, and he a man, if not of
fortune, as we estimate fortune in England, at least in what
our forefathers used to term "easy circumstances." He was
an old man when I first saw him; nearly five-and-thirty years
my senior.

In Dr Martin Hesselius, I had found my master. His knowledge was immense, his grasp of a case was an intuition. He
was the very man to inspire a young enthusiast, like me, with
awe and delight. My admiration has stood the test of time
and survived the separation of death. I am sure it was well-
founded.

For nearly twenty years I acted as his medical secretary.
His immense collection of papers he has left in my care, to be
arranged, indexed and bound. His treatment of some of these
cases is curious. He writes in two distinct characters. He describes what he saw and heard as an intelligent layman
might, and when in his style of narrative he had seen the
patient either through his own halldoor, to the light of day,
or through the gates of darkness to the caverns of the dead,
he returns upon the narrative, and in the terms of his art and
with all the force of originality of genius, proceeds to the
work of analysis, diagnosis and illustration.

Here and there a case strikes me as of a kind to amuse or
horrify a lay reader with an interest quite different from the
peculiar one which it may possess for an expert. With slight
modifications, chiefly of language, and of course a change of
names, I copy the following. The narrator is Dr Martin Hesselius. I find it among the voluminous notes of cases which he
made during a tour in England about sixty-four years ago.

It is related in series of letters to his friend Professor Van
Loo of Leyden. The professor was not a physician, but a chemist, and a man who read history and metaphysics and medicine, and had, in his day, written a play.

The narrative is therefore, if somewhat less valuable as a medical record, necessarily written in a manner more likely to interest an unlearned reader.

These letters, from a memorandum attached, appear to have been returned on the death of the professor, in 1819, to Dr Hesselius. They are written, some in English, some in French, but the greater part in German. I am a faithful, though I am conscious, by no means a graceful translator, and although here and there I omit some passages, and shorten others, and disguise names, I have interpolated nothing.

1 Dr Hesselius Relates How He Met the Rev Mr Jennings

The Rev Mr Jennings is tall and thin. He is middle-aged, and dresses with a natty, old-fashioned, high church precision. He is naturally a little stately, but not at all stiff. His features, without being handsome, are well formed, and their expression extremely kind, but also shy.

I met him one evening at Lady Mary Heyduke's. The modesty and benevolence of his countenance are extremely prepossessing.

We are but a small party, and he joined agreeably enough in the conversation. He seems to enjoy listening very much more than contributing to the talk; but what he says is always to the purpose and well said. He is a great favourite of Lady Mary's, who it seems, consults him upon many things, and thinks him the most happy and blessed person on earth. Little knows she about him.

The Rev Mr Jennings is a bachelor, and has, they say sixty thousand pounds in the funds. He is a charitable man. He is most anxious to be actively employed in his sacred profession, and yet though always tolerably well elsewhere, when he goes down to his vicarage in Warwickshire, to engage in the actual duties of his sacred calling, his health soon fails him, and in a very strange way. So says Lady Mary.

There is no doubt that Mr Jennings' health does break down in, generally, a sudden and mysterious way, sometimes in the very act of officiating in his old and pretty church at Kenlis. It may be his heart, it may be his brain. But so it has happened three or four times, or oftener, that after proceeding a certain way in the service, he has on a sudden stopped short, and after a silence, apparently quite unable to resume, he has fallen into solitary, inaudible prayer, his hands and his eyes uplifted, and then pale as death, and in the agitation of a strange shame and horror, descended trembling, and got into the vestry-room, leaving his congregation, without explanation, to themselves. This occurred when his curate was absent. When he goes down to Kenlis now, he always takes care to provide a clergyman to share his duty, and to supply his place on the instant should he become thus suddenly incapacitated.

When Mr Jennings breaks down quite, and beats a retreat from the vicarage, and returns to London, where, in a dark street off Piccadilly, he inhabits a very narrow house, Lady Mary says that he is always perfectly well. I have my own opinion about that. There are degrees of course. We shall see.

Mr Jennings is a perfectly gentlemanlike man. People, however, remark something odd. There is an impression a little ambiguous. One thing which certainly contributes to it, people I think don't remember; or, perhaps, distinctly remark. But I did, almost immediately. Mr Jennings has a way of looking sidelong upon the carpet, as if his eye followed the movements of something there. This, of course, not always. It occurs now and then. But often enough to give a certain oddity, as I have said, to his manner, and in this glance travelling along the floor there is something both shy and anxious.

A medical philosopher, as you are good enough to call me, elaborating theories by the aid of cases sought out by himself, and by him watched and scrutinised with more time at command, and consequently infinitely more minuteness than the ordinary practitioner can afford, falls insensibly into habits of observation, which accompany him everywhere, and are exercised, as some people would say, impertinently, upon every subject that presents itself with the least likelihood of rewarding inquiry.

There was a promise of this kind in the slight, timid, kindly, but reserved gentleman, whom I met for the first time at this agreeable little evening gathering. I observed, of course, more than I here set down; but I reserve all that borders on the technical for a strictly scientific paper.

I may remark, that when I here speak of medical science, I do so, as I hope some day to see it more generally understood, in a much more comprehensive sense than its generally material treatment would warrant. I believe the entire natural world is but the ultimate expression of that spiritual world from which, and in which alone, it has its life. I believe that the essential man is a spirit, that the spirit is an organised substance, but as different in point of material from what we ordinarily understand by matter, as light or electricity is; that the material body is, in the most literal sense, a vesture, and death consequently no interruption of the living man's existence, but simply his extrication from the natural body—a process which commences at the moment of what we term death, and the completion of which, at further a few days later, is the resurrection "in power."

The person who weighs the consequences of these positions will probably see their practical bearing upon medical science. This is, however, by no means the proper place for displaying the proofs and discussing the consequences of this too generally unrecognised state of facts.

In pursuit of my habit, I was covertly observing Mr Jennings, with all my caution—I think he perceived it—and I saw plainly that he was as cautiously observing me. Lady Mary happening to address me by my name, as Dr Hesselius, I saw that he glanced at me more sharply, and then became thoughtful for a few minutes.

After this, as I conversed with a gentleman at the other end of the room, I saw him look at me more steadily, and with an interest which I thought I understood. I then saw him take an opportunity of chatting with Lady Mary, and was, as one always is, perfectly aware of being the subject of a distant inquiry and answer.

This tall clergyman approached me by-and-by; and in a little time we had got into conversation. When two people, who like reading, and know books and places, having travelled, wish to converse, it is very strange if they can't find topics. It was not accident that brought him near me, and led him into conversation. He knew German and had read my Essays on

Metaphysical Medicine which suggest more than they actually say.

This courteous man, gentle, shy, plainly a man of thought and reading, who moving and talking among us, was not altogether of us, and whom I already suspected of leading a life whose transactions and alarms were carefully concealed, with an impenetrable reserve from, not only the world, but his best beloved friends—was cautiously weighing in his own mind the idea of taking a certain step with regard to me.

I penetrated his thoughts without his being aware of it, and was careful to say nothing which could betray to his sensitive vigilance my suspicions respecting his position, or my surmises about his plans respecting myself.

We chatted upon indifferent subjects for a time; but at last he said:

"I was very much interested by some papers of yours, Dr Hesselius, upon what you term Metaphysical Medicine—I read them in German, ten or twelve years ago—have they been translated?"

"No, I'm sure they have not—I should have heard. They would have asked my leave, I think."

"I asked the publishers here, a few months ago, to get the book for me in the original German; but they tell me it is out of print."

"So it is, and has been for some years; but it flatters me as an author to find that you have not forgotten my little book, although," I added, laughing, "ten or twelve years is a considerable time to have managed without it; but I suppose you have been turning the subject over again in your mind, or something has happened lately to revive your interest in it."

At this remark, accompanied by a glance of inquiry, a sudden embarrassment disturbed Mr Jennings, analogous to that which makes a young lady blush and look foolish. He dropped his eyes, and folded his hands together uneasily, and looked oddly, and you would have said, guiltily, for a moment.

I helped him out of his awkwardness in the best way, by appearing not to observe it, and going straight on, I said: "Those revivals of interest in a subject happen to me often; one book suggests another, and often sends me back on a wild-goose chase over an interval of twenty years. But if you will care to possess a copy, I shall be only too happy to provide you; I have still got two or three by me—and if you allow me to present one I shall be very much honoured."

"You are very good indeed," he said, quite at his ease again, in a moment: "I almost despaired—I don't know how to thank you."

"Pray don't say a word; the thing is really so little worth that I am only ashamed of having offered it, and if you thank me any more I shall throw it into the fire in a fit of modesty."

Mr Jennings laughed. He inquired where I was staying in London, and after a little more conversation on a variety of subjects, he took his departure.

2 *The Doctor Questions Lady Mary, and She Answers*

"I like your vicar so much, Lady Mary," said I, as soon as he was gone. "He has read, travelled, and thought, and having also suffered, he ought to be an accomplished companion."

"So he is, and, better still, he is a really good man," said she. "His advice is invaluable about my schools, and all my little undertakings at Dawlbridge, and he's so painstaking, he takes so much trouble—you have no idea—wherever he thinks he can be of use; he's so good-natured and so sensible."

"It is pleasant to hear so good an account of his neighbourly virtues. I can only testify to his being an agreeable and gentle companion, and in addition to what you have told me, I think I can tell you two or three things about him," said I.

"Really!"

"Yes, to begin with, he's unmarried."

"Yes, that's right—go on."

"He has been writing, that is he *was*, but two or three years perhaps he has not gone on with his work, and the book was upon some rather abstract subject—perhaps theology."

"Well, he was writing a book, as you say; I'm not quite sure what it was about, but only that it was nothing that I cared for; very likely you are right, and he certainly did stop—yes."

"And although he only drank a little coffee here tonight, he likes tea, at least, did like it extravagantly."

"Yes, that's *quite* true."

"He drank green tea, a good deal, didn't he?" I pursued.

"Well, that's very odd! Green tea was a subject on which we used almost to quarrel."

"But he has quite given that up," said I.

"So he has."

"And, now, one more fact. His mother or his father, did you know them?"

"Yes, both; his father is only ten years dead, and their place is near Dawlbridge. We knew them very well," she answered.

"Well, either his mother or his father—I should rather think his father, saw a ghost," said I.

"Well, you really are a conjuror, Dr Hesselius."

"Conjuror or no, haven't I said right?" I answered merrily.

"You certainly have, and it *was* his father; he was a silent, whimsical man, and he used to bore my father about his dreams, and at last he told him a story about a ghost he had seen and talked with, and a very odd story it was. I remember it particularly, because I was so afraid of him. This story was long before he died—when I was quite a child—and his ways were so silent and moping, and he used to drop in sometimes, in the dusk, when I was alone in the drawing-room, and I used to fancy there were ghosts about him."

I smiled and nodded.

"And now, having established my character as a conjuror, I think I must say goodnight," said I.

"But how *did* you find it out?"

"By the planets, of course, as the gipsies do," I answered, and so, gaily, we said goodnight.

Next morning I sent the little book he had been inquiring after, and a note to Mr Jennings, and on returning late that evening, I found that he had called at my lodgings, and left his card. He asked whether I was at home, and asked at what hour he would be most likely to find me.

Does he intend opening his case, and consulting me "professionally," as they say? I hope so. I have already conceived a theory about him. It is supported by Lady Mary's answers to my parting questions. I should like much to ascertain from his own lips. But what can I do consistently with good breeding to invite a confession? Nothing. I rather think he meditates one. At all events, my dear Van L., I shan't make myself difficult of access; I mean to return his visit tomorrow. It will be only civil in return for his politeness, to ask to see him. Perhaps something may come of it. Whether much, little, or nothing, my dear Van L, you shall hear.

3 Dr Hesselius Picks Up Something in Latin Books

Well, I have called at Blank Street.

On inquiring at the door, the servant told me that Mr Jennings was engaged very particularly with a gentleman, a clergyman from Kenlis, his parish in the country. Intending to reserve my privilege, and to call again, I merely intimated that I should try another time, and had turned to go, when the servant begged my pardon, and asked me, looking at me a little more attentively than well-bred persons of his order usually do, whether I was Dr Hesselius; and, on learning that I was, he said, "Perhaps then, sir, you would allow me to mention it to Mr Jennings, for I am sure he wishes to see you."

The servant returned in a moment, with a message from Mr Jennings, asking me to go into his study, which was in effect his back drawing-room, promising to be with me in a very few minutes.

This was really a study—almost a library. The room was lofty, with two tall slender windows, and rich dark curtains. It was much larger than I had expected, and stored with books on every side, from floor to the ceiling. The upper carpet—for to my tread it felt that there were two or three—was a Turkey carpet. My steps fell noiselessly. The bookcases standing out, placed the windows, particularly narrow ones, in deep recesses. The effect of the room was, although extremely comfortable, and even luxurious, decidedly gloomy, and aided by the silence, almost oppressive. Perhaps, however, I ought to have allowed something for association. My mind had connected peculiar ideas with Mr Jennings. I stepped into this perfectly silent room, of a very silent house, with a peculiar foreboding; and its darkness, and solemn clothing of books, for except where two narrow looking-glasses were set in the wall, they were everywhere, helped this sombre feeling.

While awaiting Mr Jennings' arrival, I amused myself by looking into some of the books with which his shelves were laden. Not among these, but immediately under them, with their backs upward, on the floor, I lighted upon a complete set of Swedenborg's *Arcana Celestia,* in the original Latin, a very fine folio set, bound in the nytty livery which theology affects, pure vellum, namely, gold letters, and carmine edges. There were paper markers in several of these volumes. I raised and placed them, one after the other upon the table, and opening where these papers were placed, I read in the solemn Latin phraseology, a series of sentences indicated by a pencilled line at the margin. Of these I copy here a few, translating them into English.

"When man's interior sight is opened, which is that of his spirit, then there appears the things of another life, which cannot possibly be made visible to the bodily sight . . ."

"By the internal sight it has been granted to me to see the things that are in the other life, more clearly than I see those that are in the world. From these considerations, it is evident that external vision exists from interior vision, and this from a vision still more interior, and so on . . ."

"There are with every man at least two evil spirits . . ."

"With wicked genii there is also a fluent speech, but harsh and grating. There is also among them a speech which is not fluent, wherein the dissent of the thoughts is perceived as something secretly creeping along within it . . ."

"The evil spirits associated with man are indeed from the hells, but when with man they are not then in hell, but are taken out thence. The place where they then are, is in the midst between heaven and hell, and is called the world of spirits—when the evil spirits who are with man, are in that world, they are not in any infernal torment, but in every thought and affection of man, and so, in all that the man himself enjoys. But when they are remitted into their hell, they return to their former state . . ."

"If evil spirits could perceive that they were associated with man, and yet that they were spirits separate from him, and if they could flow in into the things of his body, they would attempt by a thousand means to destroy him; for they hate man with a deadly hatred . . ."

"Knowing, therefore, that I was a man in the body, they were continually striving to destroy me, not as to the body only, but especially as to the soul; for to destroy any man or spirit is the very delight of the life of all who are in hell; but I have been continually protected by the Lord. Hence it appears how dangerous it is for man to be in a living consort with spirits unless he be in the good of faith . . ."

"Nothing is more carefully guarded from the knowledge of associate spirits than their being thus conjoint with a man, for if they knew it they would speak to him, with the intention to destroy him . . ."

"The delight of hell is to do evil to man, and to hasten his eternal ruin."

A long note, written with a very sharp and fine pencil, in Mr Jennings' neat hand, at the foot of the page, caught my eye. Expecting his criticism upon the text, I read a word or two, and stopped, for it was something quite different, and began with these words, *Deus misereatur mei* "May God compassionate me." Thus warned of its private nature, I averted my eyes, and shut the book, replacing all the volumes as I had found them, except one which interested me, and in which, as men studious and solitary in their habits will do, I grew so absorbed as to take no cognisance of the outer world, nor to remember where I was.

I was reading some pages which refer to "representatives" and "correspondents," in the technical language of Swedenborg, and had arrived at a passage, the substance of which is, that evil spirits, when seen by other eyes than those of their infernal associates, present themselves, by "correspondence," in the shape of the beast *(fera)* which represents their particular lust and life, in aspect direful and atrocious. This is a long passage, and particularises a number of those bestial forms.

4 Four Eyes Were Reading the Passage

I was running the head of my pencil-case along the line as I
read it, and something caused me to raise my eyes.

Directly before me was one of the mirrors I have mentioned, in which I saw reflected the tall shape of my friend,
Mr Jennings, leaning over my shoulder, and reading the page
at which I was busy, and with a face so dark and wild that I
should hardly have known him.

I turned and rose. He stood erect also, and with an effort
laughed a little, saying:

"I came in and asked you how you did, but without succeeding in awaking you from your book; so I could not re-
strain my curiosity, and very impertinently, I'm afraid,
peeped over your shoulder. This is not the first time of looking into those pages. You have looked into Swedenborg, no
doubt, long ago?"

"Oh dear, yes! I owe Swedenborg a great deal; you will discover traces of him in the little book on Metaphysical Medicine, which you were so good as to remember."

Although my friend affected a gaiety of manner, there was
a slight flush in his face, and I could perceive that he was
inwardly much perturbed.

"I'm scarcely yet qualified, I know so little of Swedenborg.
I've only had them a fortnight," he answered, "and I think
they are rather likely to make a solitary man nervous—that
is, judging from the very little I have read—I don't say that
they have made me so," he laughed; "and I'm so very much
obliged for the book. I hope you got my note?"

I made all proper acknowledgments and modest disclaim-
ers.

"I never read a book that I go with, so entirely, as that of
yours," he continued. "I saw at once there is more in it than
is quite unfolded. Do you know Dr Harley?" he asked, rather
abruptly.

In passing, the editor remarks that the physician here
named was one of the most eminent who had ever practised
in England.

I did, having had letters to him, and had experienced from

him great courtesy and considerable assistance during my
visit to England.

"I think that man one of the very greatest fools I ever met
in my life," said Mr Jennings.

This was the first time I had ever heard him say a sharp
thing of anybody, and such a term applied to so high a name
a little startled me.

"Really! and in what way?" I asked.

"In his profession," he answered.

I smiled.

"I mean this," he said: "he seems to me, one half, blind—I
mean one half of all he looks at is dark—preternaturally
bright and vivid all the rest; and the worst of it is, it seems
wilful. I can't get him—I mean he won't—I've had some experience of him as a physician, but I look on him as, in that
sense, no better than a paralytic mind, an intellect half dead.
I'll tell you—I know I shall some time—all about it," he said,
with a little agitation "You stay some months longer in England. If I should be out of town during your stay for a little
time, would you allow me to trouble you with a letter?"

"I should be only too happy," I assured him.

"Very good of you. I am so utterly dissatisfied with Harley."

"A little leaning to the materialistic school," I said.

"A *mere* materialist," he corrected me; "you can't think
how that sort of thing worries one who knows better. You
won't tell anyone—any of my friends you know—that I am
hippish; now, for instance, no one knows—not even Lady
Mary—that I have seen Dr Harley, or any other doctor. So
pray don't mention it; and, if I should have any threatening
of an attack, you'll kindly let me write, or, should I be in
town, have a little talk with you."

I was full of conjecture, and unconsciously I found I had
fixed my eyes gravely on him, for he lowered his for a moment, and he said:

"I see you think I might as well tell you now, or else you
are forming a conjecture; but you may as well give it up. If
you were guessing all the rest of your life, you will never hit
on it."

He shook his head smiling, and over that wintry sunshine a

black cloud suddenly came down, and he drew his breath in,
through his teeth as men do in pain.

"Sorry, of course, to learn that you apprehend occasion to
consult any of us; but, command me when and how you like,
and I need not assure you that your confidence is sacred."

He then talked of quite other things, and in a comparatively cheerful way and after a little time, I took my leave.

5 Dr Hesselius Is Summoned to Richmond

We parted cheerfully, but he was not cheerful, nor was I.
There are certain expressions of that powerful organ of spirit
—the human face—which, although I have seen them often,
and possess a doctor's nerve, yet disturb me profoundly. One
look of Mr Jennings' haunted me. It had seized my imagination with so dismal a power that I changed my plans for the
evening, and went to the opera, feeling that I wanted a
change of ideas.

I heard nothing of or from him for two or three days, when
a note in his hand reached me. It was cheerful, and full of
hope. He said that he had been for some little time so much
better—quite well, in fact—that he was going to make a little
experiment, and run down for a month or so to his parish, to
try whether a little work might not quite set him up. There
was in it a fervent religious expression of gratitude for his
restoration, as he now almost hoped he might call it.

A day or two later I saw Lady Mary, who repeated what his
note had announced, and told me that he was actually in
Warwickshire, having resumed his clerical duties at Kenlis;
and she added, "I begin to think that he is really perfectly
well, and that there never was anything the matter, more
than nerves and fancy; we are all nervous, but I fancy there is
nothing like a little hard work for that kind of weakness, and
he has made up his mind to try it. I should not be surprised if
he did not come back for a year."

Notwithstanding all this confidence, only two days later I
had this note, dated from his house off Piccadilly:

DEAR SIR, I have returned disappointed. If I should feel at all
able to see you, I shall write to ask you kindly to call. At
present, I am too low, and, in fact, simply unable to say all I

wish to say. Pray don't mention my name to my friends. I can
see no one. By-and-by, please God, you shall hear from me. I
mean to take a run into Shropshire, where some of my people
are. God bless you! May we, on my return, meet more happily
than I can now write.

About a week after this I saw Lady Mary at her own house,
the last person, she said, left in town, and just on the wing for
Brighton, for the London season was quite over. She told me
that she had heard from Mr Jennings' niece, Martha, in
Shropshire. There was nothing to be gathered from her letter, more than that he was low and nervous. In those words,
of which healthy people think so lightly, what a world of
suffering is sometimes hidden!

Nearly five weeks had passed without any further news of
Mr Jennings. At the end of that time I received a note from
him. He wrote:

> I have been in the country, and have had change of air,
> change of scene, change of faces, change of everything—and in
> everything—but *myself.* I have made up my mind, so far as the
> most irresolute creature on earth can do it, to tell my case
> fully to you. If your engagements will permit, pray come to me
> today, tomorrow, or the next day; but, pray defer as little as
> possible. You know not how much I need help. I have a quiet
> house at Richmond, where I now am. Perhaps you can manage
> to come to dinner, or to luncheon, or even to tea. You shall
> have no trouble in finding me out. The servant at Blank
> Street, who takes this note, will have a carriage at your door
> at any hour you please; and I am always to be found. You will
> say that I ought not to be alone. I have tried everything. Come
> and see.

I called up the servant, and decided on going out the same
evening, which accordingly I did.

He would have been much better in a lodging-house, or
hotel, I thought, as I drove up through a short double row of
sombre elms to a very old-fashioned brick house, darkened by
the foliage of these trees, which overtopped, and nearly surrounded it. It was a perverse choice, for nothing could be
imagined more triste and silent. The house, I found, belonged

to him. He had stayed for a day or two in town, and, finding it for some cause insupportable, had come out here, probably because being furnished and his own, he was relieved of the thought and delay of selection, by coming here.

The sun had already set, and the red reflected light of the western sky illuminated the scene with the peculiar effect with which we are all familiar. The hall seemed very dark, but, getting to the back drawing-room, whose windows command the west, I was again in the same dusky light.

I sat down, looking out upon the richly-wooded landscape that glowed in the grand and melancholy light which was every moment fading. The corners of the room were already dark; all was growing dim, and the gloom was insensibly toning my mind, already prepared for what was sinister. I was waiting alone for his arrival, which soon took place. The door communicating with the front room opened, and the tall figure of Mr Jennings, faintly seen in the ruddy twilight, came, with quiet stealthy steps, into the room.

We shook hands, and, taking a chair to the window, where there was still light enough to enable us to see each other's faces, he sat down beside me, and, placing his hand upon my arm, with scarcely a word of preface began his narrative.

6 How Mr Jennings Met His Companion

The faint glow of the west, the pomp of the then lonely woods of Richmond, were before us, behind and about us the darkening room, and on the stony face of the sufferer—for the character of his face, though still gentle and sweet, was changed—rested that dim, odd glow which seems to descend and produce, where it touches, lights, sudden though faint, which are lost, almost without gradation, in darkness. The silence, too, was utter: not a distant wheel, or bark, or whistle from without; and within, the depressing stillness of an invalid bachelor's house.

I guessed well the nature, though not even vaguely the particulars of the revelations I was about to receive, from that fixed face of suffering that so oddly flushed stood out, like a portrait of Schalken's, before its background of darkness.

"It began," he said, "on the 15th of October, three years

and eleven weeks ago, and two days—I keep very accurate count, for every day is torment. If I leave anywhere a chasm in my narrative, tell me.

"About four years ago I began a work, which had cost me very much thought and reading. It was upon the religious metaphysics of the ancients."

"I know," said I, "the actual religion of educated and thinking paganism, quite apart from symbolic worship? A wide and very interesting field."

"Yes, but not good for the mind—the Christian mind, I mean. Paganism is all bound together in essential unity, and, with evil sympathy, their religion involves their art, and both their manners and the subject is a degrading fascination and the Nemesis sure. God forgive me!

"I wrote a great deal; I wrote late at night. I was always thinking on the subject, walking about, wherever I was, everywhere. It thoroughly infected me. You are to remember that all the material ideas connected with it were more or less of the beautiful, the subject itself delightfully interesting, and I, then, without a care."

He sighed heavily.

"I believe that every one who sets about writing in earnest does his work, as a friend of mine phrased it, *on* something—tea, or coffee, or tobacco. I suppose there is a material waste that must be hourly supplied in such occupations, or that we should grow too abstracted, and the mind, as it were, pass out of the body, unless it were reminded often enough of the connection by actual sensation. At all events, I felt the want, and I supplied it. Tea was my companion—at first the ordinary black tea, made in the usual way, not too strong; but I drank a good deal, and increased its strength as I went on. I never experienced an uncomfortable symptom from it.

"I began to take a little green tea. I found the effect pleasanter, it cleared and intensified the power of thought so, I had come to take it frequently, but not stronger than one might take it for pleasure. I wrote a great deal out here, it was so quiet, and in this room. I used to sit up very late, and it became a habit with me to sip my tea—green tea—every now and then as my work proceeded. I had a little kettle on my table, that swung over a lamp, and made tea two or three times between eleven o'clock and two or three in the morning, my hours of going to bed.

"I used to go into town every day. I was not a monk, and, although I spent an hour or two in a library, hunting up authorities and looking out lights upon my theme, I was in no morbid state as far as I can judge. I met my friends pretty much as usual and enjoyed their society, and, on the whole, existence had never been, I think, so pleasant before.

"I had met with a man who had some odd old books, German editions in mediaeval Latin, and I was only too happy to be permitted access to them. This obliging person's books were in the City, a very out-of-the-way part of it. I had rather out-stayed my intended hour, and, on coming out, seeing no cab near, I was tempted to get into the omnibus which used to drive past this house. It was darker than this by the time the 'bus had reached an old house, you may have remarked, with four poplars at each side of the door, and there the last passenger but myself got out. We drove along rather faster. It was twilight now. I leaned back in my corner next the door ruminating pleasantly.

"The interior of the omnibus was nearly dark. I had observed in the corner opposite to me at the other side, and at the end next the horses, two small circular reflections, as it seemed to me of a reddish light. They were about two inches apart, and about the size of those small brass buttons that yachting men used to put upon their jackets. I began to speculate, as listless men will, upon this trifle, as it seemed. From what centre did that faint but deep red light come, and from what—glass beads, buttons, toy decorations—was it reflected? We were lumbering along gently, having nearly a mile still to go. I had not solved the puzzle, and it became in another minute more odd, for these two luminous points, with a sudden jerk, descended nearer and nearer the floor, keeping still their relative distance and horizontal position, and then, as suddenly they rose to the level of the seat on which I was sitting and I saw them no more.

"My curiosity was now really excited, and, before I had time to think, I saw again these two dull lamps, again together near the floor; again they disappeared, and again in their old corner I saw them.

"So, keeping my eyes upon them, I edged quietly up my own side, towards the end at which I still saw these tiny discs of red.

"There was very little light in the 'bus. It was nearly dark. I leaned forward to aid my endeavour to discover what these little circles really were. They shifted position a little as I did so. I began now to perceive an outline of something black, and I soon saw, with tolerable distinctiveness, the outline of a small black monkey, pushing its face forward in mimicry to meet mine; those were its eyes, and I now dimly saw its teeth grinning at me.

"I drew back, not knowing whether it might not meditate a spring. I fancied that one of the passengers had forgot this ugly pet, and wishing to ascertain something of its temper, though not caring to trust my fingers to it, I poked my umbrella softly towards it. It remained immovable—up to it— *through* it! For through it, and back and forward it passed, without the slightest resistance.

"I can't, in the least, convey to you the kind of horror I felt. When I had ascertained that the thing was an illusion, as I then supposed, there came a misgiving about myself and a terror that fascinated me in impotence to remove my gaze from the eyes of the brute for some moments. As I looked, it made a little skip back, quite into the corner, and I, in a panic found myself at the door, having put my head out, drawing deep breaths of the outer air, and staring at the lights and trees we were passing, too glad to reassure myself of reality.

"I stopped the 'bus and got out. I perceived the man look oddly at me as I paid him. I dare say there was something unusual in my looks and manner, for I had never felt so strangely before."

7 The Journey: First Stage

"When the omnibus drove on, and I was alone upon the road, I looked carefully round to ascertain whether the monkey had followed me. To my indescribable relief I saw it nowhere. I can't describe easily what a shock I had received, and my sense of genuine gratitude on finding myself, as I supposed, quite rid of it.

"I had got out a little before we reached this house, two or three hundred steps. A brick wall runs along the footpath, and inside the wall is a hedge of yew, or some dark evergreen of that kind, and within that again the row of fine trees which you may have remarked as you came.

"This brick wall is about as high as my shoulder, and happening to raise my eyes I saw the monkey, with that stooping gait, on all fours, walking or creeping, close beside me, on top of the wall. I stopped, looking at it with a feeling of loathing and horror. As I stopped so did it. It sat up on the wall with its long hands on its knees looking at me. There was not light enough to see it much more than in outline, nor was it dark enough to bring the peculiar light of its eyes into strong relief. I still saw, however, that red foggy light plainly enough. It did not show its teeth, nor exhibit any sign of irritation, but seemed jaded and sulky, and was observing me steadily.

"I drew back into the middle of the road. It was an unconscious recoil, and there I stood, still looking at it; it did not move.

"With an instinctive determination to try something—anything, I turned about and walked briskly towards town with askance look, all the time, watching the movements of the beast. It crept swiftly along the wall, at exactly my pace.

"Where the wall ends, near the turn of the road, it came down, and with a wiry spring or two brought itself close to my feet, and continued to keep up with me, as I quickened my pace. It was at my left side, so close to my leg that I felt every moment as if I should tread upon it.

"The road was quite deserted and silent, and it was darker every moment. I stopped, dismayed and bewildered, turning as I did so, the other way—I mean, towards this house, away from which I had been walking. When I stood still, the monkey drew back to a distance of, I suppose, about five or six yards, and remained stationary, watching me.

"I had been more agitated than I have said. I had read, of course, as everyone has, something about 'spectral illusions,' as you physicians term the phenomena of such cases. I considered my situation, and looked my misfortune in the face.

"These affections, I had read, are sometimes transitory and sometimes obstinate. I had read of cases in which the appearance, at first harmless, had, step by step, degenerated into something direful and insupportable, and ended by wearing its victim out. Still as I stood there, but for my bestial companion, quite alone, I tried to comfort myself by repeating again and again the assurance, 'the thing is purely disease, a well-known physical affection, as distinctly as small-pox or neuralgia. Doctors are all agreed on that, philosophy demonstrates it. I must not be a fool. I've been sitting up too late, and I daresay my digestion is quite wrong, and, with God's help, I shall be all right, and this is but a symptom of nervous dyspepsia.' Did I believe all this? Not one word of it, no more than any other miserable being ever did who is once seized and riveted in this satanic captivity. Against my convictions, I might say my knowledge, I was simply bullying myself into a false courage.

"I now walked homeward. I had only a few hundred yards to go. I had forced myself into a sort of resignation, but I had not got over the sickening shock and the flurry of the first certainty of my misfortune.

"I had made up my mind to pass the night at home. The brute moved close beside me, and I fancied there was the sort of anxious drawing toward the house, which one sees in tired horses or dogs, sometimes as they come toward home.

"I was afraid to go into town. I was afraid of anyone's seeing and recognising me. I was conscious of an irrepressible agitation in my manner. Also, I was afraid of any violent change in my habits, such as going to a place of amusement, or walking from home in order to fatigue myself. At the hall door it waited till I mounted the steps, and when the door was opened entered with me.

"I drank no tea that night. I got cigars and some brandy-and-water. My idea was that I should act upon my material system, and by living for a while in sensation apart from thought, send myself forcibly, as it were, into a new groove. I came up here to this drawing-room. I sat just there. The monkey then got upon a small table that then stood *there*. It looked dazed and languid. An irrepressible uneasiness as to its movements kept my eyes always upon it. Its eyes were half closed, but I could see them glow. It was looking steadily

at me. In all situations, at all hours, it is awake and looking
at me. That never changes.

"I shall not continue in detail my narrative of this particular night. I shall describe, rather, the phenomena of the first
year, which never varied, essentially. I shall describe the
monkey as it appeared in daylight. In the dark, as you shall
presently hear, there are peculiarities. It is a small monkey,
perfectly black. It had only one peculiarity—a character of
malignity—unfathomable malignity. During the first year it
looked sullen and sick. But this character of intense malice
and vigilance was always underlying that surly languor. During all that time it acted as if on a plan of giving me as little
trouble as was consistent with watching me. Its eyes were
never off me. I have never lost sight of it, except in my sleep,
light or dark, day or night, since it came here, excepting
when it withdraws for some weeks at a time, unaccountably.

"In total dark it is visible as in daylight. I do not mean
merely its eyes. It is *all* visible distinctly in a halo that resembles a glow of red embers, and which accompanies it in all
its movements.

"When it leaves me for a time, it is always at night, in the
dark, and in the same way. It grows at first uneasy, and then
furious, and then advances towards me, grinning and shaking, its paws clenched, and, at the same time, there comes the
appearance of fire in the grate. I never have any fire. I can't
sleep in the room where there is any, and it draws nearer and
nearer to the chimney, quivering, it seems, with rage, and
when its fury rises to the highest pitch, it springs into the
grate, and up the chimney, and I see it no more.

"When first this happened, I thought I was released. I was
now a new man. A day passed—a night—and no return, and
a blessed week—a week—another week. I was always on my
knees, Dr Hesselius, always, thanking God and praying. A
whole month passed of liberty, but on a sudden, it was with
me again."

8 The Second Stage

"It was with me, and the malice which before was torpid
under a sullen exterior, was now active. It was perfectly un-

changed in every other aspect. This new energy was apparent in its activity and its looks, and soon in other ways.

"For a time, you will understand, the change was shown only in an increased vivacity, and an air of menace, as if it were always brooding over some atrocious plan. Its eyes, as before, were never off me."

"Is it here now?" I asked.

"No," he replied, "it has been absent exactly a fortnight and a day—fifteen days. It has sometimes been away so long as nearly two months, once for three. Its absence always exceeds a fortnight, although it may be but by a single day. Fifteen days having past since I saw it last, it may return now at any moment."

"Is its return," I asked, "accompanied by any peculiar manifestation?"

"Nothing—no," he said. "It is simply with me again. On lifting my eyes from a book, or turning my head, I see it, as usual, looking at me, and then it remains, as before, for its appointed time. I have never told so much and so minutely before to any one."

I perceived that he was agitated, and looking like death, and he repeatedly applied his handkerchief to his forehead; I suggested that he might be tired, and told him that I would call, with pleasure, in the morning, but he said:

"No, if you don't mind hearing it all now. I have got so far, and I should prefer making one effort of it. When I spoke to Dr Harley, I had nothing like so much to tell. You are a philosophic physician. You give spirit its proper rank. If this thing is real—"

He paused, looking at me with agitated inquiry.

"We can discuss it by-and-by, and very fully. I will give you all I think," I answered, after an interval.

"Well—very well. If it is anything real, I say, it is prevailing, little by little, and drawing me more interiorly into hell. Optic nerves, he talked of. Ah! well—there are other nerves of communication. May God Almighty help me! You shall hear.

"Its power of action, I tell you, had increased. Its malice became, in a way, aggressive. About two years ago, some questions that were pending between me and the bishop hav-

ing been settled, I went down to my parish in Warwickshire,
anxious to find occupation in my profession. I was not prepared for what happened, although I have since thought I
might have apprehended something like it. The reason of my
saying so is that—"

He was beginning to speak with a great deal more effort
and reluctance, and sighed often, and seemed at times nearly
overcome. But at this time his manner was not agitated. It
was more like that of a sinking patient, who has given himself up.

"Yes, but I will first tell you about Kenlis, my parish.

"It was with me when I left this place for Dawlbridge. It
was my silent travelling companion, and it remained with me
at the vicarage. When I entered on the discharge of my duties, another change took place. The thing exhibited an atrocious determination to thwart me. It was with me in the
church—in the reading-desk—in the pulpit—within the com-
munion rails. At last, it reached this extremity, that while I
was reading to the congregation, it would spring upon the
book and squat there, so that I was unable to see the page.
This happened more than once.

"I left Dawlbridge for a time. I placed myself in Dr Harley's
hands. I did everything he told me. He gave my case a great
deal of thought. It interested him, I think. He seemed successful. For nearly three months I was perfectly free from a return. I began to think I was safe. With his full assent I returned to Dawlbridge.

"I travelled in a chaise. I was in good spirits. I was more—I
was happy and grateful. I was returning, as I thought, delivered from a dreadful hallucination, to the scene of duties
which I longed to enter upon. It was a beautiful sunny evening, everything looked serene and cheerful, and I was de-
lighted. I remember looking out of the window to see the
spire of my church at Kenlis among the trees, at the point
where one has the earliest view of it. It is exactly where the
little stream that bounds the parish passes under the road by
a culvert, and where it emerges at the roadside, a stone with
an old inscription is placed. As we passed this point, I drew
my head in and sat down, and in the corner of the chaise was
the monkey.

JOSEPH SHERIDAN LE FANU

"For a moment I felt faint, and then quite wild with despair and horror. I called to the driver, and got out, and sat down at the roadside, and prayed to God silently for mercy. A despairing resignation supervened. My companion was with me as I re-entered the vicarage. The same persecution followed. After a short struggle I submitted, and soon I left the place.

"I told you," he said, "that the beast had before this become in certain ways aggressive. I will explain a little. It seemed to be actuated by intense and increasing fury, whenever I said my prayers, or even meditated prayer. It amounted at last to a dreadful interruption. You will ask, how could a silent immaterial phantom effect that? It was thus, whenever I meditated praying; it was always before me, and nearer and nearer.

"It used to spring on a table, on the back of a chair, on the chimney-piece, and slowly to swing itself from side to side, looking at me all the time. There is in its motion an indefinable power to dissipate thought, and to contract one's attention to that monotony, till the ideas shrink, as it were, to a point, and at last to nothing—and unless I had started up and shook off the catalepsy, I have felt as if my mind were on the point of losing itself. There are other ways," he sighed heavily; "thus, for instance, while I pray with my eyes closed, it comes closer and closer, and I see it. I know it is not to be accounted for physically, but I do actually see it, though my lids are closed, and so it rocks my mind, as it were, and overpowers me, and I am obliged to rise from my knees. If you had ever yourself known this, you would be acquainted with desperation."

9 The Third Stage

"I see, Dr Hesselius, that you don't lose one word of my statement. I need not ask you to listen specially to what I am now going to tell you. They talk of the optic nerves, and of spectral illusions, as if the organ of sight was the only point assailable by the influences that have fastened upon me—I know better. For two years in my direful case that limitation prevailed. But as food is taken in softly at the lips, and then brought under the teeth, as the tip of the little finger caught

in a mill crank will draw in the hand, and the arm, and the
whole body, so the miserable mortal who has been once
caught firmly by the end of the finest fibre of his nerve, is
drawn in and in, by the enormous machinery of hell, until he
is as I am. Yes, Doctor, as *I* am, for while I talk to you, and
implore relief, I feel that my prayer is for the impossible, and
my pleading with the inexorable."

I endeavoured to calm his visibly increasing agitation, and
told him that he must not despair.

While we talked the night had overtaken us. The filmy
moonlight was wide over the scene which the window com-
manded, and I said:

"Perhaps you would prefer having candles. This light, you
know, is odd. I should wish you, as much as possible, under
your usual conditions while I make my diagnosis, shall I call
it—otherwise I don't care."

"All lights are the same to me," he said; "except when I
read or write, I care not if night were perpetual. I am going to
tell you what happened about a year ago. The thing began to
speak to me."

"Speak! How do you mean—speak as a man does, do you
mean?"

"Yes; speak in words and consecutive sentences, with perfect coherence and articulation; but there is a peculiarity. It
is not like the tone of a human voice. It is not by my ears it
reaches me—it comes like a singing through my head.

"This faculty, the power of speaking to me, will be my un-
doing. It won't let me pray, it interrupts me with dreadful
blasphemies. I dare not go on, I could not. Oh! Doctor, can the
skill, and thought, and prayers of man avail me nothing!"

"You must promise me, my dear sir, not to trouble yourself
with unnecessarily exciting thoughts; confine yourself
strictly to the narrative of *facts;* and recollect, above all, that
even if the thing that infests you be, you seem to suppose, a
reality with an actual independent life and will, yet it can
have no power to hurt you, unless it be given from above: its
access to your senses depends mainly upon your physical condition—this is, under God, your comfort and reliance: we are
all alike environed. It is only that in your case, the *paries,* the
veil of the flesh, the screen, is a little out of repair, and sights

and sounds are transmitted. We must enter on a new course, sir—be encouraged. I'll give tonight to the careful consideration of the whole case."

"You are very good, sir; you think it worth trying, you don't give me quite up; but, sir, you don't know, it is gaining such an influence over me; it orders me about, it is such a tyrant, and I'm growing so helpless. May God deliver me!"

"It orders you about—of course you mean by speech?"

"Yes, yes; it is always urging me to crimes, to injure others, or myself. You see, Doctor, the situation is urgent, it is indeed. When I was in Shropshire, a few weeks ago" (Mr Jennings was speaking rapidly and trembling now, holding my arm with one hand, and looking in my face), "I went out one day with a party of friends for a walk: my persecutor, I tell you, was with me at the time. I lagged behind the rest: the country near the Dee, you know, is beautiful. Our path happened to lie near a coal mine, and at the verge of the wood is a perpendicular shaft, they say, a hundred and fifty feet deep. My niece had remained behind with me—she knows, of course, nothing of the nature of my sufferings. She knew, however, that I had been ill, and was low, and she remained to prevent my being quite alone. As we loitered slowly on together, the brute that accompanied me was urging me to throw myself down the shaft.

"I tell you now—oh, sir, think of it!—the one consideration that saved me from that hideous death was the fear lest the shock of witnessing the occurrence should be too much for the poor girl. I asked her to go on and walk with her friends, saying that I could go no further. She made excuses, and the more I urged her the firmer she became. She looked doubtful and frightened. I suppose there was something in my looks or manner that alarmed her; but she would not go, and that literally saved me. You had no idea, sir, that a living man could be made so abject a slave of Satan," he said, with a ghastly groan and shudder.

There was a pause here, and I said, "You *were* preserved nevertheless. It was the act of God. You are in His hands and in the power of no other being: be therefore confident for the future."

10 Home

I made him have candles lighted, and saw the room looking cheery and inhabited before I left him. I told him that he must regard his illness strictly as one dependent on physical, though *subtle* physical causes. I told him that he had evidence of God's care and love in the deliverance which he had just described, and that I had perceived with pain that he seemed to regard its peculiar features as indicating that he had been delivered over to spiritual reprobation. Than such a conclusion nothing could be, I insisted, less warranted; and not only so, but more contrary to facts, as disclosed in his mysterious deliverance from that murderous influence during his Shropshire excursion. First, his niece had been retained by his side without his intending to keep her near him; and, secondly, there had been infused into his mind an irresistible repugnance to execute the dreadful suggestion in her presence.

As I reasoned this point with him, Mr Jennings wept. He seemed comforted. One promise I exacted, which was that should the monkey at any time return, I should be sent for immediately; and, repeating my assurance that I would give neither time nor thought to any other subject until I had thoroughly investigated his case, and that tomorrow he should hear the result, I took my leave.

Before getting into the carriage I told the servant that his master was far from well, and that he should make a point of frequently looking into his room.

My own arrangements I made with a view to being quite secure from interruption.

I merely called at my lodgings, and with a travelling-desk and carpet-bag, set off in a hackney-carriage for an inn about two miles out of town, called The Horns, a very quiet and comfortable house, with good thick walls. And there I resolved, without the possibility of intrusion or distraction, to devote some hours of the night, in my comfortable sitting-room, to Mr Jennings' case, and so much of the morning as it might require.

(There occurs here a careful note of Dr Hesselius' opinion

upon the case, and of the habits, dietary, and medicines which he prescribed. It is curious—some persons would say mystical. But, on the whole, I doubt whether it would sufficiently interest a reader of the kind I am likely to meet with, to warrant its being here reprinted. The whole letter was plainly written at the inn where he had hid himself for the occasion. The next letter is dated from his town lodgings.)

I left town for the inn where I slept last night at half-past nine, and did not arrive at my room in town until one o'clock this afternoon. I found a letter in Mr Jennings' hand upon my table. It had not come by post, and, on inquiry, I learned that Mr Jennings' servant had brought it, and on learning that I was not to return until today, and that no one could tell him my address, he seemed very uncomfortable, and said his orders from his master were that he was not to return without an answer.

I opened the letter and read:

DEAR DR HESSELIUS.—It is here. You had not been an hour gone when it returned. It is speaking. It knows all that has happened. It knows everything—it knows you, and is frantic and atrocious. It reviles. I send you this. It knows every word I have written—I write. This I promised, and I therefore write, but, I fear, very confused, very incoherently. I am so interrupted, disturbed.

Ever yours, sincerely yours,
ROBERT LYNDER JENNINGS.

"When did this come?" I asked.

"About eleven last night: the man was here again, and has been here thrce times today. The last time is about an hour since."

Thus answered, and with the notes I had made upon his case in my pocket, I was in a few minutes driving towards Richmond, to see Mr Jennings.

I by no means, as you perceive, despaired of Mr Jennings' case. He had himself remembered and applied, though quite in a mistaken way, the principle which I lay down in my Metaphysical Medicine, and which governs all such cases. I was about to apply it in earnest. I was profoundly interested, and very anxious to see and examine him while the "enemy" was actually present.

I drove up to the sombre house, and ran up the steps, and knocked. The door, in a little time, was opened by a tall woman in black silk. She looked ill, and as if she had been crying. She curtseyed, and heard my question, but she did not answer. She turned her face away, extending her hand towards two men who were coming downstairs; and thus having, as it were, tacitly made me over to them, she passed through a side-door hastily and shut it.

The man who was nearest the hall, I at once accosted, but being now close to him, I was shocked to see that both his hands were covered in blood.

I drew back a little, and the man, passing downstairs, merely said in a low tone, "Here's the servant, sir."

The servant had stopped on the stairs, confounded and dumb at seeing me. He was rubbing his hands in a handkerchief, and it was steeped in blood.

"Jones, what is it? what has happened?" I asked, while a sickening suspicion overpowered me.

The man asked me to come up to the lobby. I was beside him in a moment, and, frowning and pallid, with contracted eyes, he told me the horror which I already half guessed.

His master had made away with himself.

I went upstairs with him to the room—what I saw there I won't tell you. He had cut his throat with his razor. It was a frightful gash. The two men had laid him on the bed, and composed his limbs. It had happened, as the immense pool of blood on the floor declared, at some distance between the bed and the window. There was carpet round his bed, and a carpet under his dressing-table, but none on the rest of the floor, for the man said he did not like a carpet in his bedroom. In this sombre and now terrible room, one of the great elms that darkened the house was slowly moving the shadow of one of its great boughs upon this dreadful floor.

I beckoned to the servant, and we went downstairs together. I turned off the hall into an old-fashioned panelled room, and there standing, I heard all the servant had to tell. It was not a great deal.

"I concluded, sir, from your words, and looks, sir, as you

left last night, that you thought my master was seriously ill. I thought it might be that you were afraid of a fit, or something. So I attended very close to your directions. He sat up late, till past three o'clock. He was not writing or reading. He was talking a great deal to himself, but that was nothing unusual. At about that hour I assisted him to undress, and left him in his slippers and dressing-gown. I went back softly in about half-an-hour. He was in his bed, quite undressed, and a pair of candles lighted on the table beside his bed. He was leaning on his elbow, and looking out at the other side of the bed when I came in. I asked him if he wanted anything, and he said no.

"I don't know whether it was what you said to me, sir, or something a little unusual about him, but I was uneasy, uncommon uneasy about him last night.

"In another half hour, or it might be a little more, I went up again. I did not hear him talking as before. I opened the door a little. The candles were both out, which was not usual. I had a bedroom candle, and I let the light in, a little bit, looking softly round.

"I saw him sitting in that chair beside the dressing-table with his clothes on again. He turned round and looked at me. I thought it strange he should get up and dress, and put out the candles to sit in the dark, that way. But I only asked him again if I could do anything for him. He said no, rather sharp, I thought. I asked him if I might light the candles and he said, 'Do as you like, Jones.' So I lighted them, and I lingered about the room, and he said, 'Tell me truth, Jones; why did you come again—you did not hear anyone cursing?' 'No, sir,' I said, wondering what he could mean.

" 'No,' said he, after me, 'of course, no'; and I said to him, 'Wouldn't it be well, sir, you went to bed? It's just five o'clock,' and he said nothing, but, 'Very likely; goodnight, Jones.' So I went, sir, but in less than an hour I came again. The door was fast, and he heard me, and called as I thought from the bed to know what I wanted, and he desired me not to disturb him again. I lay down and slept for a little.

"It must have been between six and seven when I went up again. The door was still fast, and he made no answer, so I did not like to disturb him, and thinking he was asleep, I left him till nine. It was his custom to ring when he wished me to come, and I had no particular hour for calling him. I tapped very gently, and getting no answer, I stayed away a good while, supposing he was getting some rest then. It was not till eleven o'clock I grew really uncomfortable about him—for at the latest he was never, that I could remember, later than half-past ten. I got no answer. I knocked and called, and still no answer. So not being able to force the door, I called Thomas from the stables, and together we forced it, and found him in the shocking way you saw."

Jones had no more to tell. Poor Mr Jennings was very gentle, and very kind. All his people were fond of him. I could see that the servant was very much moved.

So, dejected and agitated, I passed from that terrible house, and its dark canopy of elms, and I hope I shall never see it more. While I write to you I feel like a man who has but half waked from a frightful and monotonous dream. My memory rejects the picture with incredulity and horror. Yet I know it is true. It is the story of the process of a poison, a poison which excites the reciprocal action of spirit and nerve, and paralyses the tissue that separates those cognate functions of the senses, the external and the interior. Thus we find strange bed-fellows, and the mortal and immortal prematurely make acquaintance.

Conclusion: A Word for Those Who Suffer

My dear Van L—, you have suffered from an affection similar to that which I have just described. You twice complained of a return of it.

Who, under God, cured you? Your humble servant, Martin Hesselius. Let me rather adopt the more emphasised piety of a certain good old French surgeon of three hundred years ago: "I treated, and God cured you."

Come, my friend, you are not to be hippish. Let me tell you a fact.

I have met with, and treated, as my book shows, fifty-seven cases of this kind of vision, which I term indifferently "sublimated," "precocious," and "interior."

There is another class of affections which are truly termed

—though commonly confounded with those which I describe —spectral illusions. These latter I look upon as being no less simply curable than a cold in the head or a trifling dyspepsia.

It is those which rank in the first category that test our promptitude of thought. Fifty-seven such cases have I encountered, neither more nor less. And in how many of these have I failed? In no single instance.

There is no one affliction of mortality more easily and certainly reducible, with a little patience, and a rational confidence in the physician. With these simple conditions, I look upon the cure as absolutely certain.

You are to remember that I had not even commenced to treat Mr Jennings' case. I have not any doubt that I should have cured him perfectly in eighteen months, or possibly it might have extended to two years. Some cases are very rapidly curable, others extremely tedious. Every intelligent physician who will give thought and diligence to the task, will effect a cure.

You know my tract on The Cardinal Functions of the Brain. I there, by the evidence of innumerable facts, prove, as I think, the high probability of a circulation arterial and venous in its mechanism, through the nerves. Of this system, thus considered, the brain is the heart. The fluid, which is propagated hence through one class of nerves, returns in an altered state through another, and the nature of that fluid is spiritual, though not immaterial, any more than, as I before remarked, light or electricity are so.

By various abuses, among which the habitual use of such agents as green tea is one, this fluid may be affected as to its quality, but it is more frequently disturbed as to equilibrium. This fluid being that which we have in common with spirits, a congestion found upon the masses of brain or nerve, connected with the interior sense, forms a surface unduly exposed, on which disembodied spirits may operate: communication is thus more or less effectually established. Between this brain circulation and the heart circulation there is an intimate sympathy. The seat, or rather the instrument of exterior vision, is the eye. The seat of interior vision is the nervous tissue and brain, immediately about and above the eyebrow.

You remember how effectually I dissipated your pictures by the simple application of iced eau-de-cologne. Few cases, however, can be treated exactly alike with anything like rapid success. Cold acts powerfully as a repellant of the nervous fluid. Long enough continued it will even produce that permanent insensibility which we call numbness, and a little longer, muscular as well as sensational paralysis.

I have not, I repeat, the slightest doubt that I should have first dimmed and ultimately sealed that inner eye which Mr Jennings had inadvertently opened. The same senses are opened in delirium tremens, and entirely shut up again when the overaction of the cerebral heart, and the prodigious nervous congestions that attend it, are terminated by a decided change in the state of the body. It is by acting steadily upon the body by a simple process, that this result is produced— and inevitably produced—I have never yet failed.

Poor Mr Jennings made away with himself. But that catastrophe was the result of a totally different malady, which, as it were, projected itself upon the disease which was established. His case was in the distinctive manner a complication, and the complaint under which he really succumbed, was a hereditary suicidal mania. Poor Mr Jennings I cannot call a patient of mine, for I had not even begun to treat his case, and he had not yet given me, I am convinced, his full and unreserved confidence. If the patient does not array himself on the side of the disease, his cure is certain.

The Damned Thing

by Ambrose Bierce

For all their monstrousness, the conventional creatures of supernatural horror share one recognizable attribute: whether ghost, vampire, werewolf, or reanimated corpse, they are recognizable deviations from human life. In "The Damned Thing" (1891), Ambrose Bierce asks readers to look beyond creatures who fall just outside the boundaries of tidy categorical distinctions and conceive instead of an entity that defies classification altogether. "The Damned Thing" is by no means the first story to suggest the existence of invisible beings, having been preceded into print by Fitz-James O'Brien's "What Was It?" and Guy de Maupassant's "The Horla." But the mindless ferocity of Bierce's monster distinguishes it from its predecessors, and conveys an almost literal image of men grappling with the unfathomable mysteries of the Unknown.

CHAPTER I

ONE DOES NOT ALWAYS EAT
WHAT IS ON THE TABLE

By the light of a tallow candle which had been placed on one end of a rough-table a man was reading something written in a book. It was an old account book, greatly worn; and the writing was not, apparently, very legible, for the man sometimes held the page close to the flame of the candle to get a stronger light on it. The shadow of the book would then throw into obscurity a half of the room, darkening a number of faces and figures; for besides the reader, eight other men were present. Seven of them sat against the rough log walls, silent, motionless, and the room being small, not very far from the table. By extending an arm anyone of them could have touched the eighth man, who lay on the table, face upward, partly covered by a sheet, his arms at his sides. He was dead.

The man with the book was not reading aloud, and no one spoke; all seemed to be waiting for something to occur; the dead man only was without expectation. From the blank darkness outside came in, through the aperture that served for a window, all the ever unfamiliar noises of night in the wilderness—the long nameless note of a distant coyote; the stilly pulsing thrill of tireless insects in trees; strange cries of night birds, so different from those of the birds of day; the drone of great blundering beetles, and all that mysterious chorus of small sounds that seem always to have been but half heard when they have suddenly ceased, as if conscious of an indiscretion. But nothing of all this was noted in that company; its members were not overmuch addicted to idle interest in matters of no practical importance; that was obvious in every line of their rugged faces—obvious even in the dim light of the single candle. They were evidently men of the vicinity—farmers and woodsmen.

The person reading was a trifle different; one would have said of him that he was of the world, worldly, albeit there was that in his attire which attested a certain fellowship with the organisms of his environment. His coat would hardly have passed muster in San Francisco; his foot-gear was not of urban origin, and the hat that lay by him on the floor (he was the only one uncovered) was such that if one had considered it as an article of mere personal adornment he would have missed its meaning. In countenance the man was rather prepossessing, with just a hint of sternness; though that he may have assumed or cultivated, as appropriate to one in authority. For he was a coroner. It was by virtue of his office that he had possession of the book in which he was reading; it had been found among the dead man's effects—in his cabin, where the inquest was now taking place.

When the coroner had finished reading he put the book into his breast pocket. At that moment the door was pushed open and a young man entered. He, clearly, was not of mountain birth and breeding: he was clad as those who dwell in cities. His clothing was dusty, however, as from travel. He had, in fact, been riding hard to attend the inquest.

The coroner nodded; no one else greeted him.

"We have waited for you," said the coroner. "It is necessary to have done with this business to-night."

The young man smiled. "I am sorry to have kept you," he said. "I went away, not to evade your summons, but to post to my newspaper an account of what I suppose I am called back to relate."

The coroner smiled.

"The account that you posted to your newspaper," he said, "differs, probably, from that which you will give here under oath."

"That," replied the other, rather hotly and with a visible flush, "is as you please. I used manifold paper and have a copy of what I sent. It was not written as news, for it is incredible, but as fiction. It may go as a part of my testimony under oath."

"But you say it is incredible."

"That is nothing to you, sir, if I also swear that it is true."

The coroner was silent for a time, his eyes upon the floor. The men about the sides of the cabin talked in whispers, but seldom withdrew their gaze from the face of the corpse. Presently the coroner lifted his eyes and said: "We will resume the inquest."

The men removed their hats. The witness was sworn.

"What is your name?" the coroner asked.

"William Harker."

"Age?"

"Twenty-seven."

"You knew the deceased, Hugh Morgan?"

"Yes."

"You were with him when he died?"

"Near him."

"How did that happen—your presence, I mean?"

"I was visiting him at this place to shoot and fish. A part of my purpose, however, was to study him and his odd, solitary way of life. He seemed a good model for a character in fiction. I sometimes write stories."

"I sometimes read them."

"Thank you."

"Stories in general—not yours."

Some of the jurors laughed. Against a sombre background humour shows high lights. Soldiers in the intervals of battle laugh easily, and a jest in the death chamber conquers by surprise.

"Relate the circumstances of this man's death," said the coroner. "You may use any notes or memoranda that you please."

The witness understood. Pulling a manuscript from his breast pocket he held it near the candle and turning the leaves until he found the passage that he wanted began to read.

CHAPTER II

WHAT MAY HAPPEN IN A FIELD OF WILD OATS

". . . The sun had hardly risen when we left the house. We were looking for quail, each with a shotgun, but we had only one dog. Morgan said that our best ground was beyond a certain ridge that he pointed out, and we crossed it by a trail through the *chaparral.* On the other side was comparatively level ground, thickly covered with wild oats. As we emerged from the *chaparral* Morgan was but a few yards in advance. Suddenly we heard, at a little distance to our right and partly in front, a noise as of some animal thrashing about in the bushes, which we could see were violently agitated.

" 'We've started a deer,' I said. 'I wish we had brought a rifle.'

"Morgan, who had stopped and was intently watching the agitated *chaparral,* said nothing, but had cocked both barrels of his gun and was holding it in readiness to aim. I thought him a trifle excited, which surprised me, for he had a reputation for exceptional coolness, even in moments of sudden and imminent peril.

" 'Oh, come,' I said. 'You are not going to fill up a deer with quailshot, are you?'

"Still he did not reply; but catching a sight of his face as he turned it slightly toward me I was struck by the intensity of his look. Then I understood that we had serious business in hand, and my first conjecture was that we had 'jumped' a grizzly. I advanced to Morgan's side, cocking my piece as I moved.

"The bushes were now quiet and the sounds had ceased, but Morgan was as attentive to the place as before.

" 'What is it? What the devil is it?' I asked.

" 'That Damned Thing!' he replied, without turning his head. His voice was husky and unnatural. He trembled visibly.

"I was about to speak further, when I observed the wild oats near the place of the disturbance moving in the most inexplicable way. I can hardly describe it. It seemed as if stirred by a streak of wind, which not only bent it, but pressed it down—crushed it so that it did not rise; and this movement was slowly prolonging itself directly toward us.

"Nothing that I had ever seen had affected me so strangely as this unfamiliar and unaccountable phenomenon, yet I am unable to recall any sense of fear. I remember—and tell it here because, singularly enough, I recollected it then—that once in looking carelessly out of an open window I momentarily mistook a small tree close at hand for one of a group of larger trees at a little distance away. It looked the same size as the others, but being more distinctly and sharply defined in mass and detail seemed out of harmony with them. It was a mere falsification of the law of aerial perspective, but it startled, almost terrified me. We so rely upon the orderly operation of familiar natural laws that any seeming suspension of them is noted as a menace to our safety, a warning of unthinkable calamity. So now the apparently causeless movement of the herbage and the slow, undeviating approach of the line of disturbance were distinctly disquieting. My companion appeared actually frightened, and I could hardly credit my senses when I saw him suddenly throw his gun to his shoulder and fire both barrels at the agitated grain! Before the smoke of the discharge had cleared away I heard a loud savage cry—a scream like that of a wild animal—and flinging his gun upon the ground Morgan sprang away and ran swiftly from the spot. At the same instant I was thrown violently to the ground by the impact of something unseen in the smoke—some soft, heavy substance that seemed thrown against me with great force.

"Before I could get upon my feet and recover my gun, which seemed to have been struck from my hands, I heard Morgan crying out as if in mortal agony, and mingling with his cries were such hoarse, savage sounds as one hears from fighting dogs. Inexpressibly terrified, I struggled to my feet and looked in the direction of Morgan's retreat; and may Heaven in mercy spare me from another sight like that! At a distance of less than thirty yards was my friend, down upon one knee, his head thrown back at a frightful angle, hatless, his long hair in disorder and his whole body in violent movement from side to side, backward and forward. His right arm was lifted and seemed to lack the hand—at least, I could see none. The other arm was invisible. At times, as my memory now reports this extraordinary scene, I could discern but a part of his body; it was as if he had been partly blotted out—I cannot otherwise express it—then a shifting of his position would bring it all into view again.

"All this must have occurred within a few seconds, yet in that time Morgan assumed all the postures of a determined wrestler vanquished by superior weight and strength. I saw nothing but him, and him not always distinctly. During the entire incident his shouts and curses were heard, as if through an enveloping uproar of such sounds of rage and fury as I had never heard from the throat of man or brute!

"For a moment only I stood irresolute, then throwing down my gun I ran forward to my friend's assistance. I had a vague belief that he was suffering from a fit, or some form of convulsion. Before I could reach his side he was down and quiet. All sounds had ceased, but with a feeling of such terror as even these awful events had not inspired I now saw again the mysterious movement of the wild oats, prolonging itself from the trampled area about the prostrate man toward the edge of a wood. It was only when it had reached the wood that I was able to withdraw my eyes and look at my companion. He was dead."

CHAPTER III

A MAN THOUGH NAKED MAY BE IN RAGS

The coroner rose from his seat and stood beside the dead man. Lifting an edge of the sheet he pulled it away, exposing the entire body, altogether naked and showing in the candle-light a clay-like yellow. It had, however, broad maculations of bluish black, obviously caused by extravasated blood from contusions. The chest and sides looked as if they had been beaten with a bludgeon. There were dreadful lacerations; the skin was torn in strips and shreds.

The coroner moved round to the end of the table and undid a silk handkerchief which had been passed under the chin and knotted on the top of the head. When the handkerchief was drawn away it exposed what had been the throat. Some of the jurors who had risen to get a better view repented their curiosity and turned away their faces. Witness Harker went to the open window and leaned out across the sill, faint and sick. Dropping the handkerchief upon the dead man's neck the coroner stepped to an angle of the room and from a pile of clothing produced one garment after another, each of which he held up a moment for inspection. All were torn, and stiff with blood. The jurors did not make a closer inspection. They seemed rather uninterested. They had, in truth, seen all this before; the only thing that was new to them being Harker's testimony.

"Gentlemen," the coroner said, "we have no more evidence, I think. Your duty has been already explained to you; if there is nothing you wish to ask you may go outside and consider your verdict."

The foreman rose—a tall, bearded man of sixty, coarsely clad.

"I shall like to ask one question, Mr. Coroner," he said. "What asylum did this yer last witness escape from?"

"Mr. Harker," said the coroner gravely and tranquilly, "from what asylum did you last escape?"

Harker flushed crimson again, but said nothing, and the seven jurors rose and solemnly filed out of the cabin.

"If you have done insulting me, sir," said Harker, as soon as he and the officer were left alone with the dead man, "I suppose I am at liberty to go?"

"Yes."

Harker started to leave, but paused, with his hand on the door latch. The habit of his profession was strong in him— stronger than his sense of personal dignity. He turned about and said:

"The book that you have there—I recognize it as Morgan's diary. You seemed greatly interested in it; you read in it while I was testifying. May I see it? The public would like—"

"The book will cut no figure in this matter," replied the official, slipping it into his coat pocket; "all the entries in it were made before the writer's death."

As Harker passed out of the house the jury re-entered and stood about the table, on which the now covered corpse showed under the sheet with sharp definition. The foreman seated himself near the candle, produced from his breast pocket a pencil and scrap of paper and wrote rather laboriously the following verdict, which with various degrees of effort all signed:

"We, the jury, do find that the remains come to their death at the hands of a mountain lion, but some of us thinks, all the same, they had fits."

CHAPTER IV

AN EXPLANATION FROM THE TOMB

In the diary of the late Hugh Morgan are certain interesting entries having, possibly, a scientific value as suggestions. At the inquest upon his body the book was not put in evidence; possibly the coroner thought it not worth while to confuse the jury. The date of the first of the entries mentioned cannot be ascertained; the upper part of the leaf is torn away; the part of the entry remaining follows:

". . . would run in a half-circle, keeping his head turned always toward the centre, and again he would stand still, barking furiously. At last he ran away into the brush as fast as he could go. I thought at first that he had gone mad, but on returning to the house found no other alteration in his manner than what was obviously due to fear of punishment.

"Can a dog see with his nose? Do odours impress some cerebral centre with images of the thing that emitted them? . . .

"*Sept. 2.*—Looking at the stars last night as they rose above the crest of the ridge east of the house, I observed them successively disappear—from left to right. Each was eclipsed but an instant, and only a few at the same time, but along the entire length of the ridge all that were within a degree or two of the crest were blotted out. It was as if something had passed along between me and them; but I could not see it, and the stars were not thick enough to define its outline. Ugh! don't like this."

Several weeks' entries are missing, three leaves being torn from the book.

"*Sept. 27.*—It has been about here again—I find evidences of its presence every day. I watched again all last night in the same cover, gun in hand, double-charged with buckshot. In the morning the fresh footprints were there, as before. Yet I would have sworn that I did not sleep—indeed, I hardly sleep at all. It is terrible, insupportable! If these amazing experiences are real I shall go mad; if they are fanciful I am mad already.

"*Oct. 3.*—I shall not go—it shall not drive me away. No, this is my house, *my* land. God hates a coward. . . .

"*Oct. 5.*—I can stand it no longer; I have invited Harker to pass a few weeks with me—he has a level head. I can judge from his manner if he thinks me mad.

"*Oct. 7.*—I have the solution of the mystery; it came to me last night—suddenly, as by revelation. How simple—how terribly simple!

"There are sounds that we cannot hear. At either end of the scale are notes that stir no chord of that imperfect instrument, the human ear. They are too high or too grave. I have observed a flock of blackbirds occupying an entire tree-top— the tops of several trees—and all in full song. Suddenly—in a moment—at absolutely the same instant—all spring into the air and fly away. How? They could not all see one another — whole tree-tops intervened. At no point could a leader have been visible to all. There must have been a signal of warning or command, high and shrill above the din, but by me unheard. I have observed, too, the same simultaneous flight when all were silent, among not only blackbirds, but other birds—quail, for example, widely separated by bushes—even on opposite sides of a hill.

"It is known to seamen that a school of whales basking or sporting on the surface of the ocean, miles apart, with the convexity of the earth between, will sometimes dive at the same instant—all gone out of sight in a moment. The signal has been sounded—too grave for the ear of the sailor at the masthead and his comrades on the deck—who nevertheless feel its vibrations in the ship as the stones of a cathedral are stirred by the bass of the organ.

"As with sounds, so with colours. At each end of the solar spectrum the chemist can detect the presence of what are known as 'actinic' rays. They represent colours—integral colours in the composition of light—which we are unable to discern. The human eye is an imperfect instrument; its range is but a few octaves of the real 'chromatic scale.' I am not mad; there are colours that we cannot see.

"And, God help me! the Damned Thing is of such a colour!"

The Yellow Sign

Robert W. Chambers

"The Yellow Sign" was first published in 1895 in The King in Yellow, *a collection that takes its title from a curious book that appears in a number of the stories and inevitably hastens its readers to extraordinary fates. Were it simply the first horror story to employ the familiar motif of "the forbidden book," it would not merit inclusion in* The Horror Hall of Fame. *But "The Yellow Sign" is a powerful exploration of the fragile border that separates nightmares from waking reality. As with dreams, no rationale is offered for the snowballing progression of events that overtakes the artist narrator and his model, nor is there any justification for the terrible fate that befalls them. Regardless, it would be difficult to find another story whose every moment is so pregnant with imminent dread.*

> Along the shore the cloud waves break,
> The twin suns sink behind the lake,
> The shadows lengthen
> > In Carcosa.
>
> Strange is the night where black stars rise,
> And strange moons circle through the skies,
> But stranger still is
> > Lost Carcosa.

> Songs that the Hyades shall sing,
> Where flap the tatters of the King,
> Must die unheard in
> > Dim Carcosa.
>
> Song of my soul, my voice is dead,
> Die thou, unsung, as tears unshed
> Shall dry and die in
> > Lost Carcosa.
>
> Cassilda's Song in *The King in Yellow.*
> > Act 1. Scene 2.

1. Being the Contents of an Unsigned Letter Sent to the Author

There are so many things which are impossible to explain! Why should certain chords in music make me think of the brown and golden tints of autumn foliage? Why should the Mass of Sainte Cécile send my thoughts wandering among caverns whose walls blaze with ragged masses of virgin silver? What was it in the roar and turmoil of Broadway at six o'clock that flashed before my eyes the picture of a still Breton forest where sunlight filtered through spring foliage and Silvia bent, half curiously, half tenderly, over a small green lizard, murmuring: "To think that this also is a little ward of God!"

When I first saw the watchman his back was toward me. I looked at him indifferently until he went into the church. I paid no more attention to him than I had to any other man who lounged through Washington Square that morning, and when I shut my window and turned back into my studio I had forgotten him. Late in the afternoon, the day being warm, I raised the window again and leaned out to get a sniff of air. A man was standing in the courtyard of the church, and I noticed him again with as little interest as I had that morning. I looked across the square to where the fountain was playing and then, with my mind filled with vague impressions of trees, asphalt drives, and the moving groups of nursemaids and holidaymakers, I started to walk back to my easel. As I turned, my listless glance included the man below in the churchyard. His face was toward me now, and with a perfectly involuntary movement I bent to see it. At the same moment he raised his head and looked at me. Instantly I thought of a coffin-worm. Whatever it was about the man that repelled me I did not know, but the impression of a plump white grave-worm was so intense and nauseating that I must have shown it in my expression, for he turned his puffy face away with a movement which made me think of a disturbed grub in a chestnut.

I went back to my easel and motioned the model to resume her pose. After working awhile I was satisfied that I was spoiling what I had done as rapidly as possible, and I took up a palette knife and scraped the color out again. The flesh tones were sallow and unhealthy, and I did not understand how I could have painted such sickly color into a study which before that had glowed with healthy tones.

I looked at Tessie. She had not changed, and the clear flush of health dyed her neck and cheeks as I frowned.

"Is it something I've done?" she said.

"No,—I've made a mess of this arm, and for the life of me I can't see how I came to paint such mud as that into the canvas," I replied.

"Don't I pose well?" she insisted.

"Of course, perfectly."

"Then it's not my fault?"

"No. It's my own."

"I'm very sorry," she said.

I told her she could rest while I applied rag and turpentine to the plague spot on my canvas, and she went off to smoke a cigarette and look over the illustrations in the *Courier Français*.

I did not know whether it was something in the turpentine or a defect in the canvas, but the more I scrubbed the more that gangrene seemed to spread. I worked like a beaver to get it out, and yet the disease appeared to creep from limb to limb of the study before me. Alarmed I strove to arrest it, but now the color on the breast changed and the whole figure seemed to absorb the infection as a sponge soaks up water.

Vigorously I plied palette knife, turpentine, and scraper, thinking all the time what a séance I should hold with Duval who had sold me the canvas; but soon I noticed that it was not the canvas which was defective nor yet the colors of Edward. "It must be the turpentine," I thought angrily, "or else my eyes have become so blurred and confused by the afternoon light that I can't see straight." I called Tessie, the model. She came and leaned over my chair blowing rings of smoke into the air.

"What *have* you been doing to it?" she exclaimed.

"Nothing," I growled, "it must be this turpentine!"

"What a horrible color it is now," she continued. "Do you think my flesh resembles green cheese?"

"No, I don't," I said angrily, "did you ever know me to paint like that before?"

"No, indeed!"

"Well, then!"

"It must be the turpentine, or something," she admitted.

She slipped on a Japanese robe and walked to the window. I scraped and rubbed until I was tired and finally picked up my brushes and hurled them through the canvas with a forcible expression, the tone alone of which reached Tessie's ears.

Nevertheless she promptly began: "That's it! Swear and act silly and ruin your brushes! You have been three weeks on that study, and now look! What's the good of ripping the canvas? What creatures artists are!"

I felt about as much ashamed as I usually did after such an outbreak, and I turned the ruined canvas to the wall. Tessie helped me clean my brushes, and then danced away to dress. From the screen she regaled me with bits of advice concerning whole or partial loss of temper, until, thinking, perhaps, I had been tormented sufficiently, she came out to implore me to button her waist where she could not reach it on the shoulder.

"Everything went wrong from the time you came back from the window and talked about that horrid-looking man you saw in the churchyard," she announced.

"Yes, he probably bewitched the picture," I said, yawning. I looked at my watch.

"It's after six, I know," said Tessie, adjusting her hat before the mirror.

"Yes," I replied, "I didn't mean to keep you so long." I leaned out of the window but recoiled with disgust, for the young man with the pasty face stood below in the church-yard. Tessie saw my gesture of disapproval and leaned from the window.

"Is that the man you don't like?" she whispered.

I nodded.

"I can't see his face, but he does look fat and soft. Someway or other," she continued, turning to look at me, "he reminds me of a dream,—an awful dream I once had. Or," she mused, looking down at her shapely shoes, "was it a dream after all?"

"How should I know?" I smiled.

Tessie smiled in reply.

"You were in it," she said, "so perhaps you might know something about it."

"Tessie! Tessie!" I protested, "don't you dare flatter by saying you dream about me!"

"But I did," she insisted; "shall I tell you about it?"

"Go ahead," I replied, lighting a cigarette.

Tessie leaned back on the open window-sill and began very seriously.

"One night last winter I was lying in bed thinking about nothing at all in particular. I had been posing for you and I was tired out, yet it seemed impossible for me to sleep. I heard the bells in the city ring ten, eleven, and midnight. I must have fallen asleep about midnight because I don't remember hearing the bells after that. It seemed to me that I had scarcely closed my eyes when I dreamed that something impelled me to go to the window. I rose, and raising the sash, leaned out. Twenty-fifth Street was deserted as far as I could see. I began to be afraid; everything outside seemed so—so black and uncomfortable. Then the sound of wheels in the distance came to my ears, and it seemed to me as though that was what I must wait for. Very slowly the wheels approached, and, finally, I could make out a vehicle moving along the street. It came nearer and nearer, and when it passed beneath my window I saw it was a hearse. Then, as I trembled with fear, the driver turned and looked straight at me. When I awoke I was standing by the open window shivering with cold, but the black-plumed hearse and the driver were gone. I dreamed this dream again in March last, and again awoke beside the open window. Last night the dream came again. You remember how it was raining; when I awoke, standing at the open window, my nightdress was soaked."

"But where did I come into the dream?" I asked.

"You—you were in the coffin; but you were not dead."

"In the coffin?"

"Yes."

"How did you know? Could you see me?"

"No; I only knew you were there."

"Had you been eating Welsh rarebits, or lobster salad?" I began laughing, but the girl interrupted me with a frightened cry.

"Hello! What's up?" I said, as she shrank into the embrasure by the window.

"The—the man below in the churchyard;—he drove the hearse."

"Nonsense," I said, but Tessie's eyes were wide with terror. I went to the window and looked out. The man was gone. "Come, Tessie," I urged, "don't be foolish. You have posed too long; you are nervous."

"Do you think I could forget that face?" she murmured. "Three times I saw the hearse pass below my window, and every time the driver turned and looked up at me. Oh, his face was so white and—and soft? It looked dead—it looked as if it had been dead a long time."

I induced the girl to sit down and swallow a glass of Marsala. Then I sat down beside her, and tried to give her some advice.

"Look here, Tessie," I said, "you go to the country for a week or two, and you'll have no more dreams about hearses. You pose all day, and when night comes your nerves are upset. You can't keep this up. Then again, instead of going to bed when your day's work is done, you run off to picnics at Sulzer's Park, or go to the Eldorado or Coney Island, and when you come down here next morning you are fagged out. There was no real hearse. That was a soft-shell crab dream."

She smiled faintly.

"What about the man in the churchyard?"

"Oh, he's only an ordinary unhealthy, everyday creature."

"As true as my name is Tessie Reardon, I swear to you, Mr. Scott, that the face of the man below in the churchyard is the face of the man who drove the hearse!"

"What of it?" I said. "It's an honest trade."

"Then you think I *did* see the hearse?"

"Oh," I said, diplomatically, "if you really did, it might not be unlikely that the man below drove it. There is nothing in that."

Tessie rose, unrolled her scented handkerchief, and taking a bit of gum from a knot in the hem, placed it in her mouth. Then drawing on her gloves she offered me her hand, with a frank, "Good-night, Mr. Scott," and walked out.

II

The next morning, Thomas, the bellboy, brought me the *Herald* and a bit of news. The church next door had been sold. I thanked Heaven for it, not that being a Catholic I had any repugnance for the congregation next door, but because my nerves were shattered by a blatant exhorter, whose every word echoed through the aisle of the church as if it had been my own rooms, and who insisted on his r's with a nasal persistence which revolted my every instinct. Then, too, there was a fiend in human shape, an organist, who reeled off some of the grand old hymns with an interpretation of his own, and I longed for the blood of a creature who could play the doxology with an amendment of minor chords which one hears only in a quartet of very young undergraduates. I believe the minister was a good man, but when he bellowed: "And the Lorrrd said unto Moses, the Lorrd is a man of war; the Lorrrd is his name. My wrath shall wax hot and I will kill you with the sworrrd!" I wondered how many centuries of purgatory it would take to atone for such a sin.

"Who bought the property?" I asked Thomas.

"Nobody that I knows, sir. They do say the gent wot owns this 'ere 'Amilton flats was lookin' at it. 'E might be a bildin' more studios."

I walked to the window. The young man with the unhealthy face stood by the churchyard gate, and at the mere
sight of him the same overwhelming repugnance took possession of me.

"By the way, Thomas," I said, "who is that fellow down
there?"

Thomas sniffed. "That there worm, sir? 'E's night-watch-
man of the church, sir. 'E maikes me tired a-sittin' out all
night on them steps and lookin' at you insultin' like. I'd a
punched 'is 'ed, sir—beg pardon, sir—"

"Go on, Thomas."

"One night a comin' 'ome with 'Arry, the other English
boy, I sees 'im a sittin' there on them steps. We 'ad Molly and
Jen with us, sir, the two girls on the tray service, an' 'e looks
so insultin' at us that I up and sez: 'Wat you looking hat, you
fat slug?'—beg pardon, sir, but that's 'ow I sez, sir. Then 'e
don't say nothin' and I sez; 'Come out and I'll punch that
puddin' 'ed.' Then I hopens the gate an' goes in, but 'e don't
say nothin', only looks insultin' like. Then I 'its 'im one, but,
ugh! 'is 'ed was that cold and mushy it ud sicken you to touch
'im."

"What did he do then?" I asked, curiously.

" 'Im? Nawthin'.' "

"And you, Thomas?"

The young fellow flushed with embarrassment and smiled
uneasily.

"Mr. Scott, sir, I ain't no coward an' I can't make it out at
all why I run. I was in the 5th Lawncers, sir, bugler at Tel-el-
Kebir, an' was shot by the wells."

"You don't mean to say you ran away?"

"Yes, sir; I run."

"Why?"

"That's just what I want to know, sir. I grabbed Molly an'
run, an' the rest was as frightened as I."

"But what were they frightened at?"

Thomas refused to answer for a while, but now my curiosity was aroused about the repulsive young man below and I
pressed him. Three years' sojourn in America had not only
modified Thomas' cockney dialect but had given him the
American's fear of ridicule.

"You won't believe me, Mr. Scott, sir?"

"Yes, I will."

"You will lawf at me, sir?"

"Nonsense!"

He hesitated. "Well, sir, it's God's truth that when I 'it 'im 'e grabbed me wrists, sir, and when I twisted 'is soft, mushy fist one of 'is fingers come off in me 'and."

The utter loathing and horror of Thomas' face must have been reflected in my own for he added:

"It's orful, an' now when I see 'im I just go away. 'E maikes me hill."

When Thomas had gone I went to the window. The man stood beside the church-railing with both hands on the gate, but I hastily retreated to my easel again, sickened and horrified, for I saw that the middle finger of his right hand was missing.

At nine o'clock Tessie appeared and vanished behind the screen with a merry "Good-morning, Mr. Scott." While she had reappeared and taken her pose upon the model-stand I started a new canvas much to her delight. She remained silent as long as I was on the drawing, but as soon as the scrape of the charcoal ceased and I took up my fixative she began to chatter.

"Oh, I had such a lovely time last night. We went to Tony Pastor's."

"Who are 'we'?" I demanded.

"Oh, Maggie, you know, Mr. Whyte's model, and Pinkie McCormick—we call her Pinkie because she's got that beautiful red hair you artists like so much—and Lizzie Burke."

I sent a shower of spray from the fixative over the canvas and said: "Well, go on."

"We saw Kelly and Baby Barnes the skirt-dancer and—and all the rest. I made a mash."

"Then you have gone back on me, Tessie?"

She laughed and shook her head.

"He's Lizzie Burke's brother, Ed. He's a perfect gen'l'man."

I felt constrained to give her some parental advice concerning mashing, which she took with a bright smile.

"Oh, I can take care of a strange mash," she said, examining her chewing gum, "but Ed is different. Lizzie is my best friend."

Then she related how Ed had come back from the stocking mill in Lowell, Massachusetts, to find her and Lizzie grown up, and what an accomplished young man he was, and how he thought nothing of squandering half a dollar for ice-cream and oysters to celebrate his entry as clerk into the woolen department of Macy's. Before she finished I began to paint, and she resumed the pose, smiling and chattering like a sparrow. By noon I had the study fairly well rubbed in and Tessie came to look at it.

"That's better," she said.

I thought so too, and ate my lunch with a satisfied feeling that all was going well. Tessie spread her lunch on a drawing table opposite me and we drank our claret from the same bottle and lighted our cigarettes from the same match. I was very much attached to Tessie. I had watched her shoot up into a slender but exquisitely formed woman from a frail, awkward child. She had posed for me during the last three years, and among all my models she was my favorite. It would have troubled me very much indeed had she become "tough" or "fly," as the phrase goes, but I never noticed any deterioration of her manner, and felt at heart that she was all right. She and I never discussed morals at all, and I had no intention of doing so, partly because I had none myself, and partly because I knew she would do what she liked in spite of me. Still I did hope she would steer clear of complications, because I wished her well, and then also I had a selfish desire to retain the best model I had. I knew that mashing, as she termed it, had no significance with girls like Tessie, and that such things in America did not resemble in the least the same things in Paris. Yet, having lived with my eyes open, I also knew that somebody would take Tessie away some day, in one manner or another, and though I professed to myself that marriage was nonsense, I sincerely hoped that, in this case, there would be a priest at the end of the vista. I am a Catholic. When I listen to high mass, when I sign myself, I feel that everything, including myself, is more cheerful, and when I confess, it does me good. A man who lives as much alone as I do, must confess to somebody. Then, again, Sylvia was Catholic, and it was reason enough for me. But I was speaking of Tessie, which is very different. Tessie also was Catholic and much more devout than I, so, taking it all in all, I had little fear for my pretty model until she should fall in love. But *then* I knew that fate alone would decide her future for her, and I prayed inwardly that fate would keep her away from men like me and throw into her path nothing but Ed Burkes and Jimmy McCormicks, bless her sweet face!

Tessie sat blowing rings of smoke up to the ceiling and tinkling the ice in her tumbler.

"Do you know, Kid, that I also had a dream last night?" I observed. I sometimes called her "the Kid."

"Not about that man," she laughed.

"Exactly. A dream similar to yours, only much worse."

It was foolish and thoughtless of me to say this, but you know how little tact the average painter has.

"I must have fallen asleep about 10 o'clock," I continued, "and after awhile I dreamt that I awoke. So plainly did I hear the midnight bells, the wind in the tree-branches, and the whistle of steamers from the bay, that even now I can scarcely believe I was not awake. I seemed to be lying in a box which had a glass cover. Dimly I saw the street lamps as I passed, for I must tell you, Tessie, the box in which I reclined appeared to lie in a cushioned wagon which jolted me over a stony pavement. After a while I became impatient and tried to move but the box was too narrow. My hands were crossed on my breast so I could not raise them to help myself. I listened and then tried to call. My voice was gone. I could hear the trample of the horses attached to the wagon and even the breathing of the driver. Then another sound broke upon my ears like the raising of a window sash. I managed to turn my head a little, and found I could look, not only through the glass cover of my box, but also through the glass panes in the side of the covered vehicle. I saw houses, empty and silent, with neither light nor life about any of them excepting one. In that house a window was open on the first floor and a figure all in white stood looking down into the street. It was you."

Tessie had turned her face away from me and leaned on the table with her elbow.

"I could see your face," I resumed, "and it seemed to me to be very sorrowful. Then we passed on and turned into a narrow black lane. Presently the horses stopped. I waited and waited, closing my eyes with fear and impatience, but all was silent as the grave. After what seemed to me hours, I began to feel uncomfortable. A sense that somebody was close to me made me unclose my eyes. Then I saw the white face of the hearse-driver looking at me through the coffin-lid—"

A sob from Tessie interrupted me. She was trembling like a leaf. I saw I had made an ass of myself and attempted to repair the damage.

"Why, Tess," I said, "I only told you this to show you what influence your story might have on another person's dreams. You don't suppose I really lay in a coffin, do you? What are you trembling for? Don't you see that your dream and my unreasonable dislike for that inoffensive watchman of the church simply set my brain working as soon as I fell asleep?"

She laid her head between her arms and sobbed as if her heart would break. What a precious triple donkey I had made of myself! But I was about to break my record. I went over and put my arm about her.

"Tessie dear, forgive me," I said; "I had no business to frighten you with such nonsense. You are too sensible a girl, too good a Catholic to believe in dreams."

Her hand tightened on mine and her head fell back upon my shoulder, but she still trembled and I petted her and comforted her.

"Come, Tess, open your eyes and smile."

Her eyes opened with a slow languid movement and met mine, but their expression was so queer that I hastened to reassure her again.

"It's all humbug, Tessie, you surely are not afraid that any harm will come to you because of that."

"No," she said, but her scarlet lips quivered.

"Then what's the matter? Are you afraid?"

"Yes. Not for myself."

"For me, then?" I demanded gayly.

"For you," she murmured in a voice almost inaudible, "I—I care—for you."

At first I started to laugh, but when I understood her, a

shock passed through me and I sat like one turned to stone. This was the crowning bit of idiocy I had committed. During the moment which elapsed between her reply and my answer I thought of a thousand responses to that innocent confession. I could pass it by with a laugh, I could misunderstand her and reassure her as to my health, I could simply point out that it was impossible she could love me. But my reply was quicker than my thoughts, and I might think and think now when it was too late, for I had kissed her on the mouth.

That evening I took my usual walk in Washington Park, pondering over the occurrences of the day. I was thoroughly committed. There was no back out now, and I stared the future straight in the face. I was not good, not even scrupulous, but I had no idea of deceiving either myself or Tessie. The one passion of my life lay buried in the sunlit forests of Brittany. Was it buried forever? Hope cried "No!" For three years I had been listening to the voice of Hope, and for three years I had waited for a footstep on my threshold. Had Sylvia forgotten? "No!" cried Hope.

I said that I was not good. That is true, but still I was not exactly a comic opera villain. I had led an easy-going reckless life, taking what invited me of pleasure, deploring and sometimes bitterly regretting consequences. In one thing alone, except my painting, was I serious, and that was something which lay hidden if not lost in the Breton forests.

It was too late now for me to regret what had occurred during the day. Whatever it had been, pity, a sudden tenderness for sorrow, or the more brutal instinct of gratified vanity, it was all the same now, and unless I wished to bruise an innocent heart my path lay marked before me. The fire and strength, the depth of passion of a love which I had never even suspected, with all my imagined experience in the world, left me no alternative but to respond or send her away. Whether because I am so cowardly about giving pain to others, or whether it was that I have little of the gloomy Puritan in me, I do not know, but I shrank from disclaiming responsibility for that thoughtless kiss, and in fact had no time to do so before the gates of her heart opened and the flood poured forth. Others who habitually do their duty and find a sullen satisfaction in making themselves and everybody else un-

happy, might have withstood it. I did not. I dared not. After
the storm had abated I did tell her that she might better have
loved Ed Burke and worn a plain gold ring, but she would not
hear of it, and I thought perhaps that as long as she had
decided to love somebody she could not marry, it had better
be me. I, at least, could treat her with an intelligent affection,
and whenever she became tired of her infatuation she could
go none the worse for it. For I was decided on that point
although I knew how hard it would be. I remembered the
usual termination of Platonic liaisons and thought how disgusted I had been whenever I heard of one. I knew I was
undertaking a great deal for so unscrupulous a man as I was,
and I dreaded the future, but never for one moment did I
doubt that she was safe with me. Had it been anybody but
Tessie I should not have bothered my head about scruples.
For it did not occur to me to sacrifice Tessie as I would have
sacrificed a woman of the world. I looked the future squarely
in the face and saw the several probable endings to the affair.
She would either tire of the whole thing, or become so unhappy that I should have either to marry her or go away. If I
married her we would be unhappy. I with a wife unsuited to
me, and she with a husband unsuitable for any woman. For
my past life could scarcely entitle me to marry. If I went
away she might either fall ill, recover, and marry some Eddie
Burke, or she might recklessly or deliberately go and do
something foolish. On the other hand if she tired of me, then
her whole life would be before her with beautiful vistas of
Eddie Burkes and marriage rings and twins and Harlem flats
and Heaven knows what. As I strolled along through the
trees by the Washington Arch, I decided that she should find
a substantial friend in me anyway and the future could take
care of itself. Then I went into the house and put on my
evening dress for the little faintly perfumed note on my
dresser said, "Have a cab at the stage door at eleven," and
the note was signed "Edith Carmichael, Metropolitan Theater, June 19th, 189—."

I took supper that night, or rather we took supper, Miss
Carmichel and I, at Solari's and the dawn was just beginning
to gild the cross on the Memorial Church as I entered Washington Square after leaving Edith at the Brunswick. There

was not a soul in the park as I passed among the trees and took the walk which leads from the Garibaldi statue to the Hamilton Apartment House, but as I passed the churchyard I saw a figure sitting on the stone steps. In spite of myself a chill crept over me at the sight of the white puffy face, and I hastened to pass. Then he said something which might have been addressed to me or might merely have been a mutter to himself, but a sudden furious anger flamed up within me that such a creature should address me. For an instant I felt like wheeling about and smashing my stick over his head, but I walked on, and entering the Hamilton went to my apartment. For some time I tossed about the bed trying to get the sound of his voice out of my ears, but could not. It filled my head, that muttering sound, like thick oily smoke from a fat-rendering vat or an odor of noisome decay. And as I lay and tossed about, the voice in my ears seemed more distinct, and I began to understand the words he had muttered. They came to me slowly as if I had forgotten them, and at last I could make some sense out of the sounds. It was this:

"Have you found the Yellow Sign?"
"Have you found the Yellow Sign?"
"Have you found the Yellow Sign?"

I was furious. What did he mean by that? Then with a curse upon him and his I rolled over and went to sleep, but when I awoke later I looked pale and haggard, for I had dreamed the dream of the night before and it troubled me more than I cared to think.

I dressed and went down into my studio. Tessie sat by the window, but as I came in she rose and put both arms around my neck for an innocent kiss. She looked so sweet and dainty that I kissed her again and then sat down before the easel.

"Hello! Where's the study I began yesterday?" I asked.

Tessie looked conscious, but did not answer. I began to hunt among the piles of canvases, saying, "Hurry up, Tess, and get ready; we must take advantage of the morning light."

When at last I gave up the search among the other canvases and turned to look around the room for the missing study I noticed Tessie standing by the screen with her clothes still on.

"What's the matter," I asked, "don't you feel well?"

"Yes."

"Then hurry."

"Do you want me to pose as—as I have always posed?"

Then I understood. Here was a new complication. I had lost, of course, the best nude model I had ever seen. I looked at Tessie. Her face was scarlet. Alas! Alas! We had eaten of the tree of knowledge, and Eden and native innocence were dreams of the past—I mean—for her.

I suppose she noticed the disappointment on my face, for she said: "I will pose if you wish. The study is behind the screen here where I put it."

"No," I said, "we will begin something new"; and I went into my wardrobe and picked out a Moorish costume which fairly blazed with tinsel. It was a genuine costume, and Tessie retired to the screen with it enchanted. When she came forth again I was astonished. Her long black hair was bound above her forehead with a circlet of turquoises, and the ends curled about her glittering girdle. Her feet were encased in the embroidered pointed slippers and the skirt of her costume, curiously wrought with arabesques in silver, fell to her ankles. The deep metallic blue vest embroidered with silver and the short Mauresque jacket spangled and sewn with turquoises became her wonderfully. She came up to me and held up her face smiling. I slipped my hand into my pocket and drawing out a gold chain with a cross attached, dropped it over her head.

"It's yours, Tessie."

"Mine?" she faltered.

"Yours. Now go and pose." Then with a radiant smile she ran behind the screen and presently reappeared with a little box on which was written my name.

"I had intended to give it to you when I went home tonight," she said, "but I can't wait now."

I opened the box. On the pink cotton inside lay a clasp of black onyx, on which was inlaid a curious symbol or letter in gold. It was neither Arabic nor Chinese, nor as I found afterwards did it belong to any human script.

"It's all I had to give you for a keepsake," she said, timidly.

I was annoyed, but I told her how much I should prize it, and promised to wear it always. She fastened it on my coat beneath the lapel.

"How foolish, Tess, to go and buy me such a beautiful thing as this," I said.

"I did not buy it," she laughed.

"Where did you get it?"

Then she told me how she had found it one day while coming from the Aquarium in the Battery, how she had advertised it and watched the papers, but at last gave up all hopes of finding the owner.

"That was last winter," she said, "the very day I had the first horrid dream about the hearse."

I remembered my dream of the previous night but said nothing, and presently my charcoal was flying over a new canvas, and Tessie stood motionless on the model-stand.

III

The day following was a disastrous one for me. While moving a framed canvas from one easel to another my foot slipped on the polished floor and I fell heavily on both wrists. They were so badly sprained that it was useless to attempt to hold a brush, and I was obliged to wander about the studio, glaring at unfinished drawings and sketches until despair seized me and I sat down to smoke and twiddle my thumbs with rage. The rain blew against the windows and rattled on the roof of the church, driving me into a nervous fit with its interminable patter. Tessie sat sewing by the window, and every now and then raised her head and looked at me with such innocent compassion that I began to feel ashamed of my irritation and looked about for something to occupy me. I had read all the papers and all the books in the library, but for the sake of something to do I went to the bookcases and shoved them open with my elbow. I knew every volume by its color and examined them all, passing slowly around the library and whistling to keep up my spirits. I was turning to go into the dining-room when my eye fell upon a book bound in yellow, standing in a corner of the top shelf of the last bookcase. I did not remember it and from the floor could not decipher the pale lettering on the back, so I went to the smoking-room and called Tessie. She came in from the studio and climbed up to reach the book.

"What is it?" I asked.

"The King in Yellow."

I was dumbfounded. Who had placed it there? How came it in my rooms? I had long ago decided that I should never open that book, and nothing on earth could have persuaded me to buy it. Fearful lest curiosity might tempt me to open it, I had never even looked at it in book-stores. If I ever had had any curiosity to read it, the awful tragedy of young Castaigne, whom I knew, prevented me from exploring its wicked pages. I had always refused to listen to any description of it, and indeed, nobody ever ventured to discuss the second part aloud, so I had absolutely no knowledge of what those leaves might reveal. I stared at the poisonous yellow binding as I would at a snake.

"Don't touch it, Tessie," I said, "come down."

Of course my admonition was enough to arouse her curiosity, and before I could prevent it she took the book and, laughing, danced away into the studio with it. I called to her but she slipped away with a tormenting smile at my helpless hands, and I followed her with some impatience.

"Tessie!" I cried, entering the library, "listen, I am serious. Put that book away. I do not wish you to open it!" The library was empty. I went into both drawing-rooms, then into the bedrooms, laundry, kitchen, and finally returned to the library and began a systematic search. She had hidden herself so well that it was half an hour later when I discovered her crouching white and silent by the latticed window in the store-room above. At the first glance I saw she had been punished for her foolishness. *The King in Yellow* lay at her feet, but the book was open at the second part. I looked at Tessie and saw it was too late. She had opened *The King in Yellow.* Then I took her by the hand and led her into the studio. She seemed dazed, and when I told her to lie down on the sofa she obeyed me without a word. After a while she closed her eyes and her breathing became regular and deep, but I could not determine whether or not she slept. For a long while I sat silently beside her, but she neither stirred nor spoke, and at last I rose and entering the unused store-room took the yellow book in my least injured hand. It seemed heavy as lead, but I carried it into the studio again, and sitting down on the rug beside the sofa, opened it and read it through from beginning to end.

When, faint with the excess of my emotions, I dropped the volume and leaned wearily back against the sofa, Tessie opened her eyes and looked at me.

We had been speaking for some time in a dull monotonous strain before I realized that we were discussing *The King in Yellow*. Oh the sin of writing such words,—words which are clear as crystal, limpid and musical as bubbling springs, words which sparkle and glow like the poisoned diamonds of the Medicis! Oh the wickedness, the hopeless damnation of a soul who could fascinate and paralyze human creatures with such words,—words understood by the ignorant and wise alike, words which are more precious than jewels, more soothing than Heavenly music, more awful than death itself.

We talked on, unmindful of the gathering shadows, and she was begging me to throw away the clasp of black onyx quaintly inlaid with what we now knew to be the Yellow Sign. I never shall know why I refused, though even at this hour, here in my bedroom as I write this confession, I should be glad to know *what* it was that prevented me from tearing the Yellow Sign from my breast and casting it into the fire. I am sure I wished to do so, but Tessie pleaded with me in vain. Night fell and the hours dragged on, but still we murmured to each other of the King and the Pallid Mask, and midnight sounded from the misty spires in the fog-wrapped city. We spoke of Hastur and of Cassilda, while outside the fog rolled against the blank window-panes as the cloud waves roll and break on the shores of Hali.

The house was very silent now and not a sound from the misty streets broke the silence. Tessie lay among the cushions, her face a gray blot in the gloom, but her hands were clasped in mine and I knew that she knew and read my thoughts as I read hers, for we had understood the mystery of the Hyades and the Phantom of Truth was laid. Then as we answered each other, swiftly, silently, thought on thought, the shadows stirred in the gloom about us, and far in the distant streets we heard a sound. Nearer and nearer it came, the dull crunching of wheels, nearer and yet nearer, and now, outside before the door it ceased, and I dragged myself to the window and saw a black-plumed hearse. The gate below opened and shut, and I crept shaking to my door and bolted it, but I knew no bolts, no locks, could keep that creature out who was coming for the Yellow Sign. And now I heard him moving very softly along the hall. Now he was at the door, and the bolts rotted at his touch. Now he had entered. With eyes starting from my head I peered into the darkness, but when he came into the room I did not see him. It was only when I felt him envelop me in his cold soft grasp that I cried out and struggled with deadly fury, but my hands were useless and he tore the onyx clasp from my coat and struck me full in the face. Then, as I fell, I heard Tessie's soft cry and her spirit fled to God, and even while falling I longed to follow her, for I knew that the King in Yellow had opened his tattered mantle and there was only Christ to cry to now.

I could tell more, but I cannot see what help it will be to the world. As for me I am past human help or hope. As I lie here, writing, careless even whether or not I die before I finish, I can see the doctor gathering up his powders and phials with a vague gesture to the good priest beside me, which I understand.

They will be very curious to know the tragedy—they of the outside world who write books and print millions of newspapers, but I shall write no more, and the father confessor will seal my last words with the seal of sanctity when his holy office is done. They of the outside world may send their creatures into wrecked homes and death-smitten firesides, and their newspapers will batten on blood and tears, but with me their spies must halt before the confessional. They know that Tessie is dead and that I am dying. They know how the people in the house, aroused by an infernal scream, rushed into my room and found one living and two dead, but they do not know what I shall tell them now; they do not know that the doctor said as he pointed to a horrible decomposed heap on the floor—the livid corpse of the watchman from the church: "I have no theory, no explanation. That man must have been dead for months!"

I think I am dying. I wish the priest would—

The Monkey's Paw

W. W. Jacobs

Originality is not an absolute necessity for an effective horror story. When W. W. Jacobs wrote "The Monkey's Paw" in 1902, the tale of the magic wish was already a staple of folklore and had given rise to fantasy tales of Aladdin and other beneficiaries of the supernatural. But Jacobs' story posited a dark side to wish fulfillment, and ever since its publication no one has been able to write a magic-wish tale without at least entertaining the potential consequences of asking for more than is one's natural lot in life. The story's enduring popularity is a measure of Jacobs' skill at sustaining dramatic tension. Though it suggests the existence of supernatural forces cruelly indifferent to human grief and implies a final horror too gruesome to be described, it also challenges the reader to prove that it is anything more than a tale of uncanny coincidence.

I

Without, the night was cold and wet, but in the small parlour of Laburnum Villa the blinds were drawn and the fire burned brightly. Father and son were at chess; the former, who possessed ideas about the game involving radical changes, putting his king into such sharp and unnecessary perils that it even provoked comment from the white-haired old lady knitting placidly by the fire.

"Hark at the wind," said Mr White, who, having seen a

fatal mistake after it was too late, was amiably desirous of preventing his son from seeing it.

"I'm listening," said the latter, grimly surveying the board as he stretched out his hand. "Check."

"I should hardly think that he'd come tonight," said his father, with his hand poised over the board.

"Mate," replied the son.

"That's the worst of living so far out," bawled Mr White, with sudden and unlooked-for violence; "of all the beastly, slushy, out-of-the-way places to live in, this is the worst. Path's a bog, and the road's a torrent. I don't know what people are thinking about. I suppose because only two houses in the road are let, they think it doesn't matter."

"Never mind, dear," said his wife soothingly; "perhaps you'll win the next one."

Mr White looked up sharply, just in time to intercept a knowing glance between mother and son. The words died away on his lips, and he hid a guilty grin in his thin grey beard.

"There he is," said Herbert White, as the gate banged to loudly and heavy footsteps came towards the door.

The old man rose with hospitable haste, and opening the door, was heard condoling with the new arrival. The new arrival also condoled with himself, so that Mrs White said, "Tut, tut!" and coughed gently as her husband entered the room, followed by a tall, burly man, beady of eye and rubicund of visage.

"Sergeant-Major Morris," he said, introducing him.

The sergeant-major shook hands, and taking the proffered seat by the fire, watched contentedly while his host got out whisky and tumblers and stood a small copper kettle on the fire.

At the third glass his eyes got brighter, and he began to talk, the little family circle regarding with eager interest this visitor from distant parts, as he squared his broad shoulders in the chair and spoke of wild scenes and doughty deeds; of wars and plagues and strange peoples.

"Twenty-one years of it," said Mr White, nodding at his wife and son. "When he went away he was a slip of a youth in the warehouse. Now look at him."

"He don't look to have taken much harm," said Mrs White politely.

"I'd like to go to India myself," said the old man, "just to look round a bit, you know."

"Better where you are," said the sergeant-major, shaking his head. He put down the empty glass, and sighing softly, shook it again.

"I should like to see those old temples and fakirs and jugglers," said the old man. "What was that you started telling me the other day about a monkey's paw or something, Morris?"

"Nothing," said the soldier hastily. "Leastways nothing worth hearing."

"Monkey's paw?" said Mrs White curiously.

"Well, it's just a bit of what you might call magic, perhaps," said the sergeant-major offhandedly.

His three listeners leaned forward eagerly. The visitor absentmindedly put his empty glass to his lips and then set it down again. His host filled it for him.

"To look at," said the sergeant-major, fumbling in his pocket, "it's just an ordinary little paw, dried to a mummy."

He took something out of his pocket and proffered it. Mrs White drew back with a grimace, but her son, taking it, examined it curiously.

"And what is there special about it?" inquired Mr White as he took it from his son, and having examined it, placed it upon the table.

"It had a spell put on it by an old fakir," said the sergeant-major, "a very holy man. He wanted to show that fate ruled people's lives, and that those who interfered with it did so to their sorrow. He put a spell on it so that three separate men could each have three wishes from it."

His manner was so impressive that his hearers were conscious that their light laughter jarred somewhat.

"Well, why don't you have three, sir?" said Herbert White cleverly.

The soldier regarded him in the way that middle age is wont to regard presumptuous youth. "I have," he said quietly, and his blotchy face whitened.

"And did you really have the three wishes granted?" asked Mrs White.

"I did," said the sergeant-major, and his glass tapped against his strong teeth.

"And has anybody else wished?" persisted the old lady.

"The first man had his three wishes. Yes," was the reply; "I don't know what the first two were, but the third was for death. That's how I got the paw."

His tones were so grave that a hush fell upon the group.

"If you've had your three wishes, it's no good to you now, then, Morris," said the old man at last. "What do you keep it for?"

The soldier shook his head. "Fancy, I suppose," he said slowly. "I did have some idea of selling it, but I don't think I will. It has caused enough mischief already. Besides, people won't buy. They think it's a fairy tale, some of them; and those who do think anything of it want to try it first and pay me afterward."

"If you could have another three wishes," said the old man, eyeing him keenly, "would you have them?"

"I don't know," said the other. "I don't know."

He took the paw, and dangling it between his forefinger and thumb, suddenly threw it upon the fire. White, with a slight cry, stooped down and snatched it off.

"Better let it burn," said the soldier solemnly.

"If you don't want it, Morris," said the other, "give it to me."

"I won't," said his friend doggedly. "I threw it on the fire. If you keep it, don't blame me for what happens. Pitch it on the fire again like a sensible man."

The other shook his head and examined his new possession closely. "How do you do it?" he inquired.

"Hold it up in your right hand and wish aloud," said the sergeant-major, "but I warn you of the consequences."

"Sounds like the *Arabian Nights,*" said Mrs White, as she rose and began to set the supper. "Don't you think you might wish for four pairs of hands for me."

Her husband drew the talisman from his pocket, and then all three burst into laughter as the sergeant-major, with a look of alarm on his face, caught him by the arm.

"If you must wish," he said gruffly, "wish for something sensible."

Mr White dropped it back in his pocket, and placing chairs, motioned his friend to the table. In the business of supper the talisman was partly forgotten, and afterward the three sat listening in an enthralled fashion to a second instalment of the soldier's adventures in India.

"If the tale about the monkey's paw is not more truthful than those he has been telling us," said Herbert, as the door closed behind their guest, just in time to catch the last train, "we shan't make much out of it."

"Did you give him anything for it, father?" inquired Mrs White, regarding her husband closely.

"A trifle," said he, colouring slightly. "He didn't want it, but I made him take it. And he pressed me again to throw it away."

"Likely," said Herbert, with pretended horror. "Why, we're going to be rich, and famous, and happy. Wish to be an emperor, father, to begin with; then you can't be henpecked."

He darted round the table, pursued by the maligned Mrs White armed with an antimacassar.

Mr White took the paw from his pocket and eyed it dubiously. "I don't know what to wish for, and that's a fact," he said slowly. "It seems to me I've got all I want."

"If you only cleared the house, you'd be quite happy, wouldn't you!" said Herbert, with his hand on his shoulder. "Well, wish for two hundred pounds, then; that'll just do it."

His father, smiling shamefacedly at his own credulity, held up the talisman, as his son, with a solemn face, somewhat marred by a wink at his mother, sat down at the piano and struck a few impressive chords.

"I wish for two hundred pounds," said the old man distinctly.

A fine crash from the piano greeted the words, interrupted by a shuddering cry from the old man. His wife and son ran toward him.

"It moved," he cried, with a glance of disgust at the object as it lay on the floor. "As I wished, it twisted in my hand like a snake."

"Well, I don't see the money," said his son, as he picked it up and placed it on the table, "and I bet I never shall."

"It must have been your fancy, father," said his wife, regarding him anxiously.

He shook his head. "Never mind, though; there's no harm done, but it gave me a shock all the same."

They sat down by the fire again while the two men finished their pipes. Outside, the wind was higher than ever, and the old man started nervously at the sound of a door banging upstairs. A silence unusual and depressing settled upon all three, which lasted until the old couple rose to retire for the night.

"I expect you'll find the cash tied up in a big bag in the middle of your bed," said Herbert, as he bade them good night, "and something horrible squatting up on top of the wardrobe watching you as you pocket your ill-gotten gains."

He sat alone in the darkness, gazing at the dying fire, and seeing faces in it. The last face was so horrible and so simian that he gazed at it in amazement. It got so vivid that, with a little uneasy laugh, he felt on the table for a glass containing a little water to throw over it. His hand grasped the monkey's paw, and with a little shiver he wiped his hand on his coat and went up to bed.

II

In the brightness of the wintry sun next morning as it streamed over the breakfast table he laughed at his fears. There was an air of prosaic wholesomeness about the room which it had lacked on the previous night, and the dirty, shrivelled little paw was pitched on the side-board with a carelessness which betokened no great belief in its virtues.

"I suppose all old soldiers are the same," said Mrs White. "The idea of our listening to such nonsense! How could wishes be granted in these days? And if they could, how could two hundred pounds hurt you, father?"

"Might drop on his head from the sky," said the frivolous Herbert.

"Morris said the things happened so naturally," said his

father, "that you might if you so wished attribute it to coincidence."

"Well, don't break into the money before I come back," said Herbert as he rose from the table. "I'm afraid it'll turn you into a mean, avaricious man, and we shall have to disown you."

His mother laughed, and following him to the door, watched him down the road; and returning to the breakfast table, was very happy at the expense of her husband's credulity. All of which did not prevent her from scurrying to the door at the postman's knock, nor prevent her from referring somewhat shortly to retired sergeant-majors of bibulous habits when she found that the post brought a tailor's bill.

"Herbert will have some more of his funny remarks, I expect, when he comes home," she said, as they sat at dinner.

"I dare say," said Mr White, pouring himself out some beer; "but for all that, the thing moved in my hand; that I'll swear to."

"You thought it did," said the old lady soothingly.

"I say it did," replied the other. "There was no thought about it; I had just— What's the matter?"

His wife made no reply. She was watching the mysterious movements of a man outside, who, peering in an undecided fashion at the house, appeared to be trying to make up his mind to enter. In mental connexion with the two hundred pounds, she noticed that the stranger was well dressed, and wore a silk hat of glossy newness. Three times he paused at the gate, and then walked on again. The fourth time he stood with his hand upon it, and then with sudden resolution flung it open and walked up the path. Mrs White at the same moment placed her hands behind her, and hurriedly unfastening the strings of her apron, put that useful article of apparel beneath the cushion of her chair.

She brought the stranger, who seemed ill at ease, into the room. He gazed at her furtively, and listened in a preoccupied fashion as the old lady apologized for the appearance of the room, and her husband's coat, a garment which he usually reserved for the garden. She then waited as patiently as her sex would permit for him to broach his business, but he was at first strangely silent.

"I—was asked to call," he said at last, and stooped and picked a piece of cotton from his trousers. "I come from 'Maw and Meggins.'"

The old lady started. "Is anything the matter?" she asked breathlessly. "Has anything happened to Herbert? What is it? What is it?"

Her husband interposed. "There, there, mother," he said hastily. "Sit down, and don't jump to conclusions. You've not brought bad news, I'm sure, sir," and he eyed the other wistfully.

"I'm sorry—" began the visitor.

"Is he hurt?" demanded the mother wildly.

The visitor bowed in assent. "Badly hurt," he said quietly, "but he is not in any pain."

"Oh, thank God!" said the old woman, clasping her hands. "Thank God for that! Thank—"

She broke off suddenly as the sinister meaning of the assurance dawned upon her and she saw the awful confirmation of her fears in the other's averted face. She caught her breath, and turning to her slower-witted husband, laid her trembling old hand upon his. There was a long silence.

"He was caught in the machinery," said the visitor at length in a low voice.

"Caught in the machinery," repeated Mr White, in a dazed fashion, "yes."

He sat staring blankly out of the window, and taking his wife's hand between his own, pressed it as he had been wont to do in their old courting days nearly forty years before.

"He was the only one left to us," he said, turning gently to the visitor. "It is hard."

The other coughed, and rising, walked slowly to the window. "The firm wished me to convey their sincere sympathy with you in your great loss," he said, without looking round. "I beg that you will understand I am only their servant and merely obeying orders."

There was no reply; the old woman's face was white, her eyes staring, and her breath inaudible; on the husband's face was a look such as his friend the sergeant might have carried into his first action.

"I was to say that Maw and Meggins disclaim all responsibility," continued the other. "They admit no liability at all, but in consideration of your son's services, they wish to present you with a certain sum as compensation."

Mr White dropped his wife's hand, and rising to his feet, gazed with a look of horror at his visitor. His dry lips shaped the words, "How much?"

"Two hundred pounds," was the answer.

Unconscious of his wife's shriek, the old man smiled faintly, put out his hands like a sightless man, and dropped, a senseless heap, to the floor.

III

In the huge new cemetery, some two miles distant, the old people buried their dead, and came back to the house steeped in shadow and silence. It was all over so quickly that at first they could hardly realize it, and remained in a state of expectation as though of something else to happen—something else which was to lighten this load, too heavy for old hearts to bear.

But the days passed, and expectation gave place to resigna tion—the hopeless resignation of the old, sometimes miscalled apathy. Sometimes they hardly exchanged a word, for now they had nothing to talk about, and their days were long to weariness.

It was about a week after that the old man, waking suddenly in the night, stretched out his hand and found himself alone. The room was in darkness, and the sound of subdued weeping came from the window. He raised himself in bed and listened.

"Come back," he said tenderly. "You will be cold."

"It is colder for my son," said the old woman, and wept afresh.

The sound of her sobs died away on his ears. The bed was warm, and his eyes heavy with sleep. He dozed fitfully, and then slept until a sudden wild cry from his wife awoke him with a start.

"The paw!" she cried wildly. "The monkey's paw!"

He started up in alarm. "Where? Where is it? What's the matter?"

She came stumbling across the room toward him. "I want it," she said quietly. "You've not destroyed it?"

"It's in the parlour, on the bracket," he replied, marvelling. "Why?"

She cried and laughed together, and bending over, kissed his cheek.

"I only just thought of it," she said hysterically. "Why didn't I think of it before? Why didn't *you* think of it?"

"Think of what?" he questioned.

"The other two wishes," she replied rapidly. "We've only had one."

"Was not that enough?" he demanded fiercely.

"No," she cried triumphantly; "we'll have one more. Go down and get it quickly, and wish our boy alive again."

The man sat up in bed and flung the bedclothes from his quaking limbs. "Good God, you are mad!" he cried, aghast.

"Get it," she panted; "get it quickly, and wish— Oh, my boy, my boy!"

Her husband struck a match and lit the candle. "Get back to bed," he said unsteadily. "You don't know what you are saying."

"We had the first wish granted," said the old woman feverishly; "why not the second?"

"A coincidence," stammered the old man.

"Go and get it and wish," cried his wife, quivering with excitement.

The old man turned and regarded her, and his voice shook. "He has been dead ten days, and besides he—I would not tell you else, but—I could only recognize him by his clothing. If he was too terrible for you to see then, how now?"

"Bring him back," cried the old woman, and dragged him towards the door. "Do you think I fear the child I have nursed?"

He went down in the darkness, and felt his way to the parlour, and then to the mantelpiece. The talisman was in its place, and a horrible fear that the unspoken wish might bring his mutilated son before him ere he could escape from the room seized upon him, and he caught his breath as he found that he had lost the direction of the door. His brow cold with sweat, he felt his way round the table, and groped along the wall until he found himself in the small passage with the unwholesome thing in his hand.

Even his wife's face seemed changed as he entered the room. It was white and expectant, and to his fears seemed to have an unnatural look upon it. He was afraid of her.

"*Wish!*" she cried, in a strong voice.

"It is foolish and wicked," he faltered.

"*Wish!*" repeated his wife.

He raised his hand. "I wish my son alive again."

The talisman fell to the floor, and he regarded it fearfully. Then he sank trembling into a chair as the old woman, with burning eyes, walked to the window and raised the blind.

He sat until he was chilled with the cold, glancing occasionally at the figure of the old woman peering through the window. The candle-end, which had burned below the rim of the china candlestick, was throwing pulsating shadows on the ceiling and walls, until, with a flicker larger than the rest, it expired. The old man, with an unspeakable sense of relief at the failure of the talisman, crept back to his bed, and a minute or two afterward the old woman came silently and apathetically beside him.

Neither spoke, but lay silently listening to the ticking of the clock. A stair creaked, and a squeaky mouse scurried noisily through the wall. The darkness was oppressive, and after lying for some time screwing up his courage, he took the box of matches, and striking one, went downstairs for a candle.

At the foot of the stairs the match went out, and he paused to strike another; and at the same moment a knock, so quiet and stealthy as to be scarcely audible, sounded on the front door.

The matches fell from his hand and spilled in the passage. He stood motionless, his breath suspended until the knock was repeated. Then he turned and fled swiftly back to his room, and closed the door behind him. A third knock sounded through the house.

"*What's that?*" cried the old woman, starting up.

"A rat," said the old man in shaking tones—"a rat. It passed me on the stairs."

His wife sat up in bed listening. A loud knock resounded through the house.

"It's Herbert!" she screamed. "It's Herbert!"

She ran to the door, but her husband was before her, and catching her by the arm, held her tightly.

"What are you going to do?" he whispered hoarsely.

"It's my boy; it's Herbert!" she cried, struggling mechanically. "I forgot it was two miles away. What are you holding me for? Let go. I must open the door."

"For God's sake don't let it in," cried the old man, trembling.

"You're afraid of your own son," she cried, struggling. "Let me go. I'm coming, Herbert; I'm coming."

There was another knock, and another. The old woman with a sudden wrench broke free and ran from the room. Her husband followed to the landing, and called after her appealingly as she hurried downstairs. He heard the chain rattle back and the bottom bolt drawn slowly and stiffly from the socket. Then the old woman's voice, strained and panting.

"The bolt," she cried loudly. "Come down. I can't reach it."

But her husband was on his hands and knees groping wildly on the floor in search of the paw. If he could only find it before the thing outside got in. A perfect fusillade of knocks reverberated through the house, and he heard the scraping of a chair as his wife put it down in the passage against the door. He heard the creaking of the bolt as it came slowly back, and at the same moment he found the monkey's paw, and frantically breathed his third and last wish.

The knocking ceased suddenly, although the echoes of it were still in the house. He heard the chair drawn back, and the door opened. A cold wind rushed up the staircase, and a long loud wail of disappointment and misery from his wife gave him courage to run down to her side, and then to the gate beyond. The street lamp flickering opposite shone on a quiet and deserted road.

The White People

Arthur Machen

*Though not original to the horror genre, the theme of inno-
cence imperiled is one whose roots are sunk firmly in the
bedrock of the Gothic tradition. Arthur Machen worked a
memorable variation on its usual villain/heroine treatment in
"The White People" (1904) by making a naive child the
emissary for creatures profane beyond description. Horror
writers have always grappled (and not always successfully)
with effective ways to render their "indescribable" horrors
believable, and the ingenuity of Machen's tale lies in the
sincerity with which its inexperienced narrator describes in
her limited vocabulary experiences that would leave her
adult guardians speechless with terror. "The White People"
is one of several stories in which Machen suggested that the
pleasant folk images of "the little people" mercifully ob-
scures their true foulness. It is generally proclaimed one of
the best horror stories in the English language and has influenced the best writers of succeeding generations, among
them H P. Lovecraft and T.E.D. Klein.*

Prologue

"Sorcery and sanctity," said Ambrose, "these are the only
realities. Each is an ecstasy, a withdrawal from the common
life."

Cotgrave listened, interested. He had been brought by a

friend to this moldering house in a northern suburb, through
an old garden to the room where Ambrose the recluse dozed
and dreamed over his books.

"Yes," he went on, "magic is justified of her children. There
are many, I think, who eat dry crusts and drink water, with a
joy infinitely sharper than anything within the experience of
the 'practical' epicure."

"You are speaking of the saints?"

"Yes, and of the sinners, too. I think you are falling into the
very general error of confining the spiritual world to the supremely good; but the supremely wicked, necessarily, have
their portion in it. The merely carnal, sensual man can no
more be a great sinner than he can be a great saint. Most of
us are just indifferent, mixed-up creatures; we muddle
through the world without realizing the meaning and the inner sense of things, and consequently, our wickedness and
our goodness are alike second-rate, unimportant."

"And you think the great sinner, then, will be an ascetic, as
well as the great saint?"

"Great people of all kinds forsake the imperfect copies and
go to the perfect originals. I have no doubt but that many of
the very highest among the saints have never done a 'good
action' (using the words in their ordinary sense). And, on the
other hand, there have been those who have sounded the very
depths of sin, who all their lives have never done an 'ill
deed.'"

He went out of the room for a moment, and Cotgrave, in
high delight, turned to his friend and thanked him for the
introduction.

"He's grand," he said. "I never saw that kind of lunatic
before."

Ambrose returned with more whiskey and helped the two
men in a liberal manner. He abused the teetotal sect with
ferocity, as he handed out the seltzer, and pouring out a glass
of water for himself, was about to resume his monologue,
when Cotgrave broke in—

"I can't stand it, you know," he said, "your paradoxes are
too monstrous. A man may be a great sinner and yet never do
anything sinful! Come!"

"You're quite wrong," said Ambrose. "I never make paradoxes; I wish I could. I merely said that a man may have an exquisite taste in Romanée Conti, and yet never have even smelt sour ale. That's all, and it's more like a truism than a paradox, isn't it? Your surprise at my remark is due to the fact that you haven't realized what sin is. Oh, yes, there is a sort of connection between Sin with the capital letter, and actions which are commonly called sinful: with murder, theft, adultery, and so forth. Much the same connection that there is between the A, B, C and fine literature. But I believe that the misconception—it is all but universal—arises in great measure from our looking at the matter through social spectacles. We think that a man who does evil to *us* and to his neighbors must be very evil. So he is, from a social standpoint; but can't you realize that Evil in its essence is a lonely thing, a passion of the solitary, individual soul? Really, the average murderer, *qua* murderer, is not by any means a sinner in the true sense of the word. He is simply a wild beast that we have to get rid of to save our own necks from his knife. I should class him rather with tigers than with sinners."

"It seems a little strange."

"I think not. The murderer murders not from positive qualities, but from negative ones; he lacks something which nonmurderers possess. Evil, of course, is wholly positive—only it is on the wrong side. You may believe me that sin in its proper sense is very rare; it is probable that there have been far fewer sinners than saints. Yes, your standpoint is all very well for practical, social purposes; we are naturally inclined to think that a person who is very disagreeable to us must be a very great sinner! It is very disagreeable to have one's pocket picked, and we pronounce the thief to be a very great sinner. In truth, he is merely an undeveloped man. He cannot be a saint, of course; but he may be, and often is, an infinitely better creature than thousands who have never broken a single commandment. He is a great nuisance to *us*, I admit, and we very properly lock him up if we catch him; but between his troublesome and unsocial action and evil—Oh, the connection is of the weakest."

It was getting very late. The man who had brought Cotgrave had probably heard all this before, since he assisted with a bland and judicious smile, but Cotgrave began to think that his "lunatic" was turning into a sage.

"Do you know," he said, "you interest me immensely? You think, then, that we do not understand the real nature of evil?"

"No, I don't think we do. We overestimate it and we underestimate it. We take the very numerous infractions of our social 'bylaws'—the very necessary and very proper regulations which keep the human company together—and we get frightened at the prevalence of 'sin' and 'evil.' But this is really nonsense. Take theft, for example. Have you any *horror* at the thought of Robin Hood, of the Highland caterans of the seventeenth century, of the mosstroopers, of the company promoters of our day?

"Then, on the other hand, we underrate evil. We attach such an enormous importance to the 'sin' of meddling with our pockets (and our wives) that we have quite forgotten the awfulness of real sin."

"And what is sin?" said Cotgrave.

"I think I must reply to your question by another. What would your feelings be, seriously, if your cat or your dog began to talk to you, and to dispute with you in human accents? You would be overwhelmed with horror. I am sure of it. And if the roses in your garden sang a weird song, you would go mad. And suppose the stones in the road began to swell and grow before your eyes, and if the pebble that you noticed at night had shot out stony blossoms in the morning?

"Well, these examples may give you some notion of what sin really is."

"Look here," said the third man, hitherto placid, "you two seem pretty well wound up. But I'm going home. I've missed my tram, and I shall have to walk."

Ambrose and Cotgrave seemed to settle down more profoundly when the other had gone out into the early misty morning and the pale light of the lamps.

"You astonish me," said Cotgrave. "I have never thought of that. If that is really so, one must turn everything upside down. Then the essence of sin really is—"

"In the taking of heaven by storm, it seems to me," said Ambrose. "It appears to me that it is simply an attempt to penetrate into another and higher sphere in a forbidden manner. You can understand why it is so rare. There are few, indeed, who wish to penetrate into other spheres, higher or lower, in ways allowed or forbidden. Men, in the mass, are amply content with life as they find it. Therefore there are few saints, and sinners (in the proper sense) are fewer still, and men of genius, who partake sometimes of each character, are rare also. Yes, on the whole, it is, perhaps, harder to be a great sinner than a great saint."

"There is something profoundly unnatural about sin? Is that what you mean?"

"Exactly. Holiness requires as great, or almost as great, an effort; but holiness works on lines that *were* natural once; it is an effort to recover the ecstasy that was before the Fall. But sin is an effort to gain the ecstasy and the knowledge that pertain alone to angels, and in making this effort man becomes a demon. I told you that the mere murderer is not *therefore* a sinner; that is true, but the sinner is sometimes a murderer. Gilles de Raiz is an instance. So you see that while the good and the evil are unnatural to man as he now is—to man the social, civilized being—evil is unnatural in a much deeper sense than good. The saint endeavors to recover a gift which he has lost; the sinner tries to obtain something which was never his. In brief, he repeats the Fall."

"But are you a Catholic?" said Cotgrave.

"Yes, I am a member of the persecuted Anglican Church."

"Then, how about those texts which seem to reckon as sin that which you would set down as a mere trivial dereliction?"

"Yes, but in one place the word 'sorcerers' comes in the same sentence, doesn't it? That seems to me to give the keynote. Consider: can you imagine for a moment that a false statement which saves an innocent man's life is a sin? No. Very good, then, it is not the mere liar who is excluded by those words; it is, above all, the 'sorcerers' who use the material life, who use the failings incidental to material life as instruments to obtain their infinitely wicked ends. And let me tell you this: our higher senses are so blunted, we are so drenched with materialism, that we should probably fail to recognize real wickedness if we encountered it."

"But shouldn't we experience a certain horror—a terror

such as you hinted we would experience if a rose tree sang—
in the mere presence of an evil man?"

"We should if we were natural: children and women feel
this horror you speak of, even animals experience it. But with
most of us convention and civilization and education have
blinded and deafened and obscured the natural reason. No,
sometimes we may recognize evil by its hatred of the good—
one doesn't need much penetration to guess at the influence
which dictated, quite unconsciously, the 'Blackwood' review
of Keats—but this is purely incidental; and, as a rule, I suspect that Hierarchs of Tophet pass quite unnoticed, or, perhaps, in certain cases, as good but mistaken men."

"But you used the word 'unconscious' just now, of Keats'
reviewers. Is wickedness ever unconscious?"

"Always. It must be so. It is like holiness and genius in this
as in other points; it is a certain rapture or ecstasy of the
soul; a transcendent effort to surpass the ordinary bounds. So,
surpassing these, it surpasses also the understanding, the
faculty that takes note of that which comes before it. No, a
man may be infinitely and horribly wicked and never suspect
it. But I tell you, evil in this, its certain and true sense, is
rare, and I think it is growing rarer."

"I am trying to get hold of it all," said Cotgrave. "From
what you say, I gather that the true evil differs generically
from that which we call evil?"

"Quite so. There is, no doubt, an analogy between the two;
a resemblance such as enables us to use, quite legitimately,
such terms as the 'foot of the mountain' and the 'leg of the
table.' And, sometimes, of course, the two speak, as it were, in
the same language. The rough miner, or 'puddler,' the un-
trained, undeveloped 'tiger-man,' heated by a quart or two
above his usual measure, comes home and kicks his irritating
and injudicious wife to death. He is a murderer. And Gilles de
Raiz was a murderer. But you see the gulf that separates the
two? The 'word,' if I may so speak, is accidentally the same in
each case, but the 'meaning' is utterly different. It is flagrant
'Hobson Jobson' to confuse the two, or rather, it is as if one
supposed that Juggernaut and the Argonauts had something
to do etymologically with one another. And no doubt the
same weak likeness, or analogy, runs between all the 'social'

sins and the real spiritual sins, and in some cases, perhaps, the lesser may be 'schoolmasters' to lead one on to the greater—from the shadow to the reality. If you are anything of a theologian, you will see the importance of all this."

"I am sorry to say," remarked Cotgrave, "that I have devoted very little of my time to theology. Indeed, I have often wondered on what grounds theologians have claimed the title of Science of Sciences for their favorite study; since the 'theological' books I have looked into have always seemed to me to be concerned with feeble and obvious pieties, or with the kings of Israel and Judah. I do not care to hear about those kings."

Ambrose grinned.

"We must try to avoid theological discussion," he said. "I perceive that you would be a bitter disputant. But perhaps the 'dates of the kings' have as much to do with theology as the hobnails of the murderous puddler with evil."

"Then, to return to our main subject, you think that sin is an esoteric, occult thing?"

"Yes. It is the infernal miracle as holiness is the supernal. Now and then it is raised to such a pitch that we entirely fail to suspect its existence; it is like the note of the great pedal pipes of the organ, which is so deep that we cannot hear it. In other cases it may lead to the lunatic asylum, or to still stranger issues. But you must never confuse it with mere social misdoing. Remember how the apostle, speaking of the 'other side,' distinguishes between 'charitable' actions and charity. And as one may give all one's goods to the poor, and yet lack charity; so, remember, one may avoid every crime and yet be a sinner."

"Your psychology is very strange to me," said Cotgrave, "but I confess I like it, and I suppose that one might fairly deduce from your premises the conclusion that the real sinner might very possibly strike the observer as a harmless enough personage?"

"Certainly, because the true evil has nothing to do with social life or social laws, or if it has, only incidentally and accidentally. It is a lonely passion of the soul—or a passion of the lonely soul—whichever you like. If, by chance, we understand it, and grasp its full significance, then, indeed, it will fill us with horror and with awe. But this emotion is widely distinguished from the fear and the disgust with which we regard the ordinary criminal, since this latter is largely or entirely founded on the regard which we have for our own skins or purses. We hate a murderer, because we know that we should hate to be murdered, or to have anyone that we like murdered. So, on the 'other side,' we venerate the saints, but we don't 'like' them as we like our friends. Can you persuade yourself that you would have 'enjoyed' St. Paul's company? Do you think that you and I would have 'got on' with Sir Galahad?

"So with the sinners, as with the saints. If you met a very evil man, and recognized his evil, he would, no doubt, fill you with horror and awe; but there is no reason why you should 'dislike' him. On the contrary, it is quite possible that if you could succeed in putting the sin out of your mind you might find the sinner capital company, and in a little while you might have to reason yourself back into horror. Still, how awful it is. If the roses and the lilies suddenly sang on this coming morning; if the furniture began to move in procession, as in de Maupassant's tale!"

"I am glad you have come back to that comparison," said Cotgrave, "because I wanted to ask you what it is that corresponds in humanity to these imaginary feats of inanimate things. In a word—what is sin? You have given me, I know, an abstract definition, but I should like a concrete example."

"I told you it was very rare," said Ambrose, who appeared willing to avoid the giving of a direct answer. "The materialism of the age, which has done a good deal to suppress sanctity, has done perhaps more to suppress evil. We find the earth so very comfortable that we have no inclination either for ascents or descents. It would seem as if the scholar who decided to 'specialize' in Tophet, would be reduced to purely antiquarian researches. No paleontologist could show you a *live* pterodactyl."

"And yet you, I think, have 'specialized,' and I believe that your researches have descended to our modern times."

"You are really interested, I see. Well, I confess, that I have dabbled a little, and if you like I can show you something that bears on the very curious subject we have been discussing."

Ambrose took a candle and went away to a far, dim corner
of the room. Cotgrave saw him open a venerable bureau that
stood there, and from some secret recess he drew out a parcel,
and came back to the window where they had been sitting.

Ambrose undid a wrapping of paper, and produced a green
pocketbook.

"You will take care of it?" he said. "Don't leave it lying
about. It is one of the choicer pieces in my collection, and I
should be very sorry if it were lost."

He fondled the faded binding.

"I knew the girl who wrote this," he said. "When you read
it, you will see how it illustrates the talk we have had tonight. There is a sequel, too, but I won't talk of that.

"There was an odd article in one of the reviews some
months ago," he began again, with the air of a man who
changes the subject. "It was written by a doctor—Dr. Coryn, I
think, was the name. He says that a lady, watching her little
girl playing at the drawing-room window, suddenly saw the
heavy sash give way and fall on the child's fingers. The lady
fainted, I think, but at any rate the doctor was summoned,
and when he had dressed the child's wounded and maimed
fingers he was summoned to the mother. She was groaning
with pain, and it was found that three fingers of her hand,
corresponding with those that had been injured on the child's
hand, were swollen and inflamed, and later, in the doctor's
language, purulent sloughing set in."

Ambrose still handled delicately the green volume.

"Well, here it is," he said at last, parting with difficulty, it
seemed, from his treasure.

"You will bring it back as soon as you have read it," he said,
as they went out into the hall, into the old garden, faint with
the odor of white lilies.

There was a broad red band in the east as Cotgrave turned
to go, and from the high ground where he stood he saw that
awful spectacle of London in a dream.

The Green Book

The morocco binding of the book was faded, and the color
had grown faint, but there were no stains nor bruises nor

marks of usage. The book looked as if it had been bought "on a visit to London" some seventy or eighty years ago, and had somehow been forgotten and suffered to lie away out of sight. There was an old, delicate, lingering odor about it, such an odor as sometimes haunts an ancient piece of furniture for a century or more. The end papers, inside the binding, were oddly decorated with colored patterns and faded gold. It looked small, but the paper was fine, and there were many leaves, closely covered with minute, painfully formed characters.

I found this book (the manuscript began) in a drawer in the old bureau that stands on the landing. It was a very rainy day and I could not go out, so in the afternoon I got a candle and rummaged in the bureau. Nearly all the drawers were full of old dresses, but one of the small ones looked empty, and I found this book hidden right at the back. I wanted a book like this, so I took it to write in. It is full of secrets. I have a great many other books of secrets I have written, hidden in a safe place, and I am going to write here many of the old secrets and some new ones; but there are some I shall not put down at all. I must not write down the real names of the days and months which I found out a year ago, nor the way to make the Aklo letters, or the Chian language, or the great beautiful Circles, nor the Mao Games, nor the chief songs. I may write something about all these things but not the way to do them, for peculiar reasons. And I must not say who the Nymphs are, or the Dôls, or Jeelo, or what voolas mean. All these are most secret secrets, and I am glad when I remember what they are, and how many wonderful languages I know, but there are some things that I call the secrets of the secrets of the secrets that I dare not think of unless I am quite alone, and then I shut my eyes, and put my hands over them and whisper the word, and the Alala comes. I only do this at night in my room or in certain woods that I know, but I must not describe them, as they are secret woods. Then there are the Ceremonies, which are all of them important, but some are more delightful than others—there are the White Ceremonies, and the Green Ceremonies, and the Scarlet Ceremonies. The Scarlet Ceremonies are the best, but there is only one place where they can be performed properly, though there is a very nice imitation which I have done in other places. Besides these, I have the dances, and the Comedy, and I have done the Comedy sometimes when the others were looking, and they didn't understand anything about it. I was very little when I first knew about these things.

When I was very small, and mother was alive, I can remember remembering things before that, only it has all got confused. But I remember when I was five or six I heard them talking about me when they thought I was not noticing. They were saying how queer I was a year or two before, and how nurse had called my mother to come and listen to me talking all to myself, and I was saying words that nobody could understand. I was speaking the Xu language, but I only remember a very few of the words, as it was about the little white faces that used to look at me when I was lying in my cradle. They used to talk to me, and I learned their language and talked to them in it about some great white place where they lived, where the trees and the grass were all white, and there were white hills as high up as the moon, and a cold wind. I have often dreamed of it afterwards, but the faces went away when I was very little. But a wonderful thing happened when I was about five. My nurse was carrying me on her shoulder; there was a field of yellow corn, and we went through it; it was very hot. Then we came to a path through a wood, and a tall man came after us, and went with us till we came to a place where there was a deep pool, and it was very dark and shady. Nurse put me down on the soft moss under a tree, and she said: "She can't get to the pond now." So they left me there, and I sat quite still and watched, and out of the water and out of the wood came two wonderful white people, and they began to play and dance and sing. They were a kind of creamy white like the old ivory figure in the drawing-room; one was a beautiful lady with kind dark eyes, and a grave face, and long black hair, and she smiled such a strange sad smile at the other, who laughed and came to her. They played together, and danced round and round the pool, and they sang a song till I fell asleep.

Nurse woke me up when she came back, and she was looking something like the lady had looked, so I told her all about

it, and asked her why she looked like that. At first she cried,
and then she looked very frightened, and turned quite pale.
She put me down on the grass and stared at me, and I could
see she was shaking all over. Then she said I had been dreaming, but I knew I hadn't. Then she made me promise not to
say a word about it to anybody, and if I did I should be thrown
into the black pit. I was not frightened at all, though nurse
was, and I never forgot about it, because when I shut my eyes
and it was quite quiet, and I was all alone, I could see them
again, very faint and far away, but very splendid; and little
bits of the song they sang came into my head, but I couldn't
sing it.

I was thirteen, nearly fourteen, when I had a very singular
adventure, so strange that the day on which it happened is
always called the White Day. My mother had been dead for
more than a year, and in the morning I had lessons, but they
let me go out for walks in the afternoon. And this afternoon I
walked a new way, and a little brook led me into a new country, but I tore my frock getting through some of the difficult
places, as the way was through many bushes, and beneath
the low branches of trees, and up thorny thickets on the hills,
and by dark woods full of creeping thorns. And it was a long,
long way. It seemed as if I was going on forever and ever, and
I had to creep by a place like a tunnel where a brook must
have been, but all the water had dried up, and the floor was
rocky, and the bushes had grown overhead till they met, so
that it was quite dark. And I went on and on through that
dark place; it was a long, long way. And I came to a hill that I
never saw before. I was in a dismal thicket full of black
twisted boughs that tore me as I went through them, and I
cried out because I was smarting all over, and then I found
that I was climbing, and I went up and up a long way, till at
last the thicket stopped and I came out crying just under the
top of a big bare place, where there were ugly gray stones
lying all about on the grass, and here and there a little
twisted, stunted tree came out from under a stone, like a
snake. And I went up, right to the top, a long way. I never
saw such big ugly stones before; they came out of the earth
some of them, and some looked as if they had been rolled to
where they were, and they went on and on as far as I could

see, a long, long way. I looked out from them and saw the
country, but it was strange. It was winter time, and there
were black terrible woods hanging from the hills all round; it
was like seeing a large room hung with black curtains, and
the shape of the trees seemed quite different from any I had
ever seen before. I was afraid. Then beyond the woods there
were other hills round in a great ring, but I had never seen
any of them; it all looked black, and everything had a voor
over it. It was all so still and silent, and the sky was heavy
and gray and sad, like a wicked voorish dome in Deep Dendo.
I went on into the dreadful rocks. There were hundreds and
hundreds of them. Some were like horrid-grinning men; I
could see their faces as if they would jump at me out of the
stone, and catch hold of me, and drag me with them back into
the rock, so that I should always be there. And there were
other rocks that were like animals, creeping, horrible animals, putting out their tongues, and others were like words
that I could not say, and others like dead people lying on the
grass. I went on among them, though they frightened me, and
my heart was full of wicked songs that they put into it; and I
wanted to make faces and twist myself about in the way they
did, and I went on and on a long way till at last I liked the
rocks, and they didn't frighten me any more. I sang the songs
I thought of; songs full of words that must not be spoken or
written down. Then I made faces like the faces on the rocks,
and I twisted myself about like the twisted ones, and I lay
down flat on the ground like the dead ones, and I went up to
one that was grinning, and put my arms round him and
hugged him. And so I went on and on through the rocks till I
came to a round mound in the middle of them. It was higher
than a mound; it was nearly as high as our house, and it was
like a great basin turned upside down, all smooth and round
and green, with one stone, like a post, sticking up at the top. I
climbed up the sides, but they were so steep I had to stop or I
should have rolled all the way down again, and I should have
knocked against the stones at the bottom, and perhaps been
killed. But I wanted to get up to the very top of the big round
mound, so I lay down flat on my face, and took hold of the
grass with my hands and drew myself up, bit by bit, till I was
at the top. Then I sat down on the stone in the middle, and

looked all about. I felt I had come such a long, long way, just as if I were a hundred miles from home, or in some other country, or in one of the strange places I had read about in the *Tale of the Genie* and the *Arabian Nights,* or as if I had gone across the sea, far away, for years and I had found another world that nobody had ever seen or heard of before, or as if I had somehow flown through the sky and fallen on one of the stars I had read about where everything is dead and cold and gray, and there is no air, and the wind doesn't blow. I sat on the stone and looked all round and down and round about me. It was just as if I was sitting on a tower in the middle of a great empty town, because I could see nothing all around but the gray rocks on the ground. I couldn't make out their shapes any more, but I could see them on and on for a long way, and I looked at them, and they seemed as if they had been arranged into patterns, and shapes, and figures. I knew they couldn't be, because I had seen a lot of them coming right out of the earth, joined to the deep rocks below, so I looked again, but still I saw nothing but circles, and small circles inside big ones, and pyramids, and domes, and spires, and they seemed all to go round and round the place where I was sitting, and the more I looked, the more I saw great big rings of rocks, getting bigger and bigger, and I stared so long that it felt as if they were all moving and turning, like a great wheel, and I was turning, too, in the middle. I got quite dizzy and queer in the head, and everything began to be hazy and not clear, and I saw little sparks of blue light, and the stones looked as if they were springing and dancing and twisting as they went round and round and round. I was frightened again, and I cried aloud, and jumped up from the stone I was sitting on, and fell down. When I got up I was so glad they all looked still, and I sat down on the top and slid down the mound, and went on again. I danced as I went in the peculiar way the rocks had danced when I got giddy, and I was so glad I could do it quite well, and I danced and danced along, and sang extraordinary songs that came into my head. At last I came to the edge of that great flat hill, and there were no more rocks, and the way went again through a dark thicket in a hollow. It was just as bad as the other one I went through climbing up, but I didn't mind this one, because I was so glad

I had seen those singular dances and could imitate them. I went down, creeping through the bushes, and a tall nettle stung me on my leg, and made me burn, but I didn't mind it, and I tingled with the boughs and the thorns, but I only laughed and sang. Then I got out of the thicket into a close valley, a little secret place like a dark passage that nobody ever knows of, because it was so narrow and deep and the woods were so thick round it. There is a steep bank with trees hanging over it, and there the ferns keep green all through the winter, when they are dead and brown upon the hill, and the ferns there have a sweet, rich smell like what oozes out of fir trees. There was a little stream of water running down this valley, so small that I could easily step across it. I drank the water with my hand, and it tasted like bright, yellow wine, and it sparkled and bubbled as it ran down over beautiful red and yellow and green stones, so that it seemed alive and all colors at once. I drank it, and I drank more with my hand, but I couldn't drink enough, so I lay down and bent my head and sucked the water up with my lips. It tasted much better, drinking it that way, and a ripple would come up to my mouth and give me a kiss, and I laughed, and drank again, and pretended there was a nymph, like the one in the old picture at home, who lived in the water and was kissing me. So I bent low down to the water, and put my lips softly to it, and whispered to the nymph that I would come again. I felt sure it could not be common water. I was so glad when I got up and went on; and I danced again and went up and up the valley, under hanging hills. And when I came to the top, the ground rose up in front of me, tall and steep as a wall, and there was nothing but the green wall and the sky. I thought of "forever and forever, world without end, Amen"; and I thought I must have really found the end of the world, because it was like the end of everything, as if there could be nothing at all beyond, except the kingdom of Voor, where the light goes when it is put out, and the water goes when the sun takes it away. I began to think of all the long, long way I had journeyed, how I had found a brook and followed it, and followed it on, and gone through bushes and thorny thickets, and dark woods full of creeping thorns. Then I had crept up a tunnel under trees, and climbed a thicket, and seen all the gray rocks, and sat in the middle of them when they turned round, and then I had gone on through the gray rocks and come down the hill through the stinging thicket and up the dark valley, all a long, long way. I wondered how I should get home again, if I could ever find the way, and if my home was there any more, or if it were turned and everybody in it into gray rocks, as in the *Arabian Nights*. So I sat down on the grass and thought what I should do next. I was tired, and my feet were hot with walking, and as I looked about I saw there was a wonderful well just under the high, steep wall of grass. All the ground round it was covered with bright, green, dripping moss; there was every kind of moss there, moss like beautiful little ferns, and like palms and fir trees, and it was all green as jewelry, and drops of water hung on it like diamonds. And in the middle was the great well, deep and shining and beautiful, so clear that it looked as if I could touch the red sand at the bottom, but it was far below. I stood by it and looked in, as if I were looking in a glass. At the bottom of the well, in the middle of it, the red grains of sand were moving and stirring all the time, and I saw how the water bubbled up, but at the top it was quite smooth, and full and brimming. It was a great well, large like a bath, and with the shining, glittering green moss about it, it looked like a great white jewel, with green jewels all round. My feet were so hot and tired that I took off my boots and stockings, and let my feet down into the water, and the water was soft and cold, and when I got up I wasn't tired any more, and I felt I must go on, farther and farther, and see what was on the other side of the wall. I climbed up it very slowly, going sideways all the time, and when I got to the top and looked over, I was in the queerest country I had seen, stranger even than the hill of the gray rocks. It looked as if earth-children had been playing there with their spades, as it was all hills and hollows, and castles and walls made of earth and covered with grass. There were two mounds like big beehives, round and great and solemn, and then hollow basins, and then a steep mounting wall like the ones I saw once by the seaside where the big guns and the soldiers were. I nearly fell into one of the round hollows, it went away from under my feet so suddenly, and I ran fast down the side and stood at the bottom and looked up.

It was strange and solemn to look up. There was nothing but the gray, heavy sky and the sides of the hollow; everything else had gone away, and the hollow was the whole world, and I thought that at night it must be full of ghosts and moving shadows and pale things when the moon shone down to the bottom at the dead of the night, and the wind wailed up above. It was so strange and solemn and lonely, like a hollow temple of dead heathen gods. It reminded me of a tale my nurse had told me when I was quite little; it was the same nurse that took me into the wood where I saw the beautiful white people. And I remembered how nurse had told me the story one winter night, when the wind was beating the trees against the wall, and crying and moaning in the nursery chimney. She said there was, somewhere or other, a hollow pit, just like the one I was standing in, everybody was afraid to go into it or near it, it was such a bad place. But once upon a time there was a poor girl who said she would go into the hollow pit, and everybody tried to stop her, but she would go. And she went down into the pit and came back laughing, and said there was nothing there at all, except green grass and red stones, and white stones and yellow flowers. And soon after, people saw she had most beautiful emerald earrings, and they asked how she got them, as she and her mother were quite poor. But she laughed, and said her earrings were not made of emeralds at all, but only of green grass. Then, one day, she wore on her breast the reddest ruby that anyone had ever seen, and it was as big as a hen's egg, and glowed and sparkled like a hot burning coal of fire. And they asked how she got it, as she and her mother were quite poor. But she laughed, and said it was not a ruby at all, but only a red stone. Then one day she wore round her neck the loveliest necklace that anyone had ever seen, much finer than the queen's finest, and it was made of great bright diamonds, hundreds of them, and they shone like all the stars on a night in June. So they asked her how she got it, as she and her mother were quite poor. But she laughed, and said they were not diamonds at all, but only white stones. And one day she went to the Court, and she wore on her head a crown of pure angel-gold, so nurse said, and it shone like the sun, and it was much more splendid than the crown the king was wearing

himself, and in her ears she wore the emeralds, and the big
ruby was the brooch on her breast, and the great diamond
necklace was sparkling on her neck. And the king and queen
thought she was some great princess from a long way off, and
got down from their thrones and went to meet her, but somebody told the king and queen who she was, and that she was
quite poor. So the king asked why she wore a gold crown, and
how she got it, as she and her mother were so poor. And she
laughed, and said it wasn't a gold crown at all, but only some
yellow flowers she had put in her hair. And the king thought
it was very strange, and said she should stay at the Court,
and they would see what would happen next. And she was so
lovely that everybody said that her eyes were greener than
the emeralds, that her lips were redder than the ruby, and
her skin was whiter than the diamonds, and that her hair
was brighter than the golden crown. So the king's son said he
would marry her, and the king said he might. And the bishop
married them, and there was a great supper, and afterwards
the king's son went to his wife's room. But just when he had
his hand on the door, he saw a tall, black man, with a dreadful face, standing in front of the door, and a voice said—

> Venture not upon your life,
> This is mine own wedded wife.

Then the king's son fell down on the ground in a fit. And
they came and tried to get into the room, but they couldn't,
and they hacked at the door with hatchets, but the wood had
turned hard as iron, and at last everybody ran away, they
were so frightened at the screaming and laughing and shrieking and crying that came out of the room. But next day they
went in, and found there was nothing in the room but thick
black smoke, because the black man had come and taken her
away. And on the bed there were two knots of faded grass and
a red stone, and some white stones, and some faded yellow
flowers. I remembered this tale of nurse's while I was standing at the bottom of the deep hollow; it was so strange and
solitary there, and I felt afraid. I could not see any stones or
flowers, but I was afraid of bringing them away without
knowing, and I thought I would do a charm that came into

my head to keep the black man away. So I stood right in the very middle of the hollow, and I made sure that I had none of those things on me, and then I walked round the place, and touched my eyes, and my lips, and my hair in a peculiar manner, and whispered some queer words that nurse taught me to keep bad things away. Then I felt safe and climbed up out of the hollow, and went on through all those mounds and hollows and walls, till I came to the end, which was high above all the rest, and I could see that all the different shapes of the earth were arranged in patterns, something like the gray rocks, only the pattern was different. It was getting late, and the air was indistinct, but it looked from where I was standing something like two great figures of people lying on the grass. And I went on, and at last I found a certain wood, which is too secret to be described, and nobody knows of the passage into it, which I found out in a very curious manner, by seeing some little animal run into the wood through it. So I went after the animal by a very narrow dark way, under thorns and bushes, and it was almost dark when I came to a kind of open place in the middle. And there I saw the most wonderful sight I have ever seen, but it was only for a minute, as I ran away directly, and crept out of the wood by the passage I had come by, and ran as fast as ever I could, because I was afraid, what I had seen was so wonderful and so strange and beautiful. But I wanted to get home and think of it, and I did not know what might not happen if I stayed by the wood. I was hot all over and trembling, and my heart was beating, and strange cries that I could not help came from me as I ran from the wood. I was glad that a great white moon came up from over a round hill and showed me the way, so I went back through the mounds and hollows and down the close valley, and up through the thicket over the place of the gray rocks, and so at last I got home again. My father was busy in his study, and the servants had not told about my not coming home, though they were frightened, and wondered what they ought to do, so I told them I had lost my way, but I did not let them find out the real way I had been. I went to bed and lay awake all through the night, thinking of what I had seen. When I came out of the narrow way, and it looked all shining, though the air was dark, it seemed so certain, and all the way home I was quite sure that I had seen it, and I wanted to be alone in my room, and be glad over it all to myself, and shut my eyes and pretend it was there, and do all the things I would have done if I had not been so afraid. But when I shut my eyes the sight would not come, and I began to think about my adventures all over again, and I remembered how dusky and queer it was at the end, and I was afraid it must be all a mistake, because it seemed impossible it could happen. It seemed like one of nurse's tales, which I didn't really believe in, though I was frightened at the bottom of the hollow; and the stories she told me when I was little came back into my head, and I wondered whether it was really there what I thought I had seen, or whether any of her tales could have happened a long time ago. It was so queer; I lay awake there in my room at the back of the house, and the moon was shining on the other side toward the river, so the bright light did not fall upon the wall. And the house was quite still. I had heard my father come upstairs, and just after the clock struck twelve, and after the house was still and empty, as if there was nobody alive in it. And though it was all dark and indistinct in my room, a pale glimmering kind of light shone in through the white blind, and once I got up and looked out, and there was a great black shadow of the house covering the garden, looking like a prison where men are hanged; and then beyond it was all white; and the wood shone white with black gulfs between the trees. It was still and clear, and there were no clouds in the sky. I wanted to think of what I had seen but I couldn't, and I began to think of all the tales that nurse had told me so long ago that I thought I had forgotten, but they all came back, and mixed up with the thickets and the gray rocks and the hollows in the earth and the secret wood, till I hardly knew what was new and what was old, or whether it was not all dreaming. And then I remembered that hot summer afternoon, so long ago, when nurse left me by myself in the shade, and the white people came out of the water and out of the wood, and played, and danced, and sang, and I began to fancy that nurse told me about something like it before I saw them, only I couldn't recollect exactly what she told me. Then I wondered whether she had been the white lady, as I remembered she was just as

white and beautiful, and had the same dark eyes and black
hair; and sometimes she smiled and looked like the lady had
looked, when she was telling me some of her stories, beginning with "Once on a time," or "In the time of the fairies."
But I thought she couldn't be the lady, as she seemed to have
gone a different way into the wood, and I didn't think the
man who came after us could be the other, or I couldn't have
seen that wonderful secret in the secret wood. I thought of
the moon; but it was afterwards when I was in the middle of
the wild land, where the earth was made into the shape of
great figures, and it was all walls, and mysterious hollows,
and smooth round mounds, that I saw the great white moon
come up over a round hill. I was wondering about all these
things, till at last I got quite frightened, because I was afraid
something had happened to me, and I remembered nurse's
tale of the poor girl who went into the hollow pit, and was
carried away at last by the black man. I knew I had gone into
a hollow pit too, and perhaps it was the same, and I had done
something dreadful. So I did the charm over again, and
touched my eyes and my lips and my hair in a peculiar manner, and said the old words from the fairy language, so that I
might be sure I had not been carried away. I tried again to
see the secret wood, and to creep up the passage and see what
I had seen there, but somehow I couldn't, and I kept on thinking of nurse's stories. There was one I remembered about a
young man who once upon a time went hunting, and all the
day he and his hounds hunted everywhere, and they crossed
the rivers and went into all the woods, and went round the
marshes, but they couldn't find anything at all, and they
hunted all day till the sun sank down and began to set behind
the mountain. And the young man was angry because he
couldn't find anything, and he was going to turn back, when
just as the sun touched the mountain, he saw come out of a
brake in front of him a beautiful white stag. And he cheered
to his hounds, but they whined and would not follow, and he
cheered to his horse, but it shivered and stood stock still, and
the young man jumped off the horse and left the hounds and
began to follow the white stag all alone. And soon it was quite
dark, and the sky was black, without a single star shining in
it, and the stag went away into the darkness. And though the

man had brought his gun with him he never shot at the stag,
because he wanted to catch it, and he was afraid he would
lose it in the night. But he never lost it once, though the sky
was so black and the air was so dark, and the stag went on
and on till the young man didn't know a bit where he was.
And they went through enormous woods where the air was
full of whispers and a pale, dead light came out from the
rotten trunks that were lying on the ground, and just as the
man thought he had lost the stag, he would see it all white
and shining in front of him, and he would run fast to catch it,
but the stag always ran faster, so he did not catch it. And
they went through the enormous woods, and they swam
across rivers, and they waded through black marshes where
the ground bubbled, and the air was full of will-o'-the-wisps,
and the stag fled away down into rocky narrow valleys, where
the air was like the smell of a vault, and the man went after
it. And they went over the great mountain and the man
heard the wind come down from the sky, and the stag went
on and the man went after. At last the sun rose and the
young man found he was in a country that he had never seen
before; it was a beautiful valley with a bright stream running
through it, and a great, big round hill in the middle. And the
stag went down the valley, towards the hill, and it seemed to
be getting tired and went slower and slower, and though the
man was tired, too, he began to run faster, and he was sure he
would catch the stag at last. But just as they got to the bottom of the hill, and the man stretched out his hand to catch
the stag, it vanished into the earth, and the man began to cry;
he was so sorry that he had lost it after all his long hunting.
But as he was crying he saw there was a door in the hill, just
in front of him, and he went in, and it was quite dark, but he
went on, as he thought he would find the white stag. And all
of a sudden it got light, and there was the sky, and the sun
shining, and birds singing in the trees, and there was a beautiful fountain. And by the fountain a lovely lady was sitting,
who was the queen of the fairies, and she told the man that
she had changed herself into a stag to bring him there because she loved him so much. Then she brought out a great
gold cup, covered with jewels, from her fairy palace, and she
offered him wine in the cup to drink. And he drank, and the

more he drank the more he longed to drink, because the wine
was enchanted. So he kissed the lovely lady, and she became
his wife and he stayed all that day and all that night in the
hill where she lived, and when he woke he found he was lying
on the ground, close to where he had seen the stag first, and
his horse was there and his hounds were there waiting, and
he looked up, and the sun sank behind the mountain. And he
went home and lived a long time, but he would never kiss any
other lady because he had kissed the queen of the fairies, and
he would never drink common wine any more, because he
had drunk enchanted wine. And sometimes nurse told me
tales that she had heard from her great-grandmother, who
was very old, and lived in a cottage on the mountain all
alone, and most of these tales were about a hill where people
used to meet at night long ago, and they used to play all sorts
of strange games and do queer things that nurse told me of,
but I couldn't understand, and now, she said, everybody but
her great-grandmother had forgotten all about it, and nobody
knew where the hill was, not even her great-grandmother.
But she told me one very strange story about the hill, and I
trembled when I remembered it. She said that people always
went there in summer, when it was very hot, and they had to
dance a good deal. It would be all dark at first, and there were
trees there, which made it much darker, and people would
come, one by one, from all directions, by a secret path which
nobody else knew, and two persons would keep the gate, and
every one as they came up had to give a very curious sign,
which nurse showed me as well as she could, but she said she
couldn't show me properly. And all kinds of people would
come; there would be gentle folks and village folks, and some
old people and the boys and girls, and quite small children,
who sat and watched. And it would all be dark as they came
in, except in one corner where someone was burning something that smelt strong and sweet, and made them laugh, and
there one would see a glaring of coals, and the smoke mounting up red. So they would all come in, and when the last had
come there was no door any more, so that no one else could
get in, even if they knew there was anything beyond. And
once a gentleman who was a stranger and had ridden a long
way, lost his path at night, and his horse took him into the

very middle of the wild country, where everything was upside down, and there were dreadful marshes and great stones everywhere, and holes underfoot, and the trees looked like gibbet-posts, because they had great black arms that stretched out across the way. And this strange gentleman was very frightened, and his horse began to shiver all over, and at last it stopped and wouldn't go any farther, and the gentleman got down and tried to lead the horse, but it wouldn't move, and it was all covered with a sweat, like death. So the gentleman went on all alone, going farther and farther into the wild country, till at last he came to a dark place, where he heard shouting and singing and crying, like nothing he had ever heard before. It all sounded quite close to him, but he couldn't get in, and so he began to call, and while he was calling, something came behind him, and in a minute his mouth and arms and legs were all bound up, and he fell into a swoon. And when he came to himself, he was lying by the roadside, just where he had first lost his way, under a blasted oak with a black trunk, and his horse was tied beside him. So he rode on to the town and told the people there what had happened, and some of them were amazed; but others knew. So when once everybody had come, there was no door at all for anybody else to pass in by. And when they were all inside, round in a ring, touching each other, someone began to sing in the darkness, and someone else would make a noise like thunder with a thing they had on purpose, and on still nights people would hear the thundering noise far, far away beyond the wild land, and some of them, who thought they knew what it was, used to make a sign on their breasts when they woke up in their beds at dead of night and heard that terrible deep noise, like thunder on the mountains. And the noise and the singing would go on and on for a long time, and the people who were in a ring swayed a little to and fro; and the song was in an old, old language that nobody knows now, and the tune was queer. Nurse said her great-grandmother had known someone who remembered a little of it, when she was quite a little girl, and nurse tried to sing some of it to me, and it was so strange a tune that I turned all cold and my flesh crept as if I had put my hand on something dead. Sometimes it was a man that sang and sometimes it was a woman, and

sometimes the one who sang it did it so well that two or three
of the people who were there fell to the ground shrieking and
tearing with their hands. The singing went on, and the people
in the ring kept swaying to and fro for a long time, and at last
the moon would rise over a place they called the Tole Deol,
and came up and showed them swinging and swaying from
side to side, with the sweet thick smoke curling up from the
burning coals, and floating in circles all around them. Then
they had their supper. A boy and a girl brought it to them;
the boy carried a great cup of wine, and the girl carried a
cake of bread, and they passed the bread and the wine round
and round, but they tasted quite different from common
bread and common wine, and changed everybody that tasted
them. Then they all rose up and danced, and secret things
were brought out of some hiding place, and they played extraordinary games, and danced round and round and round
in the moonlight, and sometimes people would suddenly disappear and never be heard of afterwards, and nobody knew
what had happened to them. And they drank more of that
curious wine, and they made images and worshipped them,
and nurse showed me how the images were made one day
when we were out for a walk, and we passed by a place where
there was a lot of wet clay. So nurse asked me if I would like
to know what those things were like that they made on the
hill, and I said yes. Then she asked me if I would promise
never to tell a living soul a word about it, and if I did I was to
be thrown into the black pit with the dead people, and I said I
wouldn't tell anybody, and she said the same thing again and
again, and I promised. So she took my wooden spade and dug
a big lump of clay and put it in my tin bucket, and told me to
say if anyone met us that I was going to make pies when I
went home. Then we went on a little way till we came to a
little brake growing right down into the road, and nurse
stopped, and looked up the road and down it, and then peeped
through the hedge into the field on the other side, and then
she said, "Quick!" and we ran into the brake, and crept in
and out among the bushes till we had gone a good way from
the road. Then we sat down under a bush, and I wanted so
much to know what nurse was going to make with the clay,
but before she would begin she made me promise again not to

say a word about it, and she went again and peeped through
the bushes on every side, though the lane was so small and
deep that hardly anybody ever went there. So we sat down,
and nurse took the clay out of the bucket, and began to knead
it with her hands, and do queer things with it, and turn it
about. And she hid it under a big dock leaf for a minute or
two and then she brought it out again, and then she stood up
and sat down, and walked round the clay in a peculiar manner, and all the time she was softly singing a sort of rhyme,
and her face got very red. Then she sat down again, and took
the clay in her hands and began to shape it into a doll, but
not like the dolls I have at home, and she made the queerest,
doll I had ever seen, all out of the wet clay, and hid it under a
bush to get dry and hard, and all the time she was making it
she was singing these rhymes to herself, and her face got
redder and redder. So we left the doll there, hidden away in
the bushes where nobody would ever find it. And a few days
later we went the same walk, and when we came to that
narrow, dark part of the lane where the brake runs down to
the bank, nurse made me promise all over again, and she
looked about, just as she had done before, and we crept into
the bushes till we got to the green place where the little clay
man was hidden. I remember it all so well, though I was only
eight, and it is eight years ago now as I am writing it down,
but the sky was a deep violet blue, and in the middle of the
brake where we were sitting there was a great elder tree
covered with blossoms, and on the other side there was a
clump of meadowsweet, and when I think of that day the
smell of the meadowsweet and elder blossom seems to fill the
room, and if I shut my eyes I can see the glaring blue sky,
with little clouds very white floating across it, and nurse who
went away long ago sitting opposite me and looking like the
beautiful white lady in the wood. So we sat down and nurse
took out the clay doll from the secret place where she had
hidden it, and she said we must "pay our respects," and she
would show me what to do, and I must watch her all the time.
So she did all sorts of queer things with the little clay man,
and I noticed she was all streaming with perspiration, though
we had walked so slowly, and then she told me to "pay my
respects," and I did everything she did because I liked her,

and it was such an odd game. And she said that if one loved
very much, the clay man was very good, if one did certain
things with it, and if one hated very much, it was just as good,
only one had to do different things, and we played with it a
long time, and pretended all sorts of things. Nurse said her
great-grandmother had told her all about these images, but
what we did was no harm at all, only a game. But she told me
a story about these images that frightened me very much,
and that was what I remembered that night when I was lying
awake in my room in the pale, empty darkness, thinking of
what I had seen and the secret wood. Nurse said there was
once a young lady of the high gentry, who lived in a great
castle. And she was so beautiful that all the gentlemen
wanted to marry her, because she was the loveliest lady that
anybody had ever seen, and she was kind to everybody, and
everybody thought she was very good. But though she was
polite to all the gentlemen who wished to marry her, she put
them off, and said she couldn't make up her mind, and she
wasn't sure she wanted to marry anybody at all. And her
father, who was a very great lord, was angry, though he was
so fond of her, and he asked her why she wouldn't choose a
bachelor out of all the handsome young men who came to the
castle. But she only said she didn't love any of them very
much, and she must wait, and if they pestered her, she said
she would go and be a nun in a nunnery. So all the gentlemen
said they would go away and wait for a year and a day, and
when a year and a day were gone, they would come back
again and ask her to say which one she would marry. So the
day was appointed and they all went away; and the lady had
promised that in a year and a day it would be her wedding
day with one of them. But the truth was, that she was the
queen of the people who danced on the hill on summer nights,
and on the proper nights she would lock the door of her room,
and she and her maid would steal out of the castle by a secret
passage that only they knew of, and go away up to the hill in
the wild land. And she knew more of the secret things than
anyone else, and more than anyone knew before or after, because she would not tell anybody the most secret secrets. She
knew how to do all the awful things, how to destroy young
men, and how to put a curse on people, and other things that

I could not understand. And her real name was the Lady
Avelin, but the dancing people called her Cassap, which
meant somebody very wise, in the old language. And she was
whiter than any of them and taller, and her eyes shone in the
dark like burning rubies; and she could sing songs that none
of the others could sing, and when she sang they all fell down
on their faces and worshipped her. And she could do what
they called the shib-show, which was a very wonderful en-
chantment. She would tell the great lord, her father, that she
wanted to go into the woods to gather flowers, so he let her go,
and she and her maid went into the woods where nobody
came, and the maid would keep watch. Then the lady would
lie down under the trees and begin to sing a particular song,
and she stretched out her arms, and from every part of the
wood great serpents would come, hissing and gliding in and
out among the trees, and shooting out their forked tongues as
they crawled up to the lady. And they all came to her, and
twisted round her, round her body, and her arms, and her
neck, till she was covered with writhing serpents, and there
was only her head to be seen. And she whispered to them,
and she sang to them, and they writhed round and round,
faster and faster, till she told them to go. And they all went
away directly, back to their holes, and on the lady's breast
there would be a most curious, beautiful stone, shaped something like an egg, and colored dark blue and yellow, and red
and green, marked like a serpent's scales. It was called a
glame stone, and with it one could do all sorts of wonderful
things, and nurse said her great-grandmother had seen a
glame stone with her own eyes, and it was for all the world
shiny and scaly like a snake. And the lady could do a lot of
other things as well, but she was quite fixed that she would
not be married. And there were a great many gentlemen who
wanted to marry her, but there were five of them who were
chief, and their names were Sir Simon, Sir John, Sir Oliver,
Sir Richard, and Sir Rowland. All the others believed she
spoke the truth, and that she would choose one of them to be
her man when a year and a day was done; it was only Sir
Simon, who was very crafty, who thought she was deceiving
them all, and he vowed he would watch and try if he could
find out anything. And though he was very wise he was very

young, and he had a smooth, soft face like a girl's, and he
pretended, as the rest did, that he would not come to the
castle for a year and a day, and he said he was going away
beyond the sea to foreign parts. But he really only went a
very little way, and came back dressed like a servant girl, and
so he got a place in the castle to wash the dishes. And he
waited and watched, and he listened and said nothing, and he
hid in dark places, and woke up at night and looked out, and
he heard things and he saw things that he thought were very
strange. And he was so sly that he told the girl that waited on
the lady that he was really a young man, and that he had
dressed up as a girl because he loved her so very much and
wanted to be in the same house with her, and the girl was so
pleased that she told him many things, and he was more than
ever certain that the Lady Avelin was deceiving him and the
others. And he was so clever, and told the servant so many
lies, that one night he managed to hide in the Lady Avelin's
room behind the curtains. And he stayed quite still and never
moved, and at last the lady came. And she bent down under
the bed, and raised up a stone, and there was a hollow place
underneath, and out of it she took a waxen image, just like
the clay one that I and nurse had made in the brake. And
all the time her eyes were burning like rubies. And she took
the little wax doll up in her arms and held it to her breast,
and she whispered and she murmured, and she took it up and
she laid it down again, and she held it high, and she held it
low, and she laid it down again. And she said, "Happy is he
that begat the bishop, that ordered the clerk, that married
the man, that had the wife, that fashioned the hive, that har-
bored the bee, that gathered the wax that my own true love
was made of." And she brought out of a pantry a great golden
bowl, and she brought out of a closet a great jar of wine, and
she poured some of the wine into the bowl, and she laid her
manikin very gently in the wine, and washed it in the wine
all over. Then she went to a cupboard and took a small round
cake and laid it on the image's mouth, and then she bore it
softly and covered it up. And Sir Simon, who was watching
all the time, though he was terribly frightened, saw the lady
bend down and stretch out her arms and whisper and sing,
and then Sir Simon saw beside her a handsome young man,

who kissed her on the lips. And they drank wine out of the
golden bowl together, and they ate the cake together. But
when the sun rose there was only the little wax doll, and the
lady hid it again under the bed in the hollow place. So Sir
Simon knew quite well what the lady was, and he waited and
he watched, till the time she had said was nearly over, and in
a week the year and a day would be done. And one night,
when he was watching behind the curtains in her room, he
saw her making more wax dolls. And she made five, and hid
them away. And the next night she took one out, and held it
up, and filled the golden bowl with water, and took the doll by
the neck and held it under the water. Then she said—

> Sir Dickon, Sir Dickon, your day is done,
> You shall be drowned in the water wan.

And the next day news came to the castle that Sir Richard
had been drowned at the ford. And at night she took another
doll and tied a violet cord round its neck and hung it up on a
nail. Then she said—

> Sir Rowland, your life has ended its span,
> High on a tree I see you hang.

And the next day news came to the castle that Sir Rowland
had been hanged by robbers in the wood. And at night she
took another doll, and drove her bodkin right into its heart.
Then she said—

> Sir Noll, Sir Noll, so cease your life,
> Your heart piercèd with the knife.

And the next day news came to the castle that Sir Oliver had
fought in a tavern, and a stranger had stabbed him to the
heart. And at night she took another doll, and held it to a fire
of charcoal till it was melted. Then she said—

> Sir John, return, and turn to clay,
> In fire of fever you waste away.

And the next day news came to the castle that Sir John had died in a burning fever. So then Sir Simon went out of the castle and mounted his horse and rode away to the bishop and told him everything. And the bishop sent his men, and they took the Lady Avelin, and everything she had done was found out. So on the day after the year and a day, when she was to have been married, they carried her through the town in her smock, and they tied her to a great stake in the marketplace, and burned her alive before the bishop with her wax image hung round her neck. And people said the wax man screamed in the burning of the flames. And I thought of this story again and again as I was lying awake in my bed, and I seemed to see the Lady Avelin in the marketplace, with the yellow flames eating up her beautiful white body. And I thought of it so much that I seemed to get into the story myself, and I fancied I was the lady, and that they were coming to take me to be burnt with fire, with all the people in the town looking at me. And I wondered whether she cared, after all the strange things she had done, and whether it hurt very much to be burned at the stake. I tried again and again to forget nurse's stories, and to remember the secret I had seen that afternoon, and what was in the secret wood, but I could only see the dark and a glimmering in the dark, and then it went away, and I only saw myself running, and then a great moon came up white over a dark round hill. Then all the old stories came back again, and the queer rhymes that nurse used to sing to me; and there was one beginning "Halsy cumsy Helen musty," that she used to sing very softly when she wanted me to go to sleep. And I began to sing it to myself inside of my head, and I went to sleep.

The next morning I was very tired and sleepy, and could hardly do my lessons, and I was very glad when they were over and I had had my dinner, as I wanted to go out and be alone. It was a warm day, and I went to a nice turfy hill by the river, and sat down on my mother's old shawl that I had brought with me on purpose. The sky was gray, like the day before, but there was a kind of white gleam behind it, and from where I was sitting I could look down on the town, and it was all still and quiet and white, like a picture. I remembered that it was on that hill that nurse taught me to play an old

game called "Troy Town," in which one had to dance, and
wind in and out on a pattern in the grass, and then when one
had danced and turned long enough the other person asks
you questions, and you can't help answering whether you
want to or not, and whatever you are told to do you feel you
have to do it. Nurse said there used to be a lot of games like
that that some people knew of, and there was one by which
people could be turned into anything you liked, and an old
man her great-grandmother had seen had known a girl who
had been turned into a large snake. And there was another
very ancient game of dancing and winding and turning, by
which you could take a person out of himself and hide him
away as long as you liked, and his body went walking about
quite empty, without any sense in it. But I came to that hill
because I wanted to think of what had happened the day
before, and of the secret of the wood. From the place where I
was sitting I could see beyond the town, into the opening I
had found, where a little brook had led me into an unknown
country. And I pretended I was following the brook over
again, and I went all the way in my mind, and at last I found
the wood, and crept into it under the bushes, and then in the
dusk I saw something that made me feel as if I were filled
with fire, as if I wanted to dance and sing and fly up into the
air, because I was changed and wonderful. But what I saw
was not changed at all, and had not grown old, and I wondered again and again how such things could happen, and
whether nurse's stories were really true, because in the day-
time in the open air everything seemed quite different from
what it was at night, when I was frightened, and thought I
was to be burned alive. I once told my father one of her little
tales, which was about a ghost, and asked him if it was true,
and he told me it was not true at all, and that only common,
ignorant people believed in such rubbish. He was very angry
with nurse for telling me the story, and scolded her, and after
that I promised her I would never whisper a word of what she
told me, and if I did I should be bitten by the great black
snake that lived in the pool in the wood. And all alone on the
hill I wondered what was true. I had seen something very
amazing and very lovely, and I knew a story, and if I had
really seen it, and not made it up out of the dark, and the

black bough, and the bright shining that was mounting up to
the sky from over the great round hill, but had really seen it
in truth, then there were all kinds of wonderful and lovely
and terrible things to think of, so I longed and trembled, and
I burned and got cold. And I looked down on the town, so
quiet and still, like a little white picture, and I thought over
and over if it could be true. I was a long time before I could
make up my mind to anything; there was such a strange fluttering at my heart that seemed to whisper to me all the time
that I had not made it up out of my head, and yet it seemed
quite impossible, and I knew my father and everybody would
say it was dreadful rubbish. I never dreamed of telling him or
anybody else a word about it, because I knew it would be of no
use, and I should only get laughed at or scolded, so for a long
time I was very quiet, and went about thinking and wondering; and at night I used to dream of amazing things, and
sometimes I woke up in the early morning and held out my
arms with a cry. And I was frightened, too, because there
were dangers, and some awful thing would happen to me,
unless I took great care, if the story were true. These old tales
were always in my head, night and morning, and I went over
them and told them to myself over and over again, and went
for walks in the places where nurse had told them to me; and
when I sat in the nursery by the fire in the evenings I used to
fancy nurse was sitting in the other chair, and telling me
some wonderful story in a low voice, for fear anybody should
be listening. But she used to like best to tell me about things
when we were right out in the country, far from the house,
because she said she was telling me such secrets, and walls
have ears. And if it was something more-than-ever secret, we
had to hide in brakes or woods; and I used to think it was
such fun creeping along a hedge, and going very softly, and
then we would get behind the bushes or run into the wood all
of a sudden, when we were sure that none was watching us;
so we knew that we had our secrets quite all to ourselves, and
nobody else at all knew anything about them. Now and then,
when we had hidden ourselves as I have described, she used
to show me all sorts of odd things. One day, I remember, we
were in a hazel brake, overlooking the brook, and we were so
snug and warm, as though it was April; the sun was quite hot,

and the leaves were just coming out. Nurse said she would show me something funny that would make me laugh, and then she showed me, as she said, how one could turn a whole house upside down, without anybody being able to find out, and the pots and pans would jump about, and the china would be broken, and the chairs would tumble over of themselves. I tried it one day in the kitchen, and I found I could do it quite well, and a whole row of plates on the dresser fell off it, and cook's little worktable tilted up and turned right over "before her eyes," as she said, but she was so frightened and turned so white that I didn't do it again, as I liked her. And afterward, in the hazel copse, when she had shown me how to make things tumble about, she showed me how to make rapping noises, and I learned how to do that, too. Then she taught me rhymes to say on certain occasions, and peculiar marks to make on other occasions, and other things that her great-grandmother had taught her when she was a little girl herself. And these were all the things I was thinking about in those days after the strange walk when I thought I had seen a great secret, and I wished nurse were there for me to ask her about it, but she had gone away more than two years before, and nobody seemed to know what had become of her, or where she had gone. But I shall always remember those days if I live to be quite old, because all the time I felt so strange, wondering and doubting, and feeling quite sure at one time, and making up my mind, and then I would feel quite sure that such things couldn't happen really, and it began all over again. But I took great care not to do certain things that might be very dangerous. So I waited and wondered for a long time, and though I was not sure at all, I never dared to try to find out. But one day I became sure that all that nurse said was quite true, and I was all alone when I found it out. I trembled all over with joy and terror, and as fast as I could I ran into one of the old brakes where we used to go—it was the one by the lane, where nurse made the little clay man—and I ran into it, and I crept into it; and when I came to the place where the elder was, I covered up my face with my hands and lay down flat on the grass, and I stayed there for two hours without moving, whispering to myself delicious, terrible things, and saying some words over and over again. It was all true and wonderful and splendid, and when I remembered the story I knew and thought of what I had really seen, I got hot and cold, and the air seemed full of scent, and flowers, and singing. And first I wanted to make a little clay man, like the one nurse had made so long ago, and I had to invent plans and stratagems, and to look about, and to think of things beforehand, because nobody must dream of anything that I was doing or going to do, and I was too old to carry clay about in a tin bucket. At last I thought of a plan, and I brought the wet clay to the brake, and did everything that nurse had done, only I made a much finer image than the one she had made; and when it was finished I did everything that I could imagine and much more than she did, because it was the likeness of something far better. And a few days later, when I had done my lessons early, I went for the second time by the way of the little brook that had led me into a strange country. And I followed the brook, and went through the bushes, and beneath the low branches of trees, and up thorny thickets on the hill, and by dark woods full of creeping thorns, a long, long way. Then I crept through the dark tunnel where the brook had been and the ground was stony, till at last I came to the thicket that climbed up the hill, and though the leaves were coming out upon the trees, everything looked almost as black as it was on the first day that I went there. And the thicket was just the same, and I went up slowly till I came out on the big bare hill, and began to walk among the wonderful rocks. I saw the terrible voor again on everything, for though the sky was brighter, the ring of wild hills all around was still dark, and the hanging woods looked dark and dreadful, and the strange rocks were as gray as ever; and when I looked down on them from the great mound, sitting on the stone, I saw all their amazing circles and rounds within rounds, and I had to sit quite still and watch them as they began to turn about me, and each stone danced in its place, and they seemed to go round and round in a great whirl, as if one were in the middle of all the stars and heard them rushing through the air. So I went down among the rocks to dance with them and to sing extraordinary songs; and I went down through the other thicket, and drank from the bright stream in the close and secret valley, putting my lips down to the bubbling water; and then I went on till I came to the deep, brimming well among the glittering moss, and I sat down. I looked before me into the secret darkness of the valley, and behind me was the great high wall of grass, and all around me there were the hanging woods that made the valley such a secret place. I knew there was nobody here at all besides myself, and that no one could see me. So I took off my boots and stockings, and let my feet down into the water, saying the words I knew. And it was not cold at all, as I expected, but warm and very pleasant, and when my feet were in it I felt as if they were in silk, or as if the nymph were kissing them. So when I had done, I said the other words and made the signs, and then I dried my feet with a towel I had brought on purpose, and put on my stockings and boots. Then I climbed up the steep wall, and went into the place where there are the hollows, and the two beautiful mounds, and the round ridges of land, and all the strange shapes. I did not go down into the hollow this time, but I turned at the end, and made out the figures quite plainly, as it was lighter, and I had remembered the story I had quite forgotten before, and in the story the two figures are called Adam and Eve, and only those who know the story understand what they mean. So I went on and on till I came to the secret wood which must not be described, and I crept into it by the way I had found. And when I had gone about halfway I stopped, and turned round, and got ready, and I bound the handkerchief tightly round my eyes, and made quite sure that I could not see at all, not a twig, nor the end of a leaf, nor the light of the sky, as it was an old red silk handkerchief with large yellow spots, that went round twice and covered my eyes, so that I could see nothing. Then I began to go on, step by step, very slowly. My heart beat faster and faster, and something rose in my throat that choked me and made me want to cry out, but I shut my lips, and went on. Boughs caught in my hair as I went, and great thorns tore me; but I went on to the end of the path. Then I stopped, and held out my arms and bowed, and I went round the first time, feeling with my hands, and there was nothing. I went round the second time, feeling with my hands, and there was nothing. Then I went round the third time, feeling with my hands, and the story was all true, and I wished that the years were

gone by, and that I had not so long a time to wait before I was
happy forever and ever.

Nurse must have been a prophet like those we read of in
the Bible. Everything that she said began to come true, and
since then other things that she told me of have happened.
That was how I came to know that her stories were true and
that I had not made up the secret myself out of my own head.
But there was another thing that happened that day. I went a
second time to the secret place. It was at the deep brimming
well, and when I was standing on the moss I bent over and
looked in, and then I knew who the white lady was that I had
seen come out of the water in the wood long ago when I was
quite little. And I trembled all over, because that told me
other things. Then I remembered how sometime after I had
seen the white people in the wood, nurse asked me more
about them, and I told her all over again, and she listened,
and said nothing for a long, long time, and at last she said,
"You will see her again." So I understood what had happened
and what was to happen. And I understood about the
nymphs; how I might meet them in all kinds of places, and
they would always help me, and I must always look for them,
and find them in all sorts of strange shapes and appearances.
And without the nymphs I could never have found the secret,
and without them none of the other things could happen.
Nurse had told me all about them long ago, but she called
them by another name, and I did not know what she meant,
or what her tales of them were about, only that they were
very queer. And there were two kinds, the bright and the
dark, and both were very lovely and very wonderful, and
some people saw only one kind, and some only the other, but
some saw them both. But usually the dark appeared first, and
the bright ones came afterwards, and there were extraordinary tales about them. It was a day or two after I had come
home from the secret place that I first really knew the
nymphs. Nurse had shown me how to call them, and I had
tried, but I did not know what she meant, and so I thought it
was all nonsense. But I made up my mind I would try again,
so I went to the wood where the pool was, where I saw the
white people, and I tried again. The dark nymph, Alanna,
came, and she turned the pool of water into a pool of fire. . . .

Epilogue

"That's a very queer story," said Cotgrave, handing back the green book to the recluse, Ambrose. "I see the drift of a good deal, but there are many things that I do not grasp at all. On the last page, for example, what does she mean by 'nymphs'?"

"Well, I think there are references throughout the manuscript to certain 'processes' which have been handed down by tradition from age to age. Some of these processes are just beginning to come within the purview of science, which has arrived at them—or rather at the steps which lead to them—by quite different paths. I have interpreted the reference to 'nymphs' as a reference to one of these processes."

"And you believe that there are such things?"

"Oh, I think so. Yes, I believe I could give you convincing evidence on that point. I am afraid you have neglected the study of alchemy? It is a pity, for the symbolism, at all events, is very beautiful, and moreover if you were acquainted with certain books on the subject, I could recall to your mind phrases which might explain a good deal in the manuscript that you have been reading."

"Yes, but I want to know whether you seriously think that there is any foundation of fact beneath these fancies. Is it not all a department of poetry; a curious dream with which man has indulged himself?"

"I can only say that it is no doubt better for the great mass of people to dismiss it all as a dream. But if you ask my veritable belief—that goes quite the other way. No, I should not say belief, but rather knowledge. I may tell you that I have known cases in which men have stumbled quite by accident on certain of these 'processes,' and have been astonished by wholly unexpected results. In the cases I am thinking of there could have been no possibility of 'suggestion' or subconscious action of any kind. One might as well suppose a schoolboy 'suggesting' the existence of AEschylus to himself, while he plods mechanically through the declensions.

"But you have noticed the obscurity," Ambrose went on, "and in this particular case it must have been dictated by instinct, since the writer never thought that her manuscripts would fall into other hands. But the practice is universal, and for most excellent reasons. Powerful and sovereign medicines, which are, of necessity, virulent poisons also, are kept in a locked cabinet. The child may find the key by chance, and drink herself dead; but in most cases the search is educational, and the phials contain precious elixirs for him who has patiently fashioned the key for himself."

"You do not care to go into details?"

"No, frankly, I do not. No, you must remain unconvinced. But you saw how the manuscript illustrates the talk we had last week?"

"Is this girl still alive?"

"No. I was one of those who found her. I knew the father well; he was a lawyer, and had always left her very much to herself. He thought of nothing but deeds and leases, and the news came to him as an awful surprise. She was missing one morning; I suppose it was about a year after she had written what you have read. The servants were called, and they told things, and put the only natural interpretation on them—a perfectly erroneous one.

"They discovered that green book somewhere in her room, and I found her in the place that she described with so much dread, lying on the ground before the image."

"It was an image?"

"Yes, it was hidden by the thorns and the thick undergrowth that had surrounded it. It was a wild, lonely country; but you know what it was like by her description, though of course you will understand that the colors have been heightened. A child's imagination always makes the heights higher and the depths deeper than they really are; and she had, unfortunately for herself, something more than imagination. One might say, perhaps, that the picture in her mind which she succeeded in a measure in putting into words, was the scene as it would have appeared to an imaginative artist. But it is a strange, desolate land."

"And she was dead?"

"Yes. She had poisoned herself—in time. No, there was not a word to be said against her in the ordinary sense. You may recollect a story I told you the other night about a lady who saw her child's fingers crushed by a window?"

"And what was this statue?"

"Well, it was of Roman workmanship, of a stone that with the centuries had not blackened, but had become white and luminous. The thicket had grown up about it and concealed it, and in the Middle Ages the followers of a very old tradition had known how to use it for their own purposes. In fact it had been incorporated into the monstrous mythology of the Sabbath. You will have noted that those to whom a sight of that shining whiteness had been vouchsafed by chance, or rather, perhaps, by apparent chance, were required to blindfold themselves on their second approach. That is very significant."

"And is it there still?"

"I sent for tools, and we hammered it into dust and fragments.

"The persistence of tradition never surprises me," Ambrose went on after a pause. "I could name many an English parish where such traditions as that girl had listened to in her childhood are still existent in occult but unabated vigor. No, for me, it is the 'story' not the 'sequel,' which is strange and awful, for I have always believed that wonder is of the soul."

The Willows

Algernon Blackwood

*The concept of the sublime was much debated in the eigh-
teenth century and was defined during the European Romantic movement as an emotional reaction that combined
respectful awe and terror. Though much Gothic horror pur-
ported to achieve the sublime through its evocation of the
supernatural, Algernon Blackwood's "The Willows" (1907) is
perhaps the closest horror literature has come to producing a
tale of truly sublime terror, one in which characters are presented with mind-boggling proof of the existence of supreme
beings and thus forced to acknowledge their own insignificance. Blackwood had an almost pantheistic reverence for
the natural world, and when he applied it to his descriptions
of the Austrian countryside, it produced a memorable portrait of a landscape where inexorable forces rule and Man is
the outsider. His tale grew out of actual boat trips down the
Danube he had made several years before. How much of it is
based in fact is probably best left to the imagination.*

I

After leaving Vienna, and long before you come to Buda-
Pesth, the Danube enters a region of singular loneliness and
desolation, where its waters spread away on all sides regardless of a main channel, and the country becomes a swamp for
miles upon miles, covered by a vast sea of low willow-bushes.

On the big maps this deserted area is painted in a fluffy blue, growing fainter in color as it leaves the banks, and across it may be seen in large straggling letters the word *Sümpfe,* meaning marshes.

In high flood this great acreage of sand, shingle-beds, and willow-grown islands is almost topped by the water, but in normal seasons the bushes bend and rustle in the free winds, showing their silver leaves to the sunshine in an ever-moving plain of bewildering beauty. These willows never attain to the dignity of trees; they have no rigid trunks; they remain humble bushes, with rounded tops and soft outline, swaying on slender stems that answer to the least pressure of the wind; supple as grasses, and so continually shifting that they somehow give the impression that the entire plain is moving and *alive.* For the wind sends waves rising and falling over the whole surface, waves of leaves instead of waves of water, green swells like the sea, too, until the branches turn and lift, and then silvery white as their under-side turns to the sun.

Happy to slip beyond the control of stern banks, the Danube here wanders about at will among the intricate network of channels intersecting the islands everywhere with broad avenues down which the waters pour with a shouting sound; making whirlpools, eddies, and foaming rapids; tearing at the sandy banks; carrying away masses of shore and willow-clumps; and forming new islands innumerable which shift daily in size and shape and possess at best an impermanent life, since the flood-time obliterates their very existence.

Properly speaking, this fascinating part of the river's life begins soon after leaving Pressburg, and we, in our Canadian canoe, with gipsy tent and frying-pan on board, reached it on the crest of a rising flood about mid-July. That very same morning, when the sky was reddening before sunrise, we had slipped swiftly through still-sleeping Vienna, leaving it a couple of hours later a mere patch of smoke against the blue hills of the Wienerwald on the horizon; we had breakfasted below Fischeramend under a grove of birch trees roaring in the wind; and had then swept on the tearing current past Orth, Hainburg, Petronell (the old Roman Carnuntum of Marcus Aurelius), and so under the frowning heights of Theben on a spur of the Carpathians, where the March steals in quietly from the left and the frontier is crossed between Austria and Hungary.

Racing along at twelve kilometers an hour soon took us well into Hungary, and the muddy waters—sure sign of flood—sent us aground on many a shingle-bed, and twisted us like a cork in many a sudden belching whirlpool before the towers of Pressburg (Hungarian, Poszony) showed against the sky; and then the canoe, leaping like a spirited horse, flew at top speed under the gray walls, negotiated safely the sunken chain of the Fliegende Brücke ferry, turned the corner sharply to the left, and plunged on yellow foam into the wilderness of islands, sand-banks, and swamp-land beyond—the land of the willows.

The change came suddenly, as when a series of bioscope pictures snaps down on the streets of a town and shifts without warning into the scenery of lake and forest. We entered the land of desolation on wings, and in less than half an hour there was neither boat nor fishing-hut nor red roof, nor any single sign of human habitation and civilization within sight. The sense of remoteness from the world of human kind, the utter isolation, the fascination of this singular world of willows, winds, and waters, instantly laid its spell upon us both, so that we allowed laughingly to one another that we ought by rights to have held some special kind of passport to admit us, and that we had, somewhat audaciously, come without asking leave into a separate little kingdom of wonder and magic—a kingdom that was reserved for the use of others who had a right to it, with everywhere unwritten warnings to trespassers for those who had the imagination to discover them.

Though still early in the afternoon, the ceaseless buffetings of a most tempestuous wind made us feel weary, and we at once began casting about for a suitable camping-ground for the night. But the bewildering character of the islands made landing difficult; the swirling flood carried us in-shore and then swept us out again; the willow branches tore our hands as we seized them to stop the canoe, and we pulled many a yard of sandy bank into the water before at length we shot with a great sideways blow from the wind into a backwater and managed to beach the bows in a cloud of spray. Then we

lay panting and laughing after our exertions on hot yellow
sand, sheltered from the wind, and in the full blaze of a
scorching sun, a cloudless blue sky above, and an immense
army of dancing, shouting willow bushes, closing in from all
sides, shining with spray and clapping their thousand little
hands as though to applaud the success of our efforts.

"What a river!" I said to my companion, thinking of all the
way we had traveled from the source in the Black Forest, and
how we had often been obliged to wade and push in the upper
shallows at the beginning of June.

"Won't stand much nonsense now, will it?" he said, pulling
the canoe a little farther into safety up the sand, and then
composing himself for a nap.

I lay by his side, happy and peaceful in the bath of the
elements—water, wind, sand, and the great fire of the sun—
thinking of the long journey that lay behind us, and of the
great stretch before us to the Black Sea, and how lucky I was
to have such a delightful and charming traveling companion
as my friend, the Swede.

We had made many similar journeys together, but the Danube, more than any other river I knew, impressed us from the
very beginning with its *aliveness*. From its tiny bubbling entry into the world among the pinewood gardens of
Donaueschingen, until this moment when it began to play
the great river-game of losing itself among the deserted
swamps, unobserved, unrestrained, it had seemed to us like
following the growth of some living creature. Sleepy at first,
but later developing violent desires as it became conscious of
its deep soul, it rolled, like some huge fluid being, through all
the countries we had passed, holding our little craft on its
mighty shoulders, playing roughly with us sometimes, yet always friendly and well-meaning, till at length we had come
inevitably to regard it as a Great Personage.

How, indeed, could it be otherwise, since it told us so much
of its secret life? At night we heard it singing to the moon as
we lay in our tent, uttering that odd sibilant note peculiar to
itself and said to be caused by the rapid tearing of the pebbles
along its bed, so great is its hurrying speed. We knew, too, the
voice of its gurgling whirlpools, suddenly bubbling up on a
surface previously quite calm; the roar of its shallows and

swift rapids; its constant steady thundering below all mere surface sounds; and that ceaseless tearing of its icy waters at the banks. How it stood up and shouted when the rains fell flat upon its face! And how its laughter roared out when the wind blew upstream and tried to stop its growing speed! We knew all its sounds and voices, its tumblings and foamings, its unnecessary splashing against the bridges; that self-conscious chatter when there were hills to look on; the affected dignity of its speech when it passed through the little towns, far too important to laugh; and all these faint, sweet whisperings when the sun caught it fairly in some slow curve and poured down upon it till the steam rose.

It was full of tricks, too, In Its early life before the great world knew it. There were places in the upper reaches among the Swabian forests, when yet the first whispers of its destiny had not reached it, where it elected to disappear through holes in the ground, to appear again on the other side of the porous limestone hills and start a new river with another name; leaving, too, so little water in its own bed that we had to climb out and wade and push the canoe through miles of shallows!

And a chief pleasure, in those early days of its irresponsible youth, was to lie low, like Brer Fox, just before the little turbulent tributaries came to join it from the Alps, and to refuse to acknowledge them when in, but to run for miles side by side, the dividing line well marked, the very levels different, the Danube utterly declining to recognize the newcomer. Below Passau, however, it gave up this particular trick, for there the Inn comes in with a thundering power impossible to ignore, and so pushes and incommodes the parent river that there is hardly room for them in the long twisting gorge that follows, and the Danube is shoved this way and that against the cliffs, and forced to hurry itself with great waves and much dashing to and fro in order to get through in time. And during the fight our canoe slipped down from its shoulder to its breast, and had the time of its life among the struggling waves. But the Inn taught the old river a lesson, and after Passau it no longer pretended to ignore new arrivals.

This was many days back, of course, and since then we had come to know other aspects of the great creature, and across

the Bavarian wheat plain of Straubing she wandered so
slowly under the blazing June sun that we could well imagine
only the surface inches were water, while below there moved
concealed as by a silken mantle, a whole army of Undines,
passing silently and unseen down to the sea, and very leisurely too, lest they be discovered.

Much, too, we forgave her because of her friendliness to the
birds and animals that haunted the shores. Cormorants lined
the banks in lonely places in rows like short black palings;
gray crows crowded the shingle-beds; storks stood fishing in
the vistas of shallower water that opened up between the
islands, and hawks, swans, and marsh birds of all sorts filled
the air with glinting wings and singing, petulant cries. It was
impossible to feel annoyed with the river's vagaries after seeing a deer leap with a splash into the water at sunrise and
swim past the bows of the canoe; and often we saw fawns
peering at us from the underbrush, or looked straight into
the brown eyes of a stag as we charged full tilt round a corner
and entered another reach of the river. Foxes, too, everywhere haunted the banks, tripping daintily among the driftwood and disappearing so suddenly that it was impossible to
see how they managed it.

But now, after leaving Pressburg, everything changed a little, and the Danube became more serious. It ceased trifling. It
was halfway to the Black Sea, within scenting distance almost of other, stranger countries where no tricks would be
permitted or understood. It became suddenly grown-up, and
claimed our respect and even our awe. It broke out into three
arms, for one thing, that only met again a hundred kilometers farther down, and for a canoe there were no indications
which one was intended to be followed.

"If you take a side channel," said the Hungarian officer we
met in the Pressburg shop while buying provisions, "you may
find yourselves, when the flood subsides, forty miles from
anywhere, high and dry, and you may easily starve. There
are no people, no farms, no fishermen. I warn you not to continue. The river, too, is still rising, and this wind will increase."

The rising river did not alarm us in the least, but the matter of being left high and dry by a sudden subsidence of the

waters might be serious, and we had consequently laid in an extra stock of provisions. For the rest, the officer's prophecy held true, and the wind, blowing down a perfectly clear sky, increased steadily till it reached the dignity of a westerly gale.

It was earlier than usual when we camped, for the sun was a good hour or two from the horizon, and leaving my friend still asleep on the hot sand, I wandered about in desultory examination of our hotel. The island, I found, was less than an acre in extent, a mere sandy bank standing some two or three feet above the level of the river. The far end, pointing into the sunset, was covered with flying spray which the tremendous wind drove off the crests of the broken waves. It was triangular in shape, with the apex upstream.

I stood there for several minutes, watching the impetuous crimson flood bearing down with a shouting roar, dashing in waves against the bank as though to sweep it bodily away, and then swirling by in two foaming streams on either side. The ground seemed to shake with the shock and rush, while the furious movement of the willow bushes as the wind poured over them increased the curious illusion that the island itself actually moved. Above, for a mile or two, I could see the great river descending upon me: it was like looking up the slope of a sliding hill, white with foam, and leaping up everywhere to show itself to the sun.

The rest of the island was too thickly grown with willows to make walking pleasant, but I made the tour, nevertheless. From the lower end the light, of course, changed, and the river looked dark and angry. Only the backs of the flying waves were visible, streaked with foam, and pushed forcibly by the great puffs of wind that fell upon them from behind. For a short mile it was visible, pouring in and out among the islands, and then disappearing with a huge sweep into the willows, which closed about it like a herd of monstrous antediluvian creatures crowding down to drink. They made me think of gigantic sponge-like growths that sucked the river up into themselves. They caused it to vanish from sight. They herded there together in such overpowering numbers.

Altogether it was an impressive scene, with its utter loneliness, its bizarre suggestion; and as I gazed, long and curiously, a singular emotion began to stir somewhere in the depths of me. Midway in my delight of the wild beauty, there crept, unbidden and unexplained, a curious feeling of disquietude, almost of alarm.

A rising river, perhaps, always suggests something of the ominous: many of the little islands I saw before me would probably have been swept away by the morning; this resistless, thundering flood of water touched the sense of awe. Yet I was aware that my uneasiness lay deeper far than the emotions of awe and wonder. It was not that I felt. Nor had it directly to do with the power of the driving wind—this shouting hurricane that might almost carry up a few acres of willows into the air and scatter them like so much chaff over the landscape. The wind was simply enjoying itself, for nothing rose out of the flat landscape to stop it, and I was conscious of sharing its great game with a kind of pleasurable excitement. Yet this novel emotion had nothing to do with the wind. Indeed, so vague was the sense of distress I experienced, that it was impossible to trace it to its source and deal with it accordingly, though I was aware somehow that it had to do with my realization of our utter insignificance before this unrestrained power of the elements about me. The huge-grown river had something to do with it too—a vague, unpleasant idea that we had somehow trifled with these great elemental forces in whose power we lay helpless every hour of the day and night. For here, indeed, they were gigantically at play together, and the sight appealed to the imagination.

But my emotion, so far as I could understand it, seemed to attach itself more particularly to the willow bushes, to these acres and acres of willows, crowding, so thickly growing there, swarming everywhere the eye could reach, pressing upon the river as though to suffocate it, standing in dense array mile after mile beneath the sky, watching, waiting, listening. And, apart quite from the elements, the willows connected themselves subtly with my malaise, attacking the mind insidiously somehow by reason of their vast numbers, and contriving in some way or other to represent to the imagination a new and mighty power, a power, moreover, not altogether friendly to us.

Great revelations of nature, of course, never fail to impress in one way or another, and I was no stranger to moods of the kind. Mountains overawe and oceans terrify, while the mystery of great forests exercises a spell peculiarly its own. But all these, at one point or another, somewhere link on intimately with human life and human experience. They stir comprehensible, even if alarming, emotions. They tend on the whole to exalt.

With this multitude of willows, however, it was something far different, I felt. Some essence emanated from them that besieged the heart. A sense of awe awakened, true, but of awe touched somewhere by a vague terror. Their serried ranks growing everywhere darker about me as the shadows deepened, moving furiously yet softly in the wind, woke in me the curious and unwelcome suggestion that we had trespassed here upon the borders of an alien world, a world where we were intruders, a world where we were not wanted or invited to remain—where we ran grave risks perhaps!

The feeling, however, though it refused to yield its meaning entirely to analysis, did not at the time trouble me by passing into menace. Yet it never left me quite, even during the very practical business of putting up the tent in a hurricane of wind and building a fire for the stew-pot. It remained, just enough to bother and perplex, and to rob a most delightful camping-ground of a good portion of its charm. To my companion, however, I said nothing, for he was a man I considered devoid of imagination. In the first place, I could never have explained to him what I meant, and in the second, he would have laughed stupidly at me if I had.

There was a slight depression in the center of the island, and here we pitched the tent. The surrounding willows broke the wind a bit.

"A poor camp," observed the imperturbable Swede when at last the tent stood upright; "no stones and precious little firewood. I'm for moving on early to-morrow—eh? This sand won't hold anything."

But the experience of a collapsing tent at midnight had taught us many devices, and we made the cosy gipsy house as safe as possible, and then set about collecting a store of wood to last till bedtime. Willow bushes drop no branches, and driftwood was our only source of supply. We hunted the shores pretty thoroughly. Everywhere the banks were crumbling as the rising flood tore at them and carried away great portions with a splash and a gurgle.

"The island's much smaller than when we landed," said the accurate Swede. "It won't last long at this rate. We'd better drag the canoe close to the tent, and be ready to start at a moment's notice. *I* shall sleep in my clothes."

He was a little distance off, climbing along the bank, and I heard his rather jolly laugh as he spoke.

"By Jove!" I heard him call, a moment later, and turned to see what had caused his exclamation; but for the moment he was hidden by the willows, and I could not find him.

"What in the world's this?" I heard him cry again, and this time his voice had become serious.

I ran up quickly and joined him on the bank. He was looking over the river, pointing at something in the water.

"Good Heavens, it's a man's body!" he cried excitedly. "Look!"

A black thing, turning over and over in the foaming waves, swept rapidly past. It kept disappearing and coming up to the surface again. It was about twenty feet from the shore, and just as it was opposite to where we stood it lurched round and looked straight at us. We saw its eyes reflecting the sunset, and gleaming an odd yellow as the body turned over. Then it gave a swift, gulping plunge, and dived out of sight in a flash.

"An otter, by gad!" we exclaimed in the same breath, laughing.

It *was* an otter, alive, and out on the hunt; yet it had looked exactly like the body of a drowned man turning helplessly in the current. Far below, it came to the surface once again, and we saw its black skin, wet and shining in the sunlight.

Then, too, just as we turned back, our arms full of driftwood, another thing happened to recall us to the river bank. This time it really was a man, and what was more, a man in a boat. Now a small boat on the Danube was an unusual sight at any time, but here in this deserted region, and at flood time, it was so unexpected as to constitute a real event. We stood and stared.

Whether it was due to the slanting sunlight, or the refraction from the wonderfully illumined water, I cannot say, but, whatever the cause, I found it difficult to focus my sight properly upon the flying apparition. It seemed, however, to be a man standing upright in a sort of flat-bottomed boat, steering with a long oar, and being carried down the opposite shore at a tremendous pace. He apparently was looking across in our direction, but the distance was too great and the light too uncertain for us to make out very plainly what he was about. It seemed to me that he was gesticulating and making signs at us. His voice came across the water to us shouting something furiously but the wind drowned it so that no single word was audible. There was something curious about the whole appearance—man, boat, signs, voice—that made an impression on me out of all proportion to its cause.

"He's crossing himself!" I cried. "Look, he's making the sign of the cross!"

"I believe you're right," the Swede said, shading his eyes with his hand and watching the man out of sight. He seemed to be gone in a moment, melting away down there into the sea of willows where the sun caught them in the bend of the river and turned them into a great crimson wall of beauty. Mist, too, had begun to rise, so that the air was hazy.

"But what in the world is he doing at nightfall on this flooded river?" I said, half to myself. "Where is he going at such a time, and what did he mean by his signs and shouting? D'you think he wished to warn us about something?"

"He saw our smoke, and thought we were spirits probably," laughed my companion. "These Hungarians believe in all sorts of rubbish: you remember the shopwoman at Pressburg warning us that no one ever landed here because it belonged to some sort of beings outside man's world! I suppose they believe in fairies and elementals, possibly demons too. That peasant in the boat saw people on the islands for the first time in his life," he added, after a slight pause, "and it scared him, that's all." The Swede's tone of voice was not convincing, and his manner lacked something that was usually there. I noted the change instantly while he talked, though without being able to label it precisely.

"If they had enough imagination," I laughed loudly—I remember trying to make as much *noise* as I could—"they might well people a place like this with the old gods of antiq-

uity. The Romans must have haunted all this region more or
less with their shrines and sacred groves and elemental deities."

The subject dropped and we returned to our stew-pot, for
my friend was not given to imaginative conversation as a
rule. Moreover, just then I remember feeling distinctly glad
that he was not imaginative; his stolid, practical nature suddenly seemed to me welcome and comforting. It was an admi-
rable temperament, I felt: he could steer down rapids like a
red Indian, shoot dangerous bridges and whirlpools better
than any white man I ever saw in a canoe. He was a grand
fellow for an adventurous trip, a tower of strength when un-
toward things happened. I looked at his strong face and light
curly hair as he staggered along under his pile of driftwood
(twice the size of mine!), and I experienced a feeling of relief.
Yes, I was distinctly glad just then that the Swede was—what
he was, and that he never made remarks that suggested more
than they said.

"The river's still rising, though," he added, as if following
out some thoughts of his own, and dropping his load with a
gasp. "This island will be under water in two days if it goes
on."

"I wish the *wind* would go down," I said. "I don't care a fig
for the river."

The flood, indeed, had no terrors for us; we could get off at
ten minutes' notice, and the more water the better we liked
it. It meant an increasing current and the obliteration of the
treacherous shingle-beds that so often threatened to tear the
bottom out of our canoe.

Contrary to our expectations, the wind did not go down
with the sun. It seemed to increase with the darkness, howling overhead and shaking the willows round us like straws.
Curious sounds accompanied it sometimes, like the explosion
of heavy guns, and it fell upon the water and the island in
great flat blows of immense power. It made me think of the
sounds a planet must make, could we only hear it, driving
along through space.

But the sky kept wholly clear of clouds, and soon after supper the full moon rose up in the east and covered the river
and the plain of shouting willows with a light like the day.

We lay on the sandy patch beside the fire, smoking, listening to the noises of the night round us, and talking happily of the journey we had already made, and of our plans ahead. The map lay spread in the door of the tent, but the high wind made it hard to study, and presently we lowered the curtain and extinguished the lantern. The firelight was enough to smoke and see each other's face by, and the sparks flew about overhead like fireworks. A few yards beyond, the river gurgled and hissed, and from time to time a heavy splash announced the falling away of further portions of the bank.

Our talk, I noticed, had to do with the far-away scenes and incidents of our first camps in the Black Forest, or of other subjects altogether remote from the present setting, for neither of us spoke of the actual moment more than was necessary—almost as though we had agreed tacitly to avoid discussion of the camp and its incidents. Neither the otter nor the boatman, for instance, received the honor of a single mention, though ordinarily these would have furnished discussion for the greater part of the evening. They were, of course, distinct events in such a place.

The scarcity of wood made it a business to keep the fire going, for the wind, that drove the smoke in our faces wherever we sat, helped at the same time to make a forced draught. We took it in turn to make foraging expeditions into the darkness, and the quantity the Swede brought back always made me feel that he took an absurdly long time finding it; for the fact was I did not care much about being left alone, and yet it always seemed to be my turn to grub about among the bushes or scramble along the slippery banks in the moonlight. The long day's battle with wind and water—such wind and such water!—had tired us both, and an early bed was the obvious program. Yet neither of us made the move for the tent. We lay there, tending the fire, talking in desultory fashion, peering about us into the dense willow bushes, and listening to the thunder of wind and river. The loneliness of the place had entered our very bones, and silence seemed natural, for after a bit the sound of our voices became a trifle unreal and forced; whispering would have been the fitting mode of communication, I felt, and the human voice, always rather absurd amid the roar of the elements, now carried with it something almost illegitimate. It was like talking out loud in church, or in some place where it was not lawful, perhaps not quite *safe*, to be overheard.

The eeriness of this lonely island, set among a million willows, swept by a hurricane, and surrounded by hurrying deep waters, touched us both, I fancy. Untrodden by man, almost unknown to man, it lay there beneath the moon, remote from human influence, on the frontier of another world, an alien world, a world tenanted by willows only and the souls of willows. And we, in our rashness, had dared to invade it, even to make use of it! Something more than the power of its mystery stirred in me as I lay on the sand, feet to fire, and peered up through the leaves at the stars. For the last time I rose to get firewood.

"When this has burnt up," I said firmly, "I shall turn in," and my companion watched me lazily as I moved off into the surrounding shadows.

For an unimaginative man I thought he seemed unusually receptive that night, unusually open to suggestion of things other than sensory. He too was touched by the beauty and loneliness of the place. I was not altogether pleased, I remember, to recognize this slight change in him, and instead of immediately collecting sticks, I made my way to the far point of the island where the moonlight on plain and river could be seen to better advantage. The desire to be alone had come suddenly upon me; my former dread returned in force; there was a vague feeling in me I wished to face and probe to the bottom.

When I reached the point of sand jutting out among the waves, the spell of the place descended upon me with a positive shock. No mere "scenery" could have produced such an effect. There was something more here, something to alarm.

I gazed across the waste of wild waters; I watched the whispering willows; I heard the ceaseless beating of the tireless wind; and, one and all, each in its own way, stirred in me this sensation of a strange distress. But the *willows* especially; for ever they went on chattering and talking among themselves, laughing a little, shrilly crying out, sometimes sighing—but what it was they made so much to-do about belonged to the secret life of the great plain they inhabited. And it was utterly alien to the world I knew, or to that of the wild yet kindly elements. They made me think of a host of beings from another plane of life, another evolution altogether, perhaps, all discussing a mystery known only to themselves. I watched them moving busily together, oddly shaking their big bushy heads, twirling their myriad leaves even when there was no wind. They moved of their own will as though alive, and they touched, by some incalculable method, my own keen sense of the *horrible*.

There they stood in the moonlight, like a vast army surrounding our camp, shaking their innumerable silver spears defiantly, formed all ready for an attack.

The psychology of places, for some imaginations at least, is very vivid; for the wanderer, especially, camps have their "note" either of welcome or rejection. At first it may not always be apparent, because the busy preparations of tent and cooking prevent, but with the first pause—after supper usually—it comes and announces itself. And the note of this willow-camp now became unmistakably plain to me: we were interlopers, trespassers; we were not welcomed. The sense of unfamiliarity grew upon me as I stood there watching. We touched the frontier of a region where our presence was resented. For a night's lodging we might perhaps be tolerated; but for a prolonged and inquisitive stay—No! by all the gods of the trees and the wilderness, no! We were the first human influences upon this island, and we were not wanted. *The willows were against us.*

Strange thoughts like these, bizarre fancies, borne I know not whence, found lodgment in my mind as I stood listening. What, I thought, if, after all, these crouching willows proved to be alive; if suddenly they should rise up, like a swarm of living creatures, marshaled by the gods whose territory we had invaded, sweep towards us off the vast swamps, booming overhead in the night—and then *settle down!* As I looked it was so easy to imagine they actually moved, crept nearer, retreated a little, huddled together in masses, hostile, waiting for the great wind that should finally start them a-running. I could have sworn their aspect changed a little, and their ranks deepened and pressed more closely together.

The melancholy shrill cry of a night bird sounded over-

head, and suddenly I nearly lost my balance as the piece of
bank I stood upon fell with a great splash into the river, un-
dermined by the flood. I stepped back just in time, and went
on hunting for firewood again, half laughing at the odd fancies that crowded so thickly into my mind and cast their spell
upon me. I recalled the Swede's remark about moving on
next day, and I was just thinking that I fully agreed with
him, when I turned with a start and saw the subject of my
thoughts standing immediately in front of me. He was quite
close. The roar of the elements had covered his approach.

"You've been gone so long," he shouted above the wind, "I
thought something must have happened to you."

But there was that in his tone, and a certain look in his
face as well, that conveyed to me more than his actual words,
and in a flash I understood the real reason for his coming. It
was because the spell of the place had entered his soul too,
and he did not like being alone.

"River still rising," he cried, pointing to the flood in the
moonlight, "and the wind's simply awful."

He always said the same things, but it was the cry for com-
panionship that gave the real importance to his words.

"Lucky," I cried back, "our tent's in the hollow. I think it'll
hold all right." I added something about the difficulty of finding wood, in order to explain my absence, but the wind
caught my words and flung them across the river, so that he
did not hear, but just looked at me through the branches,
nodding his head.

"Lucky if we get away without disaster!" he shouted, or
words to that effect; and I remember feeling half angry with
him for putting the thought into words, for it was exactly
what I felt myself. There was disaster impending somewhere,
and the sense of presentiment lay unpleasantly upon me.

We went back to the fire and made a final blaze, poking it
up with our feet. We took a last look round. But for the wind
the heat would have been unpleasant. I put this thought into
words, and I remember my friend's reply struck me oddly:
that he would rather have the heat, the ordinary July
weather, than this "diabolical wind."

Everything was snug for the night; the canoe lying turned
over beside the tent, with both yellow paddles beneath her;

the provision sack hanging from a willow stem, and the washed-up dishes removed to a safe distance from the fire, all ready for the morning meal.

We smothered the embers of the fire with sand, and then turned in. The flap of the tent door was up, and I saw the branches and the stars and the white moonlight. The shaking willows and the heavy buffetings of the wind against our taut little house were the last things I remembered as sleep came down and covered all with its soft and delicious forgetfulness.

II

Suddenly I found myself lying awake, peering from my sandy mattress through the door of the tent. I looked at my watch pinned against the canvas, and saw by the bright moonlight that it was past twelve o'clock—the threshold of a new day—and I had therefore slept a couple of hours. The Swede was asleep still beside me; the wind howled as before; something plucked at my heart and made me feel afraid. There was a sense of disturbance in my immediate neighborhood.

I sat up quickly and looked out. The trees were swaying violently to and fro as the gusts smote them, but our little bit of green canvas lay snugly safe in the hollow, for the wind passed over it without meeting enough resistance to make it vicious. The feeling of disquietude did not pass, however, and I crawled quietly out of the tent to see if our belongings were safe. I moved carefully so as not to waken my companion. A curious excitement was on me.

I was halfway out, kneeling on all fours, when my eye first took in that the tops of the bushes opposite, with their moving tracery of leaves, made shapes against the sky. I sat back on my haunches and stared. It was incredible, surely, but there, opposite and slightly above me, were shapes of some indeterminate sort among the willows, and as the branches swayed in the wind they seemed to group themselves about these shapes, forming a series of monstrous outlines that shifted rapidly beneath the moon. Close, about fifty feet in front of me, I saw these things.

My first instinct was to waken my companion, that he too

might see them, but something made me hesitate—the sudden realization, probably, that I should not welcome corroboration; and meanwhile I crouched there staring in amazement with smarting eyes. I was wide awake. I remember saying to myself that I was *not* dreaming.

They first became properly visible, these huge figures, just within the tops of the bushes—immense, bronze-colored, moving, and wholly independent of the swaying of the branches. I saw them plainly and noted, now I came to examine them more calmly, that they were very much larger than human, and indeed that something in their appearance proclaimed them to be *not human* at all. Certainly they were not merely the moving tracery of the branches against the moonlight. They shifted independently. They rose upwards in a continuous stream from earth to sky, vanishing utterly as soon as they reached the dark of the sky. They were interlaced one with another, making a great column, and I saw their limbs and huge bodies melting in and out of each other, forming this serpentine line that bent and swayed and twisted spirally with the contortions of the wind-tossed trees. They were nude, fluid shapes, passing up the bushes, *within* the leaves almost—rising up in a living column into the heavens. Their faces I never could see. Unceasingly they poured upwards, swaying in great bending curves, with a hue of dull bronze upon their skins.

I stared, trying to force every atom of vision from my eyes. For a long time I thought they *must* every moment disappear and resolve themselves into the movements of the branches and prove to be an optical illusion. I searched everywhere for a proof of reality, when all the while I understood quite well that the standard of reality had changed. For the longer I looked the more certain I became that these figures were real and living, though perhaps not according to the standards that the camera and the biologist would insist upon.

Far from feeling fear, I was possessed with a sense of awe and wonder such as I have never known. I seemed to be gazing at the personified elemental forces of this haunted and primeval region. Our intrusion had stirred the powers of the place into activity. It was we who were the cause of the disturbance, and my brain filled to bursting with stories and legends of the spirits and deities of places that have been acknowledged and worshiped by men in all ages of the world's history. But, before I could arrive at any possible explanation, something impelled me to go farther out, and I crept forward on to the sand and stood upright. I felt the ground still warm under my bare feet; the wind tore at my hair and face; and the sound of the river burst upon my ears with a sudden roar. These things, I knew, were real, and proved that my senses were acting normally. Yet the figures still rose from the earth to heaven, silent, majestically, in a great spiral of grace and strength that overwhelmed me at length with a genuine deep emotion of worship. I felt that I must fall down and worship—absolutely worship.

Perhaps in another minute I might have done so, when a gust of wind swept against me with such force that it blew me sideways, and I nearly stumbled and fell. It seemed to shake the dream violently out of me. At least it gave me another point of view somehow. The figures still remained, still ascended into heaven from the heat of the night, but my reason at last began to assert itself. It must be a subjective experience, I argued—none the less real for that, but still subjective. The moonlight and the branches combined to work out these pictures upon the mirror of my imagination, and for some reason I projected them outwards and made them appear objective. I knew this must be the case, of course. I was the subject of a vivid and interesting hallucination. I took courage, and began to move forward across the open patches of sand. By Jove, though, was it all hallucination? Was it merely subjective? Did not my reason argue in the old futile way from the little standard of the known?

I only know that great column of figures ascended darkly into the sky for what seemed a very long period of time, and with a very complete measure of reality as most men are accustomed to gauge reality. Then suddenly they were gone!

And, once they were gone and the immediate wonder of their great presence had passed, fear came down upon me with a cold rush. The esoteric meaning of this lonely and haunted region suddenly flamed up within me and I began to tremble dreadfully. I took a quick look round—a look of horror that came near to panic—calculating vainly ways of escape; and then, realizing how helpless I was to achieve anything really effective, I crept back silently into the tent and lay down again upon my sandy mattress, first lowering the door-curtain to shut out the sight of the willows in the moonlight, and then burying my head as deeply as possible beneath the blankets to deaden the sound of the terrifying wind.

III

As though further to convince me that I had not been dreaming, I remember that it was a long time before I fell again into a troubled and restless sleep; and even then only the upper crust of me slept, and underneath there was something that never quite lost consciousness, but lay alert and on the watch.

But this second time I jumped up with a genuine start of terror. It was neither the wind nor the river that woke me, but the slow approach of something that caused the sleeping portion of me to grow smaller and smaller till at last it vanished altogether, and I found myself sitting bolt upright—listening.

Outside there was a sound of multitudinous little patterings. They had been coming, I was aware, for a long time, and in my sleep they had first become audible. I sat there nervously wide awake as though I had not slept at all. It seemed to me that my breathing came with difficulty, and that there was a great weight upon the surface of my body. In spite of the hot night, I felt clammy with cold and shivered. Something surely was pressing steadily against the sides of the tent and weighing down upon it from above. Was it the body of the wind? Was this the pattering rain, the dripping of the leaves? The spray blown from the river by the wind and gathering in big drops? I thought quickly of a dozen things.

Then suddenly the explanation leaped into my mind: a bough from the poplar, the only large tree on the island, had fallen with the wind. Still half caught by the other branches, it would fall with the next gust and crush us, and meanwhile its leaves brushed and tapped upon the tight canvas surface of the tent. I raised the loose flap and rushed out, calling to the Swede to follow.

But when I got out and stood upright I saw that the tent was free. There was no hanging bough; there was no rain or spray; nothing approached.

A cold, gray light filtered down through the bushes and lay on the faintly gleaming sand. Stars still crowded the sky directly overhead, and the wind howled magnificently, but the fire no longer gave out any glow, and I saw the east reddening in streaks through the trees. Several hours must have passed since I stood there before, watching the ascending figures, and the memory of it now came back to me horribly, like an evil dream. Oh, how tired it made me feel, that ceaseless raging wind! Yet, though the deep lassitude of a sleepless night was on me, my nerves were tingling with the activity of an equally tireless apprehension, and all idea of repose was out of the question. The river, I saw, had risen further. Its thunder filled the air, and a fine spray made itself felt through my thin sleeping shirt.

Yet nowhere did I discover the slightest evidences of anything to cause alarm. This deep, prolonged disturbance in my heart remained wholly unaccounted for.

My companion had not stirred when I called him, and there was no need to waken him now. I looked about me carefully, noting everything: the turned-over canoe; the yellow paddles—two of them, I'm certain; the provision sack and the extra lantern hanging together from the tree; and, crowding everywhere about me, enveloping all, the willows, those endless, shaking willows. A bird uttered its morning cry, and a string of ducks passed with whirring flight overhead in the twilight. The sand whirled, dry and stinging, about my bare feet in the wind.

I walked round the tent and then went out a little way into the bush, so that I could see across the river to the farther landscape, and the same profound yet indefinable emotion of distress seized upon me again as I saw the interminable sea of bushes stretching to the horizon, looking ghostly and unreal in the wan light of dawn. I walked softly here and there, still puzzling over that odd sound of infinite pattering, and of that pressure upon the tent that had wakened me. It *must* have been the wind, I reflected—the wind beating upon the loose, hot sand, driving the dry particles smartly against the taut canvas—the wind dropping heavily upon our fragile roof.

Yet all the time my nervousness and malaise increased appreciably.

I crossed over to the farther shore and noted how the coast line had altered in the night, and what masses of sand the river had torn away. I dipped my hands and feet into the cool current, and bathed my forehead. Already there was a glow of sunrise in the sky and the exquisite freshness of coming day. On my way back I passed purposely beneath the very bushes where I had seen the column of figures rising into the air, and midway among the clumps I suddenly found myself overtaken by a sense of vast terror. From the shadows a large figure went swiftly by. Some one passed me, as sure as ever a man did. . . .

It was a great staggering blow from the wind that helped me forward again, and once out in the more open space, the sense of terror diminished strangely. The winds were about and walking, I remember saying to myself; for the winds often move like great presences under the trees. And altogether the fear that hovered about me was such an unknown and immense kind of fear, so unlike anything I had ever felt before, that it woke a sense of awe and wonder in me that did much to counteract its worst effects; and when I reached a high point in the middle of the island from which I could see the wide stretch of river, crimson in the sunrise, the whole magical beauty of it all was so overpowering that a sort of wild yearning woke in me and almost brought a cry up into the throat.

But this cry found no expression, for as my eyes wandered from the plain beyond to the island round me and noted our little tent half hidden among the willows, a dreadful discovery leaped out at me, compared to which my terror of the walking winds seemed as nothing at all.

For a change, I thought, had somehow come about in the arrangement of the landscape. It was not that my point of vantage gave me a different view, but that an alteration had apparently been effected in the relation of the tent to the willows, and of the willows to the tent. Surely the bushes now crowded much closer—unnecessarily, unpleasantly close. *They had moved nearer.*

Creeping with silent feet over the shifting sands, drawing imperceptibly nearer by soft, unhurried movements, the willows had come closer during the night. But had the wind moved them, or had they moved of themselves? I recalled the sound of infinite small patterings and the pressure upon the tent and upon my own heart that caused me to wake in terror. I swayed for a moment in the wind like a tree, finding it hard to keep my upright position on the sandy hillock. There was a suggestion here of personal agency, of deliberate intention, of aggressive hostility, and it terrified me into a sort of rigidity.

Then the reaction followed quickly. The idea was so bizarre, so absurd, that I felt inclined to laugh. But the laughter came no more readily than the cry, for the knowledge that my mind was so receptive to such dangerous imaginings brought the additional terror that it was through our minds and not through our physical bodies that the attack would come, and was coming.

The wind buffeted me about, and, very quickly it seemed, the sun came up over the horizon, for it was after four o'clock, and I must have stood on that little pinnacle of sand longer than I knew, afraid to come down at close quarters with the willows. I returned quietly, creepily, to the tent, first taking another exhaustive look round and—yes, I confess it—making a few measurements. I paced out on the warm sand the distances between the willows and the tent, making a note of the shortest distance particularly.

I crawled stealthily into my blankets. My companion, to all appearances, still slept soundly, and I was glad that this was so. Provided my experiences were not corroborated, I could find strength somehow to deny them, perhaps. With the daylight I could persuade myself that it was all a subjective hallucination, a fantasy of the night, a projection of the excited imagination.

Nothing further came to disturb me, and I fell asleep almost at once, utterly exhausted, yet still in dread of hearing again that weird sound of multitudinous pattering, or of feeling the pressure upon my heart that had made it difficult to breathe.

IV

The sun was high in the heavens when my companion woke me from a heavy sleep and announced that the porridge was cooked and there was just time to bathe. The grateful smell of frizzling bacon entered the tent door.

"River still rising," he said, "and several islands out in midstream have disappeared altogether. Our own island's much smaller."

"Any wood left?" I asked sleepily.

"The wood and the island will finish to-morrow in a dead heat," he laughed, "but there's enough to last us till then."

I plunged in the river from the point of the island, which had indeed altered a lot in size and shape during the night, and was swept down in a moment to the landing place opposite the tent. The water was icy, and the banks flew by like the country from an express train. Bathing under such conditions was an exhilarating operation, and the terror of the night seemed cleansed out of me by a process of evaporation in the brain. The sun was blazing hot; not a cloud showed itself anywhere; the wind, however, had not abated one little jot.

Quite suddenly then the implied meaning of the Swede's words flashed across me, showing that he no longer wished to leave post-haste, and had changed his mind. "Enough to last till to-morrow"—he assumed we should stay on the island another night. It struck me as odd. The night before he was so positive the other way. How had the change come about?

Great crumblings of the banks occurred at breakfast, with heavy splashings and clouds of spray which the wind brought into our frying-pan, and my fellow-traveler talked incessantly about the difficulty the Vienna-Pesth steamers must have to find the channel in flood. But the state of his mind interested and impressed me far more than the state of the river or the difficulties of the steamers. He had changed somehow since the evening before. His manner was different —a trifle excited, a trifle shy, with a sort of suspicion about his voice and gestures. I hardly know how to describe it now in cold blood, but at the time I remember being quite certain of one thing, viz., that he had become frightened!

He ate very little breakfast, and for once omitted to smoke his pipe. He had the map spread open beside him, and kept studying its markings.

"We'd better get off sharp in an hour," I said presently, feeling for an opening that must bring him indirectly to a partial confession at any rate. And his answer puzzled me uncomfortably: "Rather! If they'll let us."

"Who'll let us? The elements?" I asked quickly, with affected indifference.

"The powers of this awful place, whoever they are," he replied, keeping his eyes on the map. "The gods are here, if they are anywhere at all in the world."

"The elements are always the true immortals," I replied, laughing as naturally as I could manage, yet knowing quite well that my face reflected my true feelings when he looked up gravely at me and spoke across the smoke:

"We shall be fortunate if we get away without further disaster."

This was exactly what I had dreaded, and I screwed myself up to the point of the direct question. It was like agreeing to allow the dentist to extract the tooth; it *had* to come anyhow in the long run, and the rest was all pretense.

"Further disaster! Why, what's happened?"

"For one thing—the steering paddle's gone," he said quietly.

"The steering paddle gone!" I repeated, greatly excited, for this was our rudder, and the Danube in flood without a rudder was suicide. "But what——"

"And there's a tear in the bottom of the canoe," he added, with a genuine little tremor in his voice.

I continued staring at him, able only to repeat the words in his face somewhat foolishly. There, in the heat of the sun, and on this burning sand, I was aware of a freezing atmosphere descending round us. I got up to follow him, for he merely nodded his head gravely and led the way towards the tent a few yards on the other side of the fireplace. The canoe still lay there as I had last seen her in the night, ribs uppermost, the paddles, or rather, *the* paddle, on the sand beside her.

"There's only one," he said, stooping to pick it up. "And here's the rent in the base-board."

It was on the tip of my tongue to tell him that I had clearly noticed *two* paddles a few hours before, but a second impulse made me think better of it, and I said nothing. I approached to see.

There was a long, finely made tear in the bottom of the canoe where a little slither of wood had been neatly taken clean out; it looked as if the tooth of a sharp rock or snag had eaten down her length, and investigation showed that the hole went through. Had we launched out in her without observing it we must inevitably have foundered. At first the water would have made the wood swell so as to close the hole, but once out in midstream the water must have poured in, and the canoe, never more than two inches above the surface, would have filled and sunk very rapidly.

"There, you see, an attempt to prepare a victim for the sacrifice," I heard him saying, more to himself than to me, "two victims rather," he added as he bent over and ran his fingers along the slit.

I began to whistle—a thing I always do unconsciously when utterly nonplussed—and purposely paid no attention to his words. I was determined to consider them foolish.

"It wasn't there last night," he said presently, straightening up from his examination and looking anywhere but at me.

"We must have scratched her in landing, of course," I stopped whistling to say. "The stones are very sharp——"

I stopped abruptly, for at that moment he turned round and met my eye squarely. I knew just as well as he did how impossible my explanation was. There were no stones, to begin with.

"And then there's this to explain too," he added quietly, handing me the paddle and pointing to the blade.

A new and curious emotion spread freezingly over me as I took and examined it. The blade was scraped down all over, beautifully scraped, as though someone had sand-papered it with care, making it so thin that the first vigorous stroke must have snapped it off at the elbow.

"One of us walked in his sleep and did this thing," I said feebly, "or—or it has been filed by the constant stream of sand particles blown against it by the wind, perhaps."

"Ah," said the Swede, turning away, laughing a little, "you can explain everything!"

"The same wind that caught the steering paddle and flung it so near the bank that it fell in with the next lump that crumbled," I called out after him, absolutely determined to find an explanation for everything he showed me.

"I see," he shouted back, turning his head to look at me before disappearing among the willow bushes.

Once alone with these perplexing evidences of personal agency, I think my first thought took the form of "One of us must have done this thing, and it certainly was not I." But my second thought decided how impossible it was to suppose, under all the circumstances, that either of us had done it. That my companion, the trusted friend of a dozen similar expeditions, could have knowingly had a hand in it, was a suggestion not to be entertained for a moment. Equally absurd seemed the explanation that this imperturbable and densely practical nature had suddenly become insane and was busied with insane purposes.

Yet the fact remained that what disturbed me most, and kept my fear actively alive even in this blaze of sunshine and wild beauty, was the clear certainty that some curious alteration had come about in his *mind*—that he was nervous, timid, suspicious, aware of goings on he did not speak about, watching a series of secret and hitherto unmentionable events—waiting, in a word, for a climax that he expected, and, I thought, expected very soon. This grew up in my mind intuitively—I hardly knew how.

I made a hurried examination of the tent and its surroundings, but the measurements of the night remained the same. There were deep hollows formed in the sand, I now noticed for the first time, basin-shaped and of various depths and sizes, varying from that of a teacup to a large bowl. The wind, no doubt, was responsible for these miniature craters, just as it was for lifting the paddle and tossing it towards the water.

The rent in the canoe was the only thing that seemed quite inexplicable; and, after all, it *was* conceivable that a sharp point had caught it when we landed. The examination I made of the shore did not assist this theory, but all the same I clung to it with that diminishing portion of my intelligence which I called my "reason." An explanation of some kind was an absolute necessity, just as some working explanation of the universe is necessary—however absurd—to the happiness of every individual who seeks to do his duty in the world and face the problems of life. The simile seemed to me at the time an exact parallel.

I at once set the pitch melting, and presently the Swede joined me at the work, though under the best conditions in the world the canoe could not be safe for traveling till the following day. I drew his attention casually to the hollows in the sand.

"Yes," he said, "I know. They're all over the island. But *you* can explain them, no doubt!"

"Wind, of course," I answered without hesitation. "Have you never watched those little whirlwinds in the street that twist and twirl everything into a circle? This sand's loose enough to yield, that's all."

He made no reply, and we worked on in silence for a bit. I watched him surreptitiously all the time, and I had an idea he was watching me. He seemed, too, to be always listening attentively to something I could not hear, or perhaps for something that he expected to hear, for he kept turning about and staring into the bushes, and up into the sky, and out across the water where it was visible through the openings among the willows. Sometimes he even put his hand to his ear and held it there for several minutes. He said nothing to me, however, about it, and I asked no questions. And meanwhile, as he mended that torn canoe with the skill and address of a red Indian, I was glad to notice his absorption in the work, for there was a vague dread in my heart that he would speak of the changed aspect of the willows. And, if he had noticed *that,* my imagination could no longer be held a sufficient explanation of it.

At length, after a long pause, he began to talk.

"Queer thing," he added in a hurried sort of voice, as

though he wanted to say something and get it over. "Queer thing, I mean, about that otter last night."

I had expected something so totally different that he caught me with surprise, and I looked up sharply.

"Shows how lonely this place is. Otters are awfully shy things—"

"I don't mean that, of course," he interrupted. "I mean—do you think—did you think it really *was* an otter?"

"What else, in the name of heaven, what else?"

"You know, I saw it before you did, and at first it seemed—so *much* bigger than an otter."

"The sunset as you looked upstream magnified it, or something," I replied.

He looked at me absently a moment, as though his mind were busy with other thoughts.

"It had such extraordinary yellow eyes," he went on half to himself.

"That was the sun too," I laughed, a trifle boisterously. "I suppose you'll wonder next if that fellow in the boat——"

I suddenly decided not to finish the sentence. He was in the act again of listening, turning his head to the wind, and something in the expression of his face made me halt. The subject dropped, and we went on with our caulking. Apparently he had not noticed my unfinished sentence. Five minutes later, however, he looked at me across the canoe, the smoking pitch in his hand, his face exceedingly grave.

"I *did* rather wonder, if you want to know," he said slowly, "what that thing in the boat was. I remember thinking at the time it was not a man. The whole business seemed to rise quite suddenly out of the water."

I laughed again boisterously in his face, but this time there was impatience, and a strain of anger too, in my feeling.

"Look here now," I cried, "this place is quite queer enough without going out of our way to imagine things! That boat was an ordinary boat, and the man in it was an ordinary man, and they were both going downstream as fast as they could lick. And that otter *was* an otter, so don't let's play the fool about it!"

He looked steadily at me with the same grave expression.

He was not in the least annoyed. I took courage from his silence.

"And for heaven's sake," I went on, "don't keep pretending you hear things, because it only gives me the jumps, and there's nothing to hear but the river and this cursed old thundering wind."

"You *fool!*" he answered in a low, shocked voice, "you utter fool. That's just the way all victims talk. As if you didn't understand just as well as I do!" he sneered with scorn in his voice, and a sort of resignation. "The best thing you can do is to keep quiet and try to hold your mind as firm as possible. This feeble attempt at self-deception only makes the truth harder when you're forced to meet it."

My little effort was over, and I found nothing more to say, for I knew quite well his words were true, and that *I* was the fool, not *he*. Up to a certain stage in the adventure he kept ahead of me easily, and I think I felt annoyed to be out of it, to be thus proved less psychic, less sensitive than himself to these extraordinary happenings, and half ignorant all the time of what was going on under my very nose. *He knew* from the very beginning, apparently. But at the moment I wholly missed the point of his words about the necessity of there being a victim, and that we ourselves were destined to satisfy the want. I dropped all pretense thenceforward, but thenceforward likewise my fear increased steadily to the climax.

"But you're quite right about one thing," he added, before the subject passed, "and that is that we're wiser not to talk about it, or even to think about it, because what one *thinks* finds expression in words, and what one *says*, happens."

That afternoon, while the canoe dried and hardened, we spent trying to fish, testing the leak, collecting wood, and watching the enormous flood of rising water. Masses of driftwood swept near our shores sometimes, and we fished for them with long willow branches. The island grew perceptibly smaller as the banks were torn away with great gulps and splashes. The weather kept brilliantly fine till about four o'clock, and then for the first time for three days the wind showed signs of abating. Clouds began to gather in the southwest, spreading thence slowly over the sky.

This lessening of the wind came as a great relief, for the

incessant roaring, banging, and thundering had irritated our nerves. Yet the silence that came about five o'clock with its sudden cessation was in a manner quite as oppressive. The booming of the river had everything its own way then: it filled the air with deep murmurs, more musical than the wind noises, but infinitely more monotonous. The wind held many notes, rising, falling, always beating out some sort of great elemental tune; whereas the river's song lay between three notes at most—dull pedal notes, that held a lugubrious quality foreign to the wind, and somehow seemed to me, in my then nervous state, to sound wonderfully well the music of doom.

It was extraordinary, too, how the withdrawal suddenly of bright sunlight took everything out of the landscape that made for cheerfulness; and since this particular landscape had already managed to convey the suggestion of something sinister, the change of course was all the more unwelcome and noticeable. For me, I know, the darkening outlook became distinctly more alarming, and I found myself more than once calculating how soon after sunset the full moon would get up in the east, and whether the gathering clouds would greatly interfere with her lighting of the little island.

With this general hush of the wind—though it still indulged in occasional brief gusts—the river seemed to me to grow blacker, the willows to stand more densely together. The latter, too, kept up a sort of independent movement of their own, rustling among themselves when no wind stirred, and shaking oddly from the roots upwards. When common objects in this way become charged with the suggestion of horror, they stimulate the imagination far more than things of unusual appearance; and these bushes, crowding huddled about us, assumed for me in the darkness a bizarre *grotesquerie* of appearance that lent to them somehow the aspect of purposeful and living creatures. Their very ordinariness, I felt, masked what was malignant and hostile to us. The forces of the region drew nearer with the coming of night. They were focusing upon our island, and more particularly upon ourselves. For thus, somehow, in the terms of the imagination, did my really indescribable sensations in this extraordinary place present themselves.

I had slept a good deal in the early afternoon, and had thus recovered somewhat from the exhaustion of a disturbed night, but this only served apparently to render me more susceptible than before to the obsessing spell of the haunting. I fought against it, laughing at my feelings as absurd and childish, with very obvious physiological explanations, yet, in spite of every effort, they gained in strength upon me so that I dreaded the night as a child lost in a forest must dread the approach of darkness.

The canoe we had carefully covered with a waterproof sheet during the day, and the one remaining paddle had been securely tied by the Swede to the base of a tree, lest the wind should rob us of that too. From five o'clock onwards I busied myself with the stew-pot and preparations for dinner, it being my turn to cook that night. We had potatoes, onions, bits of bacon fat to add flavour, and a general thick residue from former stews at the bottom of the pot; with black bread broken up into it, the result was most excellent, and it was followed by a stew of plums with sugar and a brew of strong tea with dried milk. A good pile of wood lay close at hand, and the absence of wind made my duties easy. My companion sat lazily watching me, dividing his attentions between cleaning his pipe and giving useless advice—an admitted privilege of the off-duty man. He had been very quiet all the afternoon, engaged in re-caulking the canoe, strengthening the tent ropes, and fishing for driftwood while I slept. No more talk about undesirable things had passed between us, and I think his only remarks had to do with the gradual destruction of the island, which he declared was now fully a third smaller than when we first landed.

The pot had just begun to bubble when I heard his voice calling to me from the bank, where he had wandered away without my noticing. I ran up.

"Come and listen," he said, "and see what you make of it." He held his hand cupwise to his ear, as so often before.

"*Now* do you hear anything?" he asked, watching me curiously.

We stood there, listening attentively together. At first I heard only the deep note of the water and the hissings rising from its turbulent surface. The willows, for once, were motionless and silent. Then a sound began to reach my ears faintly, a peculiar sound—something like the humming of a distant gong. It seemed to come across to us in the darkness from the waste of swamps and willows opposite. It was repeated at regular intervals, but it was certainly neither the sound of a bell nor the hooting of a distant steamer. I can liken it to nothing so much as to the sound of an immense gong, suspended far up in the sky, repeating incessantly its muffled metallic note, soft and musical, as it was repeatedly struck. My heart quickened as I listened.

"I've heard it all day," said my companion. "While you slept this afternoon it came all round the island. I hunted it down, but could never get near enough to see—to localize it correctly. Sometimes it was overhead, and sometimes it seemed under the water. Once or twice, too, I could have sworn it was not outside at all, but *within myself*— you know —the way a sound in the fourth dimension is supposed to come."

I was too much puzzled to pay much attention to his words. I listened carefully, striving to associate it with any known familiar sound I could think of, but without success. It changed in direction, too, coming nearer, and then sinking utterly away into remote distance. I cannot say that it was ominous in quality, because to me it seemed distinctly musical, yet I must admit it set going a distressing feeling that made me wish I had never heard it.

"The wind blowing in those sand-funnels," I said, determined to find an explanation, "or the bushes rubbing together after the storm perhaps."

"It comes off the whole swamp," my friend answered. "It comes from everywhere at once." He ignored my explanations. "It comes from the willow bushes somehow——"

"But now the wind has dropped," I objected. "The willows can hardly make a noise by themselves, can they?"

His answer frightened me, first because I had dreaded it, and secondly, because I knew intuitively it was true.

"It is *because* the wind has dropped we now hear it. It was drowned before. It is the cry, I believe of the——"

I dashed back to my fire, warned by a sound of bubbling that the stew was in danger, but determined at the same time to escape from further conversation. I was resolute, if possible, to avoid the exchanging of views. I dreaded, too, that he would begin again about the gods, or the elemental forces, or something else disquieting, and I wanted to keep myself well in hand for what might happen later. There was another night to be faced before we escaped from this distressing place, and there was no knowing yet what it might bring forth.

"Come and cut up bread for the pot," I called to him, vigorously stirring the appetizing mixture. That stew-pot held sanity for us both, and the thought made me laugh.

He came over slowly and took the provision sack from the tree, fumbling in its mysterious depths, and then emptying the entire contents upon the ground-sheet at his feet.

"Hurry up!" I cried; "it's boiling."

The Swede burst out into a roar of laughter that startled me. It was forced laughter, not artificial exactly, but mirthless.

"There's nothing here!" he shouted, holding his sides.

"Bread, I mean."

"It's gone. There is no bread. They've taken it!"

I dropped the long spoon and ran up. Everything the sack contained lay upon the ground-sheet, but there was no loaf.

The whole dead weight of my growing fear fell upon me and shook me. Then I burst out laughing too. It was the only thing to do: and the sound of my own laughter also made me understand his. The strain of psychical pressure caused it— this explosion of unnatural laughter in both of us; it was an effort of repressed forces to seek relief; it was a temporary safety valve. And with both of us it ceased quite suddenly.

"How criminally stupid of me!" I cried, still determined to be consistent and find an explanation. "I clean forgot to buy a loaf at Pressburg. That chattering woman put everything out of my head, and I must have left it lying on the counter or——"

"The oatmeal, too, is much less than it was this morning," the Swede interrupted.

Why in the world need he draw attention to it? I thought angrily.

"There's enough for to-morrow," I said, stirring vigorously, "and we can get lots more at Komorn or Gran. In twenty-four hours we shall be miles from here."

"I hope so—to God," he muttered, putting the things back into the sack, "unless we're claimed first as victims for the sacrifice," he added with a foolish laugh. He dragged the sack into the tent, for safety's sake, I suppose, and I heard him mumbling on to himself, but so indistinctly that it seemed quite natural for me to ignore his words.

Our meal was beyond question a gloomy one, and we ate it almost in silence, avoiding one another's eyes, and keeping the fire bright. Then we washed up and prepared for the night, and, once smoking, our minds unoccupied with any definite duties, the apprehension I had felt all day long became more and more acute. It was not then active fear, I think, but the very vagueness of its origin distressed me far more than if I had been able to ticket and face it squarely. The curious sound I have likened to the note of a gong became now almost incessant, and filled the stillness of the night with a faint, continuous ringing rather than a series of distinct notes. At one time it was behind and at another time in front of us. Sometimes I fancied it came from the bushes on our left, and then again from the clumps on our right. More often it hovered directly overhead like the whirring of wings. It was really everywhere at once, behind, in front, at our sides and over our heads, completely surrounding us. The sound really defies description. But nothing within my knowledge is like that ceaseless muffled humming rising off the deserted world of swamps and willows.

We sat smoking in comparative silence, the strain growing every minute greater. The worst feature of the situation seemed to me that we did not know what to expect, and could therefore make no sort of preparation by way of defense. We could anticipate nothing. My explanations made in the sunshine, moreover, now came to haunt me with their foolish and wholly unsatisfactory nature, and it was more and more clear to me that some kind of plain talk with my companion was inevitable, whether I liked it or not. After all, we had to spend the night together, and to sleep in the same tent side by side. I saw that I could not get along much longer without the support of his mind, and for that, of course, plain talk was

imperative. As long as possible, however, I postponed this little climax, and tried to ignore or laugh at the occasional sentences he flung into the emptiness.

Some of these sentences, moreover, were confoundedly disquieting to me, coming as they did to corroborate much that I
felt myself: corroboration, too—which made it so much more
convincing—from a totally different point of view. He composed such curious sentences, and hurled them at me in such
an inconsequential sort of way, as though his main line of
thought was secret to himself, and these fragments were the
bits he found it impossible to digest. He got rid of them by
uttering them. Speech relieved him. It was like being sick.

"There are things about us, I'm sure, that make for disorder, disintegration, destruction, *our* destruction," he said
once, while the fire blazed between us. "We've strayed out of a
safe line somewhere."

And another time, when the gong sounds had come nearer,
ringing much louder than before, and directly over our heads,
he said, as though talking to himself:

"I don't think a phonograph would show any record of that.
The sound doesn't come to me by the ears at all. The vibrations reach me in another manner altogether, and seem to be
within me, which is precisely how a fourth dimension sound
might be supposed to make itself heard."

I purposely made no reply to this, but I sat up a little closer
to the fire and peered about me into the darkness. The clouds
were massed all over the sky and no trace of moonlight came
through. Very still, too, everything was, so that the river and
the frogs had things all their own way.

"It has that about it," he went on, "which is utterly out of
common experience. It is *unknown.* Only one thing describes
it really: it is a non-human sound; I mean a sound outside
humanity."

Having rid himself of this indigestible morsel, he lay quiet
for a time; but he had so admirably expressed my own feeling
that it was a relief to have the thought out, and to have confined it by the limitation of words from dangerous wandering
to and fro in the mind.

The solitude of that Danube camping-place, can I ever forget it? The feeling of being utterly alone on an empty planet!

My thoughts ran incessantly upon cities and the haunts of men. I would have given my soul, as the saying is, for the "feel" of those Bavarian villages we had passed through by the score; for the normal, human commonplaces: peasants drinking beer, tables beneath the trees, hot sunshine, and a ruined castle on the rocks behind the red-roofed church. Even the tourists would have been welcome.

Yet what I felt of dread was no ordinary ghostly fear. It was infinitely greater, stranger, and seemed to arise from some dim ancestral sense of terror more profoundly disturbing than anything I had known or dreamed of. We had "strayed," as the Swede put it, into some region or some set of conditions where the risks were great, yet unintelligible to us; where the frontiers of some unknown world lay close about us. It was a spot held by the dwellers in some outer space, a sort of peep-hole whence they could spy upon the earth, themselves unseen, a point where the veil between had worn a little thin. As the final result of too long a sojourn here, we should be carried over the border and deprived of what we called "our lives," yet by mental, not physical, processes. In that sense, as he said, we should be the victims of our adventure—a sacrifice.

It took us in different fashion, each according to the measure of his sensitiveness and powers of resistance. I translated it vaguely into a personification of the mightily disturbed elements, investing them with the horror of a deliberate and malefic purpose, resentful of our audacious intrusion into their breeding-place; whereas my friend threw it into the unoriginal form at first of a trespass on some ancient shrine, some place where the old gods still held sway, where the emotional forces of former worshipers still clung, and the ancestral portion of him yielded to the old pagan spell.

At any rate, here was a place unpolluted by men, kept clean by the winds from coarsening human influences, a place where spiritual agencies were within reach and aggressive. Never, before or since, have I been so attacked by indescribable suggestions of a "beyond region," of another scheme of life, another evolution not parallel to the human. And in the end our minds would succumb under the weight of the awful spell, and we should be drawn across the frontier into *their* world.

Small things testified to this amazing influence of the place, and now in the silence round the fire they allowed themselves to be noted by the mind. The very atmosphere had proved itself a magnifying medium to distort every indication: the otter rolling in the current, the hurrying boatman making signs, the shifting willows, one and all had been robbed of its natural character, and revealed in something of its other aspect—as it existed across the border in that other region. And this changed aspect I felt was new not merely to me, but to the race. The whole experience whose verge we touched was unknown to humanity at all. It was a new order of experience, and in the true sense of the word *unearthly*.

"It's the deliberate, calculating purpose that reduces one's courage to zero," the Swede said suddenly, as if he had been actually following my thoughts. "Otherwise imagination might count for much. But the paddle, the canoe, the lessening food——"

"Haven't I explained all that once?" I interrupted viciously.

"You have," he answered dryly; "you have indeed."

He made other remarks too, as usual, about what he called the "plain determination to provide a victim"; but, having now arranged my thoughts better, I recognized that his was simply the cry of his frightened soul against the knowledge that he was being attacked in a vital part, and that he would be somehow taken or destroyed. The situation called for a courage and calmness of reasoning that neither of us could compass, and I have never before been so clearly conscious of two persons in me—the one that explained everything, and the other that laughed at such foolish explanations, yet was horribly afraid.

Meanwhile, in the pitchy night the fire died down and the woodpile grew small. Neither of us moved to replenish the stock, and the darkness consequently came up very close to our faces. A few feet beyond the circle of firelight it was inky black. Occasionally a stray puff of wind set the willows shivering about us, but apart from this not very welcome sound a deep and depressing silence reigned, broken only by the gurgling of the river and the humming in the air overhead.

We both missed, I think, the shouting company of the winds.

At length, at a moment when a stray puff prolonged itself as though the wind were about to rise again, I reached the point for me of saturation, the point where it was absolutely necessary to find relief in plain speech, or else to betray myself by some hysterical extravagance that must have been far worse in its effect upon both of us. I kicked the fire into a blaze, and turned to my companion abruptly. He looked up with a start.

"I can't disguise it any longer," I said; "I don't like this place, and the darkness, and the noises, and the awful feelings I get. There's something here that beats me utterly. I'm in a blue funk, and that's the plain truth. If the other shore was—different, I swear I'd be inclined to swim for it!"

The Swede's face turned very white beneath the deep tan of sun and wind. He stared straight at me and answered quietly, but his voice betrayed his huge excitement by its unnatural calmness. For the moment, at any rate, he was the strong man of the two. He was more phlegmatic, for one thing.

"It's not a physical condition we can escape from by running away," he replied, in the tone of a doctor diagnosing some grave disease; "we must sit tight and wait. There are forces close here that could kill a herd of elephants in a second as easily as you or I could squash a fly. Our only chance is to keep perfectly still. Our insignificance perhaps may save us."

I put a dozen questions into my expression of face, but found no words. It was precisely like listening to an accurate description of a disease whose symptoms had puzzled me.

"I mean that so far, although aware of our disturbing presence, they have not *found* us—not 'located' us, as the Americans say," he went on. "They're blundering about like men hunting for a leak of gas. The paddle and canoe and provisions prove that. I think they *feel* us, but cannot actually see us. We must keep our minds quiet—it's our minds they feel. We must control our thoughts, or it's all up with us."

"Death you mean?" I stammered, icy with the horror of his suggestion.

"Worse—by far," he said. "Death, according to one's belief, means either annihilation or release from the limitations of the senses, but it involves no change of character. *You* don't suddenly alter just because the body's gone. But this means a radical alteration, a complete change, a horrible loss of oneself by substitution—far worse than death, and not even annihilation. We happen to have camped in a spot where their region touches ours, where the veil between has worn thin"— horrors! he was using my very own phrase, my actual words —"so that they are aware of our being in their neighborhood."

"But *who* are aware?" I asked.

I forgot the shaking of the willows in the windless calm, the humming overhead, everything except that I was waiting for an answer that I dreaded more than I can possibly explain.

He lowered his voice at once to reply, leaning forward a little over the fire, an indefinable change in his face that made me avoid his eyes and look down upon the ground.

"All my life," he said, "I have been strangely, vividly, conscious of another region—not far removed from our own world in one sense, yet wholly different in kind—where great things go on unceasingly, where immense and terrible personalities hurry by, intent on vast purposes compared to which earthly affairs, the rise and fall of nations, the destinies of empires, the fate of armies and continents, are all as dust in the balance; vast purposes, I mean, that deal directly with the soul, and not indirectly with mere expressions of the soul——"

"I suggest just now—" I began, seeking to stop him, feeling as though I was face to face with a madman. But he instantly overbore me with his torrent that *had* to come.

"You think," he said, "it is the spirits of the elements, and I thought perhaps it was the old gods. But I tell you now it is — *neither*. These would be comprehensible entities, for they have relations with men, depending upon them for worship or sacrifice, whereas these beings who are now about us have absolutely nothing to do with mankind, and it is mere chance that their space happens just at this spot to touch our own."

The mere conception, which his words somehow made so convincing, as I listened to them there in the dark stillness of that lonely island, set me shaking a little all over. I found it impossible to control my movements.

"And what do you propose?" I began again.

"A sacrifice, a victim, might save us by distracting them until we could get away," he went on, "just as the wolves stop to devour the dogs and give the sleigh another start. But—I see no chance of any other victim now."

I stared blankly at him. The gleam in his eyes was dreadful. Presently he continued.

"It's the willows, of course. The willows *mask* the others, but the others are feeling about for us. If we let our minds betray our fear, we're lost, lost utterly." He looked at me with an expression so calm, so determined, so sincere, that I no longer had any doubts as to his sanity. He was as sane as any man ever was. "If we can hold out through the night," he added, "we may get off in the daylight unnoticed, or rather, *undiscovered.*"

"But you really think a sacrifice would——"

That gong-like humming came down very close over our heads as I spoke, but it was my friend's scared face that really stopped my mouth.

"Hush!" he whispered, holding up his hand. "Do not mention them more than you can help. Do not refer to them *by name.* To name is to reveal: it is the inevitable clue, and our only hope lies in ignoring them, in order that they may ignore us."

"Even in thought?" He was extraordinarily agitated.

"Especially in thought. Our thoughts make spirals in their world. We must keep them *out of our minds* at all costs if possible."

I raked the fire together to prevent the darkness having everything its own way. I never longed for the sun as I longed for it then in the awful blackness of that summer night.

"Were you awake all last night?" he went on suddenly.

"I slept badly a little after dawn," I replied evasively, trying to follow his instructions, which I knew instinctively were true, "but the wind, of course——"

"I know. But the wind won't account for all the noises."

"Then you heard it too?"

"The multiplying countless little footsteps I heard," he said, adding, after a moment's hesitation, "and that other sound——"

"You mean above the tent, and the pressing down upon us of something tremendous, gigantic?"

He nodded significantly.

"It was like the beginning of a sort of inner suffocation?" I said.

"Partly, yes. It seemed to me that the weight of the atmosphere had been altered—had increased enormously, so that we should be crushed."

"And *that,*" I went on, determined to have it all out, pointing upwards where the gong-like note hummed ceaselessly, rising and falling like wind. "What do you make of that?"

"It's *their* sound," he whispered gravely. "It's the sound of their world, the humming in their region. The division here is so thin that it leaks through somehow. But, if you listen carefully, you'll find it's not above so much as around us. It's in the willows. It's the willows themselves humming, because here the willows have been made symbols of the forces that are against us."

I could not follow exactly what he meant by this, yet the thought and idea in my mind were beyond question the thought and idea in his. I realized what he realized, only with less power of analysis than his. It was on the tip of my tongue to tell him at last about my hallucination of the ascending figures and the moving bushes, when he suddenly thrust his face again close into mine across the firelight and began to speak in a very earnest whisper. He amazed me by his calmness and pluck, his apparent control of the situation. This man I had for years deemed unimaginative, stolid!

"Now listen," he said. "The only thing for us to do is to go on as though nothing had happened, follow our usual habits, go to bed, and so forth; pretend we feel nothing and notice nothing. It is a question wholly of the mind, and the less we think about them the better our chance of escape. Above all, don't *think,* for what you think happens!"

"All right," I managed to reply, simply breathless with his words and the strangeness of it all; "all right, I'll try, but tell me one thing more first. Tell me what you make of those hollows in the ground all about us, those sand-funnels?"

"No!" he cried, forgetting to whisper in his excitement. "I dare not, simply dare not, put the thought into words. If you have not guessed, I am glad. Don't try to. *They* have put it into my mind; try your hardest to prevent their putting it into yours."

He sank his voice again to a whisper before he finished, and I did not press him to explain. There was already just about as much horror in me as I could hold. The conversation came to an end, and we smoked our pipes busily in silence.

Then something happened, something unimportant apparently, as the way it is when the nerves are in a very great state of tension, and this small thing for a brief space gave me an entirely different point of view. I chanced to look down at my sand-shoe—the sort we used for the canoe—and something to do with the hole at the toe suddenly recalled to me the London shop where I had bought them, the difficulty the man had in fitting me, and other details of the uninteresting but practical operation. At once, in its train, followed a wholesome view of the modern skeptical world I was accustomed to move in at home. I thought of roast beef and ale, motor-cars, policemen, brass bands, and a dozen other things that proclaimed the soul of ordinariness or utility. The effect was immediate and astonishing even to myself. Psychologically, I suppose, it was simply a sudden and violent reaction after the strain of living in an atmosphere of things that to the normal consciousness must seem impossible and incredible. But, whatever the cause, it momentarily lifted the spell from my heart, and left me for the short space of a minute feeling free and utterly unafraid. I looked up at my friend opposite.

"You damned old pagan!" I cried, laughing aloud in his face. "You imaginative idiot! You superstitious idolator! You——"

I stopped in the middle, seized anew by the old horror. I tried to smother the sound of my voice as something sacrilegious. The Swede, of course, heard it too—that strange cry overhead in the darkness—and that sudden drop in the air as though something had come nearer.

He had turned ashen white under the tan. He stood bolt upright in front of the fire, stiff as a rod, staring at me.

"After that," he said in a sort of helpless, frantic way, "we must go! We can't stay now; we must strike camp this very instant and go on—down the river."

He was talking, I saw, quite wildly, his words dictated by abject terror—the terror he had resisted so long, but which had caught him at last.

"In the dark?" I exclaimed, shaking with fear after my hysterical outburst, but still realizing our position better than he did. "Sheer madness. The river's in flood, and we've only got a single paddle. Besides, we only go deeper into their country! There's nothing ahead for fifty miles but willows, willows, willows!"

He sat down again in a state of semi-collapse. The positions, by one of those kaleidoscopic changes nature loves, were suddenly reversed, and the control of our forces passed over into my hands. His mind at last had reached the point where it was beginning to weaken.

"What on earth possessed you to do such a thing?" he whispered, with awe of genuine terror in his voice and face.

I crossed round to his side of the fire. I took both his hands in mine, kneeling down beside him and looking straight into his frightened eyes.

"We'll make one more blaze," I said firmly, "and then turn in for the night. At sunrise we'll be off full speed for Komorn. Now, pull yourself together a bit, and remember your own advice about *not thinking fear!*"

He said no more, and I saw that he would agree and obey. In some measure, too, it was a sort of relief to get up and make an excursion into the darkness for more wood. We kept close together, almost touching, groping among the bushes and along the bank. The humming overhead never ceased, but seemed to me to grow louder as we increased our distance from the fire. It was shivery work!

We were grubbing away in the middle of a thickish clump of willows where some driftwood from a former flood had caught high among the branches, when my body was seized in a grip that made me half drop upon the sand. It was the

Swede. He had fallen against me, and was clutching me for support. I heard his breath coming and going in short gasps.

"Look! By my soul!" he whispered, and for the first time in my experience I knew what it was to hear tears of terror in a human voice. He was pointing to the fire, some fifty feet away. I followed the direction of his finger, and I swear my heart missed a beat.

There, in front of the dim glow, *something was moving.*

I saw it through a veil that hung before my eyes like the gauze drop-curtain used at the back of a theater—hazily a little. It was neither a human figure nor an animal. To me it gave the strange impression of being as large as several animals grouped together, like horses, two or three, moving slowly. The Swede, too, got a similar result, though expressing it differently, for he thought it was shaped and sized like a clump of willow bushes, rounded at the top, and moving all over upon its surface—"coiling upon itself like smoke," he said afterwards.

"I watched it settle downwards through the bushes," he sobbed at me. "Look, by God! It's coming this way! Oh, oh!"— he gave a kind of whistling cry. *"They've found us."*

I gave one terrified glance, which just enabled me to see that the shadowy form was swinging towards us through the bushes, and then I collapsed backwards with a crash into the branches. These failed, of course, to support my weight, so that with the Swede on the top of me we fell in a struggling heap upon the sand. I really hardly knew what was happening. I was conscious only of a sort of enveloping sensation of icy fear that plucked the nerves out of their fleshly covering, twisted them this way and that, and replaced them quivering. My eyes were tightly shut; something in my throat choked me; a feeling that my consciousness was expanding, extending out into space, swiftly gave way to another feeling that I was losing it altogether, and about to die.

An acute spasm of pain passed through me, and I was aware that the Swede had hold of me in such a way that he hurt me abominably. It was the way he caught at me in falling.

But it was this pain, he declared afterwards, that saved me: it caused me to *forget them* and think of something else at the

very instant when they were about to find me. It concealed
my mind from them at the moment of discovery, yet just in
time to evade their terrible seizing of me. He himself, he says,
actually swooned at the same moment, and that was what
saved him.

I only know that at a later time, how long or short is impossible to say, I found myself scrambling up out of the slippery
network of willow branches, and saw my companion standing
in front of me holding out a hand to assist me. I stared at him
in a dazed way, rubbing the arm he had twisted for me. Nothing came to me to say, somehow.

"I lost consciousness for a moment or two," I heard him
say. "That's what saved me. It made me stop thinking about
them."

"You nearly broke my arm in two," I said, uttering my only
connected thought at the moment. A numbness came over
me.

"That's what saved *you!*" he replied. "Between us, we've
managed to set them off on a false track somewhere. The
humming has ceased. It's gone—for the moment at any rate!"

A wave of hysterical laughter seized me again, and this
time spread to my friend too—great healing gusts of shaking
laughter that brought a tremendous sense of relief in their
train. We made our way back to the fire and put the wood on
so that it blazed at once. Then we saw that the tent had fallen
over and lay in a tangled heap upon the ground.

We picked it up, and during the process tripped more than
once and caught our feet in sand.

"It's those sand-funnels," exclaimed the Swede, when the
tent was up again and the firelight lit up the ground for several yards about us. "And look at the size of them!"

All round the tent and about the fireplace where we had
seen the moving shadows there were deep funnel-shaped hollows in the sand, exactly similar to the ones we had already
found over the island, only far bigger and deeper, beautifully
formed, and wide enough in some instances to admit the
whole of my foot and leg.

Neither of us said a word. We both knew that sleep was the
safest thing we could do, and to bed we went accordingly
without further delay, having first thrown sand on the fire

and taken the provision sack and the paddle inside the tent with us. The canoe, too, we propped in such a way at the end of the tent that our feet touched it, and the least motion would disturb and wake us.

In case of emergency, too, we again went to bed in our clothes, ready for a sudden start.

V

It was my firm intention to lie awake all night and watch, but the exhaustion of nerves and body decreed otherwise, and sleep after a while came over me with a welcome blanket of oblivion. The fact that my companion also slept quickened its approach. At first he fidgeted and constantly sat up, asking me if I "heard this" or "heard that." He tossed about on his cork mattress, and said the tent was moving and the river had risen over the point of the island; but each time I went out to look I returned with the report that all was well, and finally he grew calmer and lay still. Then at length his breathing became regular and I heard unmistakable sounds of snoring—the first and only time in my life when snoring has been a welcome and calming influence.

This, I remember, was the last thought in my mind before dozing off.

A difficulty in breathing woke me, and I found the blanket over my face. But something else besides the blanket was pressing upon me, and my first thought was that my companion had rolled off his mattress on to my own in his sleep. I called to him and sat up, and at the same moment it came to me that the tent was *surrounded*. That sound of multitudinous soft pattering was again audible outside, filling the night with horror.

I called again to him, louder than before. He did not answer, but I missed the sound of his snoring, and also noticed that the flap of the tent door was down. This was the unpardonable sin. I crawled out in the darkness to hook it back securely, and it was then for the first time I realized positively that the Swede was not there. He had gone.

I dashed out in a mad run, seized by a dreadful agitation, and the moment I was out I plunged into a sort of torrent of humming that surrounded me completely and came out of every quarter of the heavens at once. It was that same familiar humming—gone mad! A swarm of great invisible bees might have been about me in the air. The sound seemed to thicken the very atmosphere, and I felt that my lungs worked with difficulty.

But my friend was in danger, and I could not hesitate.

The dawn was just about to break, and a faint whitish light spread upwards over the clouds from a thin strip of clear horizon. No wind stirred. I could just make out the bushes and river beyond, and the pale sandy patches. In my excitement I ran frantically to and fro about the island, calling him by name, shouting at the top of my voice the first words that came into my head. But the willows smothered my voice, and the humming muffled it, so that the sound only traveled a few feet round me. I plunged among the bushes, tripping headlong, tumbling over roots, and scraping my face as I tore this way and that among the preventing branches.

Then, quite unexpectedly, I came out upon the island's point and saw a dark figure outlined between the water and the sky. It was the Swede. And already he had one foot in the river! A moment more and he would have taken the plunge.

I threw myself upon him, flinging my arms about his waist and dragging him shorewards with all my strength. Of course he struggled furiously, making a noise all the time just like that cursed humming, and using the most outlandish phrases in his anger about "going *inside* to Them," and "taking the way of the water and the wind," and God only knows what more besides, that I tried in vain to recall afterwards, but which turned me sick with horror and amazement as I listened. But in the end I managed to get him into the comparative safety of the tent, and flung him breathless and cursing upon the mattress, where I held him until the fit had passed.

I think the suddenness with which it all went and he grew calm, coinciding as it did with the equally abrupt cessation of the humming and pattering outside—I think this was almost the strangest part of the whole business perhaps. For he just opened his eyes and turned his tired face up to me so that the dawn threw a pale light upon it through the doorway, and said, for all the world just like a frightened child:

"My life, old man—it's my life I owe you. But it's all over now anyhow. They've found a victim in our place!"

Then he dropped back upon his blankets and went to sleep literally under my eyes. He simply collapsed, and began to snore again as healthily as though nothing had happened and he had never tried to offer his own life as a sacrifice by drowning. And when the sunlight woke him three hours later— hours of ceaseless vigil for me—it became so clear to me that he remembered absolutely nothing of what he had attempted to do that I deemed it wise to hold my peace and ask no dangerous questions.

He woke naturally and easily, as I have said, when the sun was already high in a windless hot sky, and he at once got up and set about the preparation of the fire for breakfast. I followed him anxiously at bathing, but he did not attempt to plunge in, merely dipping his head and making some remark about the extra coldness of the water.

"River's falling at last," he said, "and I'm glad of it."

"The humming has stopped too," I said.

He looked up at me quietly with his normal expression. Evidently he remembered everything except his own attempt at suicide.

"Everything has stopped," he said, "because——"

He hesitated. But I knew some reference to that remark he had made just before he fainted was in his mind, and I was determined to know it.

"Because 'They've found another victim'?" I said, forcing a little laugh.

"Exactly," he answered, "exactly! I feel as positive of it as though—as though—I feel quite safe again, I mean," he finished.

He began to look curiously about him. The sunlight lay in hot patches on the sand. There was no wind. The willows were motionless. He slowly rose to his feet.

"Come," he said; "I think if we look, we shall find it."

He started off on a run, and I followed him. He kept to the banks, poking with a stick among the sandy bays and caves and little back-waters, myself always close on his heels.

"Ah!" he exclaimed presently, "ah!"

The tone of his voice somehow brought back to me a vivid

sense of the horror of the last twenty-four hours, and I hurried up to join him. He was pointing with his stick at a large black object that lay half in the water and half on the sand. It appeared to be caught by some twisted willow roots so that the river could not sweep it away. A few hours before the spot must have been under water.

"See," he said quietly, "the victim that made our escape possible!"

And when I peered across his shoulder I saw that his stick rested on the body of a man. He turned it over. It was the corpse of a peasant, and the face was hidden in the sand. Clearly the man had been drowned but a few hours before, and his body must have been swept down upon our island somewhere about the hour of the dawn—*at the very time the fit had passed.*

"We must give it a decent burial, you know."

"I suppose so," I replied. I shuddered a little in spite of myself, for there was something about the appearance of that poor drowned man that turned me cold.

The Swede glanced up sharply at me, and began clambering down the bank. I followed him more leisurely. The current, I noticed, had torn away much of the clothing from the body, so that the neck and part of the chest lay bare.

Halfway down the bank my companion suddenly stopped and held up his hand in warning; but either my foot slipped, or I had gained too much momentum to bring myself quickly to a halt, for I bumped into him and sent him forward with a sort of leap to save himself. We tumbled together on to the hard sand so that our feet splashed into the water. And, before anything could be done, we had collided a little heavily against the corpse.

The Swede uttered a sharp cry. And I sprang back as if I had been shot.

At the moment we touched the body there arose from its surface the loud sound of humming—the sound of several hummings—which passed with a vast commotion as of winged things in the air about us and disappeared upwards into the sky, growing fainter and fainter till they finally ceased in the distance. It was exactly as though we had disturbed some living yet invisible creatures at work.

My companion clutched me, and I think I clutched him, but before either of us had time properly to recover from the unexpected shock, we saw that a movement of the current was turning the corpse round so that it became released from the grip of the willow roots. A moment later it had turned completely over, the dead face uppermost, staring at the sky. It lay on the edge of the main stream. In another moment it would be swept away.

The Swede started to save it, shouting again something I did not catch about a "proper burial" and then abruptly dropped upon his knees on the sand and covered his eyes with his hands. I was beside him in an instant.

I saw what he had seen.

For just as the body swung round to the current the face and the exposed chest turned full towards us, and showed plainly how the skin and flesh were indented with small hollows, beautifully formed, and exactly similar in shape and kind to the sand-funnels that we had found all over the island.

"Their mark!" I heard my companion mutter under his breath. "Their awful mark!"

And when I turned my eyes again from his ghastly face to the river, the current had done its work, and the body had been swept away into midstream and was already beyond our reach and almost out of sight, turning over and over on the waves like an otter.

Casting the Runes

M. R. James

M. R. James was one of the first writers to set down guide-lines for the writing of an effective ghost story. In his opinion, readers were most affected by tales in which the settings were familiar, the characters ordinary, and the ghosts malevolent. James also advocated "reticence" in the rendering of horrors, an attitude that determined his handling of events in "Casting the Runes" (1911). There is probably no more unlikely setting for a supernatural tale than the archives of the British Museum, or a more unimaginative group of characters than the stodgy academics who work there. Yet, through allusion to inexplicable events that occur before and after those actually related in the story, James gives the impression of a powerful supernatural menace ready to erupt through the tale's banal surface. "Casting the Runes" is an example of the antiquarian ghost tale, an enormously popular type of horror story perfected by James in which scholarly investigators uncover hidden truths not meant to be known. For every reader familiar with this classic tale of supernatural vengeance, probably hundreds more know it through its adaptation as Jacques Tourneur's 1958 film The Night of the Demon.

April 15th, 190—.

DEAR SIR,—I am requested by the Council of the —— Association to return to you the draft of a paper on *The Truth of Alchemy,* which you have been good enough to

offer to read at our forthcoming meeting and to inform
you that the Council do not see their way to including it
in the programme.

> I am,
> Yours faithfully,
> ——*Secretary.*

April 18th.

DEAR SIR,—I am sorry to say that my engagements do not
permit of my affording you an interview on the subject of
your proposed paper. Nor do our laws allow of your discussing the matter with a Committee of our Council, as you suggest. Please allow me to assure you that the fullest consideration was given to the draft which you submitted, and that it
was not declined without having been referred to the judgment of a most competent authority. No personal question (it
can hardly be necessary for me to add) can have had the
slightest influence on the decision of the Council.

> Believe me *(ut supra).*

April 20th.

THE SECRETARY of the —— Association begs respectfully to
inform Mr. Karswell that it is impossible for him to commu-
nicate the name of any person or persons to whom the draft
of Mr. Karswell's paper may have been submitted; and further desires to intimate that he cannot undertake to reply to
any further letters on this subject.

"AND WHO *is* Mr. Karswell?" inquired the Secretary's wife.
She had called at his office, and (perhaps unwarrantably) had
picked up the last of these three letters, which the typist had
just brought in.

"Why, my dear, just at present Mr. Karswell is a very angry man. But I don't know much about him otherwise, except
that he is a person of wealth, his address is Lufford Abbey,
Warwickshire, and he's an alchemist, apparently, and wants
to tell us all about it; and that's about all—except that I don't
want to meet him for the next week or two. Now, if you're
ready to leave this place, I am."

"What have you been doing to make him angry?" asked Mrs. Secretary.

"The usual thing, my dear, the usual thing: he sent in a draft of a paper he wanted to read at the next meeting, and we referred it to Edward Dunning—almost the only man in England who knows about these things—and he said it was perfectly hopeless, so we declined it. So Karswell has been pelting me with letters ever since. The last thing he wanted was the name of the man we referred his nonsense to; you saw my answer to that. But don't you say anything about it, for goodness' sake."

"I should think not, indeed. Did I ever do such a thing? I do hope, though, he won't get to know that it was poor Mr. Dunning."

"Poor Mr. Dunning? I don't know why you call him that; he's a very happy man, is Dunning. Lots of hobbies and a comfortable home, and all his time to himself."

"I only meant I should be sorry for him if this man got hold of his name, and came and bothered him."

"Oh, ah! yes. I dare say he would be poor Mr. Dunning then."

The Secretary and his wife were lunching out, and the friends to whose house they were bound were Warwickshire people. So Mrs. Secretary had already settled it in her own mind that she would question them judiciously about Mr. Karswell. But she was saved the trouble of leading up to the subject, for the hostess said to the host, before many minutes had passed, "I saw the Abbot of Lufford this morning." The host whistled. *"Did* you? What in the world brings him up to town?" "Goodness knows; he was coming out of the British Museum gate as I drove past." It was not unnatural that Mrs. Secretary should inquire whether this was a real Abbot who was being spoken of. "Oh no, my dear: only a neighbour of ours in the country who bought Lufford Abbey a few years ago. His real name is Karswell." "Is he a friend of yours?" asked Mr. Secretary, with a private wink to his wife. The question let loose a torrent of declamation. There was really nothing to be said for Mr. Karswell. Nobody knew what he did with himself: his servants were a horrible set of people; he had invented a new religion for himself, and practised no one could tell what appalling rites; he was very easily offended, and never forgave anybody: he had a dreadful face (so the lady insisted, her husband somewhat demurring); he never did a kind action, and whatever influence he did exert was mischievous. "Do the poor man justice, dear," the husband interrupted. "You forget the treat he gave the school children." "Forget it, indeed! But I'm glad you mentioned it, because it gives an idea of the man. Now, Florence, listen to this. The first winter he was at Lufford this delightful neighbour of ours wrote to the clergyman of his parish (he's not ours, but we know him very well) and offered to show the school children some magic-lantern slides. He said he had some new kinds, which he thought would interest them. Well, the clergyman was rather surprised, because Mr. Karswell had shown himself inclined to be unpleasant to the children —complaining of their trespassing, or something of the sort; but of course he accepted, and the evening was fixed, and our friend went himself to see that everything went right. He said he never had been so thankful for anything as that his own children were all prevented from being there: they were at a children's party at our house, as a matter of fact. Because this Mr. Karswell had evidently set out with the intention of frightening these poor village children out of their wits, and I do believe, if he had been allowed to go on, he would actually have done so. He began with some comparatively mild things. Red Riding Hood was one, and even then, Mr. Farrer said, the wolf was so dreadful that several of the smaller children had to be taken out: and he said Mr. Karswell began the story by producing a noise like a wolf howling in the distance, which was the most gruesome thing he had ever heard. All the slides he showed, Mr. Farrer said, were most clever; they were absolutely realistic, and where he had got them or how he worked them he could not imagine. Well, the show went on, and the stories kept on becoming a little more terrifying each time, and the children were mesmerized into complete silence. At last he produced a series which represented a little boy passing through his own park—Lufford, I mean—in the evening. Every child in the room could recognize the place from the pictures. And this poor boy was followed, and at last pursued and overtaken, and either torn in pieces or somehow made away with, by a horrible hopping creature in white, which you saw first dodging about amongst the trees, and gradually it appeared more and more plainly. Mr. Farrer said it gave him one of the worst nightmares he ever remembered, and what it must have meant to the children doesn't bear thinking of. Of course this was too much, and he spoke very sharply indeed to Mr. Karswell, and said it couldn't go on. All *he* said was: 'Oh, you think it's time to bring our little show to an end and send them home to their beds? *Very* well!' And then, if you please, he switched on another slide, which showed a great mass of snakes, centipedes, and disgusting creatures with wings, and somehow or other he made it seem as if they were climbing out of the picture and getting in amongst the audience; and this was accompanied by a sort of dry rustling noise which sent the children nearly mad, and of course they stampeded. A good many of them were rather hurt in getting out of the room, and I don't suppose one of them closed an eye that night. There was the most dreadful trouble in the village afterwards. Of course the mothers threw a good part of the blame on poor Mr. Farrer; and, if they could have got past the gates, I believe the fathers would have broken every window in the Abbey. Well, now, that's Mr. Karswell: that's the Abbot of Lufford, my dear, and you can imagine how we covet *his* society."

"Yes, I think he has all the possibilities of a distinguished criminal, has Karswell," said the host. "I should be sorry for anyone who got into his bad books."

"Is he the man, or am I mixing him up with someone else?" asked the Secretary (who for some minutes had been wearing the frown of the man who is trying to recollect something). "Is he the man who brought out a *History of Witchcraft* some time back—ten years or more?"

"That's the man; do you remember the reviews of it?"

"Certainly I do; and what's equally to the point, I knew the author of the most incisive of the lot. So did you: you must remember John Harrington; he was at John's in our time."

"Oh, very well indeed, though I don't think I saw or heard anything of him between the time I went down and the day I read the account of the inquest on him."

"Inquest?" said one of the ladies. "What happened to him?"

"Why, what happened was that he fell out of a tree and broke his neck. But the puzzle was, what could have induced him to get up there. It was a mysterious business, I must say. Here was this man—not an athletic fellow, was he? and with no eccentric twist about him that was ever noticed—walking home along a country road late in the evening—no tramps about—well known and liked in the place—and he suddenly begins to run like mad, loses his hat and stick, and finally shins up a tree—quite a difficult tree—growing in the hedgerow: a dead branch gives way, and he comes down with it and breaks his neck, and there he's found next morning with the most dreadful face of fear on him that could be imagined. It was pretty evident, of course, that he had been chased by something, and people talked of savage dogs, and beasts escaped out of menageries; but there was nothing to be made of that. That was in '89, and I believe his brother Henry (whom I remember as well at Cambridge, but *you* probably don't) has been trying to get on the track of an explanation ever since. He, of course, insists there was malice in it, but I don't know. It's difficult to see how it could have come in."

After a time the talk reverted to the *History of Witchcraft*. "Did you ever look into it?" asked the host.

"Yes, I did," said the Secretary. "I went so far as to read it."

"Was it as bad as it was made out to be?"

"Oh, in point of style and form, quite hopeless. It deserved all the pulverizing it got. But, besides that, it was an evil book. The man believed every word of what he was saying, and I'm very much mistaken if he hadn't tried the greater part of his receipts."

"Well, I only remember Harrington's review of it, and I must say if I'd been the author it would have quenched my literary ambition for good. I should never have held up my head again."

"It hasn't had that effect in the present case. But come, it's half-past three; I must be off."

On the way home the Secretary's wife said, "I do hope that horrible man won't find out that Mr. Dunning had anything to do with the rejection of his paper." "I don't think there's much chance of that," said the Secretary. "Dunning won't mention it himself, for these matters are confidential, and none of us will for the same reason. Karswell won't know his name, for Dunning hasn't published anything on the same subject yet. The only danger is that Karswell might find out, if he was to ask the British Museum people who was in the habit of consulting alchemical manuscripts: I can't very well tell them not to mention Dunning, can I? It would set them talking at once. Let's hope it won't occur to him."

However, Mr. Karswell was an astute man.

This much is in the way of prologue. On an evening rather later in the same week, Mr. Edward Dunning was returning from the British Museum, where he had been engaged in Research, to the comfortable house in a suburb where he lived alone, tended by two excellent women who had been long with him. There is nothing to be added by way of description of him to what we have heard already. Let us follow him as he takes his sober course homewards.

A train took him to within a mile or two of his house, and an electric tram a stage farther. The line ended at a point some three hundred yards from his front door. He had had enough of reading when he got into the car, and indeed the light was not such as to allow him to do more than study the advertisements on the panes of glass that faced him as he sat. As was not unnatural, the advertisements in this particular line of cars were objects of his frequent contemplation, and, with the possible exception of the brilliant and convincing dialogue between Mr. Lamplough and an eminent K.C. on the subject of Pyretic Saline, none of them afforded much scope to his imagination. I am wrong: there was one at the corner of the car farthest from him which did not seem familiar. It was in blue letters on a yellow ground, and all that he could read of it was a name—John Harrington—and something like a date. It could be of no interest to him to know more; but for all that, as the car emptied, he was just curious enough to move along the seat until he could read it well. He felt to a slight extent repaid for his trouble; the advertisement was *not* of the usual type. It ran thus: "In memory of John Harrington, F.S.A., of The Laurels, Ashbrooke. Died Sept. 18th, 1889. Three months were allowed."

The car stopped. Mr. Dunning, still contemplating the blue letters on the yellow ground, had to be stimulated to rise by a word from the conductor. "I beg your pardon," he said, "I was looking at that advertisement; it's a very odd one, isn't it?" The conductor read it slowly. "Well, my word," he said, "I never see that one before. Well, that is a cure, ain't it? Someone bin up to their jokes 'ere, I should think." He got out a duster and applied it, not without saliva, to the pane and then to the outside. "No," he said, returning, "that ain't no transfer; seems to me as if it was reg'lar *in* the glass, what I mean in the substance, as you may say. Don't you think so, sir?" Mr. Dunning examined it and rubbed it with his glove, and agreed. "Who looks after these advertisements, and gives leave for them to be put up? I wish you would inquire. I will just take a note of the words." At this moment there came a call from the driver: "Look alive, George, time's up." "All right, all right; there's something else what's up at this end. You come and look at this 'ere glass." "What's gorn with the glass?" said the driver, approaching. "Well, and oo's 'Arrington? What's it all about?" "I was just asking who was responsible for putting the advertisements up in your cars, and saying it would be as well to make some inquiry about this one." "Well, sir, that's all done at the Company's orfice, that work is: it's our Mr. Timms, I believe, looks into that. When we put up to-night I'll leave word, and per'aps I'll be able to tell you to-morrer if you 'appen to be coming this way."

This was all that passed that evening. Mr. Dunning did just go to the trouble of looking up Ashbrooke, and found that it was in Warwickshire.

Next day he went to town again. The car (it was the same car) was too full in the morning to allow of his getting a word with the conductor: he could only be sure that the curious advertisement had been made away with. The close of the day brought a further element of mystery into the transaction. He had missed the tram, or else preferred walking home, but at a rather late hour, while he was at work in his study, one of the maids came to say that two men from the tramways were very anxious to speak to him. This was a reminder of the advertisement, which he had, he says, nearly forgotten. He had the men in—they were the conductor and driver of the car—and when the matter of refreshment had been attended to, asked what Mr. Timms had had to say about the advertisement. "Well, sir, that's what we took the liberty to step round about," said the conductor. "Mr. Timms 'e give William 'ere the rough side of his tongue about that: 'cordin' to 'im there warn't no advertisement of that description sent in, nor ordered, nor paid for, nor put up, nor nothink, let alone not bein' there, and we was playing the fool takin' up his time. 'Well,' I says, 'if that's the case, all I ask of you, Mr. Timms,' I says, 'is to take and look at it for yourself,' I says. 'Of course if it ain't there,' I says, 'you may take and call me what you like.' 'Right,' he says, 'I will': and we went straight off. Now, I leave it to you, sir, if that ad., as we term 'em, with 'Arrington on it warn't as plain as ever you see anythink—blue letters on yeller glass, and as I says at the time, and you borne me out, reg'lar *in* the glass, because, if you remember, you recollect of me swabbing it with my duster." "To be sure I do, quite clearly—well?" "You may say well, I don't think. Mr. Timms he gets in that car with a light —no, he told William to 'old the light outside. 'Now,' he says, 'where's your precious ad. what we've 'eard so much about?' ' 'Ere it is,' I says, 'Mr. Timms,' and I laid my 'and on it." The conductor paused.

"Well," said Mr. Dunning, "it was gone, I suppose. Broken?"

"Broke!—not it. There warn't, if you'll believe me, no more trace of them letters—blue letters they was—on that piece o' glass, than—well, it's no good *me* talkin'. *I* never see such a thing. I leave it to William here if—but there, as I says, where's the benefit in me going on about it?"

"And what did Mr. Timms say?"

"Why 'e did what I give 'im leave to—called us pretty much anythink he liked, and I don't know as I blame him so much neither. But what we thought, William and me did, was as we seen you take down a bit of a note about that—well, that letterin'—"

"I certainly did that, and I have it now. Did you wish me to speak to Mr. Timms myself, and show it to him? Was that what you came in about?"

"There, didn't I say as much?" said William. "Deal with a

gent if you can get on the track of one, that's my word. Now perhaps, George, you'll allow as I ain't took you very far wrong to-night."

"Very well, William, very well; no need for you to go on as if you'd 'ad to frog's-march me 'ere. I come quiet, didn't I? All the same for that, we 'adn't ought to take up your time this way, sir; but if it so 'appened you could find time to step round to the Company's orfice in the morning and tell Mr. Timms what you seen for yourself, we should lay under a very 'igh obligation to you for the trouble. You see it ain't bein' called—well, one thing and another, as we mind, but if they got it into their 'ead at the orfice as we seen things as warn't there, why, one thing leads to another, and where we should be a twelvemunce 'ence—well, you can understand what I mean."

Amid further elucidations of the proposition, George, conducted by William, left the room.

The incredulity of Mr. Timms (who had a nodding acquaintance with Mr. Dunning) was greatly modified on the following day by what the latter could tell and show him; and any bad mark that might have been attached to the names of William and George was not suffered to remain on the Company's books; but explanation there was none.

Mr. Dunning's interest in the matter was kept alive by an incident of the following afternoon. He was walking from his club to the train, and he noticed some way ahead a man with a handful of leaflets such as are distributed to passers-by by agents of enterprising firms. This agent had not chosen a very crowded street for his operations: in fact, Mr. Dunning did not see him get rid of a single leaflet before he himself reached the spot. One was thrust into his hand as he passed: the hand that gave it touched his, and he experienced a sort of little shock as it did so. It seemed unnaturally rough and hot. He looked in passing at the giver, but the impression he got was so unclear that, however much he tried to reckon it up subsequently, nothing would come. He was walking quickly, and as he went on glanced at the paper. It was a blue one. The name of Harrington in large capitals caught his eye. He stopped, startled, and felt for his glasses. The next instant the leaflet was twitched out of his hand by a man who hur-

ried past, and was irrecoverably gone. He ran back a few
paces, but where was the passer-by? and where the distribu-
tor?

It was in a somewhat pensive frame of mind that Mr. Dunning passed on the following day into the Select Manuscript
Room of the British Museum, and filled up tickets for Harley
3586, and some other volumes. After a few minutes they were
brought to him, and he was settling the one he wanted first
upon the desk, when he thought he heard his own name whispered behind him. He turned round hastily, and in doing so,
brushed his little portfolio of loose papers on to the floor. He
saw no one he recognized except one of the staff in charge of
the room, who nodded to him, and he proceeded to pick up his
papers. He thought he had them all and was turning to begin
work, when a stout gentleman at the table behind him, who
was just rising to leave, and had collected his own belongings,
touched him on the shoulder, saying, "May I give you this? I
think it should be yours," and handed him a missing quire.
"It is mine, thank you," said Mr. Dunning. In another moment the man had left the room. Upon finishing his work for
the afternoon, Mr. Dunning had some conversation with the
assistant in charge, and took occasion to ask who the stout
gentleman was. "Oh, he's a man named Karswell," said the
assistant; "he was asking me a week ago who were the great
authorities on alchemy, and of course I told him you were the
only one in the country. I'll see if I can't catch him: he'd like
to meet you, I'm sure."

"For heaven's sake don't dream of it!" said Mr. Dunning,
"I'm particularly anxious to avoid him."

"Oh! very well," said the assistant, "he doesn't come here
often: I dare say you won't meet him."

More than once on the way home that day Mr. Dunning
confessed to himself that he did not look forward with his
usual cheerfulness to a solitary evening. It seemed to him
that something ill-defined and impalpable had stepped in between him and his fellow-men—had taken him in charge, as
it were. He wanted to sit close up to his neighbours in the
train and in the tram, but as luck would have it both train
and car were markedly empty. The conductor George was
thoughtful, and appeared to be absorbed in calculations as to

the number of passengers. On arriving at his house he found Dr. Watson, his medical man, on his doorstep. "I've had to upset your household arrangements, I'm sorry to say, Dunning. Both your servants are *hors de combat*. In fact, I've had to send them to the Nursing Home."

"Good heavens! What's the matter?"

"It's something like ptomaine poisoning, I should think: you've not suffered yourself, I can see, or you wouldn't be walking about. I think they'll pull through all right."

"Dear, dear! Have you any idea what brought it on?"

"Well, they tell me they bought some shellfish from a hawker at their dinnertime. It's odd. I've made inquiries, but I can't find that any hawker has been to other houses in the street. I couldn't send word to you; they won't be back for a bit yet. You come and dine with me to-night, anyhow, and we can make arrangements for going on. Eight o'clock. Don't be too anxious."

The solitary evening was thus obviated; at the expense of some distress and inconvenience, it is true. Mr. Dunning spent the time pleasantly enough with the doctor (a rather recent settler), and returned to his lonely home at about 11:30. The night he passed is not one on which he looks back with any satisfaction. He was in bed and the light was out. He was wondering if the charwoman would come early enough to get him hot water next morning, when he heard the unmistakable sound of his study door opening. No step followed it on the passage floor, but the sound must mean mischief, for he knew that he had shut the door that evening after putting his papers away in his desk. It was rather shame than courage that induced him to slip out into the passage and lean over the banister in his nightgown, listening. No light was visible; no further sound came: only a gust of warm, or even hot, air played for an instant round his shins. He went back and decided to lock himself into his room. There was more unpleasantness, however. Either an economical suburban company had decided that their light would not be required in the small hours, and had stopped working, or else something was wrong with the meter; the effect was in any case that the electric light was off. The obvious course was to find a match, and also to consult his watch: he might as well know how many hours of discomfort awaited him. So he put his hand into the well-known nook under the pillow: only, it did not get so far. What he touched was, according to his account, a mouth, with teeth, and with hair about it, and, he declares, not the mouth of a human being. I do not think it is any use to guess what he said or did; but he was in a spare room with the door locked and his ear to it before he was clearly conscious again. And there he spent the rest of a most miserable night, looking every moment for some fumbling at the door: but nothing came.

The venturing back to his own room in the morning was attended with many listenings and quiverings. The door stood open, fortunately, and the blinds were up (the servants had been out of the house before the hour of drawing them down); there was, to be short, no trace of an inhabitant. The watch, too, was in its usual place; nothing was disturbed, only the wardrobe door had swung open, in accordance with its confirmed habit. A ring at the back door now announced the charwoman, who had been ordered the night before, and nerved Mr. Dunning, after letting her in, to continue his search in other parts of the house. It was equally fruitless.

The day thus begun went on dismally enough. He dared not go to the Museum: in spite of what the assistant had said, Karswell might turn up there, and Dunning felt he could not cope with a probably hostile stranger. His own house was odious; he hated sponging on the doctor. He spent some little time in a call at the Nursing Home, where he was slightly cheered by a good report of his housekeeper and maid. Towards lunchtime he betook himself to his club, again experiencing a gleam of satisfaction at seeing the Secretary of the Association. At luncheon Dunning told his friend the more material of his woes, but could not bring himself to speak of those that weighed most heavily on his spirits. "My poor dear man," said the Secretary, "what an upset! Look here: we're alone at home, absolutely. You must put up with us. Yes! no excuse: send your things in this afternoon." Dunning was unable to stand out: he was, in truth, becoming acutely anxious, as the hours went on, as to what that night might have waiting for him. He was almost happy as he hurried home to pack up.

His friends, when they had time to take stock of him, were rather shocked at his lorn appearance, and did their best to keep him up to the mark. Not altogether without success: but, when the two men were smoking alone later, Dunning became dull again. Suddenly he said, "Gayton, I believe that alchemist man knows it was I who got his paper rejected." Gayton whistled. "What makes you think that?" he said. Dunning told of his conversation with the Museum assistant, and Gayton could only agree that the guess seemed likely to be correct. "Not that I care much," Dunning went on, "only it might be a nuisance if we were to meet. He's a bad-tempered party, I imagine." Conversation dropped again; Gayton became more and more strongly impressed with the desolateness that came over Dunning's face and bearing, and finally —though with a considerable effort—he asked him point-blank whether something serious was not bothering him. Dunning gave an exclamation of relief. "I was perishing to get it off my mind," he said. "Do you know anything about a man named John Harrington?" Gayton was thoroughly startled, and at the moment could only ask why. Then the complete story of Dunning's experiences came out—what had happened in the tramcar, in his own house, and in the street, the troubling of spirit that had crept over him, and still held him; and he ended with the question he had begun with. Gayton was at a loss how to answer him. To tell the story of Harrington's end would perhaps be right; only, Dunning was in a nervous state, the story was a grim one, and he could not help asking himself whether there were not a connecting link between these two cases, in the person of Karswell. It was a difficult concession for a scientific man, but it could be eased by the phrase "hypnotic suggestion." In the end he decided that his answer to-night should be guarded; he would talk the situation over with his wife. So he said that he had known Harrington at Cambridge, and he had died suddenly in 1889, adding a few details about the man and his published work. He did talk over the matter with Mrs. Gayton, and, as he had anticipated, she leapt at once to the conclusion which had been hovering before him. It was she who reminded him of the surviving brother, Henry Harrington, and she also who suggested that he might be got hold of by means of their hosts

of the day before. "He might be a hopeless crank," objected
Gayton. "That could be ascertained from the Bennetts, who
knew him," Mrs. Gayton retorted; and she undertook to see
the Bennetts the very next day.

It is not necessary to tell in further detail the steps by
which Henry Harrington and Dunning were brought together.

The next scene that does require to be narrated is a conversation that took place between the two. Dunning had told
Harrington of the strange ways in which the dead man's
name had been brought before him, and had said something,
besides, of his own subsequent experiences. Then he had
asked if Harrington was disposed, in return, to recall any of
the circumstances connected with his brother's death. Harrington's surprise at what he heard can be imagined: but his
reply was readily given.

"John," he said, "was in a very odd state, undeniably, from
time to time, during some weeks before, though not immediately before, the catastrophe. There were several things; the
principal notion he had was that he thought he was being
followed. No doubt he was an impressionable man, but he
never had had such fancies as this before. I cannot get it out
of my mind that there was ill will at work, and what you tell
me about yourself reminds me very much of my brother. Can
you think of any possible connecting link?"

"There is just one that has been taking shape vaguely in
my mind. I've been told that your brother reviewed a book
very severely not long before he died, and just lately I have
happened to cross the path of the man who wrote that book in
a way he would resent."

"Don't tell me the man was called Karswell."

"Why not? that is exactly his name."

Henry Harrington leant back. "That is final to my mind.
Now I must explain further. From something he said, I feel
sure that my brother John was beginning to believe—very
much against his will—that Karswell was at the bottom of
his trouble. I want to tell you what seems to me to have a
bearing on the situation. My brother was a great musician,
and used to run up to concerts in town. He came back, three

months before he died, from one of these, and gave me his
programme to look at—an analytical programme: he always
kept them. 'I nearly missed this one,' he said. 'I suppose I
must have dropped it: anyhow, I was looking for it under my
seat and in my pockets and so on, and my neighbour offered
me his: said "might he give it to me, he had no further use for
it," and he went away just afterwards. I don't know who he
was—a stout, clean-shaven man. I should have been sorry to
miss it; of course I could have bought another, but this cost
me nothing.' At another time he told me that he had been
very uncomfortable both on the way to his hotel and during
the night. I piece things together now in thinking it over.
Then, not very long after, he was going over these pro-
grammes, putting them in order to have them bound up, and
in this particular one (which by the way I had hardly glanced
at), he found quite near the beginning a strip of paper with
some very odd writing on it in red and black—most carefully
done—it looked to me more like Runic letters than anything
else. 'Why,' he said, 'this must belong to my fat neighbour. It
looks as if it might be worth returning to him; it may be a
copy of something; evidently someone has taken trouble over
it. How can I find his address?' We talked it over for a little
and agreed that it wasn't worth advertising about, and that
my brother had better look out for the man at the next concert, to which he was going very soon. The paper was lying on
the book and we were both by the fire; it was a cold, windy
summer evening. I suppose the door blew open, though I
didn't notice it: at any rate a gust—a warm gust it was—came
quite suddenly between us, took the paper and blew it
straight into the fire: it was light, thin paper, and flared and
went up the chimney in a single ash. 'Well,' I said, 'you can't
give it back now.' He said nothing for a minute: then rather
crossly, 'No, I can't; but why you should keep on saying so I
don't know.' I remarked that I didn't say it more than once.
'Not more than four times, you mean,' was all he said. I remember all that very clearly, without any good reason; and
now to come to the point. I don't know if you looked at that
book of Karswell's which my unfortunate brother reviewed.
It's not likely that you should: but I did, both before his death
and after it. The first time we made game of it together. It

was written in no style at all—split infinitives, and every sort
of thing that makes an Oxford gorge rise. Then there was
nothing that the man didn't swallow: mixing up classical
myths, and stories out of the *Golden Legend* with reports of
savage customs of to-day—all very proper, no doubt, if you
know how to use them, but he didn't: he seemed to put the
Golden Legend and the *Golden Bough* exactly on a par, and
to believe both: a pitiable exhibition, in short. Well, after the
misfortune, I looked over the book again. It was no better
than before, but the impression which it left this time on my
mind was different. I suspected—as I told you—that Karswell
had borne ill will to my brother, even that he was in some
way responsible for what had happened; and now his book
seemed to me to be a very sinister performance indeed. One
chapter in particular struck me, in which he spoke of 'casting
the Runes' on people, either for the purpose of gaining their
affection or of getting them out of the way—perhaps more
especially the latter: he spoke of all this in a way that really
seemed to me to imply actual knowledge. I've not time to go
into details, but the upshot is that I am pretty sure from
information received that the civil man at the concert was
Karswell: I suspect—I more than suspect—that the paper
was of importance: and I do believe that if my brother had
been able to give it back, he might have been alive now.
Therefore, it occurs to me to ask you whether you have anything to put beside what I have told you?"

By way of answer, Dunning had the episode in the Manuscript Room at the British Museum to relate. "Then he did
actually hand you some papers; have you examined them?
No? because we must, if you'll allow it, look at them at once,
and very carefully."

They went to the still empty house—empty, for the two
servants were not yet able to return to work. Dunning's portfolio of papers was gathering dust on the writing table. In it
were the quires of small-sized scribbling paper which he used
for his transcripts: and from one of these, as he took it up,
there slipped and fluttered out into the room with uncanny
quickness, a strip of thin light paper. The window was open,
but Harrington slammed it to, just in time to intercept the
paper, which he caught. "I thought so," he said; "it might be

the identical thing that was given to my brother. You'll have to look out, Dunning; this may mean something quite serious for you."

A long consultation took place. The paper was narrowly examined. As Harrington had said, the characters on it were more like Runes than anything else, but not decipherable by either man, and both hesitated to copy them, for fear, as they confessed, of perpetuating whatever evil purpose they might conceal. So it has remained impossible (if I may anticipate a little) to ascertain what was conveyed in this curious message or commission. Both Dunning and Harrington are firmly convinced that it had the effect of bringing its possessors into very undesirable company. That it must be returned to the source whence it came they were agreed, and further, that the only safe and certain way was that of personal service; and here contrivance would be necessary, for Dunning was known by sight to Karswell. He must, for one thing, alter his appearance by shaving his beard. But then might not the blow fall first? Harrington thought they could time it. He knew the date of the concert at which the "black spot" had been put on his brother: it was June 18th. The death had followed on Sept. 18th. Dunning reminded him that three months had been mentioned on the inscription on the car window. "Perhaps," he added, with a cheerless laugh, "mine may be a bill at three months too. I believe I can fix it by my diary. Yes, April 23rd was the day at the Museum; that brings us to July 23rd. Now, you know, it becomes extremely important to me to know anything you will tell me about the progress of your brother's trouble, if it is possible for you to speak of it." "Of course. Well, the sense of being watched whenever he was alone was the most distressing thing to him. After a time I took to sleeping in his room, and he was the better for that: still, he talked a great deal in his sleep. What about? Is it wise to dwell on that, at least before things are straightened out? I think not, but I can tell you this: two things came for him by post during those weeks, both with a London postmark, and addressed in a commercial hand. One was a woodcut of Bewick's, roughly torn out of the page: one which shows a moonlit road and a man walking along it, followed by an awful demon creature. Under it were written the lines out

of the 'Ancient Mariner' (which I suppose the cut illustrates)
about one who, having once looked round—

> *'walks on,*
> *And turns no more his head,*
> *Because he knows a frightful fiend*
> *Doth close behind him tread.'*

The other was a calendar, such as tradesmen often send. My
brother paid no attention to this, but I looked at it after his
death, and found that everything after Sept. 18 had been torn
out. You may be surprised at his having gone out alone the
evening he was killed, but the fact is that during the last ten
days or so of his life he had been quite free from the sense of
being followed or watched."

The end of the consultation was this. Harrington, who
knew a neighbour of Karswell's, thought he saw a way of
keeping a watch on his movements. It would be Dunning's
part to be in readiness to try to cross Karswell's path at any
moment, to keep the paper safe and in a place of ready access.

They parted. The next weeks were no doubt a severe strain
upon Dunning's nerves: the intangible barrier which had
seemed to rise about him on the day when he received the
paper, gradually developed into a brooding blackness that cut
him off from the means of escape to which one might have
thought he might resort. No one was at hand who was likely
to suggest them to him, and he seemed robbed of all initia-
tive. He waited with inexpressible anxiety as May, June, and
early July passed on, for a mandate from Harrington. But all
this time Karswell remained immovable at Lufford.

At last, in less than a week before the date he had come to
look upon as the end of his earthly activities, came a tele-
gram: "Leaves Victoria by boat train Thursday night. Do not
miss. I come to you to-night. Harrington."

He arrived accordingly, and they concocted plans. The
train left Victoria at nine and its last stop before Dover was
Croydon West. Harrington would mark down Karswell at
Victoria, and look out for Dunning at Croydon, calling to him
if need were by a name agreed upon. Dunning, disguised as
far as might be, was to have no label or initials on any hand
luggage, and must at all costs have the paper with him.

Dunning's suspense as he waited on the Croydon platform I need not attempt to describe. His sense of danger during the last days had only been sharpened by the fact that the cloud about him had perceptibly been lighter; but relief was an ominous symptom, and, if Karswell eluded him now, hope was gone: and there were so many chances of that. The rumour of the journey might be itself a device. The twenty minutes in which he paced the platform and persecuted every porter with inquiries as to the boat train were as bitter as any he had spent. Still, the train came, and Harrington was at the window. It was important, of course, that there should be no recognition: so Dunning got in at the farther end of the corridor carriage, and only gradually made his way to the compartment where Harrington and Karswell were. He was pleased, on the whole, to see that the train was far from full.

Karswell was on the alert, but gave no sign of recognition. Dunning took the seat not immediately facing him, and attempted, vainly at first, then with increasing command of his faculties, to reckon the possibilities of making the desired transfer. Opposite to Karswell, and next to Dunning, was a heap of Karswell's coats on the seat. It would be of no use to slip the paper into these—he would not be safe, or would not feel so, unless in some way it could be proffered by him and accepted by the other. There was a handbag, open, and with papers in it. Could he manage to conceal this (so that perhaps Karswell might leave the carriage without it), and then find and give it to him? This was the plan that suggested itself. If he could only have counselled with Harrington! but that could not be. The minutes went on. More than once Karswell rose and went out into the corridor. The second time Dunning was on the point of attempting to make the bag fall off the seat, but he caught Harrington's eye, and read in it a warning. Karswell, from the corridor, was watching: probably to see if the two men recognized each other. He returned, but was evidently restless: and, when he rose the third time, hope dawned, for something did slip off his seat and fall with hardly a sound to the floor. Karswell went out once more, and passed out of range of the corridor window. Dunning picked up what had fallen, and saw that the key was in his hands in the form of one of Cook's ticket cases, with tickets in it. These cases have a pocket in the cover, and within very few seconds the paper of which we have heard was in the pocket of this one. To make the operation more secure, Harrington stood in the doorway of the compartment and fiddled with the blind. It was done, and done at the right time, for the train was now slowing down towards Dover.

In a moment more Karswell re-entered the compartment. As he did so, Dunning, managing, he knew not how, to suppress the tremble in his voice, handed him the ticket case, saying, "May I give you this, sir? I believe it is yours." After a brief glance at the ticket inside, Karswell uttered the hoped for response, "Yes, it is; much obliged to you, sir," and he placed it in his breast pocket.

Even in the few moments that remained—moments of tense anxiety, for they knew not to what a premature finding of the paper might lead—both men noticed that the carriage seemed to darken about them and to grow warmer; that Karswell was fidgety and oppressed; that he drew the heap of loose coats near to him and cast it back as if it repelled him; and that he then sat upright and glanced anxiously at both. They, with sickening anxiety, busied themselves in collecting their belongings; but they both thought that Karswell was on the point of speaking when the train stopped at Dover Town. It was natural that in the short space between town and pier they should both go into the corridor.

At the pier they got out, but so empty was the train that they were forced to linger on the platform until Karswell should have passed ahead of them with his porter on the way to the boat, and only then was it safe for them to exchange a pressure of the hand and a word of concentrated congratulation. The effect upon Dunning was to make him almost faint. Harrington made him lean up against the wall, while he himself went forward a few yards within sight of the gangway to the boat, at which Karswell had now arrived. The man at the head of it examined his ticket, and, laden with coats, he passed down into the boat. Suddenly the official called after him, "You, sir, beg pardon, did the other gentleman show his ticket?" "What the devil do you mean by the other gentleman?" Karswell's snarling voice called back from the deck. The man bent over and looked at him. "The devil? Well, I don't know, I'm sure," Harrington heard him say to himself, and then aloud, "My mistake, sir; must have been your rugs!

ask your pardon." And then, to a subordinate near him, " 'Ad he got a dog with him, or what? Funny thing: I could 'a' swore 'e wasn't alone. Well, whatever it was, they'll 'ave to see to it aboard. She's off now. Another week and we shall be gettin' the 'oliday customers." In five minutes more there was nothing but the lessening lights of the boat, the long line of the Dover lamps, the night breeze, and the moon.

Long and long the two sat in their room at the "Lord Warden." In spite of the removal of their greatest anxiety, they were oppressed with a doubt, not of the lightest. Had they been justified in sending a man to his death, as they believed they had? Ought they not to warn him, at least? "No," said Harrington: "if he is the murderer I think him, we have done no more than is just. Still, if you think it better—but how and where can you warn him?" "He was booked to Abbeville only," said Dunning. "I saw that. If I wired to the hotels there in Joanne's Guide, 'Examine your ticket case, Dunning,' I should feel happier. This is the 21st: he will have a day. But I am afraid he has gone into the dark." So telegrams were left at the hotel office.

It is not clear whether these reached their destination, or whether, if they did, they were understood. All that is known is that, on the afternoon of the 23rd, an English traveller, examining the front of St. Wulfram's Church at Abbeville, then under extensive repair, was struck on the head and instantly killed by a stone falling from the scaffold erected round the north-western tower, there being, as was clearly proved, no workman on the scaffold at that moment: and the traveller's papers identified him as Mr. Karswell.

Only one detail shall be added. At Karswell's sale a set of Bewick, sold with all faults, was acquired by Harrington. The page with the woodcut of the traveller and the demon was, as he had expected, mutilated. Also, after a judicious interval, Harrington repeated to Dunning something of what he had heard his brother say in his sleep: but it was not long before Dunning stopped him.

The Graveyard Rats

Henry Kuttner

The pulp fiction magazines of the first half of the twentieth century emphasized thrills and chills over literary quality and helped drive a wedge between critical estimations of horror as a literary style and a form of popular fiction. Crude as pulp horror often was, it occasionally produced stories more frightening than strictly regulated literary horror would permit. "The Graveyard Rats" (1936) was first published in Weird Tales, *the magazine that had the strongest impact on the development of American horror fiction. By combining such familiar horror motifs as the cemetery, the predatory animal, the premature burial, and the living dead in a story with a completely unsympathetic protagonist, author Henry Kuttner created a harrowing tale of the horrors that lurk beneath the graveyards of old New England. The story's achievement is all the more remarkable when one considers that it was the twenty-year-old Kuttner's first professional fiction sale.*

Old Masson, the caretaker of one of Salem's oldest and most neglected cemeteries, had a feud with the rats. Generations ago they had come up from the wharves and settled in the graveyard, a colony of abnormally large rats, and when Masson had taken charge after the inexplicable disappearance of the former caretaker, he decided that they must go. At first he set traps for them and put poisoned food by their burrows, and later he tried to shoot them, but it did no good. The rats stayed, multiplying and overrunning the graveyard with their ravenous hordes.

They were large, even for the *mus decumanus,* which sometimes measures fifteen inches in length, exclusive of the naked pink and gray tail. Masson had caught glimpses of some as large as good-sized cats, and when, once or twice, the grave-diggers had uncovered their burrows, the malodorous tunnels were large enough to enable a man to crawl into them on his hands and knees. The ships that had come generations ago from distant ports to the rotting Salem wharves had brought strange cargoes.

Masson wondered sometimes at the extraordinary size of these burrows. He recalled certain vaguely disturbing legends he had heard since coming to ancient, witch-haunted Salem—tales of a moribund, inhuman life that was said to exist in forgotten burrows in the earth. The old days, when Cotton Mather had hunted down the evil cults that worshipped Hecate and the dark Magna Mater in frightful orgies, had passed; but dark gabled houses still leaned perilously toward each other over narrow cobbled streets, and blasphemous secrets and mysteries were said to be hidden in subterranean cellars and caverns, where forgotten pagan rites were still celebrated in defiance of law and sanity. Wagging their gray heads wisely, the elders declared that there were worse things than rats and maggots crawling in the unhallowed earth of the ancient Salem cemeteries.

And then, too, there was this curious dread of the rats. Masson disliked and respected the ferocious little rodents, for he knew the danger that lurked in their flashing, needle-sharp fangs; but he could not understand the inexplicable horror which the oldsters held for deserted, rat-infested houses. He had heard vague rumors of ghoulish beings that dwelt far underground, and that had the power of commanding the rats, marshaling them like horrible armies. The rats, the old men whispered, were messengers between this world and the grim and ancient caverns far below Salem. Bodies had been stolen from graves for nocturnal subterranean feasts, they said. The myth of the Pied Piper is a fable that hides a blasphemous horror, and the black pits of Avernus have brought forth hell-spawned monstrosities that never venture into the light of day.

Masson paid little attention to these tales. He did not fraternize with his neighbors, and, in fact, did all he could to hide the existence of the rats from intruders. Investigation, he realized, would undoubtedly mean the opening of many graves. And while some of the gnawed, empty coffins could be attributed to the activities of the rats, Masson might find it difficult to explain the mutilated bodies that lay in some of the coffins.

The purest gold is used in filling teeth, and this gold is not removed when a man is buried. Clothing, of course, is another matter; for usually the undertaker provides a plain broadcloth suit that is cheap and easily recognizable. But gold is another matter; and sometimes, too, there were medical students and less reputable doctors who were in need of cadavers, and not overscrupulous as to where these were obtained.

So far Masson had successfully managed to discourage investigation. He had fiercely denied the existence of the rats, even though they sometimes robbed him of his prey. Masson did not care what happened to the bodies after he had performed his gruesome thefts, but the rats inevitably dragged away the whole cadaver through the hole they gnawed in the coffin.

The size of these burrows occasionally worried Masson. Then, too, there was the curious circumstance of the coffins always being gnawed open at the end, never at the side or top. It was almost as though the rats were working under the direction of some impossibly intelligent leader.

Now he stood in an open grave and threw a last sprinkling of wet earth on the heap beside the pit. It was raining, a slow, cold drizzle that for weeks had been descending from soggy black clouds. The graveyard was a slough of yellow, sucking mud, from which the rain-washed tombstones stood up in irregular battalions. The rats had retreated to their burrows, and Masson had not seen one for days. But his gaunt, unshaved face was set in frowning lines; the coffin on which he was standing was a wooden one.

The body had been buried several days earlier, but Masson had not dared to disinter it before. A relative of the dead man had been coming to the grave at intervals, even in the drenching rain. But he would hardly come at this late hour, no matter how much grief he might be suffering, Masson thought, grinning wryly. He straightened and laid the shovel aside.

From the hill on which the ancient graveyard lay he could see the lights of Salem flickering dimly through the downpour. He drew a flashlight from his pocket. He would need light now. Taking up the spade, he bent and examined the fastenings of the coffin.

Abruptly he stiffened. Beneath his feet he sensed an unquiet stirring and scratching, as though something was moving within the coffin. For a moment a pang of superstitious fear shot through Masson, and then rage replaced it as he realized the significance of the sound. The rats had forestalled him again!

In a paroxysm of anger Masson wrenched at the fastenings of the coffin. He got the sharp edge of the shovel under the lid and pried it up until he could finish the job with his hands. Then he sent the flashlight's cold beam darting down into the coffin.

Rain spattered against the white satin lining; the coffin was empty. Masson saw a flicker of movement at the head of the case, and darted the light in that direction.

The end of the sarcophagus had been gnawed through, and a gaping hole led into darkness. A black shoe, limp and dragging, was disappearing as Masson watched, and abruptly he realized that the rats had forestalled him by only a few minutes. He fell on his hands and knees and made a hasty clutch at the shoe, and the flashlight incontinently fell into the coffin and went out. The shoe was tugged from his grasp, he heard a sharp, excited squealing, and then he had the flashlight again and was darting its light into the burrow.

It was a large one. It had to be, or the corpse could not have been dragged along it. Masson wondered at the size of the rats that could carry away a man's body, but the thought of the loaded revolver in his pocket fortified him. Probably if the corpse had been an ordinary one Masson would have left the rats with their spoils rather than venture into the narrow burrow, but he remembered an especially fine set of cuff-links he had observed, as well as a stickpin that was undoubtedly a

genuine pearl. With scarcely a pause he clipped the flashlight
to his belt and crept into the burrow.

It was a tight fit, but he managed to squeeze himself along.
Ahead of him in the flashlight's glow he could see the shoes
dragging along the wet earth of the bottom of the tunnel. He
crept along the burrow as rapidly as he could, occasionally
barely able to squeeze his lean body through the narrow
walls.

The air was overpowering with its musty stench of carrion.
If he could not reach the corpse in a minute, Masson decided,
he would turn back. Belated fears were beginning to crawl,
maggot-like, within his mind, but greed urged him on. He
crawled forward, several times passing the mouths of adjoining tunnels. The walls of the burrow were damp and slimy,
and twice lumps of dirt dropped behind him. The second time
he paused and screwed his head around to look back. He
could see nothing, of course, until he had unhooked the flashlight from his belt and reversed it.

Several clods lay on the ground behind him, and the danger
of his position suddenly became real and terrifying. With
thoughts of a cave-in making his pulse race, he decided to
abandon the pursuit, even though he had now almost overtaken the corpse and the invisible things that pulled it. But
he had overlooked one thing: the burrow was too narrow to
allow him to turn.

Panic touched him briefly, but he remembered a side tunnel he had just passed, and backed awkwardly along the tunnel until he came to it. He thrust his legs into it, backing
until he found himself able to turn. Then he hurriedly began
to retrace his way, although his knees were bruised and painful.

Agonizing pain shot through his leg. He felt sharp teeth
sink into his flesh, and kicked out frantically. There was a
shrill squealing and the scurry of many feet. Flashing the
light behind him, Masson caught his breath in a sob of fear as
he saw a dozen great rats watching him intently, their slitted
eyes glittering in the light. They were great misshapen
things, as large as cats, and behind them he caught a glimpse
of a dark shape that stirred and moved swiftly aside into the

shadow; and he shuddered at the unbelievable size of the thing.

The light had held them for a moment, but they were edging closer, their teeth dull orange in the pale light. Masson tugged at his pistol, managed to extricate it from his pocket, and aimed carefully. It was an awkward position, and he tried to press his feet into the soggy sides of the burrow so that he should not inadvertently send a bullet into one of them.

The rolling thunder of the shot deafened him, for a time, and the clouds of smoke set him coughing. When he could hear again and the smoke had cleared, he saw that the rats were gone. He put the pistol back and began to creep swiftly along the tunnel, and then with a scurry and a rush they were upon him again.

They swarmed over his legs, biting and squealing insanely, and Masson shrieked horribly as he snatched for his gun. He fired without aiming, and only luck saved him from blowing a foot off. This time the rats did not retreat so far, but Masson was crawling as swiftly as he could along the burrow, ready to fire again at the first sound of another attack.

There was a patter of feet and he sent the light stabbing back of him. A great gray rat paused and watched him. Its long ragged whiskers twitched, and its scabrous, naked tail was moving slowly from side to side. Masson shouted and the rat retreated.

He crawled on, pausing briefly, the black gap of a side tunnel at his elbow, as he made out a shapeless huddle on the damp clay a few yards ahead. For a second he thought it was a mass of earth that had been dislodged from the roof, and then he recognized it as a human body.

It was a brown and shriveled mummy, and with a dreadful unbelieving shock Masson realized that it was moving.

It was crawling toward him, and in the pale glow of the flashlight the man saw a frightful gargoyle face thrust into his own. It was the passionless, death's-head skull of a long-dead corpse, instinct with hellish life; and the glazed eyes swollen and bulbous betrayed the thing's blindness. It made a faint groaning sound as it crawled toward Masson, stretching

its ragged and granulated lips in a grin of dreadful hunger.
And Masson was frozen with abysmal fear and loathing.

Just before the Horror touched him, Masson flung himself
frantically into the burrow at his side. He heard a scrambling
noise at his heels, and the thing groaned dully as it came
after him. Masson, glancing over his shoulder, screamed and
propelled himself desperately through the narrow burrow.
He crawled along awkwardly, sharp stones cutting his hands
and knees. Dirt showered into his eyes, but he dared not
pause even for a moment. He scrambled on, gasping, cursing,
and praying hysterically.

Squealing triumphantly, the rats came at him, horrible
hunger in their eyes. Masson almost succumbed to their vicious teeth before he succeeded in beating them off. The passage was narrowing, and in a frenzy of terror he kicked and
screamed and fired until the hammer clicked on an empty
shell. But he had driven them off.

He found himself crawling under a great stone, embedded
in the roof, that dug cruelly into his back. It moved a little as
his weight struck it, and an idea flashed into Masson's fright-
crazed mind. If he could bring down the stone so that it
blocked the tunnel!

The earth was wet and soggy from the rains, and he
hunched himself half upright and dug away at the dirt
around the stone. The rats were coming closer. He saw their
eyes glowing in the reflection of the flashlight's beam. Still he
clawed frantically at the earth. The stone was giving. He
tugged at it and it rocked in its foundation.

A rat was approaching—the monster he had already
glimpsed. Gray and leprous and hideous it crept forward with
its orange teeth bared, and in its wake came the blind dead
thing, groaning as it crawled. Masson gave a last frantic tug
at the stone. He felt it slide downward, and then he went
scrambling along the tunnel.

Behind him the stone crashed down, and he heard a sudden
frightful shriek of agony. Clods showered upon his legs. A
heavy weight fell on his feet and he dragged them free with
difficulty. The entire tunnel was collapsing!

Gasping with fear, Masson threw himself forward as the
soggy earth collapsed at his heels. The tunnel narrowed until

he could barely use his hands and legs to propel himself; he wriggled forward like an eel and suddenly felt satin tearing beneath his clawing fingers, and then his head crashed against some thing that barred his path. He moved his legs, discovering that they were not pinned under the collapsed earth. He was lying flat on his stomach, and when he tried to raise himself he found that the roof was only a few inches from his back. Panic shot through him.

When the blind horror had blocked his path, he had flung himself into a side tunnel, a tunnel that had no outlet. He was *in a coffin,* an empty coffin into which he had crept through the hole the rats had gnawed in its end!

He tried to turn on his back and found that he could not. The lid of the coffin pinned him down inexorably. Then he braced himself and strained at the coffin lid. It was immovable, and even if he could escape from the sarcophagus, how could he claw his way up through five feet of hard-packed earth?

He found himself gasping. It was dreadfully fetid, unbearably hot. In a paroxysm of terror he ripped and clawed at the satin until it was shredded. He made a futile attempt to dig with his feet at the earth from the collapsed burrow that blocked his retreat. If he were only able to reverse his position he might be able to claw his way through to air . . . air . . .

White-hot agony lanced through his breast, throbbed in his eyeballs. His head seemed to be swelling, growing larger and larger; and suddenly he heard the exultant squealing of the rats. He began to scream insanely but could not drown them out. For a moment he thrashed about hysterically within his narrow prison, and then he was quiet, gasping for air. His eyelids closed, his blackened tongue protruded, and he sank down into the blackness of death with the mad squealing of the rats dinning in his ears.

Pigeons from Hell

Robert E. Howard

Southern Gothic is the term applied to stories set in the postbellum American South and concerned with decrepit plantations, fading gentry, and dark family secrets that time cannot erase. Though we generally associate the style with the work of William Faulkner, Tennessee Williams, and writers of similar caliber, Robert E. Howard wrote a handful of stories for the horror pulps that can be read as explorations of the Southern Gothic mode's more grotesque characteristics. "Pigeons from Hell" was first published in 1938, two years after Howard's tragic suicide, and it reflects the parochial attitudes that still prevailed at a time when the Civil War and Reconstruction were not yet distant memories. Beneath its gore, it is a tale of poetic justice presented in the guise of·a haunted house story.

1. The Whistler in the Dark

Griswell awoke suddenly, every nerve tingling with a premonition of imminent peril. He stared about wildly, unable at first to remember where he was, or what he was doing there. Moonlight filtered in through the dusty windows, and the great empty room with its lofty ceiling and gaping black fireplace was spectral and unfamiliar. Then as he emerged from the clinging cobwebs of his recent sleep, he remembered where he was and how he came to be there. He twisted his head and stared at his companion, sleeping on the floor near him. John Branner was but a vaguely bulking shape in the darkness that the moon scarcely grayed.

Griswell tried to remember what had awakened him. There was no sound in the house, no sound outside except the mournful hoot of an owl, far away in the piny woods. Now he had captured the illusive memory. It was a dream, a nightmare so filled with dim terror that it had frightened him awake. Recollection flooded back, vividly etching the abominable vision.

Or was it a dream? Certainly it must have been, but it had blended so curiously with recent actual events that it was difficult to know where reality left off and fantasy began.

Dreaming, he had seemed to relive his past few waking hours, in accurate detail. The dream had begun, abruptly, as he and John Branner came in sight of the house where they now lay. They had come rattling and bouncing over the stumpy, uneven old road that led through the pinelands, he and John Branner, wandering far afield from their New England home, in search of vacation pleasure. They had sighted the old house with its balustraded galleries rising amidst a wilderness of weeds and bushes, just as the sun was setting behind it. It dominated their fancy, rearing black and stark and gaunt against the low lurid rampart of sunset, barred by the black pines.

They were tired, sick of bumping and pounding all day over woodland roads. The old deserted house stimulated their imagination with its suggestion of antebellum splendor and ultimate decay. They left the automobile beside the rutty road, and as they went up the winding walk of crumbling bricks, almost lost in the tangle of rank growth, pigeons rose from the balustrades in a fluttering, feathery crowd and swept away with a low thunder of beating wings.

The oaken door sagged on broken hinges. Dust lay thick on the floor of the wide, dim hallway, on the broad steps of the stair that mounted up from the hall. They turned into a door opposite the landing, and entered a large room, empty, dusty, with cobwebs shining thickly in the corners. Dust lay thick over the ashes in the great fireplace.

They discussed gathering wood and building a fire, but decided against it. As the sun sank, darkness came quickly, the

thick, black, absolute darkness of the pinelands. They knew
that rattlesnakes and copperheads haunted Southern forests,
and they did not care to go groping for firewood in the dark.
They ate frugally from tins, then rolled in their blankets
fully clad before the empty fireplace, and went instantly to
sleep.

This, in part, was what Griswell had dreamed. He saw
again the gaunt house looming stark against the crimson
sunset; saw the flight of the pigeons as he and Branner came
up the shattered walk. He saw the dim room in which they
presently lay, and he saw the two forms that were himself
and his companion, lying wrapped in their blankets on the
dusty floor. Then from that point his dream altered subtly,
passed out of the realm of the commonplace and became
tinged with fear. He was looking into a vague, shadowy chamber, lit by the gray light of the moon which streamed in from
some obscure source. For there was no window in that room.
But in the gray light he saw three silent shapes that hung
suspended in a row, and their stillness and their outlines
woke chill horror in his soul. There was no sound, no word,
but he sensed a Presence of fear and lunacy crouching in a
dark corner. . . . Abruptly he was back in the dusty, high-
ceilinged room, before the great fireplace.

He was lying in his blankets, staring tensely through the
dim door and across the shadowy hall, to where a beam of
moonlight fell across the balustraded stair, some seven steps
up from the landing. And there was something on the stair, a
bent, misshapen, shadowy thing that never moved fully into
the beam of light. But a dim yellow blur that might have
been a face was turned toward him, as if *something* crouched
on the stair, regarding him and his companion. Fright crept
chilly through his veins, and it was then that he awoke—if
indeed he had been asleep.

He blinked his eyes. The beam of moonlight fell across the
stair just as he had dreamed it did; but no figure lurked there.
Yet his flesh still crawled from the fear the dream or vision
had roused in him; his legs felt as if they had been plunged in
ice-water. He made an involuntary movement to awaken his
companion, when a sudden sound paralyzed him.

It was the sound of whistling on the floor above. Eery and

sweet it rose, not carrying any tune, but piping shrill and melodious. Such a sound in a supposedly deserted house was alarming enough; but it was more than the fear of a physical invader that held Griswell frozen. He could not himself have defined the horror that gripped him. But Branner's blankets rustled, and Griswell saw he was sitting upright. His figure bulked dimly in the soft darkness, the head turned toward the stair as if the man were listening intently. More sweetly and more subtly evil rose that weird whistling.

"John!" whispered Griswell from dry lips. He had meant to shout—to tell Branner that there was somebody upstairs, somebody who could mean them no good; that they must leave the house at once. But his voice died dryly in his throat.

Branner had risen. His boots clumped on the floor as he moved toward the door. He stalked leisurely into the hall and made for the lower landing, merging with the shadows that clustered black about the stair.

Griswell lay incapable of movement, his mind a whirl of bewilderment. Who was that whistling upstairs? Why was Branner going up those stairs? Griswell saw him pass the spot where the moonlight rested, saw his head tilted back as if he were looking at something Griswell could not see, above and beyond the stair. But his face was like that of a sleep-walker. He moved across the bar of moonlight and vanished from Griswell's view, even as the latter tried to shout to him to come back. A ghastly whisper was the only result of his effort.

The whistling sank to a lower note, died out. Griswell heard the stairs creaking under Branner's measured tread. Now he had reached the hallway above, for Griswell heard the clump of his feet moving along it. Suddenly the footfalls halted, and the whole night seemed to hold its breath. Then an awful scream split the stillness, and Griswell started up, echoing the cry.

The strange paralysis that had held him was broken. He took a step toward the door, then checked himself. The foot-falls were resumed. Branner was coming back. He was not running. The tread was even more deliberate and measured than before. Now the stairs began to creak again. A groping hand, moving along the balustrade, came into the bar of

moonlight; then another, and a ghastly thrill went through
Griswell as he saw that the other hand gripped a hatchet—a
hatchet which dripped blackly. *Was* that Branner who was
coming down that stair?

Yes! The figure had moved into the bar of moonlight now,
and Griswell recognized it. Then he saw Branner's face, and a
shriek burst from Griswell's lips. Branner's face was bloodless, corpse-like; gouts of blood dripped darkly down it; his
eyes were glassy and set, and blood oozed from the great gash
which cleft the crown of his head!

Griswell never remembered exactly how he got out of that
accursed house. Afterward he retained a mad, confused impression of smashing his way through a dusty cobwebbed window, of stumbling blindly across the weed-choked lawn, gibbering his frantic horror. He saw the black wall of the pines,
and the moon floating in a blood-red mist in which there was
neither sanity nor reason.

Some shred of sanity returned to him as he saw the automobile beside the road. In a world gone suddenly mad, that
was an object reflecting prosaic reality; but even as he
reached for the door, a dry chilling whir sounded in his ears,
and he recoiled from the swaying undulating shape that
arched up from its scaly coils on the driver's seat and hissed
sibilantly at him, darting a forked tongue in the moonlight.

With a sob of horror he turned and fled down the road, as a
man runs in a nightmare. He ran without purpose or reason.
His numbed brain was incapable of conscious thought. He
merely obeyed the blind primitive urge to run—run—run until he fell exhausted.

The black walls of the pines flowed endlessly past him; so
he was seized with the illusion that he was getting nowhere.
But presently a sound penetrated the fog of his terror—the
steady, inexorable patter of feet behind him. Turning his
head, he saw *something* loping after him—wolf or dog, he
could not tell which, but its eyes glowed like balls of green
fire. With a gasp he increased his speed, reeled around a bend
in the road, and heard a horse snort; saw it rear and heard its
rider curse; saw the gleam of blue steel in the man's lifted
hand.

He staggered and fell, catching at the rider's stirrup.

"For God's sake, help me!" he panted. "The thing! It killed Branner—it's coming after me! *Look!*"

Twin balls of fire gleamed in the fringe of bushes at the turn of the road. The rider swore again, and on the heels of his profanity came the smashing report of his six-shooter— again and yet again. The fire-sparks vanished, and the rider, jerking his stirrup free from Griswell's grasp, spurred his horse at the bend. Griswell staggered up, shaking in every limb. The rider was out of sight only a moment; then he came galloping back.

"Took to the brush. Timber wolf, I reckon, though I never heard of one chasin' a man before. Do you know what it was?"

Griswell could only shake his head weakly.

The rider, etched in the moonlight, looked down at him, smoking pistol still lifted in his right hand. He was a compactly-built man of medium height, and his broad-brimmed planter's hat and his boots marked him as a native of the country as definitely as Griswell's garb stamped him as a stranger.

"What's all this about, anyway?"

"I don't know," Griswell answered helplessly. "My name's Griswell. John Branner—my friend who was traveling with me—we stopped at a deserted house back down the road to spend the night. Something——" at the memory he was choked by a rush of horror. "My God!" he screamed. "I must be mad! *Something* came and looked over the balustrade of the stair—something with a yellow face! I thought I dreamed it, but it must have been real. Then somebody began whistling upstairs, and Branner rose and went up the stairs walking like a man in his sleep, or hypnotized. I heard him scream—or someone screamed; then he came down the stair again with a bloody hatchet in his hand—and my God, sir, he was *dead!* His head had been split open. I saw brains and clotted blood oozing down his face, and his face was that of a dead man. *But he came down the stairs!* As God is my witness, John Branner was murdered in that dark upper hallway, and then his dead body came stalking down the stairs with a hatchet in its hand—to kill me!"

The rider made no reply; he sat his horse like a statue, outlined against the stars, and Griswell could not read his expression, his face shadowed by his hat-brim.

"You think I'm mad," he said hopelessly. "Perhaps I am."

"I don't know what to think," answered the rider. "If it was any house but the old Blassenville Manor—well, we'll see. My name's Buckner. I'm sheriff of this county. Took a prisoner over to the county-seat in the next county and was ridin' back late."

He swung off his horse and stood beside Griswell, shorter than the lanky New Englander, but much harder knit. There was a natural manner of decision and certainty about him, and it was easy to believe that he would be a dangerous man in any sort of a fight.

"Are you afraid to go back to the house?" he asked, and Griswell shuddered, but shook his head, the dogged tenacity of Puritan ancestors asserting itself.

"The thought of facing that horror again turns me sick. But poor Branner——" he choked again. "We must find his body. My God!" he cried, unmanned by the abysmal horror of the thing; *"what* will we find? If a dead man walks, what—"

"We'll see." The sheriff caught the reins in the crook of his left elbow and began filling the empty chambers of his big blue pistol as they walked along.

As they made the turn Griswell's blood was ice at the thought of what they might see lumbering up the road with a bloody, grinning death-mask, but they saw only the house looming spectrally among the pines, down the road. A strong shudder shook Griswell.

"God, how *evil* that house looks, against those black pines! It looked sinister from the very first—when we went up the broken walk and saw those pigeons fly up from the porch——"

"Pigeons?" Buckner cast him a quick glance. "You saw the pigeons?"

"Why, yes! Scores of them perching on the porch railing."

They strode on for a moment in silence, before Buckner said abruptly: "I've lived in this country all my life. I've passed the old Blassenville place a thousand times, I reckon, at all hours of the day and night. But I never saw a pigeon anywhere around it, or anywhere else in these woods."

"There were scores of them," repeated Griswell, bewildered.

"I've seen men who swore they'd seen a flock of pigeons perched along the balusters just at sundown," said Buckner slowly. "Negroes, all of them except one man. A tramp. He was buildin' a fire in the yard, aimin' to camp there that night. I passed along there about dark, and he told me about the pigeons. I came back by there the next mornin'. The ashes of his fire were there, and his tin cup, and skillet where he'd fried pork, and his blankets looked like they'd been slept in. Nobody ever saw him again. That was twelve years ago. The blacks say they can see the pigeons, but no black would pass along this road between sundown and sunup. They say the pigeons are the souls of the Blassenvilles, let out of hell at sunset. The Negroes say the red glare in the west is the light from hell, because then the gates of hell are open, and the Blassenvilles fly out."

"Who were the Blassenvilles?" asked Griswell, shivering.

"They owned all this land here. French-English family. Came here from the West Indies before the Louisiana Purchase. The Civil War ruined them, like it did so many. Some were killed in the War; most of the others died out. Nobody's lived in the Manor since 1890 when Miss Elizabeth Blassenville, the last of the line, fled from the old house one night like it was a plague spot, and never came back to it—this your auto?"

They halted beside the car, and Griswell stared morbidly at the grim house. Its dusty panes were empty and blank; but they did not seem blind to him. It seemed to him that ghastly eyes were fixed hungrily on him through those darkened panes. Buckner repeated his question.

"Yes. Be careful. There's a snake on the seat—or there was."

"Not there now," grunted Buckner, tying his horse and pulling an electric torch out of the saddle-bag. "Well, let's have a look."

He strode up the broken brick walk as matter-of-factly as if he were paying a social call on friends. Griswell followed close at his heels, his heart pounding suffocatingly. A scent of decay and moldering vegetation blew on the faint wind, and Griswell grew faint with nausea, that rose from a frantic abhorrence of these black woods, these ancient plantation houses that hid forgotten secrets of slavery and bloody pride and mysterious intrigues. He had thought of the South as a sunny, lazy land washed by soft breezes laden with spice and warm blossoms, where life ran tranquilly to the rhythm of black folk singing in sunbathed cottonfields. But now he had discovered another, unsuspected side—a dark, brooding, fear-haunted side, and the discovery repelled him.

The oaken door sagged as it had before. The blackness of the interior was intensified by the beam of Buckner's light playing on the sill. That beam sliced through the darkness of the hallway and roved up the stair, and Griswell held his breath, clenching his fists. But no shape of lunacy leered down at them. Buckner went in, walking light as a cat, torch in one hand, gun in the other.

As he swung his light into the room across from the stairway, Griswell cried out—and cried out again, almost fainting with the intolerable sickness at what he saw. A trail of blood drops led across the floor, crossing the blankets Branner had occupied, which lay between the door and those in which Griswell had lain. And Griswell's blankets had a terrible occupant. John Branner lay there, face down, his cleft head revealed in merciless clarity in the steady light. His outstretched hand still gripped the haft of a hatchet, and the blade was imbedded deep in the blanket and the floor beneath, just where Griswell's head had lain when he slept there.

A momentary rush of blackness engulfed Griswell. He was not aware that he staggered, or that Buckner caught him. When he could see and hear again, he was violently sick and hung his head against the mantel, retching miserably.

Buckner turned the light full on him, making him blink. Buckner's voice came from behind the blinding radiance, the man himself unseen.

"Griswell, you've told me a yarn that's hard to believe. I saw something chasin' you, but it might have been a timber wolf, or a mad dog.

"If you're holdin' back anything, you better spill it. What you told me won't hold up in any court. You're bound to be accused of killin' your partner. I'll have to arrest you. If you'll give me the straight goods now, it'll make it easier. Now, didn't you kill this fellow, Branner?

"Wasn't it something like this: you quarreled, he grabbed a hatchet and swung at you, but you dodged and then let *him* have it?"

Griswell sank down and hid his face in his hands, his head swimming.

"Great God, man, I didn't murder John! Why, we've been friends ever since we were children in school together. I've told you the truth. I don't blame you for not believing me. But God help me, it is the truth!"

The light swung back to the gory head again, and Griswell closed his eyes.

He heard Buckner grunt.

"I believe this hatchet in his hand is the one he was killed with. Blood and brains plastered on the blade, and hairs stickin' to it—hairs exactly the same color as his. This makes it tough for you, Griswell."

"How so?" the New Englander asked dully.

"Knocks any plea of self-defense in the head. Branner couldn't have swung at you with this hatchet after you split his skull with it. You must have pulled the ax out of his head, stuck it into the floor and clamped his fingers on it to make it look like he'd attacked you. And it would have been damned clever—if you'd used another hatchet."

"But I didn't kill him," groaned Griswell. "I have no intention of pleading self-defense."

"That's what puzzles me," Buckner admitted frankly, straightening. "What murderer would rig up such a crazy story as you've told me, to prove his innocence? Average killer would have told a logical yarn, at least. Hmmm! Blood drops leadin' from the door. The body was dragged—no, couldn't have been dragged. The floor isn't smeared. You must have carried it here, after killin' him in some other place. But in that case, why isn't there any blood on your clothes? Of course you could have changed clothes and washed your hands. But the fellow hasn't been dead long."

"He walked downstairs and across the room," said Griswell hopelessly. "He came to kill me. I knew he was coming to kill me when I saw him lurching down the stair. He struck where I would have been, if I hadn't awakened. That window—I burst out at it. You see it's broken."

"I see. But if he walked then, why isn't he walkin' now?"

"I don't know! I'm too sick to think straight. I've been fearing that he'd rise up from the floor where he lies and come at me again. When I heard that wolf running up the road after me, I thought it was John chasing me—John, running through the night with his bloody ax and his bloody head, and his death-grin!"

His teeth chattered as he lived that horror over again.

Buckner let his light play across the floor.

"The blood drops lead into the hall. Come on. We'll follow them."

Griswell cringed. "They lead upstairs."

Buckner's eyes were fixed hard on him.

"Are you afraid to go upstairs, with me?"

Griswell's face was gray.

"Yes. But I'm going, with you or without you. The thing that killed poor John may still be hiding up there."

"Stay behind me," ordered Buckner. "If anything jumps us, I'll take care of it. But for your own sake, I warn you that I shoot quicker than a cat jumps, and I don't often miss. If you've got any ideas of layin' me out from behind, forget them."

"Don't be a fool!" Resentment got the better of his apprehension, and this outburst seemed to reassure Buckner more than any of his protestations of innocence.

"I want to be fair," he said quietly. "I haven't indicted and condemned you in my mind already. If only half of what you're tellin' me is the truth, you've been through a hell of an experience, and I don't want to be too hard on you. But you can see how hard it is for me to believe all you've told me."

Griswell wearily motioned for him to lead the way, unspeaking. They went out into the hall, paused at the landing. A thin string of crimson drops, distinct in the thick dust, led up the steps.

"Man's tracks in the dust," grunted Buckner. "Go slow.

I've got to be sure of what I see, because we're obliteratin' them as we go up. Hmmm! One set goin' up, one comin' down. Same man. Not your tracks. Branner was a bigger man than you are. Blood drops all the way—blood on the bannisters like a man had laid his bloody hand there—a smear of stuff that looks—*brains*. Now what——"

"He walked down the stair, a dead man," shuddered Griswell. "Groping with one hand—the other gripping the hatchet that killed him."

"Or was carried," muttered the sheriff. "But if somebody carried him—*where are the tracks?*"

They came out into the upper hallway, a vast, empty space of dust and shadows where time-crusted windows repelled the moonlight and the ring of Buckner's torch seemed inadequate. Griswell trembled like a leaf. Here, in darkness and horror, John Branner had died.

"Somebody whistled up here," he muttered. "John came, as if he were being called."

Buckner's eyes were blazing strangely in the light.

"The footprints lead down the hall," he muttered. "Same as on the stair—one set going, one coming. Same prints— *Judas!*"

Behind him Griswell stifled a cry, for he had seen what prompted Buckner's exclamation. A few feet from the head of the stair Branner's footprints stopped abruptly, then returned, treading almost in the other tracks. And where the trail halted there was a great splash of blood on the dusty floor—and other tracks met it—tracks of bare feet, narrow but with splayed toes. They too receded in a second line from the spot.

Buckner bent over them, swearing.

"The tracks meet! And where they meet there's blood and brains on the floor! Branner must have been killed on that spot—with a blow from a hatchet. Bare feet coming out of the darkness to meet shod feet—then both turned away again; the shod feet went downstairs, the bare feet went back down the hall." He directed his light down the hall. The footprints faded into darkness, beyond the reach of the beam. On either hand the closed doors of chambers were cryptic portals of mystery.

"Suppose your crazy tale *was* true," Buckner muttered, half to himself. "These aren't your tracks. They look like a woman's. Suppose somebody did whistle, and Branner went upstairs to investigate. Suppose somebody met him here in the dark and split his head. The signs and tracks would have been, in that case, just as they really are. But if that's so, why isn't Branner lyin' here where he was killed? Could he have lived long enough to take the hatchet away from whoever killed him, and stagger downstairs with it?"

"No, no!" Recollection gagged Griswell. "I *saw* him on the stair. He was dead. No man could live a minute after receiving such a wound."

"I believe it," muttered Buckner. "But—it's madness! Or else it's *too* clever—yet, what sane man would think up and work out such an elaborate and utterly insane plan to escape punishment for murder, when a simple plea of self-defense would have been so much more effective? No court would recognize that story. Well, let's follow these other tracks. They lead down the hall—here, what's this?"

With an icy clutch at his soul, Griswell saw the light was beginning to grow dim.

"This battery is new," muttered Buckner, and for the first time Griswell caught an edge of fear in his voice. "Come on— out of here quick!"

The light had faded to a faint red glow. The darkness seemed straining into them, creeping with black cat-feet. Buckner retreated, pushing Griswell stumbling behind him as he walked backward, pistol cocked and lifted, down the dark hall. In the growing darkness Griswell heard what sounded like the stealthy opening of a door. And suddenly the blackness about them was vibrant with menace. Griswell knew Buckner sensed it as well as he, for the sheriff's hard body was tense and taut as a stalking panther's.

But without haste he worked his way to the stair and backed down it, Griswell preceding him, and fighting the panic that urged him to scream and burst into mad flight. A ghastly thought brought icy sweat out on his flesh. *Suppose the dead man were creeping up the stair behind them in the dark, face frozen in the death-grin, blood-caked hatchet lifted to strike?*

This possibility so overpowered him that he was scarcely aware when his feet struck the level of the lower hallway, and he was only then aware that the light had grown brighter as they descended, until it now gleamed with its full power—but when Buckner turned it back up the stairway, it failed to illuminate the darkness that hung like a tangible fog at the head of the stair.

"The damn thing was conjured," muttered Buckner. "Nothin' else. It couldn't act like that naturally."

"Turn the light into the room," begged Griswell. "See if John—if John is——"

He could not put the ghastly thought into words, but Buckner understood.

He swung the beam around, and Griswell had never dreamed that the sight of the gory body of a murdered man could bring such relief.

"He's still there," grunted Buckner. "If he walked after he was killed, he hasn't walked since. But that thing——"

Again he turned the light up the stair, and stood chewing his lip and scowling. Three times he half lifted his gun. Griswell read his mind. The sheriff was tempted to plunge back up that stair, take his chance with the unknown. But common sense held him back.

"I wouldn't have a chance in the dark," he muttered. "And I've got a hunch the light would go out again."

He turned and faced Griswell squarely.

"There's no use dodgin' the question. There's somethin' hellish in this house, and I believe I have an inklin' of what it is. I don't believe you killed Branner. Whatever killed him is up there—now. There's a lot about your yarn that don't sound sane; but there's nothin' sane about a flashlight goin' out like this one did. I don't believe that thing upstairs is human. I never met anything I was afraid to tackle in the dark before, but I'm not goin' up there until daylight. It's not long until dawn. We'll wait for it out there on that gallery."

The stars were already paling when they came out on the broad porch. Buckner seated himself on the balustrade, facing the door, his pistol dangling in his fingers. Griswell sat down near him and leaned back against a crumbling pillar. He shut his eyes, grateful for the faint breeze that seemed to cool his throbbing brain. He experienced a dull sense of unreality. He was a stranger in a strange land, a land that had become suddenly imbued with black horror. The shadow of the noose hovered above him, and in that dark house lay John Branner, with his butchered head—like the figments of a dream these facts spun and eddied in his brain until all merged in a gray twilight as sleep came uninvited to his weary soul.

He awoke to a cold white dawn and full memory of the horrors of the night. Mists curled about the stems of the pines, crawled in smoky wisps up the broken walk. Buckner was shaking him.

"Wake up! It's daylight."

Griswell rose, wincing at the stiffness of his limbs. His face was gray and old.

"I'm ready. Let's go upstairs."

"I've already been!" Buckner's eyes burned in the early dawn. "I didn't wake you up. I went as soon as it was light. I found nothin'."

"The tracks of the bare feet——"

"Gone!"

"Gone?"

"Yes, gone! The dust had been disturbed all over the hall, from the point where Branner's tracks ended; swept into corners. No chance of trackin' anything there now. Something obliterated those tracks while we sat here, and I didn't hear a sound. I've gone through the whole house. Not a sign of anything."

Griswell shuddered at the thought of himself sleeping alone on the porch while Buckner conducted his exploration.

"What shall we do?" he asked listlessly. "With those tracks gone there goes my only chance of proving my story."

"We'll take Branner's body into the county-seat," answered Buckner. "Let me do the talkin'. If the authorities knew the facts as they appear, they'd insist on you being confined and indicted. I don't believe you killed Branner—but neither a district attorney, judge nor jury would believe what you told me, or what happened to us last night. I'm handlin' this thing my own way. I'm not goin' to arrest you until I've exhausted every other possibility.

"Say nothin' about what's happened here, when we get to town. I'll simply tell the district attorney that John Branner was killed by a party or parties unknown, and that I'm workin' on the case.

"Are you game to come back with me to this house and spend the night here, sleepin' in that room as you and Branner slept last night?"

Griswell went white, but answered as stoutly as his ancestors might have expressed their determination to hold their cabins in the teeth of the Pequots: "I'll do it."

"Let's go then; help me pack the body out to your auto."

Griswell's soul revolted at the sight of John Branner's bloodless face in the chill white dawn, and the feel of his clammy flesh. The gray fog wrapped wispy tentacles about their feet as they carried their grisly burden across the lawn.

2. *The Snake's Brother*

Again the shadows were lengthening over the pinelands, and again two men came bumping along the old road in a car with a New England license plate.

Buckner was driving. Griswell's nerves were too shattered for him to trust himself at the wheel. He looked gaunt and haggard, and his face was still pallid. The strain of the day spent at the county-seat was added to the horror that still rode his soul like the shadow of a black-winged vulture. He had not slept, had not tasted what he had eaten.

"I told you I'd tell you about the Blassenvilles," said Buckner. "They were proud folks, haughty, and pretty damn ruthless when they wanted their way. They didn't treat their slaves as well as the other planters did—got their ideas in the West Indies, I reckon. There was a streak of cruelty in them—especially Miss Celia, the last one of the family to come to these parts. That was long after the slaves had been freed, but she used to whip her mulatto maid just like she was a slave, the old folks say. . . . The Negroes said when a Blassenville died, the devil was always waitin' for him out in the black pines.

"Well, after the Civil War they died off pretty fast, livin' in poverty on the plantation which was allowed to go to ruin.

Finally only four girls were left, sisters, livin' in the old house and ekin' out a bare livin', with a few blacks livin' in the old slave huts and workin' the fields on the share. They kept to themselves, bein' proud, and ashamed of their poverty. Folks wouldn't see them for months at a time. When they needed supplies they sent a Negro to town after them.

"But folks knew about it when Miss Celia came to live with them. She came from somewhere in the West Indies, where the whole family originally had its roots—a fine, handsome woman, they say, in the early thirties. But she didn't mix with folks any more than the girls did. She brought a mulatto maid with her, and the Blassenville cruelty cropped out in her treatment of this maid. I knew an old man years ago, who swore he saw Miss Celia tie this girl up to a tree, stark naked, and whip her with a horsewhip. Nobody was surprised when she disappeared. Everybody figured she'd run away, of course.

"Well, one day in the spring of 1890 Miss Elizabeth, the youngest girl, came in to town for the first time in maybe a year. She came after supplies. Said the blacks had all left the place. Talked a little more, too, a bit wild. Said Miss Celia had gone, without leaving any word. Said her sisters thought she'd gone back to the West Indies, but she believed her aunt *was still in the house.* She didn't say what she meant. Just got her supplies and pulled out for the Manor.

"A month went past, and a black came into town and said that Miss Elizabeth was livin' at the Manor alone. Said her three sisters weren't there any more, that they'd left one by one without givin' any word or explanation. She didn't know where they'd gone, and was afraid to stay there alone, but didn't know where else to go. She'd never known anything but the Manor, and had neither relatives nor friends. But she was in mortal terror of *something.* The black said she locked herself in her room at night and kept candles burnin' all night. . . .

"It was a stormy spring night when Miss Elizabeth came tearin' into town on the one horse she owned, nearly dead from fright. She fell from her horse in the square; when she could talk she said she'd found a secret room in the Manor that had been forgotten for a hundred years. And she said that there she found her three sisters, dead, and hangin' by their necks from the ceilin'. She said *something* chased her and nearly brained her with an ax as she ran out the front door, but somehow she got to the horse and got away. She was nearly crazy with fear, and didn't know what it was that chased her—said it looked like a woman with a yellow face.

"About a hundred men rode out there, right away. They searched the house from top to bottom, but they didn't find any secret room, or the remains of the sisters. But they did find a hatchet stickin' in the doorjamb downstairs, with some of Miss Elizabeth's hairs stuck on it, just as she'd said. She wouldn't go back there and show them how to find the secret door; almost went crazy when they suggested it.

"When she was able to travel, the people made up some money and loaned it to her—she was still too proud to accept charity—and she went to California. She never came back, but later it was learned, when she sent back to repay the money they'd loaned her, that she'd married out there.

"Nobody ever bought the house. It stood there just as she'd left it, and as the years passed folks stole all the furnishings out of it, poor white trash, I reckon. A Negro wouldn't go about it. But they came after sun-up and left long before sundown."

"What did the people think about Miss Elizabeth's story?" asked Griswell.

"Well, most folks thought she'd gone a little crazy, livin' in that old house alone. But some people believed that mulatto girl, Joan, didn't run away, after all. They believed she'd hidden in the woods, and glutted her hatred of the Blassenvilles by murderin' Miss Celia and the three girls. They beat up the woods with bloodhounds, but never found a trace of her. If there was a secret room in the house, she might have been hidin' there—if there was anything to that theory."

"She couldn't have been hiding there all these years," muttered Griswell. "Anyway, the thing in the house now isn't human."

Buckner wrenched the wheel around and turned into a dim trace that left the main road and meandered off through the pines.

"Where are you going?"

"There's an old Negro that lives off this way a few miles. I want to talk to him. We're up against something that takes more than white man's sense. The black people know more than we do about some things. This old man is nearly a hundred years old. His master educated him when he was a boy, and after he was freed he traveled more extensively than most white men do. They say he's a voodoo man."

Griswell shivered at the phrase, staring uneasily at the green forest walls that shut them in. The scent of the pines was mingled with the odors of unfamiliar plants and blossoms. But underlying all was a reek of rot and decay. Again a sick abhorrence of these dark mysterious woodlands almost overpowered him.

"Voodoo!" he muttered. "I'd forgotten about that—I never could think of black magic in connection with the South. To me witchcraft was always associated with old crooked streets in waterfront towns, overhung by gabled roofs that were old when they were hanging witches in Salem; dark musty alleys where black cats and other things might steal at night. Witchcraft always meant the old towns of New England, to me—but all this is more terrible than any New England legend—these somber pines, old deserted houses, lost plantations, mysterious black people, old tales of madness and horror—God, what frightful, ancient terrors there are on this continent fools call 'young'!"

"Here's old Jacob's hut," announced Buckner, bringing the automobile to a halt.

Griswell saw a clearing and a small cabin squatting under the shadows of the huge trees. The pines gave way to oaks and cypresses, bearded with gray trailing moss, and behind the cabin lay the edge of a swamp that ran away under the dimness of the trees, choked with rank vegetation. A thin wisp of blue smoke curled up from the stick-and-mud chimney.

He followed Buckner to the tiny stoop, where the sheriff pushed open the leather-hinged door and strode in. Griswell blinked in the comparative dimness of the interior. A single small window let in a little daylight. An old Negro crouched beside the hearth, watching a pot stew over the open fire. He looked up as they entered, but did not rise. He seemed incredibly old. His face was a mass of wrinkles, and his eyes, dark and vital, were filmed momentarily at times as if his mind wandered.

Buckner motioned Griswell to sit down in a string-bottomed chair, and himself took a rudely-made bench near the hearth, facing the old man.

"Jacob," he said bluntly, "the time's come for you to talk. I know you know the secret of Blassenville Manor. I've never questioned you about it, because it wasn't in my line. But a man was murdered there last night, and this man here may hang for it, unless you tell me what haunts that old house of the Blassenvilles."

The old man's eyes gleamed, then grew misty as if clouds of extreme age drifted across his brittle mind.

"The Blassenvilles," he murmured, and his voice was mellow and rich, his speech not the patois of the piny woods darky. "They were proud people, sirs—proud and cruel. Some died in the war, some were killed in duels—the menfolks, sirs. Some died in the Manor—the old Manor——" His voice trailed off into unintelligible mumblings.

"What of the Manor?" asked Buckner patiently.

"Miss Celia was the proudest of them all," the old man muttered. "The proudest and the cruelest. The black people hated her; Joan most of all. Joan had white blood in her, and she was proud, too. Miss Celia whipped her like a slave."

"What is the secret of Blassenville Manor?" persisted Buckner.

The film faded from the old man's eyes; they were dark as moonlit wells.

"What secret, sir? I do not understand."

"Yes, you do. For years that old house has stood there with its mystery. You know the key to its riddle."

The old man stirred the stew. He seemed perfectly rational now.

"Sir, life is sweet, even to an old black man."

"You mean somebody would kill you if you told me?"

But the old man was mumbling again, his eyes clouded.

"Not somebody. No human. No human being. The black gods of the swamps. My secret is inviolate, guarded by the Big Serpent, the god above all gods. He would send a little

brother to kiss me with his cold lips—a little brother with a
white crescent moon on his head. I sold my soul to the Big
Serpent when he made me maker of *zuvembies*——"

Buckner stiffened.

"I heard that word once before," he said softly, "from the
lips of a dying black man, when I was a child. What does it
mean?"

Fear filled the eyes of old Jacob.

"What have I said? No—no! I said nothing."

"Zuvembies," prompted Buckner.

"Zuvembies," mechanically repeated the old man, his eyes
vacant. "A *zuvembie* was once a woman—on the Slave Coast
they know of them. The drums that whisper by night in the
hills of Haiti tell of them. The makers of *zuvembies* are honored of the people of Damballah. It is death to speak of it to a
white man—it is one of the Snake God's forbidden secrets."

"You speak of the *zuvembies,*" said Buckner softly.

"I must not speak of it," mumbled the old man, and Griswell realized that he was thinking aloud, too far gone in his
dotage to be aware that he was speaking at all. "No white
man must know that I danced in the Black Ceremony of the
voodoo, and was made a maker of *zombies* and *zuvembies*. The
Big Snake punishes loose tongues with death."

"A *zuvembie* is a woman?" prompted Buckner.

"Was a woman," the old Negro muttered. *"She* knew I was
a maker of *zuvembies*—she came and stood in my hut and
asked for the awful brew—the brew of ground snake-bones,
and the blood of vampire bats, and the dew from a night-
hawk's wings, and other elements unnamable. She had
danced in the Black Ceremony—she was ripe to become a
zuvembie—the Black Brew was all that was needed—the
other was beautiful—I could not refuse her."

"Who?" demanded Buckner tensely, but the old man's head
was sunk on his withered breast, and he did not reply. He
seemed to slumber as he sat. Buckner shook him. "You gave a
brew to make a woman a *zuvembie*—what is a *zuvembie?*"

The old man stirred resentfully and muttered drowsily.

"A *zuvembie* is no longer human. It knows neither relatives
nor friends. It is one with the people of the Black World. It
commands the natural demons—owls, bats, snakes and were-

wolves, and can fetch darkness to blot out a little light. It can
be slain by lead or steel, but unless it is slain thus, it lives for
ever, and it eats no such food as humans eat. It dwells like a
bat in a cave or an old house. Time means naught to the
zuvembie; an hour, a day, a year, all is one. It cannot speak
human words, nor think as a human thinks, but it can hypno-
tize the living by the sound of its voice, and when it slays a
man, it can command his lifeless body until the flesh is cold.
As long as the blood flows, the corpse is its slave. Its pleasure
lies in the slaughter of human beings."

"And why should one become a *zuvembie?*" asked Buckner
softly.

"Hate," whispered the old man. "Hate! Revenge!"

"Was her name Joan?" murmured Buckner.

It was as if the name penetrated the fogs of senility that
clouded the voodoo-man's mind. He shook himself and the
film faded from his eyes, leaving them hard and gleaming as
wet black marble.

"Joan?" he said slowly. "I have not heard that name for the
span of a generation. I seem to have been sleeping, gentlemen; I do not remember—I ask your pardon. Old men fall
asleep before the fire, like old dogs. You asked me of Blassenville Manor? Sir, if I were to tell you why I cannot answer
you, you would deem it mere superstition. Yet the white
man's God be my witness——"

As he spoke he was reaching across the hearth for a piece
of firewood, groping among the heaps of sticks there. And his
voice broke in a scream, as he jerked back his arm convul-
sively. And a horrible, thrashing, trailing *thing* came with it.
Around the voodoo-man's arm a mottled length of that shape
was wrapped, and a wicked wedge-shaped head struck again
in silent fury.

The old man fell on the hearth, screaming, upsetting the
simmering pot and scattering the embers, and then Buckner
caught up a billet of firewood and crushed that flat head.
Cursing, he kicked aside the knotting, twisting trunk, glaring
briefly at the mangled head. Old Jacob had ceased screaming
and writhing; he lay still, staring glassily upward.

"Dead?" whispered Griswell.

"Dead as Judas Iscariot," snapped Buckner, frowning at

the twitching reptile. "That infernal snake crammed enough poison into his veins to kill a dozen men his age. But I think it was the shock and fright that killed him."

"What shall we do?" asked Griswell, shivering.

"Leave the body on that bunk. Nothin' can hurt it, if we bolt the door so the wild hogs can't get in, or any cat. We'll carry it into town tomorrow. We've got work to do tonight. Let's get goin'."

Griswell shrank from touching the corpse, but he helped Buckner lift it on the rude bunk, and then stumbled hastily out of the hut. The sun was hovering above the horizon, visible in dazzling red flame through the black stems of the trees.

They climbed into the car in silence, and went bumping back along the stumpy train.

"He said the Big Snake would send one of his brothers," muttered Griswell.

"Nonsense!" snorted Buckner. "Snakes like warmth, and that swamp is full of them. It crawled in and coiled up among that firewood. Old Jacob disturbed it, and it bit him. Nothin' supernatural about that." After a short silence he said, in a different voice, "That was the first time I ever saw a rattler strike without singin'; and the first time I ever saw a snake *with a white crescent moon on its head.*"

They were turning in to the main road before either spoke again.

"You think that the mulatto Joan has skulked in the house all these years?" Griswell asked.

"You heard what old Jacob said," answered Buckner grimly. "Time means nothin' to a *zuvembie.*"

As they made the last turn in the road, Griswell braced himself against the sight of Blassenville Manor looming black against the red sunset. When it came into view he bit his lip to keep from shrieking. The suggestion of cryptic horror came back in all its power.

"Look!" he whispered from dry lips as they came to a halt beside the road. Buckner grunted.

From the balustrades of the gallery rose a whirling cloud of pigeons that swept away into the sunset, black against the lurid glare. . . .

3. The Call of Zuvembie

Both men sat rigid for a few moments after the pigeons had flown.

"Well, I've seen them at last," muttered Buckner.

"Only the doomed see them perhaps," whispered Griswell. "That tramp saw them——"

"Well, we'll see," returned the Southerner tranquilly, as he climbed out of the car, but Griswell noticed him unconsciously hitch forward his scabbarded gun.

The oaken door sagged on broken hinges. Their feet echoed on the broken brick walk. The blind windows reflected the sunset in sheets of flame. As they came into the broad hall Griswell saw the string of black marks that ran across the floor and into the chamber, marking the path of a dead man.

Buckner had brought blankets out of the automobile. He spread them before the fireplace.

"I'll lie next to the door," he said. "You lie where you did last night."

"Shall we light a fire in the grate?" asked Griswell, dreading the thought of the blackness that would cloak the woods when the brief twilight had died.

"No. You've got a flashlight and so have I. We'll lie here in the dark and see what happens. Can you use that gun I gave you?"

"I suppose so. I never fired a revolver, but I know how it's done."

"Well, leave the shootin' to me, if possible." The sheriff seated himself cross-legged on his blankets and emptied the cylinder of his big blue Colt, inspecting each cartridge with a critical eye before he replaced it.

Griswell prowled nervously back and forth, begrudging the slow fading of the light as a miser begrudges the waning of his gold. He leaned with one hand against the mantelpiece, staring down into the dust-covered ashes. The fire that produced those ashes must have been built by Elizabeth Blassenville, more than forty years before. The thought was depressing. Idly he stirred the dusty ashes with his toe. Something came to view among the charred debris—a bit of paper, stained and yellowed. Still idly he bent and drew it out of the ashes. It was a note-book with moldering cardboard backs.

"What have you found?" asked Buckner, squinting down the gleaming barrel of his gun.

"Nothing but an old note-book. Looks like a diary. The pages are covered with writing—but the ink is so faded, and the paper is in such a state of decay that I can't tell much about it. How do you suppose it came in the fireplace, without being burned up?"

"Thrown in long after the fire was out," surmised Buckner. "Probably found and tossed in the fireplace by somebody who was in here stealin' furniture. Likely somebody who couldn't read."

Griswell fluttered the crumbling leaves listlessly, straining his eyes in the fading light over the yellowed scrawls. Then he stiffened.

"Here's an entry that's legible! Listen!" He read:

" 'I know someone is in the house besides myself. I can hear someone prowling about at night when the sun has set and the pines are black outside. Often in the night I hear *it* fumbling at my door. *Who* is it? Is it one of my sisters? Is it Aunt Celia? If it is either of these, why does she steal so subtly about the house? Why does she tug at my door, and glide away when I call to her? Shall I open the door and go out to her? No, no! I dare not! I am afraid. Oh God, what shall I do? I dare not stay here—but where am I to go?' "

"By God!" ejaculated Buckner. "That must be Elizabeth Blassenville's diary! Go on!"

"I can't make out the rest of the page," answered Griswell. "But a few pages further on I can make out some lines." He read:

" 'Why did the Negroes all run away when Aunt Celia disappeared? My sisters are dead. I know they are dead. I seem to sense that they died horribly, in fear and agony. But why? *Why?* If someone murdered Aunt Celia, why should that person murder my poor sisters? They were always kind to the black people. Joan——' " He paused, scowling futilely.

"A piece of the page is torn out. Here's another entry under another date—at least I judge it's a date; I can't make it out for sure.

" '——the awful thing that the old Negress hinted at? She named Jacob Blount, and Joan, but she would not speak plainly; perhaps she feared to——' Part of it gone here; then: 'No, no! How can it be? *She* is dead—or gone away. Yet—she was born and raised in the West Indies, and from hints she let fall in the past, I know she delved into the mysteries of the voodoo. I believe she even danced in one of their horrible ceremonies—how could she have been such a beast? And this —this horror. God, can such things be? I know not what to think. If it is *she* who roams the house at night, who fumbles at my door, who *whistles* so weirdly and sweetly—no, no, I must be going mad. If I stay here alone I shall die as hideously as my sisters must have died. Of that I am convinced.' "

The incoherent chronicle ended as abruptly as it had begun. Griswell was so engrossed in deciphering the scraps that he was not aware that darkness had stolen upon them, hardly aware that Buckner was holding his electric torch for him to read by. Waking from his abstraction he started and darted a quick glance at the black hallway.

"What do you make of it?"

"What I've suspected all the time," answered Buckner. "That mulatto maid Joan turned *zuvembie* to avenge herself on Miss Celia. Probably hated the whole family as much as she did her mistress. She'd taken part in voodoo ceremonies on her native island until she was 'ripe,' as old Jacob said. All she needed was the Black Brew—he supplied that. She killed Miss Celia and the three older girls, and would have gotten Elizabeth but for chance. She's been lurkin' in this old house all these years, like a snake in a ruin."

"But why should she murder a stranger?"

"You heard what old Jacob said," reminded Buckner. "A *zuvembie* finds satisfaction in the slaughter of humans. She called Branner up the stair and split his head and stuck the hatchet in his hand, and sent him downstairs to murder you. No court will ever believe that, but if we can produce her body, that will be evidence enough to prove your innocence.

My word will be taken, that she murdered Branner. Jacob
said a *zuvembie* could be killed . . . in reporting this affair I
don't have to be too accurate in detail."

"She came and peered over the balustrade of the stair at
us," muttered Griswell. "But why didn't we find her tracks on
the stair?"

"Maybe you dreamed it. Maybe a *zuvembie* can project her
spirit—hell! why try to rationalize something that's outside
the bounds of rationality? Let's begin our watch."

"Don't turn out the light!" exclaimed Griswell involuntarily. Then he added: "Of course. Turn it out. We must be in
the dark as"—he gagged a bit—"as Branner and I were."

But fear like a physical sickness assailed him when the
room was plunged in darkness. He lay trembling and his
heart beat so heavily he felt as if he would suffocate.

"The West Indies must be the plague spot of the world,"
muttered Buckner, a blur on his blankets. "I've heard of *zombies*. Never knew before what a *zuvembie* was. Evidently
some drug concocted by the voodoo-men to induce madness in
women. That doesn't explain the other things, though: the
hypnotic powers, the abnormal longevity, the ability to control corpses—no, a *zuvembie* can't be merely a mad-woman.
It's a monster, something more and less than a human being,
created by the magic that spawns in black swamps and jun-
gles—well, we'll see."

His voice ceased, and in the silence Griswell heard the
pounding of his own heart. Outside in the black woods a wolf
howled eerily, and owls hooted. Then silence fell again like a
black fog.

Griswell forced himself to lie still on his blankets. Time
seemed at a standstill. He felt as if he were choking. The
suspense was growing unendurable; the effort he made to
control his crumbling nerves bathed his limbs in sweat. He
clenched his teeth until his jaws ached and almost locked,
and the nails of his fingers bit deeply into his palms.

He did not know what he was expecting. The fiend would
strike again—but how? Would it be a horrible, sweet
whistling, bare feet stealing down the creaking steps, or a
sudden hatchet-stroke in the dark? Would it choose him or
Buckner? *Was Buckner already dead?* He could see nothing in

the blackness, but he heard the man's steady breathing. The Southerner must have nerves of steel. Or was that Buckner breathing beside him, separated by a narrow strip of darkness? Had the fiend already struck in silence, and taken the sheriff's place, there to lie in ghoulish glee until it was ready to strike?—a thousand hideous fancies assailed Griswell tooth and claw.

He began to feel that he would go mad if he did not leap to his feet, screaming, and burst frenziedly out of that accursed house—not even the fear of the gallows could keep him lying there in the darkness any longer—the rhythm of Buckner's breathing was suddenly broken, and Griswell felt as if a bucket of ice-water had been poured over him. From somewhere above them rose a sound of weird, sweet whistling. . . .

Griswell's control snapped, plunging his brain into darkness deeper than the physical blackness which engulfed him. There was a period of absolute blankness, in which a realization of *motion* was his first sensation of awakening consciousness. He was running, madly, stumbling over an incredibly rough road. All was darkness about him, and he ran blindly. Vaguely he realized that he must have bolted from the house, and fled for perhaps miles before his overwrought brain began to function. He did not care; dying on the gallows for a murder he never committed did not terrify him half as much as the thought of returning to that house of horror. He was overpowered by the urge to run—run—run as he was running now, blindly, until he reached the end of his endurance. The mist had not yet fully lifted from his brain, but he was aware of a dull wonder that he could not see the stars through the black branches. He wished vaguely that he could see where he was going. He believed he must be climbing a hill, and that was strange, for he knew there were no hills within miles of the Manor. Then above and ahead of him a dim glow began.

He scrambled toward it, over ledge-like projections that were more and more taking on a disquieting symmetry. Then he was horror-stricken to realize that a sound was impacting on his ears—*a weird mocking whistle.* The sound swept the mists away. Why, what was this? *Where was he?* Awakening and realization came like the stunning stroke of a butcher's maul. He was not fleeing along a road, or climbing a hill; he was mounting a stair. He was still in Blassenville Manor! *And he was climbing the stair!*

An inhuman scream burst from his lips. Above it the mad whistling rose in a ghoulish piping of demoniac triumph. He tried to stop—to turn back—even to fling himself over the balustrade. His shrieking rang unbearably in his own ears. But his will-power was shattered to bits. It did not exist. He had no will. He had dropped his flashlight, and he had forgotten the gun in his pocket. He could not command his own body. His legs, moving stiffly, worked like pieces of mechanism detached from his brain, obeying an outside will. Clumping methodically they carried him shrieking up the stair toward the witch-fire glow shimmering above him.

"Buckner!" he screamed. "Buckner! Help, for God's sake!"

His voice strangled in his throat. He had reached the upper landing. He was tottering down the hallway. The whistling sank and ceased, but its impulsion still drove him on. He could not see from what source the dim glow came. It seemed to emanate from no central focus. But he saw a vague figure shambling toward him. It looked like a woman, but no human woman ever walked with that skulking gait, and no human woman ever had that face of horror, that leering yellow blur of lunacy—he tried to scream at the sight of that face, at the glint of keen steel in the uplifted claw-like hand—but his tongue was frozen.

Then something crashed deafeningly behind him; the shadows were split by a tongue of flame which lit a hideous figure falling backward. Hard on the heels of the report rang an inhuman squawk.

In the darkness that followed the flash Griswell fell to his knees and covered his face with his hands. He did not hear Buckner's voice. The Southerner's hand on his shoulder shook him out of his swoon.

A light in his eyes blinded him. He blinked, shaded his eyes, looked up into Buckner's face, bending at the rim of the circle of light. The sheriff was pale.

"Are you hurt? God, man, are you hurt? There's a butcher knife there on the floor——"

"I'm not hurt," mumbled Griswell. "You fired just in time —the fiend! Where is it? Where did it go?"

"Listen!"

Somewhere in the house there sounded a sickening flopping and flapping as of something that thrashed and struggled in its death convulsions.

"Jacob was right," said Buckner grimly. "Lead can kill them. I hit her, all right. Didn't dare use my flashlight, but there was enough light. When that whistlin' started you almost walked over me gettin' out. I knew you were hypnotized, or whatever it is. I followed you up the stairs. I was right behind you, but crouchin' low so she wouldn't see me, and maybe get away again. I almost waited too long before I fired — but the sight of her almost paralyzed me. Look!"

He flashed his light down the hall, and now it shone bright and clear. And it shone on an aperture gaping in the wall where no door had showed before.

"The secret panel Miss Elizabeth found!" Buckner snapped. "Come on!"

He ran across the hallway and Griswell followed him dazedly. The flopping and thrashing came from beyond that mysterious door, and now the sounds had ceased.

The light revealed a narrow, tunnel-like corridor that evidently led through one of the thick walls. Buckner plunged into it without hesitation.

"Maybe it couldn't think like a human," he muttered, shining his light ahead of him. "But it had sense enough to erase its tracks last night so we couldn't trail it to that point in the wall and maybe find the secret panel. There's a room ahead— the secret room of the Blassenvilles!"

And Griswell cried out: "My God! It's the windowless chamber I saw in my dream, with the three bodies hanging— ahhhhh!"

Buckner's light playing about the circular chamber became suddenly motionless. In that wide ring of light three figures appeared, three dried, shriveled, mummy-like shapes, still clad in the moldering garments of the last century. Their slippers were clear of the floor as they hung by their withered necks from chains suspended from the ceiling.

"The three Blassenville sisters!" muttered Buckner. "Miss Elizabeth wasn't crazy, after all."

"Look!" Griswell could barely make his voice intelligible. "There—over there in the corner!"

The light moved, halted.

"Was that thing a woman once?" whispered Griswell. "God, look at that face, even in death. Look at those claw-like hands, with black talons like those of a beast. Yes, it was human, though—even the rags of an old ballroom gown. Why should a mulatto maid wear such a dress, I wonder?"

"This has been her lair for over forty years," muttered Buckner, brooding over the grinning grisly thing sprawling in the corner. "This clears you, Griswell—a crazy woman with a hatchet—that's all the authorities need to know. God, what a revenge!—what a foul revenge! Yet what a bestial nature she must have had, in the beginnin', to delve into voodoo as she must have done——"

"The mulatto woman?" whispered Griswell, dimly sensing a horror that overshadowed all the rest of the terror.

Buckner shook his head. "We misunderstood old Jacob's maunderin's, and the things Miss Elizabeth wrote—*she* must have known, but family pride sealed her lips. Griswell, I understand now; the mulatto woman had her revenge, but not as we'd supposed. She didn't drink the Black Brew old Jacob fixed for her. It was for somebody else, to be given secretly in her food, or coffee, no doubt. Then Joan ran away, leavin' the seeds of the hell she'd sowed to grow."

"That—that's not the mulatto woman?" whispered Griswell.

"When I saw her out there in the hallway I knew she was no mulatto. And those distorted features still reflect a family likeness. I've seen her portrait, and I can't be mistaken. There lies the creature that was once Celia Blassenville."

It

Theodore Sturgeon

In her novel Frankenstein; or, The Modern Prometheus
*(1818), Mary Shelley created the horror archetype that critic
James Twitchell has dubbed "the hulk without a name." Yet
it must be admitted that Shelley's monster was more pitiable
than frightening, less the victimizer than the victim. In "It"
(1940), Theodore Sturgeon took the bare bones of Shelley's
tale and used them to fashion a truly terrifying monster out of
immortal clay. Over fifty years after they were written, the
scenes in which the reader sees events from the monster's
point of view remain unsettling. Lacking the strong moral
orientation of* Frankenstein, *"It" is a powerful tale of ordinary
people forced to cope with an onslaught of the extraordinary.*

It walked in the woods.

It was never born. It existed. Under the pine needles the
fires burn, deep and smokeless in the mold. In heat and in
darkness and decay there is growth. There is life and there is
growth. It grew, but it was not alive. It walked unbreathing
through the woods, and thought and saw and was hideous
and strong, and it was not born and it did not live. It grew
and moved about without living.

It crawled out of the darkness and hot damp mold into the
cool of a morning. It was huge. It was lumped and crusted
with its own hateful substances, and pieces of it dropped off

as it went its way, dropped off and lay writhing, and stilled, and sank putrescent into the forest loam.

It had no mercy, no laughter, no beauty. It had strength and great intelligence. And—perhaps it could not be destroyed. It crawled out of its mound in the wood and lay pulsing in the sunlight for a long moment. Patches of it shone wetly in the golden glow, parts of it were nubbled and flaked. And whose dead bones had given it the form of a man?

It scrabbled painfully with its half-formed hands, beating the ground and the bole of a tree. It rolled and lifted itself up on its crumbling elbows, and it tore up a great handful of herbs and shredded them against its chest, and it paused and gazed at the gray-green juices with intelligent calm. It wavered to its feet, and seized a young sapling and destroyed it, folding the slender trunk back on itself again and again, watching attentively the useless, fibered splinters. And it squealed, snatching up a fear-frozen field-creature, crushing it slowly, letting blood and pulpy flesh and fur ooze from between its fingers, run down and rot on the forearms.

It began searching.

Kimbo drifted through the tall grasses like a puff of dust, his bushy tail curled tightly over his back and his long jaws agape. He ran with an easy lope, loving his freedom and the power of his flanks and furry shoulders. His tongue lolled listlessly over his lips. His lips were black and serrated, and each tiny pointed liplet swayed with his doggy gallop. Kimbo was all dog, all healthy animal.

He leaped high over a boulder and landed with a startled yelp as a long-eared cony shot from its hiding place under the rock. Kimbo hurtled after it, grunting with each great thrust of his legs. The rabbit bounced just ahead of him, keeping its distance, its ears flattened on its curving back and its little legs nibbling away at a distance hungrily. It stopped, and Kimbo pounced, and the rabbit shot away at a tangent and popped into a hollow log. Kimbo yelped again and rushed snuffling at the log, and knowing his failure, curvetted but once around the stump and ran on into the forest. The thing that watched from the wood raised its crusted arms and waited for Kimbo.

Kimbo sensed it there, standing dead-still by the path. To him it was a bulk which smelled of carrion not fit to roll in, and he snuffled distastefully and ran to pass it.

The thing let him come abreast and dropped a heavy twisted fist on him. Kimbo saw it coming and curled up tight as he ran, and the hand clipped stunningly on his rump, sending him rolling and yipping down the slope. Kimbo straddled to his feet, shook his head, shook his body with a deep growl, came back to the silent thing with green murder in his eyes. He walked stiffly, straight-legged, his tail as low as his lowered head and a ruff of fury round his neck. The thing raised its arms again, waited.

Kimbo slowed, then flipped himself through the air at the monster's throat. His jaws closed on it; his teeth clicked together through a mass of filth, and he fell choking and snarling at its feet. The thing leaned down and struck twice, and after the dog's back was broken, it sat beside him and began to tear him apart.

"Be back in an hour or so," said Alton Drew, picking up his rifle from the corner behind the wood box. His brother laughed.

"Old Kimbo 'bout runs your life, Alton," he said.

"Ah, I know the ol' devil," said Alton. "When I whistle for him for half an hour and he don't show up, he's in a jam or he's treed something wuth shootin' at. The ol' son of a gun calls me by not answerin'."

Cory Drew shoved a full glass of milk over to his nine-year-old daughter and smiled. "You think as much o' that houn'-dog o' yours as I do of Babe here."

Babe slid off her chair and ran to her uncle. "Gonna catch me the bad fella, Uncle Alton?" she shrilled. The "bad fella" was Cory's invention—the one who lurked in corners ready to pounce on little girls who chased the chickens and played around mowing machines and hurled green apples with a powerful young arm at the sides of the hogs, to hear the synchronized thud and grunt; little girls who swore with an Austrian accent like an ex-hired man they had had; who dug caves in haystacks till they tipped over, and kept pet crawfish in tomorrow's milk cans, and rode work horses to a lather in the night pasture.

"Get back here and keep away from Uncle Alton's gun!" said Cory. "If you see the bad fella, Alton, chase him back here. He has a date with Babe here for that stunt of hers last night." The preceding evening, Babe had kind-heartedly poured pepper on the cows' salt block.

"Don't worry, kiddo," grinned her uncle, "I'll bring you the bad fella's hide if he don't get me first."

Alton Drew walked up the path toward the wood, thinking about Babe. She was a phenomenon—a pampered farm child. Ah well—she had to be. They'd both loved Clissa Drew, and she'd married Cory, and they had to love Clissa's child. Funny thing, love. Alton was a man's man, and thought things out that way; and his reaction to love was a strong and frightened one. He knew what love was because he felt it still for his brother's wife and would feel it as long as he lived for Babe. It led him through his life, and yet he embarrassed himself by thinking of it. Loving a dog was an easy thing, because you and the old devil could love one another completely without talking about it. The smell of gun smoke and the smell of wet fur in the rain were perfume enough for Alton Drew, a grunt of satisfaction and the scream of something hunted and hit were poetry enough. They weren't like love for a human, that choked his throat so he could not say words he could not have thought of anyway. So Alton loved his dog Kimbo and his Winchester for all to see, and let his love for his brother's women, Clissa and Babe, eat at him quietly and unmentioned.

His quick eyes saw the fresh indentations in the soft earth behind the boulder, which showed where Kimbo had turned and leaped with a single surge, chasing the rabbit. Ignoring the tracks, he looked for the nearest place where a rabbit might hide, and strolled over to the stump. Kimbo had been there, he saw, and had been there too late. "You're an ol' fool," muttered Alton. "Y' can't catch a cony by chasin' it. You want to cross him up some way." He gave a peculiar trilling whistle, sure that Kimbo was digging frantically under some nearby stump for a rabbit that was three counties away by now. No answer. A little puzzled, Alton went back to the path. "He never done this before," he said softly. There was something about this he didn't like.

He cocked his .32-40 and cradled it. At the county fair someone had once said of Alton Drew that he could shoot at a handful of salt and pepper thrown in the air and hit only the pepper. Once he split a bullet on the blade of a knife and put two candles out. He had no need to fear anything that could be shot at. That's what he believed.

The thing in the woods looked curiously down at what it had done to Kimbo, and moaned the way Kimbo had before he died. It stood a minute storing away facts in its foul, unemotional mind. Blood was warm. The sunlight was warm. Things that moved and bore fur had a muscle to force the thick liquid through tiny tubes in their bodies. The liquid coagulated after a time. The liquid on rooted green things was thinner and the loss of a limb did not mean loss of life. It was very interesting, but the thing, the mold with a mind, was not pleased. Neither was it displeased. Its accidental urge was a thirst for knowledge, and it was only—interested.

It was growing late, and the sun reddened and rested awhile on the hilly horizon, teaching the clouds to be inverted flames. The thing threw up its head suddenly, noticing the dusk. Night was ever a strange thing, even for those of us who have known it in life. It would have been frightening for the monster had it been capable of fright, but it could only be curious; it could only reason from what it had observed.

What was happening? It was getting harder to see. Why? It threw its shapeless head from side to side. It was true— things were dim, and growing dimmer. Things were changing shape, taking on a new and darker color. What did the creatures it had crushed and torn apart see? How did they see? The larger one, the one that had attacked, had used two organs in its head. That must have been it, because after the thing had torn off two of the dog's legs it had struck at the hairy muzzle; and the dog, seeing the blow coming, had dropped folds of skin over the organs—closed its eyes. Ergo, the dog saw with its eyes. But then after the dog was dead, and its body still, repeated blows had had no effect on the eyes. They remained open and staring. The logical conclusion

was, then, that a being that had ceased to live and breathe
and move about lost the use of its eyes. It must be that to lose
sight was, conversely, to die. Dead things did not walk about.
They lay down and did not move. Therefore the thing in the
wood concluded that it must be dead, and so it lay down by
the path, not far away from Kimbo's scattered body, lay down
and believed itself dead.

Alton Drew came up through the dusk to the wood. He was
frankly worried. He whistled again, and then called, and
there was still no response, and he said again, "The ol' flea-
bus never done this before," and shook his heavy head. It was
past milking time, and Cory would need him. "Kimbo!" he
roared. The cry echoed through the shadows, and Alton
flipped on the safety catch of his rifle and put the butt on the
ground beside the path. Leaning on it, he took off his cap and
scratched the back of his head, wondering. The rifle butt sank
into what he thought was soft earth; he staggered and
stepped into the chest of the thing that lay beside the path.
His foot went up to the ankle in its yielding rottenness, and
he swore and jumped back.

"Whew! Sompn sure dead as hell there! Ugh!" He swabbed
at his boot with a handful of leaves while the monster lay in
the growing blackness with the edges of the deep footprint in
its chest sliding into it, filling it up. It lay there regarding
him dimly out of its muddy eyes, thinking it was dead because of the darkness, watching the articulation of Alton
Drew's joints, wondering at this new uncautious creature.

Alton cleaned the butt of his gun with more leaves and
went on up the path, whistling anxiously for Kimbo.

Clissa Drew stood in the door of the milk shed, very lovely
in red-checked gingham and a blue apron. Her hair was clean
yellow, parted in the middle and stretched tautly back to a
heavy braided knot. "Cory! Alton!" she called a little sharply.

"Well?" Cory responded gruffly from the barn, where he
was stripping off the Ayrshire. The dwindling streams of milk
plopped pleasantly into the froth of a full pail.

"I've called and called," said Clissa. "Supper's cold, and
Babe won't eat until you come. Why—where's Alton?"

Cory grunted, heaved the stool out of the way, threw over the stanchion lock and slapped the Ayrshire on the rump. The cow backed and filled like a towboat, clattered down the line and out into the barnyard. "Ain't back yet."

"Not back?" Clissa came in and stood beside him as he sat by the next cow, put his forehead against the warm flank. "But, Cory, he said he'd—"

"Yeh, yeh, I know. He said he'd be back fer the milkin'. I heard him. Well, he ain't."

"And you have to— Oh, Cory, I'll help you finish up. Alton would be back if he could. Maybe he's—"

"Maybe he's treed a blue jay," snapped her husband. "Him an' that damn dog." He gestured hugely with one hand while the other went on milking. "I got twenty-six head o' cows to milk. I got pigs to feed an' chickens to put to bed. I got to toss hay for the mare and turn the team out. I got harness to mend and a wire down in the night pasture. I got wood to split an' carry." He milked for a moment in silence, chewing on his lip. Clissa stood twisting her hands together, trying to think of something to stem the tide. It wasn't the first time Alton's hunting had interfered with the chores. "So I got to go ahead with it. I can't interfere with Alton's spoorin'. Every damn time that hound o' his smells out a squirrel I go without my supper. I'm gettin' sick an'—"

"Oh, I'll help you!" said Clissa. She was thinking of the spring, when Kimbo had held four hundred pounds of raging black bear at bay until Alton could put a bullet in its brain, the time Babe had found a bearcub and started to carry it home, and had fallen into a freshet, cutting her head. You can't hate a dog that has saved your child for you, she thought.

"You'll do nothin' of the kind!" Cory growled. "Get back to the house. You'll find work enough there. I'll be along when I can. Dammit, Clissa, don't cry! I didn't mean to— Oh, shucks!" He got up and put his arms around her. "I'm wrought up," he said. "Go on now. I'd no call to speak that way to you. I'm sorry. Go back to Babe. I'll put a stop to this for good tonight. I've had enough. There's work here for four farmers an' all we've got is me an' that . . . that huntsman. Go on now, Clissa."

"All right," she said into his shoulder. "But, Cory, hear him out first when he comes back. He might be unable to come back this time. Maybe he . . . he—"

"Ain't nothin' kin hurt my brother that a bullet will hit. He can take care of himself. He's got no excuse good enough this time. Go on, now. Make the kid eat."

Clissa went back to the house, her young face furrowed. If Cory quarreled with Alton now and drove him away, what with the drought and the creamery about to close and all, they just couldn't manage. Hiring a man was out of the question. Cory'd have to work himself to death, and he just wouldn't be able to make it. No one man could. She sighed and went into the house. It was seven o'clock, and the milking not done yet. Oh, why did Alton have to—

Babe was in bed at nine when Clissa heard Cory in the shed, slinging the wire cutters into a corner. "Alton back yet?" they both said at once as Cory stepped into the kitchen; and as she shook her head he clumped over to the stove, and lifting a lid, spat into the coals. "Come to bed," he said.

She lay down her stitching and looked at his broad back. He was twenty-eight, and he walked and acted like a man ten years older, and looked like a man five years younger. "I'll be up in a while," Clissa said.

Cory glanced at the corner behind the wood box where Alton's rifle usually stood, then made an unspellable, disgusted sound and sat down to take off his heavy muddy shoes.

"It's after nine," Clissa volunteered timidly. Cory said nothing, reaching for house slippers.

"Cory, you're not going to—"

"Not going to what?"

"Oh, nothing. I just thought that maybe Alton—"

"Alton!" Cory flared. "The dog goes hunting field mice. Alton goes hunting the dog. Now you want me to go hunting Alton. That's what you want?"

"I just— He was never this late before."

"I won't do it! Go out lookin' for him at nine o'clock in the night? I'll be damned! He has no call to use us so, Clissa."

Clissa said nothing. She went to the stove, peered into the wash boiler, set it aside at the back of the range. When she turned around, Cory had his shoes and coat on again.

"I knew you'd go," she said. Her voice smiled though she did not.

"I'll be back durned soon," said Cory. "I don't reckon he's strayed far. It is late. I ain't feared for him, but—" He broke his 12-gauge shotgun, looked through the barrels, slipped two shells in the breech and a box of them into his pocket. "Don't wait up," he said over his shoulder as he went out.

"I won't," Clissa replied to the closed door, and went back to her stitching by the lamp.

The path up the slope to the wood was very dark when Cory went up it, peering and calling. The air was chill and quiet, and a fetid odor of mold hung in it. Cory blew the taste of it out through impatient nostrils, drew it in again with the next breath, and swore. "Nonsense," he muttered. "Houn'-dog. Huntin', at ten in th' night, too. Alton!" he bellowed. "Alton Drew!" Echoes answered him, and he entered the wood. The huddled thing he passed in the dark heard him and felt the vibrations of his footsteps and did not move because it thought it was dead.

Cory strode on, looking around and ahead and not down since his feet knew the path.

"Alton!"

"That you, Cory?"

Cory Drew froze. That corner of the wood was thickly set and as dark as a burial vault. The voice he heard was choked, quiet, penetrating.

"Alton?"

"I found Kimbo, Cory."

"Where the hell have you been?" shouted Cory furiously. He disliked this pitch-blackness; he was afraid at the tense hopelessness of Alton's voice, and he mistrusted his ability to stay angry at his brother.

"I called him, Cory. I whistled at him, an' the ol' devil didn't answer."

"I can say the same for you, you . . . you louse. Why weren't you to milkin'? Where are you? You caught in a trap?"

"The houn' never missed answerin' me before, you know," said the tight, monotonous voice from the darkness.

"Alton! What the devil's the matter with you? What do I care if your mutt didn't answer? Where—"

"I guess because he ain't never died before," said Alton, refusing to be interrupted.

"You *what?*" Cory clicked his lips together twice and then said, "Alton, you turned crazy? What's that you say?"

"Kimbo's dead."

"Kim . . . oh! Oh!" Cory was seeing that picture again in his mind—Babe sprawled unconscious in the freshet, and Kimbo raging and snapping against a monster bear, holding her back until Alton could get there. "What happened, Alton?" he asked more quietly.

"I aim to find out. Someone tore him up."

"Tore him up?"

"There ain't a bit of him left tacked together, Cory. Every damn joint in his body tore apart. Guts out of him."

"Good God! Bear, you reckon?"

"No bear, nor nothin' on four legs. He's all here. None of him's been et. Whoever done it just killed him an'—tore him up."

"Good God!" Cory said again. "Who could've—" There was a long silence, then. "Come 'long home," he said almost gently. "There's no call for you to set up by him all night."

"I'll set. I aim to be here at sunup, an' I'm goin' to start trackin', an' I'm goin' to keep trackin' till I find the one done this job on Kimbo."

"You're drunk or crazy, Alton."

"I ain't drunk. You can think what you like about the rest of it. I'm stickin' here."

"We got a farm back yonder. Remember? I ain't going to milk twenty-six head o' cows again in the mornin' like I did jest now, Alton."

"Somebody's got to. I can't be there. I guess you'll just have to, Cory."

"You dirty scum!" Cory screamed. "You'll come back with me now or I'll know why!"

Alton's voice was still tight, half-sleepy. "Don't you come no nearer, Bud."

Cory kept moving toward Alton's voice.

"I said"—the voice was very quiet now—*"stop where you*

are." Cory kept coming. A sharp click told of the release of the .32-40's safety. Cory stopped.

"You got your gun on me, Alton?" Cory whispered.

"That's right, Bud. You ain't a-trompin' up these tracks for me. I need 'em at sun-up."

A full minute passed, and the only sound in the blackness was that of Cory's pained breathing. Finally:

"I got my gun, too, Alton. Come home."

"You can't see to shoot me."

"We're even on that."

"We ain't. I know just where you stand, Cory. I been here four hours."

"My gun scatters."

"My gun kills."

Without another word Cory Drew turned on his heel and stamped back to the farm.

Black and liquescent it lay in the blackness, not alive, not understanding death, believing itself dead. Things that were alive saw and moved about. Things that were not alive could do neither. It rested its muddy gaze on the line of trees at the crest of the rise, and deep within it thoughts trickled wetly. It lay huddled, dividing its new-found facts, dissecting them as it had dissected live things when there was light, comparing, concluding, pigeon-holing.

The trees at the top of the slope could just be seen, as their trunks were a fraction of a shade lighter than the dark sky behind them. At length they, too, disappeared, and for a moment sky and trees were a monotone. The thing knew it was dead now, and like many a being before it, it wondered how long it must stay like this. And then the sky beyond the trees grew a little lighter. That was a manifestly impossible occurrence, thought the thing, but it could see it and it must be so. Did dead things live again? That was curious. What about dismembered dead things? It would wait and see.

The sun came hand over hand up a beam of light. A bird somewhere made a high yawning peep, and as an owl killed a shrew, a skunk pounced on another, so that the night-shift deaths and those of day could go on without cessation. Two flowers nodded archly to each other, comparing their pretty clothes. A dragonfly nymph decided it was tired of looking serious and cracked its back open, to crawl out and dry gauzily. The first golden ray sheared down between the trees, through the grasses, passed over the mass in the shadowed bushes. "I am alive again," thought the thing that could not possibly live. "I am alive, for I see clearly." It stood up on its thick legs, up into the golden glow. In a little while the wet flakes that had grown during the night dried in the sun, and when it took its first steps, they cracked off and a little shower of them fell away. It walked up the slope to find Kimbo, to see if he, too, were alive again.

Babe let the sun come into her room by opening her eyes. Uncle Alton was gone—that was the first thing that ran through her head. Dad had come home last night and had shouted at mother for an hour. Alton was plumb crazy. He'd turned a gun on his own brother. If Alton ever came ten feet into Cory's land, Cory would fill him so full of holes he'd look like a tumbleweed. Alton was lazy, shiftless, selfish, and one or two other things of questionable taste but undoubted vividness. Babe knew her father. Uncle Alton would never be safe in this county.

She bounced out of bed in the enviable way of the very young, and ran to the window. Cory was trudging down to the night pasture with two bridles over his arm, to get the team. There were kitchen noises from downstairs.

Babe ducked her head in the washbowl and shook off the water like a terrier before she toweled. Trailing clean shirt and dungarees, she went to the head of the stairs, slid into the shirt, and began her morning ritual with the trousers. One step down was a step through the right leg. One more, and she was into the left. Then, bouncing step by step on both feet, buttoning one button per step, she reached the bottom fully dressed and ran into the kitchen.

"Didn't Uncle Alton come back a-tall, Mum?"

"Morning, Babe. No, dear." Clissa was too quiet, smiling too much, Babe thought shrewdly. Wasn't happy.

"Where'd he go, Mum?"

"We don't know, Babe. Sit down and eat your breakfast."

"What's a misbegotten, Mum?" the Babe asked suddenly.

Her mother nearly dropped the dish she was drying. "Babe! You must never say that again!"

"Oh. Well, why is Uncle Alton, then?"

"Why is he what?"

Babe's mouth muscled around an outsize spoonful of oatmeal. "A misbe—"

"Babe!"

"All right, Mum," said Babe with her mouth full. "Well, why?"

"I told Cory not to shout last night," Clissa said half to herself.

"Well, whatever it means, he isn't," said Babe with finality. "Did he go hunting again?"

"He went to look for Kimbo, darling."

"Kimbo? Oh Mummy, is Kimbo gone, too? Didn't he come back either?"

"No, dear. Oh, please, Babe, stop asking questions!"

"All right. Where do you think they went?"

"Into the north woods. Be quiet."

Babe gulped away at her breakfast. An idea struck her; and as she thought of it she ate slower and slower, and cast more and more glances at her mother from under the lashes of her tilted eyes. It would be awful if Daddy did anything to Uncle Alton. Someone ought to warn him.

Babe was halfway to the woods when Alton's .32-40 sent echoes giggling up and down the valley.

Cory was in the south thirty, riding a cultivator and cussing at the team of grays when he heard the gun. "Hoa," he called to the horses, and sat a moment to listen to the sound. "One-two-three. Four," he counted. "Saw someone, blasted away at him. Had a chance to take aim and give him another, careful. My God!" He threw up the cultivator points and steered the team into the shade of three oaks. He hobbled the gelding with swift tosses of a spare strap, and headed for the woods. "Alton a killer," he murmured, and doubled back to the house for his gun. Clissa was standing just outside the door.

"Get shells!" he snapped and flung into the house. Clissa

followed him. He was strapping his hunting knife on before she could get a box off the shelf. "Cory—"

"Hear that gun, did you? Alton's off his nut. He don't waste lead. He shot at someone just then, and he wasn't fixin' to shoot pa'tridges when I saw him last. He was out to get a man. Gimme my gun."

"Cory, Babe—"

"You keep her here. Oh, God, this is a helluva mess! I can't stand much more." Cory ran out the door.

Clissa caught his arm. "Cory, I'm trying to tell you. Babe isn't here. I've called, and she isn't here."

Cory's heavy, young-old face tautened. "Babe— Where did you last see her?"

"Breakfast." Clissa was crying now.

"She say where she was going?"

"No. She asked a lot of questions about Alton and where he'd gone."

"Did you say?"

Clissa's eyes widened, and she nodded, biting the back of her hand.

"You shouldn't ha' done that, Clissa," he gritted, and ran toward the woods. Clissa looked after him, and in that moment she could have killed herself.

Cory ran with his head up, straining with his legs and lungs and eyes at the long path. He puffed up the slope to the woods, agonized for breath after the forty-five minutes' heavy going. He couldn't even notice the damp smell of mold in the air.

He caught a movement in a thicket to his right, and dropped. Struggling to keep his breath, he crept forward until he could see clearly. There was something in there, all right. Something black, keeping still. Cory relaxed his legs and torso completely to make it easier for his heart to pump some strength back into them, and slowly raised the 12-gauge until it bore on the thing hidden in the thicket.

"Come out!" Cory said when he could speak.

Nothing happened.

"Come out or by God I'll shoot!" rasped Cory.

There was a long moment of silence, and his finger tightened on the trigger.

"You asked for it," he said, and as he fired the thing leaped sideways into the open, screaming.

It was a thin little man dressed in sepulchral black, and bearing the rosiest little baby-face Cory had ever seen. The face was twisted with fright and pain. The little man scrambled to his feet and hopped up and down saying over and over, "Oh, my hand! Don't shoot again! Oh, my hand! Don't shoot again!" He stopped after a bit, when Cory had climbed to his feet, and he regarded the farmer out of sad china-blue eyes. "You shot me," he said reproachfully, holding up a little bloody hand. "Oh, my goodness!"

Cory said, "Now, who the hell are you?"

The man immediately became hysterical, mouthing such a flood of broken sentences that Cory stepped back a pace and half-raised his gun in self-defense. It seemed to consist mostly of "I lost my papers," and "I didn't do it," and "It was horrible. Horrible. Horrible," and "The dead man," and "Oh, don't shoot again!"

Cory tried twice to ask him a question, and then he stepped over and knocked the man down. He lay on the ground writhing and moaning and blubbering and putting his bloody hand to his mouth where Cory had hit him.

The man rolled over and sat up. "I didn't do it!" he sobbed. "I didn't! I was walking along and I heard the gun and I heard some swearing and an awful scream and I went over there and peeped and I saw the dead man and I ran away and you came and I hid and you shot me and—"

"Shut up!" The man did, as if a switch had been thrown. "Now," said Cory, pointing along the path, "you say there's a dead man up there?"

The man nodded and began crying in earnest. Cory helped him up. "Follow this path back to my farmhouse," he said. "Tell my wife to fix up your hand. Don't tell her anything else. And wait there until I come. Hear?"

"Yes. Thank you. Oh, thank you. Snff."

"Go on now." Cory gave him a gentle shove in the right direction and went alone, in cold fear, up the path to the spot where he had found Alton the night before.

He found him here now, too, and Kimbo. Kimbo and Alton had spent several years together in the deepest friendship;

they had hunted and fought and slept together, and the lives
they owed each other were finished now. They were dead together.

It was terrible that they died the same way. Cory Drew was
a strong man, but he gasped and fainted dead away when he
saw what the thing of the mold had done to his brother and
his brother's dog.

The little man in black hurried down the path, whimpering
and holding his injured hand as if he rather wished he could
limp with it. After a while the whimper faded away, and the
hurried stride changed to a walk as the gibbering terror of
the last hour receded. He drew two deep breaths, said: "My
goodness!" and felt almost normal. He bound a linen handkerchief around his wrist, but the hand kept bleeding. He
tried the elbow, and that made it hurt. So he stuffed the
handkerchief back in his pocket and simply waved the hand
stupidly in the air until the blood clotted.

It wasn't much of a wound. Two of the balls of shot had
struck him, one passing through the fleshy part of his thumb
and the other scoring the side. As he thought of it, he became
a little proud that he had borne a gunshot wound. He strolled
along in the midmorning sunlight, feeling a dreamy commu-
nion with the boys at the front. "The whine of shot and
shell—" Where had he read that? Ah, what a story this would
make! "And there beside the"—what was the line?—"the em-
battled farmer stood." Didn't the awfulest things happen in
the nicest places? This was a nice forest. No screeches and
snakes and deep dark menaces. Not a story-book wood at all.
Shot by a gun. How exciting! He was now—he strutted—a
gentleman adventurer. He did not see the great moist horror
that clumped along behind him, though his nostrils crinkled
a little with its foulness.

The monster had three little holes close together on its
chest, and one little hole in the middle of its slimy forehead.
It had three close-set pits in its back and one on the back of
its head. These marks were where Alton Drew's bullets had
struck and passed through. Half of the monster's shapeless
face was sloughed away, and there was a deep indentation on
its shoulder. This was what Alton Drew's gun butt had done

after he clubbed it and struck at the thing that would not lie down after he put his four bullets through it. When these things happened the monster was not hurt or angry. It only wondered why Alton Drew acted that way. Now it followed the little man without hurrying at all, matching his stride step by step and dropping little particles of muck behind it.

The little man went on out of the wood and stood with his back against a big tree at the forest's edge, and he thought. Enough had happened to him here. What good would it do to stay and face a horrible murder inquest, just to continue this silly, vague quest? There was supposed to be the ruin of an old, old hunting lodge deep in this wood somewhere, and perhaps it would hold the evidence he wanted. But it was a vague report—vague enough to be forgotten without regret. It would be the height of foolishness to stay for all the hick-town red tape that would follow that ghastly affair back in the wood. Ergo, it would be ridiculous to follow that farmer's advice, to go to his house and wait for him. He would go back to town.

The monster was leaning against the other side of the big tree.

The little man snuffled disgustedly at a sudden overpowering odor of rot. He reached for his handkerchief, fumbled and dropped it. As he bent to pick it up, the monster's arm *whuffed* heavily in the air where his head had been—a blow that would certainly have removed that baby-faced protuberance. The man stood up and would have put the handkerchief to his nose had it not been so bloody. The creature behind the tree lifted its arms again just as the little man tossed the handkerchief away and stepped out into the field, heading across country to the distant highway that would take him back to town. The monster pounced on the handkerchief, picked it up, studied it, tore it across several times and inspected the tattered edges. Then it gazed vacantly at the disappearing figure of the little man, and finding him no longer interesting, turned back into the woods.

Babe broke into a trot at the sound of the shots. It was important to warn Uncle Alton about what her father had said, but it was more interesting to find out what he had bagged. Oh, he'd bagged it, all right. Uncle Alton never fired without killing. This was about the first time she had ever heard him blast away like that. Must be a bear, she thought excitedly, tripping over a root, sprawling, rolling to her feet again, without noticing the tumble. She'd love to have another bearskin in her room. Where would she put it? Maybe they could line it and she could have it for a blanket. Uncle Alton could sit on it and read to her in the evening— Oh, no. No. Not with this trouble between him and Dad. Oh, if she could only do something! She tried to run faster, worried and anticipating, but she was out of breath and went more slowly instead.

At the top of the rise by the edge of the woods she stopped and looked back. Far down in the valley lay the south thirty. She scanned it carefully, looking for her father. The new furrows and the old were sharply defined, and her keen eyes saw immediately that Cory had left the line with the cultivator and had angled the team over to the shade trees without finishing his row. That wasn't like him. She could see the team now, and Cory's pale-blue denim was not in sight.

A little nearer was the house; and as her gaze fell on it she moved out of the cleared pathway. Her father was coming; she had seen his shotgun and he was running. He could really cover ground when he wanted to. He must be chasing her, she thought immediately. He'd guessed that she would run toward the sound of the shots, and he was going to follow her tracks to Uncle Alton and shoot him. She knew that he was as good a woodsman as Alton; he would most certainly see her tracks. Well, she'd fix him.

She ran along the edge of the wood, being careful to dig her heels deeply into the loam. A hundred yards of this, and she angled into the forest and ran until she reached a particularly thick grove of trees. Shinnying up like a squirrel, she squirmed from one close-set tree to another until she could go no farther back toward the path, then dropped lightly to the ground and crept on her way, now stepping very gently. It would take him an hour to beat around for her trail, she thought proudly, and by that time she could easily get to Uncle Alton. She giggled to herself as she thought of the way she had fooled her father. And the little sound of laughter drowned out, for her, the sound of Alton's hoarse dying scream.

She reached and crossed the path and slid through the brush beside it. The shots came from up around here somewhere. She stopped and listened several times, and then suddenly heard something coming toward her, fast. She ducked under cover, terrified, and a little baby-faced man in black, his blue eyes wide with horror, crashed blindly past her, the leather case he carried catching on the branches. It spun a moment and then fell right in front of her. The man never missed it.

Babe lay there for a long moment and then picked up the case and faded into the woods. Things were happening too fast for her. She wanted Uncle Alton, but she dared not call. She stopped again and strained her ears. Back toward the edge of the wood she heard her father's voice, and another's—probably the man who had dropped the brief case. She dared not go over there. Filled with enjoyable terror, she thought hard, then snapped her fingers in triumph. She and Alton had played Injun many times up here; they had a whole repertoire of secret signals. She had practiced birdcalls until she knew them better than the birds themselves. What would it be? Ah—blue jay. She threw back her head and by some youthful alchemy produced a nerve-shattering screech that would have done justice to any jay that ever flew. She repeated it, and then twice more.

The response was immediate—the call of a blue jay, four times, spaced two and two. Babe nodded to herself happily. That was the signal that they were to meet immediately at The Place. The Place was a hide-out that he had discovered and shared with her, and not another soul knew of it; an angle of rock beside a stream not far away. It wasn't exactly a cave, but almost. Enough so to be entrancing. Babe trotted happily away toward the brook. She had just known that Uncle Alton would remember the call of the blue jay, and what it meant.

In the tree that arched over Alton's scattered body perched a large jay bird, preening itself and shining in the sun. Quite unconscious of the presence of death, hardly noticing the

Babe's realistic cry, it screamed again four times, two and two.

It took Cory more than a moment to recover himself from what he had seen. He turned away from it and leaned weakly against a pine, panting. Alton. That was Alton lying there, in —parts.

"God! God, God, God—"

Gradually his strength returned, and he forced himself to turn again. Stepping carefully, he bent and picked up the .32-40. Its barrel was bright and clean, but the butt and stock were smeared with some kind of stinking rottenness. Where had he seen the stuff before? Somewhere—no matter. He cleaned it off absently, throwing the befouled bandanna away afterward. Through his mind ran Alton's words—was that only last night? —*"I'm goin' to start trackin'. An' I'm goin' to keep trackin' till I find the one done this job on Kimbo."*

Cory searched shrinkingly until he found Alton's box of shells. The box was wet and sticky. That made it—better, somehow. A bullet wet with Alton's blood was the right thing to use. He went away a short distance, circled around till he found heavy footprints, then came back.

"I'm a-trackin' for you, Bud," he whispered thickly, and began. Through the brush he followed its wavering spoor, amazed at the amount of filthy mold about, gradually associating it with the thing that had killed his brother. There was nothing in the world for him any more but hate and doggedness. Cursing himself for not getting Alton home last night, he followed the tracks to the edge of the woods. They led him to a big tree there, and there he saw something else—the footprints of the little city man. Nearby lay some tattered scraps of linen, and—what was that?

Another set of prints—small ones. Small, stub-toed ones. Babe's.

"Babe!" Cory screamed. "Babe!"

No answer. The wind sighed. Somewhere a blue jay called.

Babe stopped and turned when she heard her father's voice, faint with distance, piercing.

"Listen at him holler," she crooned delightedly. "Gee, he

sounds mad." She sent a jay bird's call disrespectfully back to him and hurried to The Place.

It consisted of a mammoth boulder beside the brook. Some upheaval in the glacial age had cleft it, cutting out a huge V-shaped chunk. The widest part of the cleft was at the water's edge, and the narrowest was hidden by bushes. It made a little ceilingless room, rough and uneven and full of pot-holes and cavelets inside, and yet with quite a level floor. The open end was at the water's edge.

Babe parted the bushes and peered down the cleft.

"Uncle Alton!" she called softly. There was no answer. Oh, well, he'd be along. She scrambled in and slid down to the floor.

She loved it here. It was shaded and cool, and the chattering little stream filled it with shifting golden lights and laughing gurgles. She called again, on principle, and then perched on an outcropping to wait. It was only then she realized that she still carried the little man's brief case.

She turned it over a couple of times and then opened it. It was divided in the middle by a leather wall. On one side were a few papers in a large yellow envelope, and on the other some sandwiches, a candy bar, and an apple. With a youngster's complacent acceptance of manna from heaven, Babe fell to. She saved one sandwich for Alton, mainly because she didn't like its highly spiced bologna. The rest made quite a feast.

She was a little worried when Alton hadn't arrived, even after she had consumed the apple core. She got up and tried to skim some flat pebbles across the roiling brook, and she stood on her hands, and she tried to think of a story to tell herself, and she tried just waiting. Finally, in desperation, she turned again to the brief case, took out the papers, curled up by the rocky wall and began to read them. It was something to do, anyway.

There was an old newspaper clipping that told about strange wills that people had left. An old lady had once left a lot of money to whoever would make the trip from the Earth to the Moon and back. Another had financed a home for cats whose masters and mistresses had died. A man left thousands of dollars to the first man who could solve a certain mathematical problem and prove his solution. But one item was blue-penciled. It was:

One of the strangest of wills still in force is that of Thaddeus M. Kirk, who died in 1920. It appears that he built an elaborate mausoleum with burial vaults for all the remains of his family. He collected and removed caskets from all over the country to fill the designated niches. Kirk was the last of his line; there were no relatives when he died. His will stated that the mausoleum was to be kept in repair permanently, and that a certain sum was to be set aside as a reward for whoever could produce the body of his grandfather, Roger Kirk, whose niche is still empty. Anyone finding this body is eligible to receive a substantial fortune.

Babe yawned vaguely over this, but kept on reading because there was nothing else to do. Next was a thick sheet of business correspondence, bearing the letterhead of a firm of lawyers. The body of it ran:

In regard to your query regarding the will of Thaddeus Kirk, we are authorized to state that his grandfather was a man about five feet, five inches, whose left arm had been broken and who had a triangular silver plate set into his skull. There is no information as to the whereabouts of his death. He disappeared and was declared legally dead after the lapse of fourteen years.

The amount of the reward as stated in the will, plus accrued interest, now amounts to a fraction over sixty-two thousand dollars. This will be paid to anyone who produces the remains, providing that said remains answer descriptions kept in our private files.

There was more, but Babe was bored. She went on to the little black notebook. There was nothing in it but penciled and highly abbreviated records of visits to libraries; quotations from books with titles like *History of Angelina and Tyler Counties* and *Kirk Family History*. Babe threw that aside, too. Where could Uncle Alton be?

She began to sing tunelessly, "Tumalumalum tum, ta ta ta," pretending to dance a minuet with flowing skirts like a girl she had seen in the movies. A rustle of the bushes at the entrance to The Place stopped her. She peeped upward, saw them being thrust aside. Quickly she ran to a tiny cul-de-sac in the rock wall, just big enough for her to hide in. She giggled at the thought of how surprised Uncle Alton would be when she jumped out at him.

She heard the newcomer come shuffling down the steep slope of the crevice and land heavily on the floor. There was something about the sound—what was it? It occurred to her that though it was a hard job for a big man like Uncle Alton to get through the little opening in the bushes, she could hear no heavy breathing. She heard no breathing at all!

Babe peeped out into the main cave and squealed in utmost horror. Standing there was, not Uncle Alton, but a massive caricature of a man: a huge thing like an irregular mud doll, clumsily made. It quivered and parts of it glistened and parts of it were dried and crumbly. Half of the lower left part of its face was gone, giving it a lopsided look. It had no perceptible mouth or nose, and its eyes were crooked, one higher than the other, both a dingy brown with no whites at all. It stood quite still looking at her, its only movement a steady unalive quivering of its body.

It wondered about the queer little noise Babe had made.

Babe crept far back against a little pocket of stone, her brain running round and round in tiny circles of agony. She opened her mouth to cry out, and could not. Her eyes bulged and her face flamed with the strangling effort, and the two golden ropes of her braided hair twitched and twitched as she hunted hopelessly for a way out. If only she were out in the open—or in the wedge-shaped half-cave where the thing was —or home in bed!

The thing clumped toward her, expressionless, moving with a slow inevitability that was the sheer crux of horror. Babe lay wide-eyed and frozen, mounting pressure of terror stilling her lungs, making her heart shake the whole world. The monster came to the mouth of the little pocket, tried to walk to her and was stopped by the sides. It was such a narrow little fissure; and it was all Babe could do to get in. The thing from the wood stood straining against the rock at its shoulders, pressing harder and harder to get to Babe. She sat up slowly, so near to the thing that its odor was almost thick enough to see, and a wild hope burst through her voiceless fear. It couldn't get in! It couldn't get in because it was too big!

The substance of its feet spread slowly under the tremendous strain, and at its shoulder appeared a slight crack. It widened as the monster unfeelingly crushed itself against the rock, and suddenly a large piece of the shoulder came away and the being twisted slushily three feet farther in. It lay quietly with its muddy eyes fixed on her, and then brought one thick arm up over its head and reached.

Babe scrambled in the inch farther she had believed impossible, and the filthy clubbed hand stroked down her back, leaving a trail of muck on the blue denim of the shirt she wore. The monster surged suddenly and, lying full length now, gained the last precious inch. A black hand seized one of her braids, and for Babe the lights went out.

When she came to, she was dangling by her hair from that same crusted paw. The thing held her high, so that her face and its featureless head were not more than a foot apart. It gazed at her with a mild curiosity in its eyes, and it swung her slowly back and forth. The agony of her pulled hair did what fear could not do—gave her a voice. She screamed. She opened her mouth and puffed up her powerful young lungs, and she sounded off. She held her throat in the position of the first scream, and her chest labored and pumped more air through the frozen throat. Shrill and monotonous and infinitely piercing, her screams.

The thing did not mind. It held her as she was, and watched. When it had learned all it could from this phenomenon, it dropped her jarringly, and looked around the half-cave, ignoring the stunned and huddled Babe. It reached over and picked up the leather brief case and tore it twice across as if it were tissue. It saw the sandwich Babe had left, picked it up, crushed it, dropped it.

Babe opened her eyes, saw that she was free, and just as the thing turned back to her she dove between its legs and out into the shallow pool in front of the rock, paddled across and hit the other bank screaming. A vicious little light of fury burned in her; she picked up a grapefruit-sized stone and hurled it with all her frenzied might. It flew low and fast, and struck squashily on the monster's ankle. The thing was just taking a step toward the water; the stone caught it off balance, and its unpracticed equilibrium could not save it. It tottered for a long, silent moment at the edge and then splashed into the stream. Without a second look Babe ran shrieking away.

Cory Drew was following the little gobs of mold that somehow indicated the path of the murderer, and he was nearby when he first heard her scream. He broke into a run, dropping his shotgun and holding the .32-40 ready to fire. He ran with such deadly panic in his heart that he ran right past the huge cleft rock and was a hundred yards past it before she burst out through the pool and ran up the bank. He had to run hard and fast to catch her, because anything behind her was that faceless horror in the cave, and she was living for the one idea of getting away from there. He caught her in his arms and swung her to him, and she screamed on and on and on.

Babe didn't see Cory at all, even when he held her and quieted her.

The monster lay in the water. It neither liked nor disliked the new element. It rested on the bottom, its massive head a foot beneath the surface, and it curiously considered the facts that it had garnered. There was the little humming noise of Babe's voice that sent the monster questing into the cave. There was the black material of the brief case that resisted so much more than green things when he tore it. There was the little two-legged one who sang and brought him near, and who screamed when he came. There was this new cold moving thing he had fallen into. It was washing his body away. That had never happened before. That was interesting. The monster decided to stay and observe this new thing. It felt no urge to save itself; it could only be curious.

The brook came laughing down out of its spring, ran down from its source beckoning to the sunbeams and embracing freshets and helpful brooklets. It shouted and played with streaming little roots, and nudged the minnows and pollywogs about in its tiny backwaters. It was a happy brook. When it came to the pool by the cloven rock it found the monster there, and plucked at it. It soaked the foul substances and smoothed and melted the molds, and the waters

below the thing eddied darkly with its diluted matter. It was
a thorough brook. It washed all it touched, persistently.
Where it found filth, it removed filth; and if there were layer
on layer of foulness, then layer by foul layer it was removed.
It was a good brook. It did not mind the poison of the monster, but took it up and thinned it and spread it in little rings
around rocks downstream, and let it drift to the rootlets of
water plants, that they might grow greener and lovelier. And
the monster melted.

"I am smaller," the thing thought. "That is interesting. I
could not move now. And now this part of me which thinks is
going, too. It will stop in just a moment, and drift away with
the rest of the body. It will stop thinking and I will stop being,
and that, too, is a very interesting thing."

So the monster melted and dirtied the water, and the water
was clean again, washing and washing the skeleton that the
monster had left. It was not very big, and there was a badly
healed knot on the left arm. The sunlight flickered on the
triangular silver plate set into the pale skull, and the skeleton was very clean now. The brook laughed about it for an
age.

They found the skeleton, six grim-lipped men who came to
find a killer. No one had believed Babe, when she told her
story days later. It had to be days later because Babe had
screamed for seven hours without stopping, and had lain like
a dead child for a day. No one believed her at all, because her
story was all about the bad fella, and they knew that the bad
fella was simply a thing that her father had made up to
frighten her with. But it was through her that the skeleton
was found, and so the men at the bank sent a check to the
Drews for more money than they had ever dreamed about. It
was old Roger Kirk, sure enough, that skeleton, though it was
found five miles from where he had died and sank into the
forest floor where the hot molds built around his skeleton and
emerged—a monster.

So the Drews had a new barn and fine new livestock and
they hired four men. But they didn't have Alton. And they
didn't have Kimbo. And Babe screams at night and has
grown very thin.

Smoke Ghost

Fritz Leiber

Although horror is an endlessly imaginative fiction, most of its conventional monsters remain static, assuming the same guises and behaviors today as they did when first set down on paper centuries before. Recognizing that most horror figures of the past were totally irrelevant to the reality of the modern world, editor John W. Campbell encouraged writers for his magazine Unknown Worlds *to create horror fiction that addressed itself directly to the concerns of post-Depression America. Fritz Leiber responded in 1941 with "Smoke Ghost," a tale that reconceives one of the hoariest figures in all supernatural literature for the modern industrial cityscape. Though Leiber's story is often lumped with Theodore Sturgeon's "It" as an example of the renovation of classic horror themes that went on in the pages of* Unknown Worlds, *it has since been recognized as the tale that gave rise to the subgenre of contemporary urban horror.*

Miss Millick wondered just what had happened to Mr. Wran. He kept making the strangest remarks when she took dictation. Just this morning he had quickly turned around and asked, "Have you ever seen a ghost, Miss Millick?" And she had tittered nervously and replied, "When I was a girl there was a thing in white that used to come out of the closet in the attic bedroom when I slept there, and moan. Of course it was just my imagination. I was frightened of lots of things." And he had said, "I don't mean that kind of ghost. I mean a ghost

from the world today, with the soot of the factories on its face
and the pounding of machinery in its soul. The kind that
would haunt coal yards and slip around at night through deserted office buildings like this one. A real ghost. Not something out of books." And she hadn't known what to say.

He'd never been like this before. Of course he might be
joking, but it didn't sound that way. Vaguely Miss Millick
wondered whether he mightn't be seeking some sort of sympathy from her. Of course, Mr. Wran was married and had a
little child, but that didn't prevent her from having
daydreams. The daydreams were not very exciting, still they
helped fill up her mind. But now he was asking her another of
those unprecedented questions.

"Have you ever thought what a ghost of our times would
look like, Miss Millick? Just picture it. A smoky composite
face with the hungry anxiety of the unemployed, the neurotic
restlessness of the person without purpose, the jerky tension
of the high-pressure metropolitan worker, the uneasy resentment of the striker, the callous opportunism of the scab, the
aggressive whine of the panhandler, the inhibited terror of
the bombed civilian, and a thousand other twisted emotional
patterns. Each one overlying and yet blending with the other,
like a pile of semitransparent masks?"

Miss Millick gave a little self-conscious shiver and said,
"That would be terrible. What an awful thing to think of."

She peered furtively across the desk. She remembered having heard that there had been something impressively abnormal about Mr. Wran's childhood, but she couldn't recall what
it was. If only she could do something—laugh at his mood or
ask him what was really wrong. She shifted the extra pencils
in her left hand and mechanically traced over some of the
shorthand curlicues in her notebook.

"Yet, that's just what such a ghost or vitalized projection
would look like, Miss Millick," he continued, smiling in a
tight way. "It would grow out of the real world. It would
reflect the tangled, sordid, vicious things. All the loose ends.
And it would be very grimy. I don't think it would seem white
or wispy, or favor graveyards. It wouldn't moan. But it would
mutter unintelligibly, and twitch at your sleeve. Like a sick,
surly ape. What would such a thing want from a person, Miss

Millick? Sacrifice? Worship? Or just fear? What could you do
to stop it from troubling you?"

Miss Millick giggled nervously. There was an expression
beyond her powers of definition in Mr. Wran's ordinary, flat-
cheeked, thirtyish face, silhouetted against the dusty window. He turned away and stared out into the gray downtown
atmosphere that rolled in from the railroad yards and the
mills. When he spoke again his voice sounded far away.

"Of course, being immaterial, it couldn't hurt you physically—at first. You'd have to be peculiarly sensitive to see it,
or be aware of it at all. But it would begin to influence your
actions. Make you do this. Stop you from doing that. Although only a projection, it would gradually get its hooks into
the world of things as they are. Might even get control of
suitably vacuous minds. Then it could hurt whomever it
wanted."

Miss Millick squirmed and read back her shorthand, like
the books said you should do when there was a pause. She
became aware of the failing light and wished Mr. Wran would
ask her to turn on the overhead. She felt scratchy, as if soot
were sifting down on to her skin.

"It's a rotten world, Miss Millick," said Mr. Wran, talking
at the window. "Fit for another morbid growth of superstition. It's time the ghosts, or whatever you call them, took
over and began a rule of fear. They'd be no worse than men."

"But"—Miss Millick's diaphragm jerked, making her titter
inanely—"of course, there aren't any such things as ghosts."

Mr. Wran turned around.

"Of course there aren't, Miss Millick," he said in a loud,
patronizing voice, as if she had been doing the talking rather
than he. "Science and common sense and psychiatry all go to
prove it."

She hung her head and might even have blushed if she
hadn't felt so all at sea. Her leg muscles twitched, making her
stand up, although she hadn't intended to. She aimlessly
rubbed her hand along the edge of the desk.

"Why, Mr. Wran, look what I got off your desk," she said,
showing him a heavy smudge. There was a note of clumsily
playful reproof in her voice. "No wonder the copy I bring you

always gets so black. Somebody ought to talk to those
scrubwomen. They're skimping on your room."

She wished he would make some normal joking reply. But
instead he drew back and his face hardened.

"Well, to get back," he rapped out harshly, and began to
dictate.

When she was gone, he jumped up, dabbed his finger exper-
imentally at the smudged part of the desk, frowned worriedly
at the almost inky smears. He jerked open a drawer,
snatched out a rag, hastily swabbed off the desk, crumpled
the rag into a ball and tossed it back. There were three or
four other rags in the drawer, each impregnated with soot.

Then he went over to the window and peered out anxiously
through the dusk, his eyes searching the panorama of roofs,
fixing on each chimney and water tank.

"It's a neurosis. Must be. Compulsions. Hallucinations," he
muttered to himself in a tired, distraught voice that would
have made Miss Millick gasp. "It's that damned mental abnormality cropping up in a new form. Can't be any other
explanation. But it's so damned real. Even the soot. Good
thing I'm seeing the psychiatrist. I don't think I could force
myself to get on the elevated tonight." His voice trailed off, he
rubbed his eyes, and his memory automatically started to
grind.

It had all begun on the elevated. There was a particular
little sea of roofs he had grown into the habit of glancing at
just as the packed car carrying him homeward lurched
around a turn. A dingy, melancholy little world of tar-paper,
tarred gravel and smoky brick. Rusty tin chimneys with odd
conical hats suggested abandoned listening posts. There was
a washed-out advertisement of some ancient patent medicine
on the nearest wall. Superficially it was like ten thousand
other drab city roofs. But he always saw it around dusk, either in the smoky half-light, or tinged with red by the flat
rays of a dirty sunset, or covered by ghostly windblown white
sheets of rain-splash, or patched with blackish snow; and it
seemed unusually bleak and suggestive; almost beautifully
ugly though in no sense picturesque; dreary, but meaningful.
Unconsciously it came to symbolize for Catesby Wran certain
disagreeable aspects of the frustrated, frightened century in

which he lived, the jangled century of hate and heavy industry and total wars. The quick daily glance into the half darkness became an integral part of his life. Oddly, he never saw
it in the morning, for it was then his habit to sit on the other
side of the car, his head buried in the paper.

One evening toward winter he noticed what seemed to be a
shapeless black sack lying on the third roof from the tracks.
He did not think about it. It merely registered as an addition
to the well-known scene and his memory stored away the
impression for further reference. Next evening, however, he
decided he had been mistaken in one detail. The object was a
roof nearer than he had thought. Its color and texture, and
the grimy stains around it, suggested that it was filled with
coal dust, which was hardly reasonable. Then, too, the following evening it seemed to have been blown against a rusty
ventilator by the wind—which could hardly have happened if
it were at all heavy. Perhaps it was filled with leaves. Catesby
was surprised to find himself anticipating his next daily
glance with a minor note of apprehension. There was something unwholesome in the posture of the thing that stuck in
his mind—a bulge in the sacking that suggested a misshaped
head peering around the ventilator. And his apprehension
was justified, for that evening the thing was on the nearest
roof, though on the farther side, looking as if it had just
flopped down over the low brick parapet.

Next evening the sack was gone. Catesby was annoyed at
the momentary feeling of relief that went through him, because the whole matter seemed too unimportant to warrant
feelings of any sort. What difference did it make if his imagination had played tricks on him, and he'd fancied that the
object was slowly crawling and hitching itself closer across
the roofs? That was the way any normal imagination worked.
He deliberately chose to disregard the fact that there were
reasons for thinking his imagination was by no means a normal one. As he walked home from the elevated, however, he
found himself wondering whether the sack was really gone.
He seemed to recall a vague, smudgy trail leading across the
gravel to the nearer side of the roof, which was masked by a
parapet. For an instant an unpleasant picture formed in his

mind—that of an inky, humped creature crouched behind the parapet, waiting.

The next time he felt the familiar grating lurch of the car, he caught himself trying not to look out. That angered him. He turned his head quickly. When he turned it back, his compact face was definitely pale. There had been only time for a fleeting rearward glance at the escaping roof. Had he actually seen in silhouette the upper part of a head of some sort peering over the parapet? Nonsense, he told himself. And even if he had seen something, there were a thousand explanations which did not involve the supernatural or even true hallucination. Tomorrow he would take a good look and clear up the whole matter. If necessary, he would visit the roof personally, though he hardly knew where to find it and disliked in any case the idea of pampering a silly fear.

He did not relish the walk home from the elevated that evening, and visions of the thing disturbed his dreams, and were in and out of his mind all next day at the office. It was then that he first began to relieve his nerves by making jokingly serious remarks about the supernatural to Miss Millick, who seemed properly mystified. It was on the same day, too, that he became aware of a growing antipathy to grime and soot. Everything he touched seemed gritty, and he found himself mopping and wiping at his desk like an old lady with a morbid fear of germs. He reasoned that there was no real change in his office, and that he'd just now become sensitive to the dirt that had always been there, but there was no denying an increasing nervousness. Long before the car reached the curve, he was straining his eyes through the murky twilight, determined to take in every detail.

Afterward he realized he must have given a muffled cry of some sort, for the man beside him looked at him curiously, and the woman ahead gave him an unfavorable stare. Conscious of his own pallor and uncontrollable trembling, he stared back at them hungrily, trying to regain the feeling of security he had completely lost. They were the usual reassuringly wooden-faced people everyone rides home with on the elevated. But suppose he had pointed out to one of them what he had seen—that sodden, distorted face of sacking and coal dust, that boneless paw which waved back and forth, unmistakably in his direction, as if reminding him of a future appointment—he involuntarily shut his eyes tight. His thoughts were racing ahead to tomorrow evening. He pictured this same windowed oblong of light and packed humanity surging around the curve—then an opaque monstrous form leaping out from the roof in a parabolic swoop—an unmentionable face pressed close against the window, smearing it with wet coal dust—huge paws fumbling sloppily at the glass—

Somehow he managed to turn off his wife's anxious inquiries. Next morning he reached a decision and made an appointment for that evening with a psychiatrist a friend had told him about. It cost him a considerable effort, for Catesby had a well-grounded distaste for anything dealing with psychological abnormality. Visiting a psychiatrist meant raking up an episode in his past which he had never fully described even to his wife. Once he had made the decision, however, he felt considerably relieved. The psychiatrist, he told himself, would clear everything up. He could almost fancy him saying, "Merely a bad case of nerves. However, you must consult the oculist whose name I'm writing down for you, and you must take two of these pills in water every four hours," and so on. It was almost comforting, and made the coming revelation he would have to make seem less painful.

But as the smoky dusk rolled in, his nervousness had returned and he had let his joking mystification of Miss Millick run away with him until he had realized he wasn't frightening anyone but himself.

He would have to keep his imagination under better control, he told himself, as he continued to peer out restlessly at the massive, murky shapes of the downtown office buildings. Why, he had spent the whole afternoon building up a kind of neo-medieval cosmology of superstition. It wouldn't do. He realized then that he had been standing at the window much longer than he'd thought, for the glass panel in the door was dark and there was no noise coming from the outer office. Miss Millick and the rest must have gone home.

It was then he made the discovery that there would have been no special reason for dreading the swing around the curve that night. It was, as it happened, a horrible discovery.

For, on the shadowed roof across the street and four stories
below, he saw the thing huddle and roll across the gravel and,
after one upward look of recognition, merge into the blackness beneath the water tank.

As he hurriedly collected his things and made for the elevator, fighting the panicky impulse to run, he began to think of
hallucination and mild psychosis as very desirable conditions. For better or for worse, he pinned all his hopes on the
psychiatrist.

"So you find yourself growing nervous and . . . er . . .
jumpy, as you put it," said Dr. Trevethick, smiling with digni-
fied geniality. "Do you notice any more definite physical
symptoms? Pain? Headache? Indigestion?"

Catesby shook his head and wet his lips. "I'm especially
nervous while riding in the elevated," he murmured swiftly.

"I see. We'll discuss that more fully. But I'd like you first to
tell me about something you mentioned earlier. You said
there was something about your childhood that might predis-
pose you to nervous ailments. As you know, the early years
are critical ones in the development of an individual's behav-
ior pattern."

Catesby studied the yellow reflections of frosted globes in
the dark surface of the desk. The palm of his left hand aimlessly rubbed the thick nap of the armchair. After a while he
raised his head and looked straight into the doctor's small
brown eyes.

"From perhaps my third to my ninth year," he began,
choosing the words with care, "I was what you might call a
sensory prodigy."

The doctor's expression did not change. "Yes?" he inquired
politely.

"What I mean is that I was supposed to be able to see
through walls, read letters through envelopes and books
through their covers, fence and play ping-pong blindfolded,
find things that were buried, read thoughts." The words tumbled out.

"And could you?" The doctor's voice was toneless.

"I don't know. I don't suppose so," answered Catesby, long-
lost emotions flooding back into his voice. "It's all confused

now. I thought I could, but then they were always encouraging me. My mother . . . was . . . well . . . interested in psychic phenomena. I was . . . exhibited. I seem to remember seeing things other people couldn't. As if most opaque objects were transparent. But I was very young. I didn't have any scientific criteria for judgment."

He was reliving it now. The darkened rooms. The earnest assemblages of gawking, prying adults. Himself alone on a little platform, lost in a straight-backed wooden chair. The black silk handkerchief over his eyes. His mother's coaxing, insistent questions. The whispers. The gasps. His own hate of the whole business, mixed with hunger for the adulation of adults. Then the scientists from the university, the experiments, the big test. The reality of those memories engulfed him and momentarily made him forget the reason why he was disclosing them to a stranger.

"Do I understand that your mother tried to make use of you as a medium for communicating with the . . . er . . . other world?"

Catesby nodded eagerly.

"She tried to, but she couldn't. When it came to getting in touch with the dead, I was a complete failure. All I could do—or thought I could do—was see real, existing, three-dimensional objects beyond the vision of normal people. Objects anyone could have seen except for distance, obstruction, or darkness. It was always a disappointment to Mother."

He could hear her sweetish, patient voice saying, "Try again, dear, just this once. Katie was your aunt. She loved you. Try to hear what she's saying." And he had answered, "I can see a woman in a blue dress standing on the other side of Dick's house." And she had replied, "Yes, I know, dear. But that's not Katie. Katie's a spirit. Try again. Just this once, dear." The doctor's voice gently jarred him back into the softly gleaming office.

"You mentioned scientific criteria for judgment, Mr. Wran. As far as you know, did anyone ever try to apply them to you?"

Catesby's nod was emphatic.

"They did. When I was eight, two young psychologists from the university got interested in me. I guess they did it for a joke at first, and I remember being very determined to show them I amounted to something. Even now I seem to recall how the note of polite superiority and amused sarcasm drained out of their voices. I suppose they decided at first that it was very clever trickery, but somehow they persuaded Mother to let them try me out under controlled conditions. There were lots of tests that seemed very businesslike after Mother's slipshod little exhibitions. They found I was clair-voyant—or so they thought. I got worked up and on edge. They were going to demonstrate my supernormal sensory powers to the university psychology faculty. For the first time I began to worry about whether I'd come through. Perhaps they kept me going at too hard a pace, I don't know. At any rate, when the test came, I couldn't do a thing. Everything became opaque. I got desperate and made things up out of my imagination. I lied. In the end I failed utterly, and I believe the two young psychologists got into a lot of hot water as a result."

He could hear the brusque, bearded man saying, "You've been taken in by a child, Flaxman, a mere child. I'm greatly disturbed. You've put yourself on the same plane as common charlatans. Gentlemen, I ask you to banish from your minds this whole sorry episode. It must never be referred to." He winced at the recollection of his feeling of guilt. But at the same time he was beginning to feel exhilarated and almost light-hearted. Unburdening his long-repressed memories had altered his whole viewpoint. The episodes on the elevated be-gan to take on what seemed their proper proportions as merely the bizarre workings of overwrought nerves and an overly suggestible mind. The doctor, he anticipated confi-dently, would disentangle the obscure subconscious causes, whatever they might be. And the whole business would be finished off quickly, just as his childhood experience—which was beginning to seem a little ridiculous now—had been fin-ished off.

"From that day on," he continued, "I never exhibited a trace of my supposed powers. My mother was frantic and tried to sue the university. I had something like a nervous breakdown. Then the divorce was granted, and my father got custody of me. He did his best to make me forget it. We went on long outdoor vacations and did a lot of athletics, associated with normal matter-of-fact people. I went to business college eventually. I'm in advertising now. But," Catesby paused, "now that I'm having nervous symptoms, I've wondered if there mightn't be a connection. It's not a question of whether I was really clairvoyant or not. Very likely my mother taught me a lot of unconscious deceptions, good enough to fool even young psychology instructors. But don't you think it may have some important bearing on my present condition?"

For several moments the doctor regarded him with a professional frown. Then he said quietly, "And is there some . . . er . . . more specific connection between your experiences then and now? Do you by any chance find that you are once again beginning to . . . er . . . see things?"

Catesby swallowed. He had felt an increasing eagerness to unburden himself of his fears, but it was not easy to make a beginning, and the doctor's shrewd question rattled him. He forced himself to concentrate. The thing he thought he had seen on the roof loomed up before his inner eye with unexpected vividness. Yet it did not frighten him. He groped for words.

Then he saw that the doctor was not looking at him but over his shoulder. Color was draining out of the doctor's face and his eyes did not seem so small. Then the doctor sprang to his feet, walked past Catesby, threw up the window and peered into the darkness.

As Catesby rose, the doctor slammed down the window and said in a voice whose smoothness was marred by a slight, persistent gasping, "I hope I haven't alarmed you. I saw the face of . . . er . . . a Negro prowler on the fire escape. I must have frightened him, for he seems to have gotten out of sight in a hurry. Don't give it another thought. Doctors are frequently bothered by *voyeurs* . . . er . . . Peeping Toms."

"A Negro?" asked Catesby, moistening his lips.

The doctor laughed nervously. "I imagine so, though my first odd impression was that it was a white man in blackface. You see, the color didn't seem to have any brown in it. It was dead-black."

Catesby moved toward the window. There were smudges on the glass. "It's quite all right, Mr. Wran." The doctor's voice had acquired a sharp note of impatience, as if he were trying hard to reassume his professional authority. "Let's continue our conversation. I was asking you if you were"—he made a face—"seeing things."

Catesby's whirling thoughts slowed down and locked into place. "No, I'm not seeing anything that other people don't see, too. And I think I'd better go now. I've been keeping you too long." He disregarded the doctor's half-hearted gesture of denial. "I'll phone you about the physical examination. In a way you've already taken a big load off my mind." He smiled woodenly. "Goodnight, Dr. Trevethick."

Catesby Wran's mental state was a peculiar one. His eyes searched every angular shadow, he glanced sideways down each chasm-like alley and barren basement passageway, and kept stealing looks at the irregular line of the roofs, yet he was hardly conscious of where he was going. He pushed away the thoughts that came into his mind, and kept moving. He became aware of a slight sense of security as he turned into a lighted street where there were people and high buildings and blinking signs. After a while he found himself in the dim lobby of the structure that housed his office. Then he realized why he couldn't go home, why he daren't go home—after what had happened at the office of Dr. Trevethick.

"Hello, Mr. Wran," said the night elevator man, a burly figure in overalls, sliding open the grille-work door to the old-fashioned cage. "I didn't know you were working nights now, too."

Catesby stepped in automatically. "Sudden rush of orders," he murmured inanely. "Some stuff that has to be gotten out."

The cage creaked to a stop at the top floor. "Be working very late, Mr. Wran?"

He nodded vaguely, watched the car slide out of sight, found his keys, swiftly crossed the outer office, and entered his own. His hand went out to the light switch, but then the thought occurred to him that the two lighted windows, standing out against the dark bulk of the building, would indicate his whereabouts and serve as a goal toward which something could crawl and climb. He moved his chair so that the back was against the wall and sat down in the semidarkness. He did not remove his overcoat.

For a long time he sat there motionless, listening to his own breathing and the faraway sounds from the streets below: the thin metallic surge of the crosstown streetcar, the farther one of the elevated, faint lonely cries and honkings, indistinct rumblings. Words he had spoken to Miss Millick in nervous jest came back to him with the bitter taste of truth. He found himself unable to reason critically or connectedly, but by their own volition thoughts rose up into his mind and gyrated slowly and rearranged themselves with the inevitable movement of planets.

Gradually his mental picture of the world was transformed. No longer a world of material atoms and empty space, but a world in which the bodiless existed and moved according to its own obscure laws or unpredictable impulses. The new picture illuminated with dreadful clarity certain general facts which had always bewildered and troubled him and from which he had tried to hide: the inevitability of hate and war, the diabolically timed mischances which wreck the best of human intentions, the walls of willful misunderstanding that divide one man from another, the eternal vitality of cruelty and ignorance and greed. They seemed appropriate now, necessary parts of the picture. And superstition only a kind of wisdom.

Then his thoughts returned to himself and the question he had asked Miss Millick, "What would such a thing want from a person? Sacrifices? Worship, Or just fear? What could you do to stop it from troubling you?" It had become a practical question.

With an explosive jangle, the phone began to ring. "Cate, I've been trying everywhere to get you," said his wife. "I never thought you'd be at the office. What are you doing? I've been worried."

He said something about work.

"You'll be home right away?" came the faint anxious question. "I'm a little frightened. Ronny just had a scare. It woke him up. He kept pointing to the window saying, 'Black man, black man.' Of course it's something he dreamed. But I'm frightened. You will be home? What's that, dear? Can't you hear me?"

"I will. Right away," he said. Then he was out of the office, buzzing the night bell and peering down the shaft.

He saw it peering up the shaft at him from the deep shadows three floors below, the sacking face pressed against the iron grille-work. It started up the stair at a shockingly swift, shambling gait, vanishing temporarily from sight as it swung into the second corridor below.

Catesby clawed at the door to the office, realized he had not locked it, pushed it in, slammed and locked it behind him, retreated to the other side of the room, cowered between the filing cases and the wall. His teeth were clicking. He heard the groan of the rising cage. A silhouette darkened the frosted glass of the door, blotting out part of the grotesque reverse of the company name. After a little the door opened.

The big-globed overhead light flared on and, standing inside the door, her hand on the switch, was Miss Millick.

"Why, Mr. Wran," she stammered vacuously, "I didn't know you were here. I'd just come in to do some extra typing after the movie. I didn't . . . but the lights weren't on. What were you—"

He stared at her. He wanted to shout in relief, grab hold of her, talk rapidly. He realized he was grinning hysterically.

"Why, Mr. Wran, what's happened to you?" she asked embarrassedly, ending with a stupid titter. "Are you feeling sick? Isn't there something I can do for you?"

He shook his head jerkily and managed to say, "No, I'm just leaving. I was doing some extra work myself."

"But you *look* sick," she insisted, and walked over toward him. He inconsequentially realized she must have stepped in mud, for her high-heeled shoes left neat black prints.

"Yes, I'm sure you must be sick. You're so terribly pale." She sounded like an enthusiastic, incompetent nurse. Her face brightened with a sudden inspiration. "I've got something in my bag, that'll fix you up right away," she said. "It's for indigestion."

She fumbled at her stuffed oblong purse. He noticed that she was absentmindedly holding it shut with one hand while she tried to open it with the other. Then, under his very eyes, he saw her bend back the thick prongs of metal locking the purse as if they were tinfoil, or as if her fingers had become a pair of steel pliers.

Instantly his memory recited the words he had spoken to Miss Millick that afternoon. "It couldn't hurt you physically —at first . . . gradually get its hooks into the world . . . might even get control of suitably vacuous minds. Then it could hurt whomever it wanted." A sickish, cold feeling grew inside him. He began to edge toward the door.

But Miss Millick hurried ahead of him.

"You don't have to wait, Fred," she called. "Mr. Wran's decided to stay a while longer."

The door to the cage shut with a mechanical rattle. The cage creaked. Then she turned around in the door.

"Why, Mr. Wran," she gurgled reproachfully, "I just couldn't think of letting you go home now. I'm sure you're terribly unwell. Why, you might collapse in the street. You've just got to stay here until you feel different."

The creaking died away. He stood in the center of the office, motionless. His eyes traced the coal-black course of Miss Millick's footprints to where she stood blocking the door. Then a sound that was almost a scream was wrenched out of him, for it seemed to him that the blackness was creeping up her legs under the thin stockings.

"Why, Mr. Wran," she said, "you're acting as if you were crazy. You must lie down for a while. Here, I'll help you off with your coat."

The nauseously idiotic and rasping note was the same; only it had been intensified. As she came toward him he turned and ran through the storeroom, clattered a key desperately at the lock of the second door to the corridor.

"Why, Mr. Wran," he heard her call, "are you having some kind of a fit? You must let me help you."

The door came open and he plunged out into the corridor and up the stairs immediately ahead. It was only when he reached the top that he realized the heavy steel door in front of him led to the roof. He jerked up the catch.

"Why, Mr. Wran, you mustn't run away. I'm coming after you."

Then he was out on the gritty gravel of the roof. The night sky was clouded and murky, with a faint pinkish glow from the neon signs. From the distant mills rose a ghostly spurt of flame. He ran to the edge. The street lights glared dizzily upward. Two men were tiny round blobs of hat and shoulders. He swung around.

The thing was in the doorway. The voice was no longer solicitous but moronically playful, each sentence ending in a titter.

"Why, Mr. Wran, why have you come up here? We're all alone. Just think, I might push you off."

The thing came slowly toward him. He moved backward until his heels touched the low parapet. Without knowing why, or what he was going to do, he dropped to his knees. He dared not look at the face as it came nearer, a focus for the worst in the world, a gathering point for poisons from everywhere. Then the lucidity of terror took possession of his mind, and words formed on his lips.

"I will obey you. You are my god," he said. "You have supreme power over man and his animals and his machines. You rule this city and all others. I recognize that."

Again the titter, closer. "Why, Mr. Wran, you never talked like this before. Do you mean it?"

"The world is yours to do with as you will, save or tear to pieces," he answered fawningly, the words automatically fitting themselves together in vaguely liturgical patterns. "I recognize that. I will praise, I will sacrifice. In smoke and soot I will worship you for ever."

The voice did not answer. He looked up. There was only Miss Millick, deathly pale and swaying drunkenly. Her eyes were closed. He caught her as she wobbled toward him. His knees gave way under the added weight and they sank down together on the edge of the roof.

After a while she began to twitch. Small noises came from her throat and her eyelids edged open.

"Come on, we'll go downstairs," he murmured jerkily, trying to draw her up. "You're feeling bad."

"I'm terribly dizzy," she whispered. "I must have fainted, I didn't eat enough. And then I'm so nervous lately, about the war and everything, I guess. Why, we're on the roof! Did you bring me up here to get some air? Or did I come up without knowing it? I'm awfully foolish. I used to walk in my sleep, my mother said."

As he helped her down the stairs, she turned and looked at him. "Why, Mr. Wran," she said, faintly, "you've got a big black smudge on your forehead. Here, let me get it off for you." Weakly she rubbed at it with her handkerchief. She started to sway again and he steadied her.

"No, I'll be all right," she said. "Only I feel cold. What happened, Mr. Wran? Did I have some sort of fainting spell?"

He told her it was something like that.

Later, riding home in the empty elevated car, he wondered how long he would be safe from the thing. It was a purely practical problem. He had no way of knowing, but instinct told him he had satisfied the brute for some time. Would it want more when it came again? Time enough to answer that question when it arose. It might be hard, he realized, to keep out of an insane asylum. With Helen and Ronny to protect, as well as himself, he would have to be careful and tightlipped. He began to speculate as to how many other men and women had seen the thing or things like it.

The elevated slowed and lurched in a familiar fashion. He looked at the roofs near the curve. They seemed very ordinary, as if what made them impressive had gone away for a while.

Yours Truly, Jack the Ripper

Robert Bloch

Horror tales tend to reflect anxieties prevalent at the time of their writing. However, some figures of horror lend themselves to endless resurrection as they take the imprint of the fears of each new age. Though Jack the Ripper's trail of bloody murders began and ended on the streets of London's Whitechapel district in the summer and fall of 1888, he was never apprehended. Speculations about the Ripper's identity and fate have produced several collections' worth of horror stories, but Robert Bloch's 1943 tale "Yours Truly, Jack the Ripper" was the first to imagine the Ripper as an immortal spirit of the age of the serial killer. With its sequels "A Toy for Juliette" and "The Prowler in the City at the Edge of the World" (written by Harlan Ellison), it forms a trilogy of horror and science fiction stories concerned with the relationship between society and the monsters it produces. Readers unfamiliar with the story or its numerous radio and television adaptations are forewarned that when it comes to endings, Bloch is the O. Henry of the horror tale.

I looked at the stage Englishman. He looked at me.

"Sir Guy Hollis?" I asked.

"Indeed. Have I the pleasure of addressing John Carmody, the psychiatrist?"

I nodded. My eyes swept over the figure of my distinguished visitor. Tall, lean, sandy-haired—with the traditional tufted mustache. And the tweeds. I suspected a monocle concealed in a vest pocket, and wondered if he'd left his umbrella in the outer office.

But more than that, I wondered what the devil had impelled Sir Guy Hollis of the British Embassy to seek out a total stranger here in Chicago.

Sir Guy didn't help matters any as he sat down. He cleared his throat, glanced around nervously, tapped his pipe against the side of the desk. Then he opened his mouth.

"Mr. Carmody," he said, "have you ever heard of—Jack the Ripper?"

"The murderer?" I asked.

"Exactly. The greatest monster of them all. Worse than Springheel Jack or Crippen. Jack the Ripper. Red Jack."

"I've heard of him," I said.

"Do you know his history?"

"I don't think we'll get any place swapping old wives' tales about famous crimes of history."

He took a deep breath.

"This is no old wives' tale. It's a matter of life or death."

He was so wrapped up in his obsession he even talked that way. Well—I was willing to listen. We psychiatrists get paid for listening.

"Go ahead," I told him. "Let's have the story."

Sir Guy lit a cigarette and began to talk.

"London, 1888," he began. "Late summer and early fall. That was the time. Out of nowhere came the shadowy figure of Jack the Ripper—a stalking shadow with a knife, prowling through London's East End. Haunting the squalid dives of Whitechapel, Spitalfields. Where he came from no one knew. But he brought death. Death in a knife.

"Six times that knife descended to slash the throats and bodies of London's women. Drabs and alley sluts. August 7th was the date of the first butchery. They found her body lying there with thirty-nine stab wounds. A ghastly murder. On August 31st, another victim. The press became interested. The slum inhabitants were more deeply interested still.

"Who was this unknown killer who prowled in their midst and struck at will in the deserted alleyways of night-town? And what was more important—when would he strike again?

"September 8th was the date. Scotland Yard assigned special deputies. Rumors ran rampant. The atrocious nature of the slayings was the subject for shocking speculation.

"The killer used a knife—expertly. He cut throats and removed—certain portions—of the bodies after death. He chose victims and settings with a fiendish deliberation. No one saw him or heard him. But watchmen making their gray rounds in the dawn would stumble across the hacked and horrid thing that was the Ripper's handiwork.

"Who was he? What was he? A mad surgeon? A butcher? An insane scientist? A pathological degenerate escaped from an asylum? A deranged nobleman? A member of the London police?

"Then the poem appeared in the newspapers. The anonymous poem, designed to put a stop to speculations—but which only aroused public interest to a further frenzy. A mocking little stanza:

> *I'm not a butcher, I'm not a Yid*
> *Nor yet a foreign skipper,*
> *But I'm your own true loving friend,*
> *Yours truly—Jack the Ripper.*

"And on September 30th, two more throats were slashed open. There was silence, then, in London for a time. Silence, and a nameless fear. When would Red Jack strike again? They waited through October. Every figment of fog concealed his phantom presence. Concealed it well—for nothing was learned of the Ripper's identity, or his purpose. The drabs of London shivered in the raw wind of early November. Shivered, and were thankful for the coming of each morning's sun.

"November 9th. They found her in her room. She lay there very quietly, limbs neatly arranged. And beside her, with equal neatness, were laid her breasts and heart. The Ripper had outdone himself in execution.

"Then, panic. But needless panic. For though press, police, and populace alike waited in sick dread, Jack the Ripper did not strike again.

"Months passed. A year. The immediate interest died, but

not the memory. They said Jack had skipped to America. That he had committed suicide. They said—and they wrote. They've written ever since. Theories, hypotheses, arguments, treatises. But to this day no one knows who Jack the Ripper was. Or why he killed. Or why he stopped killing."

Sir Guy was silent. Obviously he expected some comment from me.

"You tell the story well," I remarked. "Though with a slight emotional bias."

"I suppose you want to know why I'm interested?" he snapped.

"Yes. That's exactly what I'd like to know."

"Because," said Sir Guy Hollis, "I am on the trail of Jack the Ripper now. I think he's here—in Chicago!"

"Say that again."

"Jack the Ripper is alive, in Chicago, and I'm out to find him."

He wasn't smiling. It wasn't a joke.

"See here," I said. "What was the date of these murders?"

"August to November, 1888."

"1888? But if Jack the Ripper was an able-bodied man in 1888, he'd surely be dead today! Why look, man—if he were merely born in that year, he'd be fifty-seven years old today!"

"Would he?" smiled Sir Guy Hollis. "Or should I say, 'Would she?' Because Jack the Ripper may have been a woman. Or any number of things."

"Sir Guy," I said. "You came to the right person when you looked me up. You definitely need the services of a psychiatrist."

"Perhaps. Tell me, Mr. Carmody, do you think I'm crazy?"

I looked at him and shrugged. But I had to give him a truthful answer.

"Frankly—no."

"Then you might listen to the reasons I believe Jack the Ripper is alive today."

"I might."

"I've studied these cases for thirty years. Been over the actual ground. Talked to officials. Talked to friends and acquaintances of the poor drabs who were killed. Visited with men and women in the neighborhood. Collected an entire library of material touching on Jack the Ripper. Studied all the wild theories or crazy notions.

"I learned a little. Not much, but a little. I won't bore you with my conclusions. But there was another branch of inquiry that yielded more fruitful return. I have studied unsolved crimes. Murders.

"I could show you clippings from the papers of half the world's greatest cities. San Francisco. Shanghai. Calcutta. Omsk. Paris. Berlin. Pretoria. Cairo. Milan. Adelaide.

"The trail is there, the pattern. Unsolved crimes. Slashed throats of women. With the peculiar disfigurations and removals. Yes, I've followed a trail of blood. From New York westward across the continent. Then to the Pacific. From there to Africa. During the World War of 1914–18 it was Europe. After that, South America. And since 1930, the United States again. Eighty-seven such murders—and to the trained criminologist, all bear the stigma of the Ripper's handiwork.

"Recently there were the so-called Cleveland torso slayings. Remember? A shocking series. And finally, two recent deaths in Chicago. Within the past six months. One out on South Dearborn. The other somewhere up on Halsted. Same type of crime, same technique. I tell you, there are unmistakable indications in all these affairs—indications of the work of Jack the Ripper!"

"A very tight theory," I said. "I'll not question your evidence at all, or the deductions you draw. You're the criminologist, and I'll take your word for it. Just one thing remains to be explained. A minor point, perhaps, but worth mentioning."

"And what is that?" asked Sir Guy.

"Just how could a man of, let us say, eight-five years commit these crimes? For if Jack the Ripper was around thirty in 1888 and lived, he'd be eighty-five today."

"Suppose he didn't get any older?" whispered Sir Guy.

"What's that?"

"Suppose Jack the Ripper didn't grow old? Suppose he is still a young man today?

"It's a crazy theory, I grant you," he said. "All the theories about the Ripper are crazy. The idea that he was a doctor. Or a maniac. Or a woman. The reasons advanced for such beliefs are flimsy enough. There's nothing to go by. So why should my notion be any worse?"

"Because people grow older," I reasoned with him. "Doctors, maniacs, and women alike."

"What about—*sorcerers?*"

"Sorcerers?"

"Necromancers. Wizards. Practicers of Black Magic?"

"What's the point?"

"I studied," said Sir Guy. "I studied everything. After a while I began to study the dates of the murders. The pattern those dates formed. The rhythm. The solar, lunar, stellar rhythm. The sidereal aspect. The astrological significance.

"Suppose Jack the Ripper didn't murder for murder's sake alone? Suppose he wanted to make—a sacrifice?"

"What kind of a sacrifice?"

Sir Guy shrugged. "It is said that if you offer blood to the dark gods they grant boons. Yes, if a blood offering is made at the proper time—when the moon and the stars are right—and with the proper ceremonies—they grant boons. Boons of youth. Eternal youth."

"But that's nonsense!"

"No. That's—Jack the Ripper."

I stood up. "A most interesting theory," I told him. "But why do you come here and tell it to me? I'm not an authority on witchcraft. I'm not a police official or criminologist. I'm a practicing psychiatrist. What's the connection?"

Sir Guy smiled.

"You are interested, then?"

"Well, yes. There must be some point."

"There is. But I wished to be assured of your interest first. Now I can tell you my plan."

"And just what is that plan?"

Sir Guy gave me a long look.

"John Carmody," he said, "you and I are going to capture Jack the Ripper."

2

That's the way it happened. I've given the gist of that first interview in all its intricate and somewhat boring detail, be-

cause I think it's important. It helps to throw some light on
Sir Guy's character and attitude. And in view of what happened after that—

But I'm coming to those matters.

Sir Guy's thought was simple. It wasn't even a thought.
Just a hunch.

"You know the people here," he told me. "I've inquired.
That's why I came to you as the ideal man for my purpose.
You number amongst your acquaintances many writers,
painters, poets. The so-called intelligentsia. The lunatic
fringe from the near north side.

"For certain reasons—never mind what they are—my clues
lead me to infer that Jack the Ripper is a member of that
element. He chooses to pose as an eccentric. I've a feeling
that with you to take me around and introduce me to your
set, I might hit upon the right person."

"It's all right with me," I said. "But just how are you going
to look for him? As you say, he might be anybody, anywhere.
And you have no idea what he looks like. He might be young
or old. Jack the Ripper—a Jack of all trades? Rich man, poor
man, beggar man, thief, doctor, lawyer—how will you know?"

"We shall see." Sir Guy sighed heavily. "But I must find
him. At once."

"Why the hurry?"

Sir Guy sighed again. "Because in two days he will kill
again."

"Are you sure?"

"Sure as the stars. I've plotted this chart, you see. All of the
murders correspond to certain astrological rhythm patterns.
If, as I suspect, he makes a blood sacrifice to renew his youth,
he must murder within two days. Notice the pattern of his
first crimes in London. August 7th. Then August 31st. September 8th. September 30th. November 9th. Intervals of 24
days, 9 days, 22 days—he killed two this time—and then 40
days. Of course there were crimes in between. There had to
be. But they weren't discovered and pinned on him.

"At any rate, I've worked out a pattern for him, based on
all my data. And I say that within the next two days he kills.
So I must seek him out, somehow, before then."

"And I'm still asking you what you want me to do."

"Take me out," said Sir Guy. "Introduce me to your friends. Take me to parties."

"But where do I begin? As far as I know, my artistic friends, despite their eccentricities, are all normal people."

"So is the Ripper. Perfectly normal. Except on certain nights." Again that faraway look in Sir Guy's eyes. "Then he becomes an ageless pathological monster, crouching to kill."

"All right," I said. "All right. I'll take you."

We made our plans. And that evening I took him over to Lester Baston's studio.

As we ascended to the penthouse roof in the elevator I took the opportunity to warn Sir Guy.

"Baston's a real screwball," I cautioned him. "So are his guests. Be prepared for anything and everything."

"I am." Sir Guy Hollis was perfectly serious. He put his hand in his trousers pocket and pulled out a gun.

"What the—" I began.

"If I see him I'll be ready," Sir Guy said. He didn't smile, either.

"But you can't go running around at a party with a loaded revolver in your pocket, man!"

"Don't worry, I won't behave foolishly."

I wondered. Sir Guy Hollis was not, to my way of thinking, a normal man.

We stepped out of the elevator, went toward Baston's apartment door.

"By the way," I murmured, "just how do you wish to be introduced? Shall I tell them who you are and what you are looking for?"

"I don't care. Perhaps it would be best to be frank."

"But don't you think that the Ripper—if by some miracle he or she is present—will immediately get the wind up and take cover?"

"I think the shock of the announcement that I am hunting the Ripper would provoke some kind of betraying gesture on his part," said Sir Guy.

"It's a fine theory. But I warn you, you're going to be in for a lot of ribbing. This is a wild bunch."

Sir Guy smiled.

"I'm ready," he announced. "I have a little plan of my own. Don't be shocked at anything I do."

I nodded and knocked on the door.

Baston opened it and poured out into the hall. His eyes were as red as the maraschino cherries in his Manhattan. He teetered back and forth regarding us very gravely. He squinted at my square-cut homburg hat and Sir Guy's mustache.

"Aha," he intoned. "The Walrus and the Carpenter."

I introduced Sir Guy.

"Welcome," said Baston, gesturing us inside with over-elaborate courtesy. He stumbled after us into the garish parlor.

I stared at the crowd that moved restlessly through the fog of cigarette smoke.

It was the shank of the evening for this mob. Every hand held a drink. Every face held a slightly hectic flush. Over in one corner the piano was going full blast, but the imperious strains of the *March* from *The Love for Three Oranges* couldn't drown out the profanity from the crap-game in the other corner.

Prokofieff had no chance against African polo, and one set of ivories rattled louder than the other.

Sir Guy got a monocle-full right away. He saw LaVerne Gonnister, the poetess, hit Hymie Kralik in the eye. He saw Hymie sit down on the floor and cry until Dick Pool accidentally stepped on his stomach as he walked through to the dining room for a drink.

He heard Nadia Vilinoff, the commercial artist, tell Johnny Odcutt that she thought his tattooing was in dreadful taste, and he saw Barclay Melton crawl under the dining room table with Johnny Odcutt's wife.

His zoological observations might have continued indefinitely if Lester Baston hadn't stepped to the center of the room and called for silence by dropping a vase on the floor.

"We have distinguished visitors in our midst," bawled Lester, waving his empty glass in our direction. "None other than the Walrus and the Carpenter. The Walrus is Sir Guy Hollis, a something-or-other from the British Embassy. The Carpenter, as you all know, is our own John Carmody, the prominent dispenser of libido liniment."

He turned and grabbed Sir Guy by the arm, dragging him to the middle of the carpet. For a moment I thought Hollis might object, but a quick wink reassured me. He was prepared for this.

"It is our custom, Sir Guy," said Baston, loudly, "to subject our new friends to a little cross-examination. Just a little formality at these very formal gatherings, you understand. Are you prepared to answer questions?"

Sir Guy nodded and grinned.

"Very well," Baston muttered. "Friends—I give you this bundle from Britain. Your witness."

Then the ribbing started. I meant to listen, but at that moment Lydia Dare saw me and dragged me off into the vestibule for one of those Darling-I-waited-for-your-call-all-day routines.

By the time I got rid of her and went back, the impromptu quiz session was in full swing. From the attitude of the crowd, I gathered that Sir Guy was doing all right for himself.

Then Baston himself interjected a question that upset the apple-cart.

"And what, may I ask, brings you to our midst tonight? What is your mission, oh Walrus?"

"I'm looking for Jack the Ripper."

Nobody laughed.

Perhaps it struck them all the way it did me. I glanced at my neighbors and began to *wonder*.

LaVerne Gonnister. Hymie Kralik. Harmless. Dick Pool. Nadia Vilinoff. Johnny Odcutt and his wife. Barclay Melton. Lydia Dare. All harmless.

But what a forced smile on Dick Pool's face! And that sly, self-conscious smirk that Barclay Melton wore!

Oh, it was absurd, I grant you. But for the first time I saw these people in a new light. I wondered about their lives—their secret lives beyond the scenes of parties.

How many of them were playing a part, concealing something?

Who here would worship Hecate and grant that horrid goddess the dark boon of blood?

Even Lester Baston might be masquerading.

The mood was upon us all, for a moment. I saw questions flicker in the circle of eyes around the room.

Sir Guy stood there, and I could swear he was fully conscious of the situation he'd created, and enjoyed it.

I wondered idly just what was *really* wrong with him. Why he had this odd fixation concerning Jack the Ripper. Maybe he was hiding secrets, too. . . .

Baston, as usual, broke the mood. He burlesqued it.

"The Walrus isn't kidding, friends," he said. He slapped Sir Guy on the back and put his arm around him as he orated. "Our English cousin is really on the trail of the fabulous Jack the Ripper. You all remember Jack the Ripper, I presume? Quite a cut-up in the old days, as I recall. Really had some ripping good times when he went out on a tear.

"The Walrus has some idea that the Ripper is still alive, probably prowling around Chicago with a Boy Scout knife. In fact—" Baston paused impressively and shot it out in a rasping stage whisper—"in fact, he has reason to believe that Jack the Ripper might even be right here in our midst tonight."

There was the expected reaction of giggles and grins. Baston eyed Lydia Dare reprovingly. "You girls needn't laugh," he smirked. "Jack the Ripper might be a woman, too, you know. Sort of a Jill the Ripper."

"You mean you actually suspect one of us?" shrieked LaVerne Gonnister, simpering up to Sir Guy. "But that Jack the Ripper person disappeared ages ago, didn't he? In 1888?"

"Aha!" interrupted Baston. "How do you know so much about it, young lady? Sounds suspicious! Watch her, Sir Guy —she may not be as young as she appears. These lady poets have dark pasts."

The tension was gone, the mood was shattered, and the whole thing was beginning to degenerate into a trivial party joke. The man who had played the *March* was eyeing the piano with a *scherzo* gleam in his eye that augured ill for Prokofieff. Lydia Dare was glancing at the kitchen, waiting to make a break for another drink.

Then Baston caught it.

"Guess what?" he yelled. "The Walrus has a gun."

His embracing arm had slipped and encountered the hard

outline of the gun in Sir Guy's pocket. He snatched it out before Hollis had the opportunity to protest.

I stared hard at Sir Guy, wondering if this thing had carried far enough. But he flicked a wink my way and I remembered he had told me not to be alarmed.

So I waited as Baston broached a drunken inspiration.

"Let's play fair with our friend the Walrus," he cried. "He came all the way from England to our party on this mission. If none of you is willing to confess, I suggest we give him a chance to find out—the hard way."

"What's up?" asked Johnny Odcutt.

"I'll turn out the lights for one minute. Sir Guy can stand here with his gun. If anyone in this room is the Ripper he can either run for it or take the opportunity to—well, eradicate his pursuer. Fair enough?"

It was even sillier than it sounds, but it caught the popular fancy. Sir Guy's protests went unheard in the ensuing babble. And before I could stride over and put in my two cents' worth, Lester Baston had reached the light switch.

"Don't anybody move," he announced, with fake solemnity. "For one minute we will remain in darkness—perhaps at the mercy of a killer. At the end of that time, I'll turn up the lights again and look for bodies. Choose your partners, ladies and gentlemen."

The lights went out.

Somebody giggled.

I heard footsteps in the darkness. Mutterings.

A hand brushed my face.

The watch on my wrist ticked violently. But even louder, rising above it, I heard another thumping. The beating of my heart.

Absurd. Standing in the dark with a group of tipsy fools. And yet there was real terror lurking here, rustling through the velvet blackness.

Jack the Ripper prowled in darkness like this. And Jack the Ripper had a knife. Jack the Ripper had a madman's brain and a madman's purpose.

But Jack the Ripper was dead, dead and dust these many years—by every human law.

Only there are no human laws when you feel yourself in

the darkness, when the darkness hides and protects and the outer mask slips off your face and you feel something welling up within you, a brooding shapeless purpose that is brother to the blackness.

Sir Guy Hollis shrieked.

There was a grisly thud.

Baston put the lights on.

Everybody screamed.

Sir Guy Hollis lay sprawled on the floor in the center of the room. The gun was still clutched in his hand.

I glanced at the faces, marveling at the variety of expressions human beings can assume when confronting horror.

All the faces were present in the circle. Nobody had fled. And yet Sir Guy Hollis lay there.

LaVerne Gonnister was wailing and hiding her face.

"All right."

Sir Guy rolled over and jumped to his feet. He was smiling.

"Just an experiment, eh? If Jack the Ripper *were* among those present, and thought I had been murdered, he would have betrayed himself in some way when the lights went on and he saw me lying there.

"I am convinced of your individual and collective innocence. Just a gentle spoof, my friends."

Hollis stared at the goggling Baston and the rest of them crowding in behind him.

"Shall we leave, John?" he called to me. "It's getting late, I think."

Turning, he headed for the closet. I followed him. Nobody said a word.

It was a pretty dull party after that.

3

I met Sir Guy the following evening as we agreed, on the corner of 29th and South Halsted.

After what had happened the night before, I was prepared for almost anything. But Sir Guy seemed matter-of-fact enough as he stood huddled against a grimy doorway and waited for me to appear.

"Boo!" I said, jumping out suddenly. He smiled. Only the

betraying gesture of his left hand indicated that he'd instinctively reached for his gun when I startled him.

"All ready for our wild-goose chase?" I asked.

"Yes." He nodded. "I'm glad that you agreed to meet me without asking questions," he told me. "It shows you trust my judgment." He took my arm and edged me along the street slowly.

"It's foggy tonight, John," said Sir Guy Hollis. "Like London."

I nodded.

"Cold, too, for November."

I nodded again and half-shivered my agreement.

"Curious," mused Sir Guy. "London fog and November. The place and the time of the Ripper murders."

I grinned through darkness. "Let me remind you, Sir Guy, that this isn't London, but Chicago. And it isn't November, 1888. It's over fifty years later."

Sir Guy returned my grin, but without mirth. "I'm not so sure, at that," he murmured. "Look about you. Those tangled alleys and twisted streets. They're like the East End. Mitre Square. And surely they are as ancient as fifty years, at least."

"You're in the black neighborhood of South Clark Street," I said shortly. "And why you dragged me down here I still don't know."

"It's a hunch," Sir Guy admitted. "Just a hunch on my part, John. I want to wander around down here. There's the same geographical conformation in these streets as in those courts where the Ripper roamed and slew. That's where we'll find him, John. Not in the bright lights, but down here in the darkness. The darkness where he waits and crouches."

"Isn't that why you brought a gun?" I asked. I was unable to keep a trace of sarcastic nervousness from my voice. All this talk, this incessant obsession with Jack the Ripper, got on my nerves more than I cared to admit.

"We may need a gun," said Sir Guy, gravely. "After all, tonight is the appointed night."

I sighed. We wandered on through the foggy, deserted streets. Here and there a dim light burned above a gin-mill doorway. Otherwise, all was darkness and shadow. Deep, gap-

ing alleyways loomed as we proceeded down a slanting side-
street.

We crawled through that fog, alone and silent, like two tiny
maggots floundering within a shroud.

"Can't you see there's not a soul around these streets?" I
said.

"He's bound to come," said Sir Guy. "He'll be drawn here.
This is what I've been looking for. A *genius loci.* An evil spot
that attracts evil. Always, when he slays, it's in the slums.

"You see, that must be one of his weaknesses. He has a
fascination for squalor. Besides, the women he needs for sacrifice are more easily found in the dives and stewpots of a
great city."

"Well, let's go into one of the dives or stewpots," I suggested. "I'm cold. Need a drink. This damned fog gets into
your bones. You Britishers can stand it, but I like warmth
and dry heat."

We emerged from our side street and stood upon the
threshold of an alley.

Through the white clouds of mist ahead, I discerned a dim
blue light, a naked bulb dangling from a beer sign above an
alley tavern.

"Let's take a chance," I said. "I'm beginning to shiver."

"Lead the way," said Sir Guy. I led him down the alley
passage. We halted before the door of the dive.

"What are you waiting for?" he asked.

"Just looking in," I told him. "This is a rough neighborhood, Sir Guy. Never know what you're liable to run into.
And I'd prefer we didn't get into the wrong company. Some of
these places resent white customers."

"Good idea, John."

I finished my inspection through the doorway. "Looks deserted," I murmured. "Let's try it."

We entered a dingy bar. A feeble light flickered above the
counter and railing, but failed to penetrate the further gloom
of the back booths.

A gigantic black lolled across the bar. He scarcely stirred
as we came in, but his eyes flicked open quite suddenly and I
knew he noted our presence and was judging us.

"Evening," I said.

He took his time before replying. Still sizing us up. Then, he grinned.

"Evening, gents. What's your pleasure?"

"Gin," I said. "Two gins. It's a cold night."

"That's right, gents."

He poured, I paid, and took the glasses over to one of the booths. We wasted no time in emptying them.

I went over to the bar and got the bottle. Sir Guy and I poured ourselves another drink. The big man went back into his doze, with one wary eye half-open against any sudden activity.

The clock over the bar ticked on. The wind was rising outside, tearing the shroud of fog to ragged shreds. Sir Guy and I sat in the warm booth and drank our gin.

He began to talk, and the shadows crept up about us to listen.

He rambled a great deal. He went over everything he'd said in the office when I met him, just as though I hadn't heard it before. The poor devils with obsessions are like that.

I listened very patiently. I poured Sir Guy another drink. And another.

But the liquor only made him more talkative. How he did run on! About ritual killings and prolonging the life unnaturally—the whole fantastic tale came out again. And of course, he maintained his unyielding conviction that the Ripper was abroad tonight.

I suppose I was guilty of goading him.

"Very well," I said, unable to keep the impatience from my voice. "Let us say that your theory is correct—even though we must overlook every natural law and swallow a lot of superstition to give it any credence.

"But let us say, for the sake of argument, that you are right. Jack the Ripper was a man who discovered how to prolong his own life through making human sacrifices. He did travel around the world as you believe. He is in Chicago now and he is planning to kill. In other words, let us suppose that everything you claim is gospel truth. So what?"

"What do you mean, 'so what'?" said Sir Guy.

"I mean—so what?" I answered. "If all this is true, it still doesn't prove that by sitting down in a dingy gin-mill on the

South Side, Jack the Ripper is going to walk in here and let you kill him, or turn him over to the police. And come to think of it, I don't even know now just what you intend to *do* with him if you ever did find him."

Sir Guy gulped his gin. "I'd capture the bloody swine," he said. "Capture him and turn him over to the government, together with all the papers and documentary evidence I've collected against him over a period of many years. I've spent a fortune investigating this affair, I tell you, a fortune! His capture will mean the solution of hundreds of unsolved crimes, of that I am convinced."

In vino veritas. Or was all this babbling the result of too much gin? It didn't matter. Sir Guy Hollis had another. I sat there and wondered what to do with him. The man was rapidly working up to a climax of hysterical drunkenness.

"That's enough," I said, putting out my hand as Sir Guy reached for the half-emptied bottle again. "Let's call a cab and get out of here. It's getting late and it doesn't look as though your elusive friend is going to put in his appearance. Tomorrow, if I were you, I'd plan to turn all those papers and documents over to the F.B.I. If you're so convinced of the truth of your theory, they are competent to make a very thorough investigation, and find your man."

"No." Sir Guy was drunkenly obstinate. "No cab."

"But let's get out of here anyway," I said, glancing at my watch. "It's past midnight."

He sighed, shrugged, and rose unsteadily. As he started for the door, he tugged the gun free from his pocket.

"Here, give me that!" I whispered. "You can't walk around the street brandishing that thing."

I took the gun and slipped it inside my coat. Then I got hold of his right arm and steered him out of the door. The black man didn't look up as we departed.

We stood shivering in the alleyway. The fog had increased. I couldn't see either end of the alley from where we stood. It was cold. Damp. Dark. Fog or no fog, a little wind was whispering secrets to the shadows at our backs.

Sir Guy, despite his incapacity, still stared apprehensively at the alley, as though he expected to see a figure approaching.

Disgust got the better of me.

"Childish foolishness," I snorted. "Jack the Ripper, indeed! I call this carrying a hobby too far."

"Hobby?" He faced me. Through the fog I could see his distorted face. "You call this a hobby?"

"Well, what is it?" I grumbled. "Just why else are you so interested in tracking down this mythical killer?"

My arm held his. But his stare held me.

"In London," he whispered. "In 1888 . . . one of those nameless drabs the Ripper slew . . . was my mother."

"What?"

"Later I was recognized by my father, and legitimatized. We swore to give our lives to find the Ripper. My father was the first to search. He died in Hollywood in 1926—on the trail of the Ripper. They said he was stabbed by an unknown assailant in a brawl. But I knew who that assailant was.

"So I've taken up his work, do you see, John? I've carried on. And I will carry on until I do find him and kill him with my own hands."

I believed him then. He wouldn't give up. He wasn't just a drunken babbler anymore. He was as fanatical, as determined, as relentless as the Ripper himself.

Tomorrow he'd be sober. He'd continue the search. Perhaps he'd turn those papers over to the F.B.I. Sooner or later, with such persistence—and with his motive—he'd be successful. I'd always known he had a motive.

"Let's go," I said, steering him down the alley.

"Wait a minute," said Sir Guy. "Give me back my gun." He lurched a little. "I'd feel better with the gun on me."

He pressed me into the dark shadows of a little recess.

I tried to shrug him off, but he was insistent.

"Let me carry the gun, now, John," he mumbled.

"All right," I said.

I reached into my coat, brought my hand out.

"But that's not a gun," he protested. "That's a knife."

"I know."

I bore down on him swiftly.

"John!" he screamed.

"Never mind the 'John,' " I whispered, raising the knife. "Just call me . . . Jack."

The Small Assassin

Ray Bradbury

There are many ways in which writers of supernatural horror induce the reader's willing suspension of disbelief long enough to introduce an irrational possibility into the otherwise rational world. In "The Small Assassin" (1946), Ray Bradbury uses the one figure whose irrationality is openly condoned by all: the newborn child. Although many earlier horror stories (including a number by Bradbury) had explored the Romantic notion that childern live in a world of fantastic wonders that more logically minded adults have cut themselves off from, "The Small Assassin" was one of the first to suggest that the innocence of childhood might serve as the perfect alibi for beings with malefic motives. With its portrayal of the child as an alien in our midst, Bradbury's tale can be viewed as a forerunner of novels like William March's The Bad Seed *(1954) and Thomas Tryon's* The Other *(1971) and as one of the more ingenious stories to deal with that mainstay of modern horror, the demon child.*

Just when the idea occurred to her that she was being murdered she could not tell. There had been little subtle signs, little suspicions for the past month; things as deep as sea tides in her, like looking at a perfectly calm stretch of tropic water, wanting to bathe in it and finding, just as the tide takes your body, that monsters dwell just under the surface, things unseen, bloated, many-armed, sharp-finned, malignant and inescapable.

A room floated around her in an effluvium of hysteria. Sharp instruments hovered and there were voices, and people in sterile white masks.

My name, she thought, what is it?

Alice Leiber. It came to her. David Leiber's wife. But it gave her no comfort. She was alone with these silent, whispering white people and there was great pain and nausea and death-fear in her.

I am being murdered before their eyes. These doctors, these nurses don't realize what hidden thing has happened to me. David doesn't know. Nobody knows except me and—the killer, the little murderer, the small assassin.

I am dying and I can't tell them now. They'd laugh and call me one in delirium. They'll see the murderer and hold him and never think him responsible for my death. But here I am, in front of God and man, dying, no one to believe my story, everyone to doubt me, comfort me with lies, bury me in ignorance, mourn me and salvage my destroyer.

Where is David? she wondered. In the waiting room, smoking one cigarette after another, listening to the long tickings of the very slow clock?

Sweat exploded from all of her body at once, and with it an agonized cry. Now. Now! Try and kill me, she screamed. Try, try, but I won't die! I won't!

There was a hollowness. A vacuum. Suddenly the pain fell away. Exhaustion, and dusk came around. It was over. Oh, God! She plummeted down and struck a black nothingness which gave way to nothingness and nothingness and another and still another. . . .

Footsteps. Gentle, approaching footsteps.

Far away, a voice said, "She's asleep. Don't disturb her."

An odor of tweeds, a pipe, a certain shaving lotion. David was standing over her. And beyond him the immaculate smell of Dr. Jeffers.

She did not open her eyes. "I'm awake," she said, quietly. It was a surprise, a relief to be able to speak, to not be dead.

"Alice," someone said, and it was David beyond her closed eyes, holding her tired hands.

Would you like to meet the murderer, David? she thought. I

hear your voice asking to see him, so there's nothing but for me to point him out to you.

David stood over her. She opened her eyes. The room came into focus. Moving a weak hand, she pulled aside a coverlet.

The murderer looked up at David Leiber with a small, red-faced, blue-eyed calm. Its eyes were deep and sparkling.

"Why!" cried David Leiber, smiling. "He's a *fine* baby!"

Dr. Jeffers was waiting for David Leiber the day he came to take his wife and new child home. He motioned Leiber to a chair in his office, gave him a cigar, lit one for himself, sat on the edge of his desk, puffing solemnly for a long moment. Then he cleared his throat, looked David Leiber straight on and said, "Your wife doesn't like her child, Dave."

"What!"

"It's been a hard thing for her. She'll need a lot of love this next year. I didn't say much at the time, but she was hysterical in the delivery room. The strange things she said—I won't repeat them. All I'll say is that she feels alien to the child. Now, this may simply be a thing we can clear up with one or two questions." He sucked on his cigar another moment, then said, "Is this child a 'wanted' child, Dave?"

"Why do you ask?"

"It's vital."

"Yes. Yes, it is a 'wanted' child. We planned it together. Alice was so happy, a year ago, when—"

"Mmmm—that makes it more difficult. Because if the child was unplanned, it would be a simple case of a woman hating the idea of motherhood. That doesn't fit Alice." Dr. Jeffers took his cigar from his lips, rubbed his hand across his jaw. "It must be something else, then. Perhaps something buried in her childhood that's coming out now. Or it might be the simple temporary doubt and distrust of any mother who's gone through the unusual pain and near-death that Alice has. If so, then a little time should heal that. I thought I'd tell you, though, Dave. It'll help you be easy and tolerant with her if she says anything about—well—about wishing the child had been born dead. And if things don't go well, the three of you drop in on me. I'm always glad to see old friends, eh? Here, take another cigar along for—ah—for the baby."

It was a bright spring afternoon. Their car hummed along wide, tree-lined boulevards. Blue sky, flowers, a warm wind. Dave talked a lot, lit his cigar, talked some more. Alice answered directly, softly, relaxing a bit more as the trip progressed. But she held the baby not tightly or warmly or motherly enough to satisfy the queer ache in Dave's mind. She seemed to be merely carrying a porcelain figurine.

"Well," he said, at last, smiling. "What'll we name him?"

Alice Leiber watched green trees slide by. "Let's not decide yet. I'd rather wait until we get an exceptional name for him. Don't blow smoke in his face." Her sentences ran together with no change of tone. The last statement held no motherly reproof, no interest, no irritation. She just mouthed it and it was said.

The husband, disquieted, dropped the cigar from the window. "Sorry," he said.

The baby rested in the crook of its mother's arm, shadows of sun and tree changing his face. His blue eyes opened like fresh blue spring flowers. Moist noises came from the tiny, pink, elastic mouth.

Alice gave her baby a quick glance. Her husband felt her shiver against him.

"Cold?" he asked.

"A chill. Better raise the window, David."

It was more than a chill. He rolled the window slowly up.

Suppertime.

David had brought the child from the nursery, propped him at a tiny, bewildered angle, supported by many pillows, in a newly purchased high chair.

Alice watched her knife and fork move. "He's not highchair size," she said.

"Fun having him here, anyway," said Dave, feeling fine. "Everything's fun. At the office, too. Orders up to my nose. If I don't watch myself I'll make another fifteen thousand this year. Hey, look at Junior, will you? Drooling all down his chin!" He reached over to wipe the baby's mouth with his napkin. From the corner of his eye he realized that Alice wasn't even watching. He finished the job.

"I guess it wasn't very interesting," he said, back again at his food. "But one would think a mother'd take some interest in her own child!"

Alice jerked her chin up. "Don't speak that way! Not in front of him! Later, if you must."

"Later?" he cried. "In front of, in back of, what's the difference?" He quieted suddenly, swallowed, was sorry. "All right. Okay. I know how it is."

After dinner she let him carry the baby upstairs. She didn't tell him to; she *let* him.

Coming down, he found her standing by the radio, listening to music she didn't hear. Her eyes were closed, her whole attitude one of wondering, self-questioning. She started when he appeared.

Suddenly, she was at him, against him, soft, quick; the same. Her lips found him, kept him. He was stunned. Now that the baby was gone, upstairs, out of the room, she began to breathe again, live again. She was free. She was whispering, rapidly, endlessly.

"Thank you, thank you, darling. For being yourself, always. Dependable, so very dependable!"

He had to laugh. "My father told me, 'Son, provide for your family!'"

Wearily, she rested her dark, shining hair against his neck. "You've overdone it. Sometimes I wish we were just the way we were when we were first married. No responsibilities, nothing but ourselves. No—no babies."

She crushed his hand in hers, a supernatural whiteness in her white face.

"Oh, Dave, once it was just you and me. We protected each other, and now we protect the baby, but get no protection from it. Do you understand? Lying in the hospital I had time to think a lot of things. The world is evil—"

"Is it?"

"Yes. It is. But laws protect us from it. And when there aren't laws, then love does the protecting. You're protected from my hurting you, by my love. You're vulnerable to me, of all people, but love shields you. I feel no fear of you, because love cushions all your irritations, unnatural instincts, hatreds and immaturities. But—what about the baby? It's too young to know love, or a law of love, or anything, until we teach it. And in the meantime be vulnerable to it."

"Vulnerable to a baby?" He held her away and laughed gently.

"Does a baby know the difference between right and wrong?" she asked.

"No. But it'll learn."

"But a baby is so new, so amoral, so conscience-free." She stopped. Her arms dropped from him and she turned swiftly. "That noise? What was it?"

Leiber looked around the room. "I didn't hear—"

She stared at the library door. "In there," she said, slowly.

Leiber crossed the room, opened the door and switched the library lights on and off. "Not a thing." He came back to her. "You're worn out. To bed with you—right now."

Turning out the lights together, they walked slowly up the soundless hall stairs, not speaking. At the top she apologized. "My wild talk, darling. Forgive me. I'm exhausted."

He understood, and said so.

She paused, undecided, by the nursery door. Then she fingered the brass knob sharply, walked in. He watched her approach the crib much too carefully, look down, and stiffen as if she'd been struck in the face. "David!"

Leiber stepped forward, reached the crib.

The baby's face was bright red and very moist; his small pink mouth opened and shut, opened and shut; his eyes were a fiery blue. His hands leapt about on the air.

"Oh," said Dave, "he's just been crying."

"Has he?" Alice Leiber seized the crib-railing to balance herself. "I didn't hear him."

"The door was closed."

"Is that why he breathes so hard, why his face is red?"

"Sure. Poor little guy. Crying all alone in the dark. He can sleep in our room tonight, just in case he cries."

"You'll spoil him," his wife said.

Leiber felt her eyes follow as he rolled the crib into their bedroom. He undressed silently, sat on the edge of the bed. Suddenly he lifted his head, swore under his breath, snapped his fingers. "Damn it! Forgot to tell you. I must fly to Chicago Friday."

"Oh, David." Her voice was lost in the room.

"I've put this trip off for two months, and now it's so critical I just *have* to go."

"I'm afraid to be alone."

"We'll have the new cook by Friday. She'll be here all the time. I'll only be gone a few days."

"I'm afraid. I don't know of what. You wouldn't believe me if I told you. I guess I'm crazy."

He was in bed now. She darkened the room; he heard her walk around the bed, throw back the cover, slide in. He smelled the warm woman-smell of her next to him. He said, "If you want me to wait a few days, perhaps I could—"

"No," she said, unconvinced. "You go. I know it's important. It's just that I keep thinking about what I told you. Laws and love and protection. Love protects you from me. But, the baby—" She took a breath. "What protects you from him, David?"

Before he could answer, before he could tell her how silly it was, speaking so of infants, she switched on the bed light, abruptly.

"Look," she said, pointing.

The baby lay wide awake in its crib, staring straight at him, with deep, sharp blue eyes.

The lights went out again. She trembled against him.

"It's not nice being afraid of the thing you birthed." Her whisper lowered, became harsh, fierce, swift. "He tried to kill me! He lies there, listens to us talking, waiting for you to go away so he can try to kill me again! I swear it!" Sobs broke from her.

"Please," he kept saying, soothing her. "Stop it, stop it. Please."

She cried in the dark for a long time. Very late she relaxed, shakingly, against him. Her breathing came soft, warm, regular, her body twitched its worn reflexes and she slept.

He drowsed.

And just before his eyes lidded wearily down, sinking him into deeper and yet deeper tides, he heard a strange little sound of awareness and awakeness in the room.

The sound of small, moist, pinkly elastic lips.

The baby.

And then—sleep.

In the morning, the sun blazed. Alice smiled.

David Leiber dangled his watch over the crib. "See, baby? Something bright. Something pretty. Sure. Sure. Something bright. Something pretty."

Alice smiled. She told him to go ahead, fly to Chicago, she'd be very brave, no need to worry. She'd take care of baby. Oh, yes, she'd take care of him, all right.

The airplane went east. There was a lot of sky, a lot of sun and clouds and Chicago running over the horizon. Dave was dropped into the rush of ordering, planning, banqueting, telephoning, arguing in conference. But he wrote letters each day and sent telegrams to Alice and the baby.

On the evening of his sixth day away from home he received the long-distance phone call. Los Angeles.

"Alice?"

"No, Dave. This is Jeffers speaking."

"Doctor!"

"Hold on to yourself, son. Alice is sick. You'd better get the next plane home. It's pneumonia. I'll do everything I can, boy. If only it wasn't so soon after the baby. She needs strength."

Leiber dropped the phone into its cradle. He got up, with no feet under him, and no hands and no body. The hotel room blurred and fell apart.

"Alice," he said, blindly, starting for the door.

The propellers spun about, whirled, fluttered, stopped; time and space were put behind. Under his hand, David felt the doorknob turn; under his feet the floor assumed reality, around him flowed the walls of a bedroom, and in the late-afternoon sunlight Dr. Jeffers stood, turning from a window, as Alice lay waiting in her bed, something carved from a fall of winter snow. Then Dr. Jeffers was talking, talking continuously, gently, the sound rising and falling through the lamplight, a soft flutter, a white murmur of voice.

"Your wife's too good a mother, Dave. She worried more about the baby than herself. . . ."

Somewhere in the paleness of Alice's face, there was a sudden constriction which smoothed itself out before it was realized. Then, slowly, half-smiling, she began to talk and she talked as a mother should about this, that, and the other thing, the telling detail, the minute-by-minute and hour-by-hour report of a mother concerned with a dollhouse world and the miniature life of that world. But she could not stop; the spring was wound tight, and her voice rushed on to anger, fear and the faintest touch of revulsion, which did not change Dr. Jeffers' expression, but caused Dave's heart to match the rhythm of this talk that quickened and could not stop:

"The baby wouldn't sleep. I thought he was sick. He just lay, staring, in his crib, and late at night he'd cry. So loud, he'd cry, and he'd cry all night and all night. I couldn't quiet him, and I couldn't rest."

Dr. Jeffers' head nodded slowly, slowly. "Tired herself right into pneumonia. But she's full of sulfa now and on the safe side of the whole damn thing."

Dave felt ill. "The baby, what about the baby?"

"Fit as a fiddle; cock of the walk!"

"Thanks, doctor."

The doctor walked off away and down the stairs, opened the front door faintly, and was gone.

"David!"

He turned to her frightened whisper.

"It was the baby again." She clutched his hand. "I try to lie to myself and say that I'm a fool, but the baby knew I was weak from the hospital, so he cried all night every night, and when he wasn't crying he'd be much too quiet. I knew if I switched on the light he'd be there, staring up at me."

David felt his body close in on itself like a fist. He remembered seeing the baby, feeling the baby, awake in the dark, awake very late at night when babies should be asleep. Awake and lying there, silent as thought, not crying, but watching from its crib. He thrust the thought aside. It was insane.

Alice went on. "I was going to kill the baby. Yes, I was. When you'd been gone only a day on your trip I went to his room and put my hands about his neck; and I stood there, for a long time, thinking, afraid. Then I put the covers up over his face and turned him over on his face and pressed him down and left him that way and ran out of the room."

He tried to stop her.

"No, let me finish," she said, hoarsely, looking at the wall. "When I left his room I thought, It's simple. Babies smother every day. No one'll ever know. But when I came back to see him dead, David, he was alive! Yes, alive, turned over on his back, alive and smiling and breathing. And I couldn't touch him again after that. I left him there and I didn't come back, not to feed him or look at him or do anything. Perhaps the cook tended to him. I don't know. All I know is that his crying kept me awake, and I thought all through the night, and walked around the rooms and now I'm sick." She was almost finished now. "The baby lies there and thinks of ways to kill me. Simple ways. Because he knows I know so much about him. I have no love for him; there is no protection between us; there never will be."

She was through. She collapsed inward on herself and finally slept. David Leiber stood for a long time over her, not able to move. His blood was frozen in his body, not a cell stirred anywhere, anywhere at all.

The next morning there was only one thing to do. He did it. He walked into Dr. Jeffers' office and told him the whole thing, and listened to Jeffers' tolerant replies:

"Let's take this thing slowly, son. It's quite natural for mothers to hate their children, sometimes. We have a label for it—ambivalence. The ability to hate, while loving. Lovers hate each other, frequently. Children detest their mothers—"

Leiber interrupted. "I never hated my mother."

"You won't admit it, naturally. People don't enjoy admitting hatred for their loved ones."

"So Alice hates her baby."

"Beter say she has an obsession. She's gone a step further than plain, ordinary ambivalence. A Caesarian operation brought the child into the world and almost took Alice out of it. She blames the child for her near-death and her pneumonia. She's projecting her troubles, blaming them on the handiest object she can use as a source of blame. We *all* do it. We stumble into a chair and curse the furniture, not our own clumsiness. We miss a golf-stroke and damn the turf or our club, or the make of ball. If our business fails we blame the gods, the weather, our luck. All I can tell you is what I told you before. Love her. Finest medicine in the world. Find little ways of showing your affection, give her security. Find ways of showing her how harmless and innocent the child is. Make her feel that the baby was worth the risk. After a while, she'll settle down, forget about death, and begin to love the child. If she doesn't come around in the next month or so, ask me. I'll recommend a good psychiatrist. Go on along now, and take that look off your face."

When summer came, things seemed to settle, become easier. Dave worked, immersed himself in office detail, but found much time for his wife. She, in turn, took long walks, gained strength, played an occasional light game of badminton. She rarely burst out any more. She seemed to have rid herself of her fears.

Except on one certain midnight when a sudden summer wind swept around the house, warm and swift, shaking the trees like so many shining tambourines. Alice wakened, trembling, and slid over into her husband's arms, and let him console her, and ask her what was wrong.

She said, "Something's here in the room, watching us."

He switched on the light. "Dreaming again," he said. "You're better, though. Haven't been troubled for a long time."

She sighed as he clicked off the light again, and suddenly she slept. He held her, considering what a sweet, weird creature she was, for about half an hour.

He heard the bedroom door sway open a few inches.

There was nobody at the door. No reason for it to come open. The wind had died.

He waited. It seemed like an hour he lay silently, in the dark.

Then, far away, wailing like some small meteor dying in the vast inky gulf of space, the baby began to cry in his nursery.

It was a small, lonely sound in the middle of the stars and

the dark and the breathing of this woman in his arms and the wind beginning to sweep through the trees again.

Leiber counted to one hundred, slowly. The crying continued.

Carefully disengaging Alice's arm he slipped from bed, put on his slippers, robe, and moved quietly from the room.

He'd go downstairs, he thought, fix some warm milk, bring it up, and—

The blackness dropped out from under him. His foot slipped and plunged. Slipped on something soft. Plunged into nothingness.

He thrust his hands out, caught frantically at the railing. His body stopped falling. He held. He cursed.

The "something soft" that caused his feet to slip rustled and thumped down a few steps. His head rang. His heart hammered at the base of his throat, thick and shot with pain.

Why do careless people leave things strewn about a house? He groped carefully with his fingers for the object that had almost spilled him headlong down the stairs.

His hand froze, startled. His breath went in. His heart held one or two beats.

The thing he held in his hand was a toy. A large cumbersome, patchwork doll he had bought as a joke, for—

For the baby.

Alice drove him to work the next day.

She slowed the car halfway downtown, pulled to the curb and stopped it. Then she turned on the seat and looked at her husband.

"I want to go away on a vacation. I don't know if you can make it now, darling, but if not, please let me go alone. We can get someone to take care of the baby, I'm sure. But I just have to get away. I thought I was growing out of this—this *feeling.* But I haven't. I can't stand being in the room with him. He looks up at me as if he hates me, too. I can't put my finger on it; all I know is I want to get away before something happens."

He got out on his side of the car, came around, motioned to her to move over, got in. "The only thing you're going to do is see a good psychiatrist. And if he suggests a vacation, well, okay. But this can't go on; my stomach's in knots all the time." He started the car. "I'll drive the rest of the way."

Her head was down; she was trying to keep back tears. She looked up when they reached his office building. "All right. Make the appointment. I'll go talk to anyone you want, David."

He kissed her. "Now, you're talking sense, lady. Think you can drive home okay?"

"Of course, silly."

"See you at supper, then. Drive carefully."

"Don't I always? 'Bye."

He stood on the curb, watching her drive off, the wind taking hold of her long, dark, shining hair. Upstairs, a minute later, he phoned Jeffers and arranged an appointment with a reliable neuro-psychiatrist.

The day's work went uneasily. Things fogged over; and in the fog he kept seeing Alice lost and calling his name. So much of her fear had come over to him. She actually had him convinced that the child was in some ways not quite natural.

He dictated long, uninspired letters. He checked some shipments downstairs. Assistants had to be questioned, and kept going. At the end of the day he was exhausted, his head throbbed, and he was very glad to go home.

On the way down in the elevator he wondered, What if I told Alice about the toy—that patchwork doll—I slipped on on the stairs last night? Lord, wouldn't *that* back her off? No, I won't ever tell her. Accidents are, after all, accidents.

Daylight lingered in the sky as he drove home in a taxi. In front of the house he paid the driver and walked slowly up the cement walk, enjoying the light that was still in the sky and the trees. The white colonial front of the house looked unnaturally silent and uninhabited, and then, quietly, he remembered this was Thursday, and the hired help they were able to obtain from time to time were all gone for the day.

He took a deep breath of air. A bird sang behind the house. Traffic moved on the boulevard a block away. He twisted the key in the door. The knob turned under his fingers, oiled, silent.

The door opened. He stepped in, put his hat on the chair

with his briefcase, started to shrug out of his coat, when he looked up.

Late sunlight streamed down the stairwell from the window near the top of the hall. Where the sunlight touched it took on the bright color of the patchwork doll sprawled at the bottom of the stairs.

But he paid no attention to the toy.

He could only look, and not move, and look again at Alice.

Alice lay in a broken, grotesque, pallid gesturing and angling of her thin body, at the bottom of the stairs, like a crumpled doll that doesn't want to play any more, ever.

Alice was dead.

The house remained quiet, except for the sound of his heart.

She was dead.

He held her head in his hands, he felt her fingers. He held her body. But she wouldn't live. She wouldn't even try to live. He said her name, out loud, many times, and he tried, once again, by holding her to him, to give her back some of the warmth she had lost, but that didn't help.

He stood up. He must have made a phone call. He didn't remember. He found himself, suddenly, upstairs. He opened the nursery door and walked inside and stared blankly at the crib. His stomach was sick. He couldn't see very well.

The baby's eyes were closed, but his face was red, moist with perspiration, as if he'd been crying long and hard.

"She's dead," said Leiber to the baby. "She's dead."

Then he started laughing low and soft and continuously for a long time until Dr. Jeffers walked in out of the night and slapped him again and again across the face.

"Snap out of it! Pull yourself together!"

"She fell down the stairs, Doctor. She tripped on a patchwork doll and fell. I almost slipped on it the other night, myself. And now—"

The doctor shook him.

"Doc, Doc, Doc," said Dave, hazily. "Funny thing. Funny. I —I finally thought of a name for the baby."

The doctor said nothing.

Leiber put his head back in his trembling hands and spoke the words. "I'm going to have him christened next Sunday.

Know what name I'm giving him? I'm going to call him Lucifer."

It was eleven at night. A lot of strange people had come and
gone through the house, taking the essential flame with them
—Alice.

David Leiber sat across from the doctor in the library.

"Alice wasn't crazy," he said, slowly. "She had good reason
to fear the baby."

Jeffers exhaled. "Don't follow after her! She blamed the
child for her sickness, now you blame it for her death. She
stumbled on a toy, remember that. You can't blame the
child."

"You mean Lucifer?"

"Stop calling him that!"

Leiber shook his head. "Alice heard things at night, moving in the halls. You want to know what made those noises,
Doctor? They were made by the baby. Four months old, moving in the dark, listening to us talk. Listening to every word!"
He held to the sides of the chair. "And if I turned the lights
on, a baby is so small. It can hide behind furniture, a door,
against a wall—below eye-level."

"I want you to stop this!" said Jeffers.

"Let me say what I think or I'll go crazy. When I went to
Chicago, who was it kept Alice awake, tiring her into pneumonia? The baby! And when Alice didn't die, then he tried
killing me. It was simple; leave a toy on the stairs, cry in the
night until your father goes downstairs to fetch your milk,
and stumbles. A crude trick, but effective. It didn't get me.
But it killed Alice dead."

David Leiber stopped long enough to light a cigarette. "I
should have caught on. I'd turn on the lights in the middle of
the night, many nights, and the baby'd be lying there, eyes
wide. Most babies sleep all the time. Not this one. He stayed
awake, thinking."

"Babies don't think."

"He stayed awake doing whatever he *could* do with his
brain, then. What in hell do we know about a baby's mind?
He had every reason to hate Alice; she suspected him for
what he was—certainly not a normal child. Something—dif-

ferent. What do you know of babies, Doctor? The general run,
yes. You know, of course, how babies kill their mothers at
birth. Why? Could it be resentment at being forced into a
lousy world like this one?"

Leiber leaned toward the doctor, tiredly. "It all ties up.
Suppose that a few babies out of all the millions born are
instantaneously able to move, see, hear, think, like many animals and insects can. Insects are born self-sufficient. In a few
weeks most mammals and birds adjust. But children take
years to speak and learn to stumble around on their weak
legs.

"But suppose one child in a billion is—strange? Born perfectly aware, able to think, instinctively. Wouldn't it be a perfect setup, a perfect blind for anything the baby might want
to do? He could pretend to be ordinary, weak, crying, ignorant. With just a *little* expenditure of energy he could crawl
about a darkened house, listening. And how easy to place
obstacles at the top of stairs. How easy to cry all night and
tire a mother into pneumonia. How easy, right at birth, to be
so close to the mother that *a few deft maneuvers might cause
peritonitis!*"

"For God's sake!" Jeffers was on his feet. "That's a repulsive thing to say!"

"It's a repulsive thing I'm speaking of. How many mothers
have died at the birth of their children? How many have
suckled strange little improbabilities who cause death one
way or another? Strange, red little creatures with brains that
work in a bloody darkness we can't even guess at. Elemental
little brains, warm with racial memory, hatred, and raw
cruelty, with no more thought than self-preservation. And
self-preservation in this case consisted of eliminating a
mother who realized what a horror she had birthed. I ask
you, Doctor, what is there in the world more selfish than a
baby? Nothing!"

Jeffers scowled and shook his head, helplessly.

Leiber dropped his cigarette down. "I'm not claiming any
great strength for the child. Just enough to crawl around a
little, a few months ahead of schedule. Just enough to listen
all the time. Just enough to cry late at night. That's enough,
more than enough."

Jeffers tried ridicule. "Call it murder, then. But murder must be motivated. What motive had the child?"

Leiber was ready with the answer. "What is more at peace, more dreamfully content, at ease, at rest, fed, comforted, unbothered, than an unborn child? Nothing. It floats in a sleepy, timeless wonder of nourishment and silence. Then, suddenly, it is asked to give up its berth, is forced to vacate, rushed out into a noisy, uncaring, selfish world where it is asked to shift for itself, to hunt, to feed from the hunting, to seek after a vanishing love that once was its unquestionable right, to meet confusion instead of inner silence and conservative slumber! And the child *resents* it! Resents the cold air, the huge spaces, the sudden departure from familiar things. And in the tiny filament of brain the only thing the child knows is selfishness and hatred because the spell has been rudely shattered. Who is responsible for this disenchantment, this rude breakage of the spell? The mother. So here the new child has someone to hate with all its unreasoning mind. The mother has cast it out, rejected it. And the father is no better, kill him, too! He's responsible in *his* way!"

Jeffers interrupted. "If what you say is true, then every woman in the world would have to look on her baby as something to dread, something to wonder about."

"And why not? Hasn't the child a perfect alibi? A thousand years of accepted medical belief protects him. By all natural accounts he is helpless, not responsible. The child is born hating. And things grow worse, instead of better. At first the baby gets a certain amount of attention and mothering. But then as time passes, things change. When very new, a baby has the power to make parents do silly things when it cries or sneezes, jump when it makes a noise. As the years pass, the baby feels even that small power slip rapidly, forever away, never to return. Why shouldn't it grasp all the power it can have? Why shouldn't it jockey for position while it has all the advantages? In later years it would be too late to express its hatred. *Now* would be the time to strike."

Leiber's voice was very soft, very low.

"My little boy baby, lying in his crib nights, his face moist and red and out of breath. From crying? No. From climbing slowly out of his crib, from crawling long distances through darkened hallways. My little boy baby. I want to kill him."

The doctor handed him a water glass and some pills. "You're not killing anyone. You're going to sleep for twenty-four hours. Sleep'll change your mind. Take this."

Leiber drank down the pills and let himself be led upstairs to his bedroom, crying, and felt himself being put to bed. The doctor waited until he was moving deep into sleep, then left the house.

Leiber, alone, drifted down, down.

He heard a noise. "What's—what's *that?*" he demanded, feebly.

Something moved in the hall.

David Leiber slept.

Very early the next morning, Dr. Jeffers drove up to the house. It was a good morning, and he was here to drive Leiber to the country for a rest. Leiber would still be asleep upstairs. Jeffers had given him enough sedative to knock him out for at least fifteen hours.

He rang the doorbell. No answer. The servants were probably not up. Jeffers tried the front door, found it open, stepped in. He put his medical kit on the nearest chair.

Something white moved out of sight at the top of the stairs. Just a suggestion of a movement. Jeffers hardly noticed it.

The smell of gas was in the house.

Jeffers ran upstairs, crashed into Leiber's bedroom.

Leiber lay motionless on the bed, and the room billowed with gas, which hissed from a released jet at the base of the wall near the door. Jeffers twisted it off, then forced up all the windows and ran back to Leiber's body.

The body was cold. It had been dead quite a few hours.

Coughing violently, the doctor hurried from the room, eyes watering. Leiber hadn't turned on the gas himself. He *couldn't* have. Those sedatives had knocked him out, he wouldn't have wakened until noon. It wasn't suicide. Or was there the faintest possibility?

Jeffers stood in the hall for five minutes. Then he walked to the door of the nursery. It was shut. He opened it. He walked inside and to the crib.

The crib was empty.

He stood swaying by the crib for half a minute, then he said something to nobody in particular.

"The nursery door blew shut. You couldn't get back into your crib where it was safe. You didn't plan on the door blowing shut. A little thing like a slammed door can ruin the best of plans. I'll find you somewhere in the house, hiding, pretending to be something you are not." The doctor looked dazed. He put his hand to his head and smiled palely. "Now I'm talking like Alice and David talked. But, I can't take any chances. I'm not sure of anything, but I can't take any chances."

He walked downstairs, opened his medical bag on the chair, took something out of it and held it in his hands.

Something rustled down the hall. Something very small and very quiet. Jeffers turned rapidly.

I had to operate to bring you into this world, he thought. Now I guess I can operate to take you out of it. . . .

He took half a dozen slow, sure steps forward into the hall. He raised his hand into the sunlight.

"See, baby! Something bright—something pretty!"

A scalpel.

The Whimper of Whipped Dogs

Harlan Ellison

The expression "I don't want to get involved" has become so entrenched in the vernacular that we have all but forgotten its source. On March 13, 1964, Kitty Genovese was brutally murdered in the courtyard of her Queens, New York, apartment complex while thirty-eight of her neighbors looked on. Not one of them thought to call the police. Sociological studies based on this landmark case presented it as an example of how modern urban life had drastically altered the fundamental dynamics of human social relationships. In "The Whimper of Whipped Dogs," Harlan Ellison uses the Genovese murder as the springboard for a tale of urban survival, in which city dwellers enter into an unholy pact with their environment out of necessity. A lineal descendant of the urban horrors of Fritz Leiber's "Smoke Ghost," Ellison's story epitomizes a dominant theme of postwar horror fiction —that the worst horrors wear a human face. In 1973, the Mystery Writers of America awarded the Edgar to "The Whimper of Whipped Dogs" for best short fiction of that year.

On the night after the day she had stained the louvered window shutters of her new apartment on East 52nd Street, Beth saw a woman slowly and hideously knifed to death in the

courtyard of her building. She was one of twenty-six witnesses to the ghoulish scene, and, like them, she did nothing
to stop it.

She saw it all, every moment of it, without break and with
no impediment to her view. Quite madly, the thought crossed
her mind as she watched in horrified fascination, that she
had the sort of marvelous line of observation Napoleon had
sought when he caused to have constructed at the *Comédie-
Française* theaters, a curtained box at the rear, so he could
watch the audience as well as the stage. The night was clear,
the moon was full, she had just turned off the 11:30 movie on
Channel 2 after the second commercial break, realizing she
had already seen Robert Taylor in *Westward the Women,* and
had disliked it the first time; and the apartment was quite
dark.

She went to the window, to raise it six inches for the night's
sleep, and she saw the woman stumble into the courtyard.
She was sliding along the wall, clutching her left arm with
her right hand. Con Ed had installed mercury-vapor lamps on
the poles; there had been sixteen assaults in seven months;
the courtyard was illuminated with a chill purple glow that
made the blood streaming down the woman's left arm look
black and shiny. Beth saw every detail with utter clarity, as
though magnified a thousand power under a microscope, so-
larized as if it had been a television commercial.

The woman threw back her head, as if she were trying to
scream, but there was no sound. Only the traffic on First Avenue, late cabs foraging for singles paired for the night at
Maxwell's Plum and Friday's and Adam's Apple. But that
was over there, beyond. Where *she* was, down there seven
floors below, in the courtyard, everything seemed silently suspended in an invisible force-field.

Beth stood in the darkness of her apartment, and realized
she had raised the window completely. A tiny balcony lay just
over the low sill; now not even glass separated her from the
sight; just the wrought-iron balcony railing and seven floors
to the courtyard below.

The woman staggered away from the wall, her head still
thrown back, and Beth could see she was in her mid-thirties,
with dark hair cut in a shag; it was impossible to tell if she

was pretty: terror had contorted her features and her mouth was a twisted black slash, opened but emitting no sound. Cords stood out in her neck. She had lost one shoe, and her steps were uneven, threatening to dump her to the pavement.

The man came around the corner of the building, into the courtyard. The knife he held was enormous—or perhaps it only seemed so: Beth remembered a bone-handled fish knife her father had used one summer at the lake in Maine: it folded back on itself and locked, revealing eight inches of serrated blade. The knife in the hand of the dark man in the courtyard seemed to be similar.

The woman saw him and tried to run, but he leaped across the distance between them and grabbed her by the hair and pulled her head back as though he would slash her throat in the next reaper-motion.

Then the woman screamed.

The sound skirled up into the courtyard like bats trapped in an echo chamber, unable to find a way out, driven mad. It went on and on. . . .

The man struggled with her and she drove her elbows into his sides and he tried to protect himself, spinning her around by her hair, the terrible scream going up and up and never stopping. She came loose and he was left with a fistful of hair torn out by the roots. As she spun out, he slashed straight across and opened her up just below the breasts. Blood sprayed through her clothing and the man was soaked; it seemed to drive him even more berserk. He went at her again, as she tried to hold herself together, the blood pouring down over her arms.

She tried to run, teetered against the wall, slid sidewise, and the man struck the brick surface. She was away, stumbling over a flower bed, falling, getting to her knees as he threw himself on her again. The knife came up in a flashing arc that illuminated the blade strangely with purple light. And still she screamed.

Lights came on in dozens of apartments and people appeared at windows.

He drove the knife to the hilt into her back, high on the right shoulder. He used both hands.

Beth caught it all in jagged flashes—the man, the woman,

the knife, the blood, the expressions on the faces of those watching from the windows. Then lights clicked off in the windows, but they still stood there, watching.

She wanted to yell, to scream, "What are you doing to that woman?" But her throat was frozen, two iron hands that had been immersed in dry ice for ten thousand years clamped around her neck. She could feel the blade sliding into her own body.

Somehow—it seemed impossible but there it was down there, happening somehow—the woman struggled erect and *pulled* herself off the knife. Three steps, she took three steps and fell into the flower bed again. The man was howling now, like a great beast, the sounds inarticulate, bubbling up from his stomach. He fell on her and the knife went up and came down, then again, and again, and finally it was all a blur of motion, and her scream of lunatic bats went on till it faded off and was gone.

Beth stood in the darkness, trembling and crying, the sight filling her eyes with horror. And when she could no longer bear to look at what he was doing down there to the unmoving piece of meat over which he worked, she looked up and around at the windows of darkness where the others still stood—even as she stood—and somehow she could see their faces, bruise-purple with the dim light from the mercury lamps, and there was a universal sameness to their expressions. The women stood with their nails biting into the upper arms of their men, their tongues edging from the corners of their mouths; the men were wild-eyed and smiling. They all looked as though they were at cock fights. Breathing deeply. Drawing some sustenance from the grisly scene below. An exhalation of sound, deep, deep, as though from caverns beneath the earth. Flesh pale and moist.

And it was then that she realized the courtyard had grown foggy, as though mist off the East River had rolled up 52nd Street in a veil that would obscure the details of what the knife and the man were still doing . . . endlessly doing it . . . long after there was any joy in it . . . still doing it . . . again and again . . .

But the fog was unnatural, thick and gray and filled with tiny scintillas of light. She stared at it, rising up in the empty space of the courtyard. Bach in the cathedral, stardust in a vacuum chamber.

Beth saw eyes.

There, up there, at the ninth floor and higher, two great eyes, as surely as night and the moon, there were *eyes*. And— a face? Was that a face, could she be sure, was she imagining it . . . a face? In the roiling vapors of chill fog something lived, something brooding and patient and utterly malevolent had been summoned up to witness what was happening down there in the flower bed. Beth tried to look away, but could not. The eyes, those primal burning eyes, filled with an abysmal antiquity yet frighteningly bright and anxious like the eyes of a child; eyes filled with tomb depths, ancient and new, chasm-filled, burning, gigantic and deep as an abyss, holding her, compelling her. The shadow play was being staged not only for the tenants in their windows, watching and drinking of the scene, but for some *other*. Not on frigid tundra or waste moors, not in subterranean caverns or on some faraway world circling a dying sun, but here, in the city, here the eyes of that *other* watched.

Shaking with the effort, Beth wrenched her eyes from those burning depths up there beyond the ninth floor, only to see again the horror that had brought that *other*. And she was struck for the first time by the awfulness of what she was witnessing, she was released from the immobility that had held her like a coelacanth in shale, she was filled with the blood thunder pounding against the membranes of her mind: she had *stood* there! She had done nothing, nothing! A woman had been butchered and she had said nothing, done nothing. Tears had been useless, tremblings had been pointless, she *had done nothing*!

Then she heard hysterical sounds midway between laughter and giggling, and as she stared up into that great face rising in the fog and chimneysmoke of the night, she heard *herself* making those deranged gibbon noises and from the man below a pathetic, trapped sound, like the whimper of whipped dogs.

She was staring up into that face again. She hadn't wanted to see it again—ever. But she was locked with those smoldering eyes, overcome with the feeling that they were childlike, though she *knew* they were incalculably ancient.

Then the butcher below did an unspeakable thing and Beth reeled with dizziness and caught the edge of the window before she could tumble out onto the balcony; she steadied herself and fought for breath.

She felt herself being looked at, and for a long moment of frozen terror she feared she might have caught the attention of that face up there in the fog. She clung to the window, feeling everything growing faraway and dim, and stared straight across the court. She *was* being watched. Intently. By the young man in the seventh-floor window across from her own apartment. Steadily, he was looking at her. Through the strange fog with its burning eyes feasting on the sight below, he was staring at her.

As she felt herself blacking out, in the moment before unconsciousness, the thought flickered and fled that there was something terribly familiar about his face.

It rained the next day. East 52nd Street was slick and shining with the oil rainbows. The rain washed the dog turds into the gutters and nudged them down and down to the catch-basin openings. People bent against the slanting rain, hidden beneath umbrellas, looking like enormous, scurrying black mushrooms. Beth went out to get the newspapers after the police had come and gone.

The news reports dwelled with loving emphasis on the twenty-six tenants of the building who had watched in cold interest as Leona Ciarelli, 37, of 455 Fort Washington Avenue, Manhattan, had been systematically stabbed to death by Burton H. Wells, 41, an unemployed electrician, who had been subsequently shot to death by two off-duty police officers when he burst into Michael's Pub on 55th Street, covered with blood and brandishing a knife that authorities later identified as the murder weapon.

She had thrown up twice that day. Her stomach seemed incapable of retaining anything solid, and the taste of bile lay along the back of her tongue. She could not blot the scenes of the night before from her mind; she re-ran them again and again, every movement of that reaper arm playing over and over as though on a short loop of memory. The woman's head thrown back for silent screams. The blood. Those eyes in the fog.

She was drawn again and again to the window, to stare down into the courtyard and the street. She tried to superimpose over the bleak Manhattan concrete the view from her window in Swann House at Bennington: the little yard and another white, frame dormitory; the fantastic apple trees; and from the other window the rolling hills and gorgeous Vermont countryside; her memory skittered through the change of seasons. But there was always concrete and the rain-slick streets; the rain on the pavement was black and shiny as blood.

She tried to work, rolling up the tambour closure of the old rolltop desk she had bought on Lexington Avenue and hunching over the graph sheets of choreographer's charts. But Labanotation was merely a Jackson Pollock jumble of arcane hieroglyphics to her today, instead of the careful representation of eurhythmics she had studied four years to perfect. And before that, Farmington.

The phone rang. It was the secretary from the Taylor Dance Company, asking when she would be free. She had to beg off. She looked at her hand, lying on the graph sheets of figures Laban had devised, and she saw her fingers trembling. She had to beg off. Then she called Guzman at the Downtown Ballet Company, to tell him she would be late with the charts.

"My God, lady, I have ten dancers sitting around in a rehearsal hall getting their leotards sweaty! What do you expect me to do?"

She explained what had happened the night before. And as she told him, she realized the newspapers had been justified in holding that tone against the twenty-six witnesses to the death of Leona Ciarelli. Paschal Guzman listened, and when he spoke again, his voice was several octaves lower, and he spoke more slowly. He said he understood and she could take a little longer to prepare the charts. But there was a distance in his voice, and he hung up while she was thanking him.

She dressed in an argyle sweater vest in shades of dark purple, and a pair of fitted khaki gabardine trousers. She had to go out, to walk around. To do what? To think about other things. As she pulled on the Fred Braun chunky heels, she idly wondered if that heavy silver bracelet was still in the window of Georg Jensen's. In the elevator, the young man from the window across the courtyard stared at her. Beth felt her body begin to tremble again. She went deep into the corner of the box when he entered behind her.

Between the fifth and fourth floors, he hit the *off* switch and the elevator jerked to a halt.

Beth stared at him and he smiled innocently.

"Hi. My name's Gleeson, Ray Gleeson, I'm in 714."

She wanted to demand he turn the elevator back on, by what right did he pre*sume* to do such a thing, what did he mean by this, turn it on at once or suffer the consequences. That was what she *wanted* to do. Instead, from the same place she had heard the gibbering laughter the night before, she heard her voice, much smaller and much less possessed than she had trained it to be, saying, "Beth O'Neill, I live in 701."

The thing about it, was that *the elevator was stopped.* And she was frightened. But he leaned against the paneled wall, very well dressed, shoes polished, hair combed and probably blown dry with a hand dryer, and he *talked* to her as if they were across a table at L'Argenteuil. "You just moved in, huh?"

"About two months ago."

"Where did you go to school? Bennington or Sarah Lawrence?"

"Bennington. How did you know?"

He laughed, and it was a nice laugh. "I'm an editor at a religious book publisher; every year we get half a dozen Bennington, Sarah Lawrence, Smith girls. They come hopping in like grasshoppers, ready to revolutionize the publishing industry."

"What's wrong with that? You sound like you don't care for them."

"Oh, I *love* them, they're marvelous. They think they know how to write better than the authors we publish. Had one darlin' little item who was given galleys of three books to proof, and she rewrote all three. I think she's working as a table-swabber in a Horn & Hardart's now."

She didn't reply to that. She would have pegged him as an anti-feminist, ordinarily, if it had been anyone else speaking. But the eyes. There was something terribly familiar about his face. She was enjoying the conversation; she rather liked him.

"What's the nearest big city to Bennington?"

"Albany, New York. About sixty miles."

"How long does it take to drive there?"

"From Bennington? About an hour and a half."

"Must be a nice drive, that Vermont country, really pretty. They went coed, I understand. How's that working out?"

"I don't know, really."

"You don't know?"

"It happened around the time I was graduating."

"What did you major in?"

"I was a dance major, specializing in Labanotation. That's the way you write choreography."

"It's all electives, I gather. You don't have to take anything required, like sciences, for example." He didn't change tone as he said, "That was a terrible thing last night. I saw you watching. I guess a lot of us were watching. It was a really terrible thing."

She nodded dumbly. Fear came back.

"I understand the cops got him. Some nut, they don't even know why he killed her, or why he went charging into that bar. It was really an awful thing. I'd very much like to have dinner with you one night soon, if you're not attached."

"That would be all right."

"Maybe Wednesday. There's an Argentinian place I know. You might like it."

"That would be all right."

"Why don't you turn on the elevator, and we can go," he said, and smiled again. She did it, wondering why she had stopped the elevator in the first place.

On her third date with him, they had their first fight. It was at a party thrown by a director of television commercials. He lived on the ninth floor of their building. He had just done a series of spots for *Sesame Street* (the letters "U" for Underpass, "T" for Tunnel, lowercase "b" for boats, "c" for cars; the numbers 1 to 6 and the numbers 1 to 20; the words *light* and *dark*) and was celebrating his move from the arena of commercial tawdriness (and its attendant $75,000 a year) to the sweet fields of educational programming (and its accompanying descent into low-pay respectability). There was a logic in his joy Beth could not quite understand, and when she talked with him about it, in a far corner of the kitchen, his arguments didn't seem to parse. But he seemed happy, and his girlfriend, a long-legged ex-model from Philadelphia, continued to drift to him and away from him, like some exquisite undersea plant, touching his hair and kissing his neck, murmuring words of pride and barely submerged sexuality. Beth found it bewildering, though the celebrants were all bright and lively.

In the living room, Ray was sitting on the arm of the sofa, hustling a stewardess named Luanne. Beth could tell he was hustling; he was trying to look casual. When he *wasn't* hustling, he was always intense, about everything. She decided to ignore it, and wandered around the apartment, sipping at a Tanqueray and tonic.

There were framed prints of abstract shapes clipped from a calendar printed in Germany. They were in metal Bonniers frames.

In the dining room a huge door from a demolished building somewhere in the city had been handsomely stripped, teaked and refinished. It was now the dinner table.

A Lightolier fixture attached to the wall over the bed swung out, levered up and down, tipped, and its burnished globe-head revolved a full three hundred and sixty degrees.

She was standing in the bedroom, looking out the window, when she realized *this* had been one of the rooms in which light had gone on, gone off; one of the rooms that had contained a silent watcher at the death of Leona Ciarelli.

When she returned to the living room, she looked around more carefully. With only three or four exceptions—the stewardess, a young married couple from the second floor, a stockbroker from Hemphill, Noyes—*everyone* at the party had been a witness to the slaying.

"I'd like to go," she told him.

"Why, aren't you having a good time?" asked the stewardess, a mocking smile crossing her perfect little face.

"Like all Bennington ladies," Ray said, answering for Beth, "she is enjoying herself most by not enjoying herself at all. It's a trait of the anal retentive. Being here in someone else's apartment, she can't empty ashtrays or rewind the toilet paper roll so it doesn't hang a tongue, and being tightassed, her nature demands we go.

"All right, Beth, let's say our goodbyes and take off. The Phantom Rectum strikes again."

She slapped him and the stewardess's eyes widened. But the smile remained frozen where it had appeared.

He grabbed her wrist before she could do it again. "Garbanzo beans, baby," he said, holding her wrist tighter than necessary.

They went back to her apartment, and after sparring silently with kitchen cabinet doors slammed and the television being tuned too loud, they got to her bed, and he tried to perpetuate the metaphor by fucking her in the ass. He had her on elbows and knees before she realized what he was doing; she struggled to turn over and he rode her bucking and tossing without a sound. And when it was clear to him that she would never permit it, he grabbed her breast from underneath and squeezed so hard she howled in pain. He dumped her on her back, rubbed himself between her legs a dozen times, and came on her stomach.

Beth lay with her eyes closed and an arm thrown across her face. She wanted to cry, but found she could not. Ray lay on her and said nothing. She wanted to rush to the bathroom and shower, but he did not move, till long after his semen had dried on their bodies.

"Who did you date at college?" he asked.

"I didn't date anyone very much." Sullen.

"No heavy makeouts with wealthy lads from Williams and Dartmouth . . . no Amherst intellectuals begging you to save them from creeping faggotry by permitting them to stick their carrots in your sticky little slit?"

"Stop it!"

"Come on, baby, it couldn't all have been knee socks and

little round circle-pins. You don't expect me to believe you didn't get a little mouthful of cock from time to time. It's only, what? about fifteen miles to Williamstown? I'm sure the Williams werewolves were down burning the highway to your cunt on weekends; you can level with old Uncle Ray. . . ."

"Why are you like this?!" She started to move, to get away from him, and he grabbed her by the shoulder, forced her to lie down again. Then he rose up over her and said, "I'm like this because I'm a New Yorker, baby. Because I live in this fucking city every day. Because I have to play patty-cake with the ministers and other sanctified holy-joe assholes who want their goodness and lightness tracts published by the Blessed Sacrament Publishing and Storm Window Company of 277 Park Avenue, when what I *really* want to do is toss the stupid psalm-suckers out the thirty-seventh-floor window and listen to them quote chapter-and-worse all the way down. Because I've lived in this great big snapping dog of a city all my life and I'm mad as a mudfly, for chrissakes!"

She lay unable to move, breathing shallowly, filled with a sudden pity and affection for him. His face was white and strained, and she knew he was saying things to her that only a bit too much Almadén and exact timing would have let him say.

"What do you expect from me," he said, his voice softer now, but no less intense, "do you expect kindness and gentility and understanding and a hand on *your* hand when the smog burns your eyes? I can't do it, I haven't got it. No one has it in this cesspool of a city. Look around you; what do you think is happening here? They take rats and they put them in boxes and when there are too many of them, some of the little fuckers go out of their minds and start gnawing the rest to death. *It ain't no different here, baby!* It's rat time for everybody in this madhouse. You can't expect to jam as many people into this stone thing as we do, with buses and taxis and dogs shitting themselves scrawny and noise night and day and no money and not enough places to live and no place to go to have a decent think . . . you can't do it without making the time right for some godforsaken other kind of thing to be born! You can't hate everyone around you, and

kick every beggar and nigger and *mestizo* shithead, you can't
have cabbies stealing from you and taking tips they don't
deserve, and then cursing you, you can't walk in the soot till
your collar turns black, and your body stinks with the smell
of flaking brick and decaying brains, you can't do it without
calling up some kind of awful—"

He stopped.

His face bore the expression of a man who has just received
brutal word of the death of a loved one. He suddenly lay
down, rolled over, and turned off.

She lay beside him, trembling, trying desperately to remember where she had seen his face before.

He didn't call her again, after the night of the party. And
when they met in the hall, he pointedly turned away, as
though he had given her some obscure chance and she had
refused to take it. Beth thought she understood: though Ray
Gleeson had not been her first affair, he had been the first to
reject her so completely. The first to put her not only out of
his bed and his life, but even out of his world. It was as
though she were invisible, not even beneath contempt, simply
not there.

She busied herself with other things.

She took on three new charting jobs for Guzman and a new
group that had formed on Staten Island, of all places. She
worked furiously and they gave her new assignments; they
even paid her.

She tried to decorate the apartment with a less precise
touch. Huge poster blowups of Merce Cunningham and
Martha Graham replaced the Brueghel prints that had reminded her of the view looking down the hill toward Williams. The tiny balcony outside her window, the balcony she
had steadfastly refused to stand upon since the night of the
slaughter, the night of the fog with eyes, that balcony she
swept and set about with little flower boxes in which she
planted geraniums, petunias, dwarf zinnias, and other hardy
perennials. Then, closing the window, she went to give herself, to involve herself in this city to which she had brought
her ordered life.

And the city responded to her overtures:

Seeing off an old friend from Bennington, at Kennedy International, she stopped at the terminal coffee shop to have a sandwich. The counter—like a moat—surrounded a center service island that had huge advertising cubes rising above it on burnished poles. The cubes proclaimed the delights of Fun City. *New York Is a Summer Festival,* they said, and *Joseph Papp Presents Shakespeare in Central Park* and *Visit the Bronx Zoo* and *You'll Adore Our Contentious but Lovable Cabbies.* The food emerged from a window far down the service area and moved slowly on a conveyor belt through the hordes of screaming waitresses who slathered the counter with redolent washcloths. The lunchroom had all the charm and dignity of a steel-rolling mill, and approximately the same noise level. Beth ordered a cheeseburger that cost a dollar and a quarter, and a glass of milk.

When it came, it was cold, the cheese unmelted, and the patty of meat resembling nothing so much as a dirty scouring pad. The bun was cold and untoasted. There was no lettuce under the patty.

Beth managed to catch the waitress's eye. The girl approached with an annoyed look. "Please toast the bun and may I have a piece of lettuce?" Beth said.

"We dun' do that," the waitress said, turning half away as though she would walk in a moment.

"You don't do what?"

"We dun' toass the bun here."

"Yes, but I *want* the bun toasted," Beth said firmly.

"An' you got to pay for extra lettuce."

"If I was asking for *extra* lettuce," Beth said, getting annoyed, "I would pay for it, but since there's *no* lettuce here, I don't think I should be charged extra for the first piece."

"We dun' do that."

The waitress started to walk away. "Hold it," Beth said, raising her voice just enough so the assembly-line eaters on either side stared at her. "You mean to tell me I have to pay a dollar and a quarter and I can't get a piece of lettuce or even get the bun toasted?"

"Ef you dun' like it . . ."

"Take it back."

"You gotta pay for it, you order it."

"I said take it back, I don't want the fucking thing!"

The waitress scratched it off the check. The milk cost 27¢ and tasted going-sour. It was the first time in her life that Beth had said *that* word aloud.

At the cashier's stand, Beth said to the sweating man with the felt-tip pens in his shirt pocket, "Just out of curiosity, are you interested in complaints?"

"No!" he said, snarling, quite literally snarling. He did not look up as he punched out 73¢ and it came rolling down the chute.

The city responded to her overtures:

It was raining again. She was trying to cross Second Avenue, with the light. She stepped off the curb and a car came sliding through the red and splashed her. "Hey!" she yelled.

"Eat shit, sister!" the driver yelled back, turning the corner.

Her boots, her legs and her overcoat were splattered with mud. She stood trembling on the curb.

The city responded to her overtures:

She emerged from the building at One Astor Place with her big briefcase full of Laban charts; she was adjusting her rain scarf about her head. A well-dressed man with an attaché case thrust the handle of his umbrella up between her legs from the rear. She gasped and dropped her case.

The city responded and responded and responded.

Her overtures altered quickly.

The old drunk with the stippled cheeks extended his hand and mumbled words. She cursed him and walked on up Broadway past the beaver film houses.

She crossed against the lights on Park Avenue, making hackies slam their brakes to avoid hitting her; she used *that* word frequently now.

When she found herself having a drink with a man who had elbowed up beside her in the singles' bar, she felt faint and knew she should go home.

But Vermont was so far away.

Nights later. She had come home from the Lincoln Center ballet, and gone straight to bed. Lying half-asleep in her bedroom, she heard an alien sound. One room away, in the living room, in the dark, there was a sound. She slipped out of bed and went to the door between the rooms. She fumbled silently for the switch on the lamp just inside the living room, and found it, and clicked it on. A black man in a leather car coat was trying to get *out* of the apartment. In that first flash of light filling the room she noticed the television set beside him on the floor as he struggled with the door, she noticed the police lock and bar had been broken in a new and clever manner *New York* magazine had not yet reported in a feature article on apartment ripoffs, she noticed that he had gotten his foot tangled in the telephone cord that she had requested be extra-long so she could carry the instrument into the bathroom, I don't want to miss any business calls when the shower is running; she noticed all things in perspective and one thing with sharpest clarity: the expression on the burglar's face.

There was something familiar in that expression.

He almost had the door open, but now he closed it, and slipped the police lock. He took a step toward her.

Beth went back, into the darkened bedroom.

The city responded to her overtures.

She backed against the wall at the head of the bed. Her hand fumbled in the shadows for the telephone. His shape filled the doorway, light, all light behind him.

In silhouette it should not have been possible to tell, but somehow she knew he was wearing gloves and the only marks he would leave would be deep bruises, very blue, almost black, with the tinge under them of blood that had been stopped in its course.

He came for her, arms hanging casually at his sides. She tried to climb over the bed, and he grabbed her from behind, ripping her nightgown. Then he had a hand around her neck and he pulled her backward. She fell off the bed, landed at his feet and his hold was broken. She scuttled across the floor and for a moment she had the respite to feel terror. She was going to die, and she was frightened.

He trapped her in the corner between the closet and the bureau and kicked her. His foot caught her in the thigh as she folded tighter, smaller, drawing her legs up. She was cold.

Then he reached down with both hands and pulled her

erect by her hair. He slammed her head against the wall.
Everything slid up in her sight as though running off the
edge of the world. He slammed her head against the wall
again, and she felt something go soft over her right ear.

When he tried to slam her a third time she reached out
blindly for his face and ripped down with her nails. He
howled in pain and she hurled herself forward, arms wrapping themselves around his waist. He stumbled backward
and in a tangle of thrashing arms and legs they fell out onto
the little balcony.

Beth landed on the bottom, feeling the window boxes
jammed up against her spine and legs. She fought to get to
her feet, and her nails hooked into his shirt under the open
jacket, ripping. Then she was on her feet again and they
struggled silently.

He whirled her around, bent her backward across the
wrought-iron railing. Her face was turned outward.

They were standing in their windows, watching.

Through the fog she could see them watching. Through the
fog she recognized their expressions. Through the fog she
heard them breathing in unison, bellows breathing of expectation and wonder. Through the fog.

And the black man punched her in the throat. She gagged
and started to black out and could not draw air into her
lungs. Back, back, he bent her further back and she was looking up, straight up, toward the ninth floor and higher . . .

Up there: eyes.

The words Ray Gleeson had said in a moment filled with
what he had become, with the utter hopelessness and finality
of the choice the city had forced on him, the words came back.
*You can't live in this city and survive unless you have protec-
tion . . . you can't live this way, like rats driven mad, without making the time right for some godforsaken other kind of
thing to be born . . . you can't do it without calling up some
kind of awful . . .*

God! A new God, an ancient God come again with the eyes
and hunger of a child, a deranged blood God of fog and street
violence. A God who needed worshippers and offered the
choices of death as a victim or life as an eternal witness to the

deaths of *other* chosen victims. A God to fit the times, a God of streets and people.

She tried to shriek, to appeal to Ray, to the director in the bedroom window of his ninth-floor apartment with his long-legged Philadelphia model beside him and his fingers inside her as they worshipped in their holiest of ways, to the others who had been at the party that had been Ray's offer of a chance to join their congregation. She wanted to be saved from having to make that choice.

But the black man had punched her in the throat, and now his hands were on her, one on her chest, the other in her face, the smell of leather filling her where the nausea could not. And she understood Ray had *cared,* had wanted her to take the chance offered; but she had come from a world of little white dormitories and Vermont countryside; it was not a real world. *This* was the real world and up there was the God who ruled this world, and she had rejected him, had said no to one of his priests and servitors. *Save me! Don't make me do it!*

She knew she had to call out, to make appeal, to try and win the approbation of that God. *I can't . . . save me!*

She struggled and made terrible little mewling sounds trying to summon the words to cry out, and suddenly she crossed a line, and screamed up into the echoing courtyard with a voice Leona Ciarelli had never known enough to use.

"Him! Take him! Not me! I'm yours, I love you, I'm yours! Take him, not me, please not me, take him, take him, I'm yours!"

And the black man was suddenly lifted away, wrenched off her, and off the balcony, whirled straight up into the fog-thick air in the courtyard, as Beth sank to her knees on the ruined flower boxes.

She was half-conscious, and could not be sure she saw it just that way, but up he went, end over end, whirling and spinning like a charred leaf.

And the form took firmer shape. Enormous paws with claws and shapes that no animal she had ever seen had ever possessed, and the burglar, black, poor, terrified, whimpering like a whipped dog, was stripped of his flesh. His body was opened with a thin incision, and there was a rush as all the blood poured from him like a sudden cloudburst, and yet he was still alive, twitching with the involuntary horror of a frog's leg shocked with an electric current. Twitched, and twitched again as he was torn piece by piece to shreds. Pieces of flesh and bone and half a face with an eye blinking furiously, cascaded down past Beth, and hit the cement below with sodden thuds. And still he was alive, as his organs were squeezed and musculature and bile and shit and skin were rubbed, sandpapered together and let fall. It went on and on, as the death of Leona Ciarelli had gone on and on, and she understood with the blood-knowledge of survivors *at any cost* that the reason the witnesses to the death of Leona Ciarelli had done nothing was not that they had been frozen with horror, that they didn't want to get involved, or that they were inured to death by years of television slaughter.

They were worshippers at a black mass the city had demanded be staged; not once, but a thousand times a day in this insane asylum of steel and stone.

Now she was on her feet, standing half-naked in her ripped nightgown, her hands tightening on the wrought-iron railing, begging to see more, to drink deeper.

Now she was one of them, as the pieces of the night's sacrifice fell past her, bleeding and screaming.

Tomorrow the police would come again, and they would question her, and she would say how terrible it had been, that burglar, and how she had fought, afraid he would rape her and kill her, and how he had fallen, and she had no idea how he had been so hideously mangled and ripped apart, but a seven-storey fall, after all . . .

Tomorrow she would not have to worry about walking in the streets, because no harm could come to her. Tomorrow she could even remove the police lock. Nothing in the city could do her any further evil, because she had made the only choice. She was now a dweller in the city, now wholly and richly a part of it. Now she was taken to the bosom of her God.

She felt Ray beside her, standing beside her, holding her, protecting her, his hand on her naked backside, and she watched the fog swirl up and fill the courtyard, fill the city, fill her eyes and her soul and her heart with its power. As Ray's naked body pressed tightly inside her, she drank deeply of the night, knowing whatever voices she heard from this moment forward would be the voices not of whipped dogs, but those of strong, meat-eating beasts.

At last she was unafraid, and it was so good, so very good *not* to be afraid.

"When inward life dries up, when feeling decreases and apathy increases, when one cannot affect or even genuinely touch another person, violence flares up as a daimonic necessity for contact, a mad drive forcing touch in the most direct way possible."

—Rollo May,
LOVE AND WILL

Calling Card

Ramsey Campbell

The Christmas ghost story is a venerable English tradition within the tradition of supernatural horror fiction. Although its origins extend back into the nineteenth century to the Christmas books of Charles Dickens, it is probably most closely associated with the work of M. R. James, whose stories were often written to be read to friends at the Yuletide season. Ramsey Campbell's "Calling Card" (1981) is both an homage to James's restrained tales of horror and a fine example of the changes Campbell has wrought on Jamesian principles for writing ghost stories. In the drab world of Campbell's fiction, the least upset to the boring routines of daily life is enough to plunge characters into doubt about the certainty of their surroundings. Even the garbage at the curb begins to take on an ominous cast. In the well-told Campbell story, it is impossible to determine whether characters are "done in" or succumb to their increasingly paranoid delusions.

Dorothy Harris stepped off the pavement and into her hall. As she stooped groaning to pick up the envelopes the front door opened, a yawn that wouldn't be suppressed. She wrestled it shut—she must ask Simon to see to it, though certainly not over Christmas—then she began to open the cards.

Here was Father Christmas, and here he was again, apparently after dieting. Here was a robin like a rosy apple with a beak, and here was an envelope whose handwriting staggered: Simon's and Margery's children, perhaps?

The card showed a church on a snowy hill. The hill was bare except for a smudge of ink. Though the card was unsigned, there was writing within. A Very Happy Christmas And A Prosperous New Year, the message should have said—but now it said A Very Harried Christmas And No New Year. She turned back to the picture, her hands shaking. It wasn't just a smudge of ink; someone had drawn a smeary cross on the hill: a grave.

Though the name on the envelope was a watery blur, the address was certainly hers. Suddenly the house—the kitchen and living room, the two bedrooms with her memories stacked neatly against the walls—seemed far too large and dim. Without moving from the front door she phoned Margery.

"Is it Grandma?" Margery had to hush the children while she said, "You come as soon as you like, Mummy."

Lark Lane was deserted. An unsold Christmas tree loitered in a shop doorway, a gargoyle craned out from the police station. Once Margery had moved away, the nearness of the police had been reassuring—not that Dorothy was nervous, like some of the old folk these days—but the police station was only a community center now.

The bus already sounded like a pub. She sat outside on the ferry, though the bench looked and felt like black ice. Lights fished in the Mersey, gulls drifted down like snowflakes from the muddy sky. A whitish object grabbed the rail, but of course it was only a gull. Nevertheless she was glad that Simon was waiting with the car at Woodside.

As soon as the children had been packed off to bed so that Father Christmas could get to work, she produced the card. It felt wet, almost slimy, though it hadn't before. Simon pointed out what she'd overlooked: the age of the stamp. "We weren't even living there then," Margery said. "You wouldn't think they would bother delivering it after sixty years."

"A touch of the Christmas spirit."

"I wish they hadn't bothered," Margery said. But her mother didn't mind now; the addressee must have died years ago. She turned the conversation to old times, to Margery's father. Later she gazed from her bedroom window, at the houses of Bebington sleeping in pairs. A man was creeping about the house, but it was only Simon, laden with presents.

In the morning the house was full of cries of delight, gleaming new toys, balls of wrapping paper big as cabbages. In the afternoon the adults, bulging with turkey and pudding, lolled in chairs. When Simon drove her home that night, Dorothy noticed that the unsold Christmas tree was still there, a scrawny glistening shape at the back of the shop doorway. As soon as Simon left, she found herself thinking about the unpleasant card. She tore it up, then went determinedly to bed.

Boxing Day was her busiest time, what with cooking the second version of Christmas dinner, and making sure the house was impeccable, and hiding small presents for the children to find. She wished she could see them more often, but they and their parents had their own lives to lead.

An insect clung to a tinsel globe on the tree. When she reached out to squash the insect it wasn't there, neither on the globe nor on the floor. Could it have been the reflection of someone thin outside the window? Nobody was there now.

She liked the house best when it was full of laughter, and it would be again soon: "We'll get a sitter," Margery promised, "and first-foot you on New Year's Eve." She'd used to do that when she had lived at home—she'd waited outside at midnight of the Old Year so as to be the first to cross her mother's threshold. That reminded Dorothy to offer the children a holiday treat. Everything seemed fine, even when they went to the door to leave. "Grandma, someone's left you a present," little Denise cried.

Then she cried out, and dropped the package. Perhaps the wind had snatched it from her hands. As the package, which looked wet and moldy, struck the curb it broke open. Did its contents scuttle out and sidle away into the dark? Surely that was the play of the wind, which tumbled carton and wrapping away down the street.

Someone must have used her doorway for a wastebin, that was all. Dorothy lay in bed, listening to the wind which groped around the windowless side of the house, that faced onto the alley. She kept thinking she was on the ferry, backing away from the rail, forgetting that the rail was also behind her. Her nervousness annoyed her—she was acting like an old fogey—which was why, next afternoon, she walked to Otterspool promenade.

Gulls and planes sailed over the Mersey, which was deserted except for buoys. On the far bank, tiny towns and stalks of factory chimneys stood at the foot of an enormous frieze of clouds. Sunlight slipped through to Birkenhead and Wallasey, touching up the colors of microscopic streets; specks of windows glinted. She enjoyed none of this, for the slopping of water beneath the promenade seemed to be pacing her. Worse, she couldn't make herself go to the rail to prove that there was nothing.

Really, it was heartbreaking. One vicious card and she felt nervous in her own house. A blurred voice seemed to creep behind the carols on the radio, lowing out of tune. Next day she took her washing to Lark Lane, in search of distraction as much as anything.

The Westinghouse Laundromat was deserted. O O O, the washing machines said emptily. There was only herself, and her dervishes of clothes, and a black plastic bag almost as tall as she was. If someone had abandoned it, whatever its lumpy contents were, she could see why, for it was leaking; she smelled stagnant water. It must be a draft that made it twitch feebly. Nevertheless, if she had been able to turn off her machine she might have fled.

She mustn't grow neurotic. She still had friends to visit. The following day she went to a friend whose flat overlooked Wavertree Park. It was all very convivial—a rainstorm outside made the mince pies more warming, the chat flowed as easily as the whiskey—but she kept glancing at the thin figure who stood in the park, unmoved by the downpour. The trails of rain on the window must be lending him their color, for his skin looked like a snail's.

Eventually the 68 bus, meandering like a drunkard's monologue, took her home to Aigburth. No, the man in the park hadn't really looked as though his clothes and his body had merged into a single grayish mass. Tomorrow she was taking the children for their treat, and that would clear her mind.

She took them to the aquarium. Piranhas sank stonily, their sides glittering like Christmas cards. Toads were bubbling lumps of tar. Finny humbugs swam, and darting fish wired with light. Had one of the tanks cracked? There seemed to be a stagnant smell.

In the museum everything was under glass: shrunken heads like sewn leathery handbags, a watchmaker's workshop, buses passing as though the windows were silent films. Here was a slum street, walled in by photographs of despair, real flagstones underfoot, overhung by streetlamps on brackets. She halted between a grid and a drinking fountain; she was trapped in the dimness between blind corners, and couldn't see either way. Why couldn't she get rid of the stagnant smell? Gray forlorn faces, pressed like specimens, peered out of the walls. "Come on, quickly," she said, pretending that only the children were nervous.

She was glad of the packed crowds in Church Street, even though the children kept letting go of her hands. But the stagnant smell was trailing her, and once, when she grabbed for little Denise's hand, she clutched someone else's, which felt soft and wet. It must have been nervousness which made her fingers seem to sink into the hand.

That night she returned to the aquarium and found she was locked in. Except for the glow of the tanks, the narrow room was oppressively dark. In the nearest tank a large dead fish floated toward her, out of weeds. Now she was in the tank, her nails scrabbling at the glass, and she saw that it wasn't a fish but a snail-colored hand, which closed spongily on hers. When she woke, her scream made the house sound very empty.

At least it was New Year's Eve. After tonight she could stop worrying. Why had she thought that? It only made her more nervous. Even when Margery phoned to confirm they would first-foot her, that reminded her how many hours she would be on her own. As the night seeped into the house, the emptiness grew.

A knock at the front door made her start, but it was only the Harveys, inviting her next door for sherry and sandwiches. While she dodged a sudden rainstorm, Mr. Harvey dragged at her front door, one hand through the letter box, until the latch clicked.

After several sherries Dorothy remembered something

she'd once heard. "The lady who lived next door before me—
didn't she have trouble with her son?"

"He wasn't right in the head. He got so he'd go for anyone,
even if he'd never met them before. She got so scared of him
she locked him out one New Year's Eve. They say he threw
himself in the river, though they never found the body."

Dorothy wished she hadn't asked. She thought of the body,
rotting in the depths. She must go home, in case Simon and
Margery arrived. The Harveys were next door if she needed
them.

The sherries had made her sleepy. Only the ticking of her
clock, clipping away the seconds, kept her awake. Twenty
past eleven. The splashing from the gutters sounded like wet
footsteps pacing outside the window. She had never noticed
she could smell the river in her house. She wished she had
stayed longer with the Harveys; she would have been able to
hear Simon's car.

Twenty to twelve. Surely they wouldn't wait until midnight. She switched on the radio for company. A master of
ceremonies was making people laugh; a man was laughing
thickly, sounding waterlogged. Was he a drunk in the street?
He wasn't on the radio. She mustn't brood; why, she hadn't
put out the sherry glasses; that was something to do, to dis-
tract her from the intolerably measured counting of the
clock, the silenced radio, the emptiness displaying her
sounds—

Though the knock seemed enormously loud, she didn't
start. They were here at last, though she hadn't heard the
car. It was New Year's Day. She ran, and had reached the
front door when the phone shrilled. That startled her so
badly that she snatched the door open before lifting the re-
ceiver.

Nobody was outside—only a distant uproar of cheers and
bells and horns—and Margery was on the phone. "We've been
held up, Mummy. There was an accident in the tunnel. We'll
be over as soon as we can."

Then who had knocked? It must have been a drunk; she
heard him stumbling beside the house, thumping on her window. He'd better take himself off, or she would call Mr. Har-

vey to deal with him. But she was still inside the doorway when she saw the object on her step.

Good God, was it a rat? No, just a shoe, so ancient that it looked stuffed with mold. It wasn't mold, only a rotten old sock. There was something in the sock, something that smelled of stagnant water and worse. She stooped to peer at it, and then she was struggling to close the door, fighting to make the latch click, no breath to spare for a scream. She'd had her first foot, and now—hobbling doggedly alongside the house, its hands slithering over the wall—here came the rest of the body.

Coin of the Realm

Charles L. Grant

Horror has always tended to flourish in rural settings, where pathways are less well lit, victims more helpless, and the powers of darkness less likely to be under constant surveillance. The subgenre of small-town or "suburban" horror developed in the postwar years in direct response to America's suburbanization and changing social outlook. Following the lead of Ray Bradbury, whose early horror fiction chronicled the dark side of life in the American heartland, writers turned increasingly away from monster-based horror to plumb more intimate fears concerning the home, the family, and the workplace. Charles Grant has become the major exponent of contemporary small-town horror through his series of stories set in Oxrun Station, a fictional Connecticut town in which the wealthy have an almost preternatural control over their less fortunate neighbors, and where the longings of the have-nots frequently have unpredictable consequences. In "Coin of the Realm," Grant superimposes the framework of classical myth on a tale that is concerned, at heart, with the anxieties of rootlessness and economic hardship.

It was the wrong time of year and the wrong hour of the day. In sunlight, in spring, the tollbooths that stretched eight across the highway bounced back the clean sharp air of April as though they had just been painted. Green, and gold, with red lights, green lights, guiding into the lanes beyond the cars that jerked, that halted, that separated once through and vanished down the road.

In autumn, in the afternoon, the paint on the booths mellowed in tune with the trees that flanked the tarmac, and the air was brisk and brittle and filled with the cries of Canadian geese.

But it was November, past midnight, and Wes rubbed at his heavy arms encased in khaki as he waited for the next automobile to break from the darkness and feed him its toll.

The air was damp, the stars gone, birds gone, and there seemed nothing left alive on the road except him.

He'd taken the job, though hating the night shift, when the electronics firm he'd managed folded in the dead wake of a dying space industry, and his engineering skills abruptly cheapened to less than a dime a dozen. For months he'd driven; from California to Florida to Houston and finally to a small apartment in Oxrun Station. For months he had filled with his precise small handwriting all the blanks and the boxes and the circles on applications, answered questions about his ambitions, and shook soft tanned hands that bade him wait by the telephone for that miraculous call. That never came.

"Wes?" It was a woman's voice, and he looked up and across the narrow space to the booth opposite. Terry was there, beckoning, and he shrugged.

"Can't," he said ruefully. "Pete's not out here yet."

"Oh, come on! There's no one coming. We'll get him out of the office, okay?"

She was dark, less than half his weight, an Oxrun native and mother of six who needed the money as badly as he and worked the nights because the pay was twice as high. Normally she grinned constantly even when she was silent; but now her face, too much aged, was folded into a concerned frown that bothered him. She called him again, impatiently, and he nodded, pushed open the gate that penned him in, and lumbered down the single step to the gap between them. He glanced back up the road with an uncertain shudder, saw nothing, and hurried out of the November dark into the gar-

ish fluorescent glare of the highway-authority office building
squatting green and gold between four large pines.

There were generally four on duty throughout the graveyard shift: two in the booths, to keep each other awake, and
two inside who spelled the others several times an hour . . .
to keep them all awake.

Pete Hawkins, Wes's relief, pushed past him through the
door, a punch to his arm and a smile and a nod. Wes didn't
speak to him. There was nothing to say. Hawkins had known
him for less than a week, and since they'd never shared coffee, they never shared dreams.

Terry was already sitting at a long and low table, a paper
cup in front of her, steaming grey.

Wes sat, rubbing gratefully at his stomach, scratching at
his thick neck. He remembered a time when he was reason-
ably thin, but with money tight only starches and the like
were easy to come by.

"Wes, I've been had again."

"Again?" He couldn't believe Terry would allow herself to
be cheated more than once a month. But twice? Twice in the
past two days some jokers had driven through her lane and
had given her fake coins in place of the real. And they
weren't even imitations of quarters, but only the same size
and texture. On their front a small stylized pyramid, on their
backs various designs he hadn't understood.

"Wes, what am I going to do, huh? I can't keep putting in
my own money this way. I need every penny I can get. You
know that. Four dollars' worth in the last two weeks. You
know how much I can do with four dollars and six kids?"

Wes nodded, and a strand of black hair dropped to his forehead. He pushed at it, waited with one hand poised until he
was satisfied it would stay. "They must know when you're on,
Ter," he said finally. "They must think you're a sucker—"

"I am, obviously."

"—so they'll keep at it until you tumble at the wrong time.
Wrong time for them, I mean. Don't you ever look at the
money first?"

She laughed and shook her head. "You like people too
much, Wes, and you trust them too far. Someone could hand
you a boiler plate and you wouldn't know it until they were

in Canada. Of course I look at them, but they're silvery and they weigh the same. Only when I got time to count and stack, then I notice. Damn, Wes, what am I going to do?"

You're going to get fired, he thought, when Pete finds out and tells the right people—for him—what's happening. And she must have sensed it because immediately her eyes filled with watery light.

"If Lou were still here, or Jess—"

"Or Mac or Dave," he finished. "But they're not, Terry. They're gone."

Over the past four weeks, as many workers had walked off their jobs. Wes, who had been on the booths for just over three months, had gaped in astonishment each time it happened. It was, invariably, in the middle of the shift, somewhere near three when the road was at its most still, its most invisible. The lights from the gas station a mile east were out, the goosenecked lamps overhanging the broad toll plaza had been reduced to one on either side, and all the toll lights were red save one green facing in either direction. One by one, then, the men had climbed out of their booths and into their cars. Backed them up, went through the lanes like ordinary commuter travelers or tourists, and vanished beyond the edge of the light.

Not a word to anyone, not a letter once they had gone.

And each one had passed to Terry one of the bogus coins.

"Listen, Terry," he said when the silence began to unnerve him, "tell you what I'll do. I'll switch booths with you, all right? And when one of them jerks tries anything on me, I'll . . ."

"Break their arms?"

"Sit on them," he said, and spread his arms to display his bulk.

She pushed at her hair, shaking her head but smiling in spite of herself, and Wes relaxed. It would have been a hell of a long night if he and Terry hadn't been able to call to each other from their respective stations. Jokes. Stories. About her kids, his jobs, complaints about traffic and the lack of it . . . anything at all to keep from turning on the portable radio. Radios were death in the middle of the night. The music was loud enough to keep him awake, but the jockeys kept telling him the time he didn't want to know until the sun broke over the horizon.

He supposed, he *knew,* it would have been cheaper just to keep the exact-change lane open, but there was always some idiot with a five-dollar bill . . . at four in the morning with a five-dollar bill. His eyes would be stinging by then, because instead of sleeping when the sun came up he would write his résumés and make calls and once in a while take a sick day to drive out to an interview. He had done that yesterday, in fact, and finally there was a chance that he could kiss nickels and quarters and dimes good-bye forever. He had not mentioned it to Terry, though, because he didn't want to jinx it.

He waited, instead.

And walked with her back to the road.

A yellow van was waiting in his lane, honking his horn and shouting for attention. At first Wes thought the driver might be in trouble, but when he hurried to the island and tightroped to the gate, the booth was empty.

The driver was mad.

Wes apologized for the delay, received a curse for a tip, and the quarter was thrown against his chest as the van sped away.

"Terry," he called, "do you see Pete anywhere?"

Silence. Then, "No," her voice thin in the damp air.

It wasn't the best damned job in the world, he thought as he strode angrily toward the parking lot behind the authority building, but damnit, whoever's doing it ought to do it right, for God's sake.

He heard Terry calling him, ignored her and rounded the back corner, and stopped. The lot was empty except for her station wagon and his sedan. Both of them were old, and both of them were alone.

Good God, he thought, walked back to the plaza and stared east, then west, shaking his head.

The following night there were two new takers, and one, a young blond man with a wisp for a mustache, appealed to Wes instantly. During one break, then, instead of going inside with Terry, he leaned against the booth and they talked, trading lies and histories until Wes learned that Joseph was a student looking to make ends and tuitions meet somewhere, it was hoped in the direction of a bank account.

"You're crazy, you know that?" Wes said with a grin. "How you going to study and do your papers out here, huh? You'll be dead for your classes, you know. You won't be able to stay awake."

Joseph grinned, gap-toothed and pleasant. "I'll work it out, Wes, don't worry. As long as I don't get fired for being cheated—"

"Terry told you?"

"Yeah. As a matter of fact, I got one of them things just a few minutes ago, while you were getting coffee."

He held out his palm and Wes picked at the coin clumsily, finally grabbing it and holding it close to his face. There was the pyramid, and on the opposite face . . . an odd representation of what looked to be some kind of bird. A hawk, he thought, or maybe an eagle.

"Osiris," Joseph said.

"What?"

"That's Osiris there, I think. The head, I mean."

"You're kidding," Wes said. "You mean, folks are dumping Egyptian coins on us?"

He couldn't wait to tell Terry. Not that it would do her much good . . . but he shrugged and had turned to step down from the ledge when a station wagon pulled up and a hand stuck out. He couldn't move. It was Terry. He saw her through the windshield and she was . . . not exactly crying, not exactly happy. Her lips fought to give him a smile, but as soon as Joseph had taken her toll, her hand snapped back to the steering wheel and he had to press tight against the booth to keep from being knocked off the island when she floored the accelerator and raced west toward the hills.

"Goddamn," Joseph said. "She stuck me! Do you believe it? Terry . . ." He held out his hand. The coin was there.

In the glove compartment, Wes remembered suddenly; when they had arrived simultaneously at the parking lot and he'd hurried over to greet her and help her from the wagon, she'd been fumbling in the glove compartment, had snatched back her hand as though it had been burned. She'd slid out quickly, grabbing his arm, but not before he saw the silver glitter lying on top of a folded worn map.

"Joe, cover for me," he said quickly, and without waiting for an answer, raced for his car, put it in gear, and spewed gravel and dust in his haste to get on the highway.

West of the toll plaza the road ran straight for nearly two miles, then began a sinuous curve that climbed up the sides of two consecutive mountains. At the end of the level stretch was an exit, closed now for repairs and barricaded heavily, the shoulders flush against massive boulders that would prevent a car of any size from squeezing around it. Because of the land and the trees, then, he knew there wouldn't be any way for Terry to leave the road for the next twenty-two miles. Foolish, he thought, as the speedometer climbed from fifty to sixty, sixty-five to seventy. What the hell is she running away from?

His headlights punched weak holes in the blackness, and it seemed less like he was driving, more like he was floating through air that thickened the faster he went.

He glanced down at the odometer and frowned when he realized it wasn't registering the miles he was traveling. Damn, he thought; another expense.

He looked up, suddenly wrenched at the wheel and slammed on the brakes, the car skewing to one side, the smell of burning rubber already sharp in his nostrils. When he stopped, he was shaking and he laid his forehead against the cool plastic of the wheel until his stomach calmed and his arms stopped trembling.

Then he slid out of the car.

Directly ahead of him was a soft wavering light that stretched across the road from forest to forest. It wasn't the sun, he was facing west, and it wasn't a fire because he could smell nothing but the rubber, felt no heat as he approached it. It was . . . just a light, that illuminated nothing.

He wiped his hands nervously against his shirt, telling himself he was too tired to think straight, too anxious about the possible new job to think anything through. But he walked cautiously forward until, with a step, he was in the light. In it, not beyond it. And stretched for what seemed like miles in every direction were lines of automobiles. Abandoned. Rusting. He reached out to touch one, pulled his hand back when his legs began to feel weak.

Tired, that's all.

The land was sloped down and away from him, and in the middle distance was a broad blue-white river. He could see on the near bank a small group of people straggling onto a river-craft whose bow and stern were arched high and bent down toward the center of the deck; like a double-sting scorpion, he thought. In the middle of the deck was a tiny cabin. The people, their faces dimmed by the suffusion of the light, bent and entered until they were all inside. Then, from a shadow on the bank came a tall man who stepped up the gangway, pulled it to after him, and reached out for a pole attached to a rudder. As he did so he looked up . . . and Wes blinked, turned abruptly, and ran.

The man's head was not human. It was black. It was a dog.

Suddenly the light was behind him and he was in his car, racing the engine and skidding into a U-turn. A cloud of deep black fear settled over him until, with a check in his rearview mirror, he realized that the light was gone. There was nothing behind him but the road. And it wasn't until he had stopped his sedan in the parking lot that he realized the car he'd almost touched on that congregated slope had been a station wagon, had been Terry's.

"So," Joe said near the end of the shift, "he would finish wrapping up the dead, see, and take them to something like a courthouse where they'd be judged for whatever they did when they were alive. But, Wes, I don't understand what all this has to do with Terry."

Wes smiled weakly, said nothing, and as soon as the morning shift began filing out of the office, he waved a brusque good-bye and headed for his car. He drove for several hours, aimlessly, though keeping to the back roads to minimize contact with other cars. Then, when he could no longer see without squinting, he returned to his apartment and threw himself onto the couch, one arm over his eyes.

He slept.

Did not dream.

Woke only once: when the telephone rang and a man, his

voice officiously contrite, said, *I'm sorry, Wes, but that's the way it goes. Good luck.*

It was nearly nine when he roused himself again, showered the sleep and fog from his mind, and dressed in the near-military uniform of khaki and green he was required to wear. Then he made himself a dinner of steak and potatoes, carrots and lima beans—the steak he had been saving for the celebration of freedom. He tasted almost nothing, spent most of the time chewing absently and staring at the wall clock over the counter by the sink.

I am an engineer, he told himself; I do not believe in what I saw last night.

But he could see how others might, and that's what frightened him. Times were bad—not for everyone, but for enough —and when this town becomes intolerable you look toward the next one. The same with worlds. When life is lousy, like butting against a wall that doesn't even show the marks, you look for the afterlife; it has to be better there, right? It sure as hell can't get worse. And with organized religions falling apart under the weight of secular advancement and no scientific proof, it didn't take him long to see that somewhere, someone decided that maybe the good old days might hold the answer—and in this case, those "good old days" were numbered in the thousands of years. Someone who was steeped in Egyptology. Someone who deluded himself into thinking that if this life wasn't fair, maybe the gods would be.

After all, gods don't die; they simply go into retirement until someone believes again.

And if enough people believe, if enough people are miserable . . .

"Nonsense," he snapped at his knife and fork. "Damned utter nonsense."

But, something told him, you can't deny the coins and you can't deny the light, and you can't deny the fact that Terry has gone.

He raced into the living room and scrambled for the phone book, found Terry's number and called it.

"I'm sorry," a man's voice said, "but there's no one here by that name."

"Are you sure?"

"I'm sure, believe me. I've lived here for six years."

He tried Peter Hawkins, who had lived with two friends.

"Hawkins? I'm sorry, there's no one here by that name."

He tried Dave Sparker, who lived with his parents.

"Is this a joke? We ain't never had any kids, Mac."

I'm sorry, Wes, but that's the way it goes.

He closed his eyes to imagine Terry as he'd last seen her: hands clutching the wheel, eyes determinedly straight ahead; but the look she had given him before she drove off . . . relief. Sad, but relieved.

He shook his head and left for work, found Joe already seated at the table in the break room, and slid in beside him with a cup of coffee. "I'm cracking up, kid," he said, and explained.

Joe listened attentively, tracing designs on the table's plastic top until Wes had done. "Interesting," he said. "But for crying out loud, Wes, you know it can't be true."

"I know what I saw."

The young man grinned. "You know what you think you saw, right? Look, Wes, just for the sake of argument let's assume that what you're saying is true. Then why are there still ghettos and rundown slums and unemployment and stuff like that? I mean, if life is so rotten, why haven't all those people taken this way out? It doesn't make sense. Terry just decided it was time to get out before she cracked, that's all. She was doing something for herself for a change."

"But the kids!"

"Did you ever see them?"

Wes frowned. Shook his head. "But," he said, "our whole society is based on the reach of the automobile, right? How many really poor folks have one? The car gets you out, see. You wake up one day and your fare is in the glove compartment and off you go. A little sad, maybe, because you're leaving your friends and what all, but you know it's going to be better, so you go."

Joe shook his head, grinning. "Wes, you should have been a writer or something. For an engineer, you got a hell of an imagination. But," he added quickly, a hand up to quiet him, "assuming one more time that this is all so, what do you and I have to worry about? We're not starving, are we? I'm getting good grades all the time, and you're getting more and more interviews so that you're bound to hit one sooner or later. You're too good. It's just a matter of time."

He clapped Wes on the shoulder, pointed at the clock on the wall, and reached up for the fur-lined jackets they would be wearing that night. He helped Wes into his, Wes returned the favor, and they trudged out to the tollbooths to begin the shift.

He's right, Wes thought, as he nodded to the man leaving his booth; I'm letting myself panic, that's all. I'm losing faith in myself, and I can't let that happen.

At the first break, neither of them had been handed the silver pyramid coins.

At the second, Joe had had one.

Wes decided to do some figuring and, for the next few nights, kept a record of the fake coins as they flowed into the booths. Joe was getting worried, but like Terry he replaced the fares with money of his own. So did Wes. And by the end of the month, he noted with curious calm that there was an increase in the number of cars that passed along the road between the hours of twelve and three, so much so that the authority was toying with the idea of putting on two extra men. And as the cars increased, so did the coins. There was no geometric progression, only one or two more each night, but in no case was he able to catch a glimpse of the driver after he'd realized what he'd been handed.

"If this keeps up," he said to Joe one January night, "we're both going to be broke."

"Not me," Joe said, grinning. "You'll be happy to know, sir, that this toll taker is giving his notice."

"What?"

"That's right, Wes. I just got word there's a scholarship waiting for me on the West Coast, and I'm taking the first flight to San Francisco I can get." He slapped at the table and laughed. "Done, pal. This boy is done taking quarters for the rest of his life."

"I'll kill him," the supervisor said when Joe left an hour early, laughing, shrieking his delight that his nights would now be his own. "I'll get that punk if it's the last thing I do. He can't leave me short like this, damnit! He can't!"

Wes tsked and shook his head. "Revenge is not charity," he said, unable to keep back a grin.

He slept well that day, rose just after six, and made himself breakfast. Then he checked his mail, opened one rather thick envelope, and threw the rest into the air. It had come. In Iowa, a firm was looking for an electronics man with just his qualifications; and more importantly, it had the funds to offer him a salary not much less than he'd been making with his own company. Unashamedly he stood in front of the bathroom mirror, shaving, crying, shaking his head and wishing Joe had waited one more day to hear his own fine news. And Terry; he rinsed the razor under the faucet and wondered if he would have had the nerve to ask her to marry him. It would have meant instant family, of course, but it would have . . . might have stopped her from . . .

He scowled and threw the razor into the sink, stalked into the bedroom and pulled on his clothes, so viciously that he tore two shirts at the shoulder before calming enough to get one on properly.

"Knock it off, pal," he muttered to himself as he hurried downstairs to the parking lot and his car. "You got the wrong number, and she took off someplace else. Someplace real, pal, someplace real."

Hawkins.

Sparker.

His mood grew heavy, grey, like a storm grumbling on the horizon. He snarled at everyone at the office, including his supervisor, and it was well past midnight before he was able to force himself to relax and remember the job. The job. He laughed aloud as a car pulled into the gap and a hand reached up to him. He leaned down to take the coin, still laughing until he saw Joe's face in the dim dashboard light.

The young man was unshaven, pale, perspiration running down his face as though it were the middle of summer. His jaw trembled, his lips quivered, and before his hand slapped back to the wheel as if magnetized, he gasped one word: "Supervisor."

Wes yelled as the car shot out of the gap and vanished down the black road, the taillights glaring at him redly until, abruptly, they vanished.

He had no intention of looking at his palm.

He knew what would be there.

For several minutes he stood there numbly, unthinking, then snapping back to the day Joe had quit and the supervisor had ranted for the rest of the night.

Wes groaned and threw the coin away.

Joe *believed*. Joe *knew*.

That Wes's intellectual game-playing was not playing at all, that he was right about the depression that had fallen on people, the need to escape, the need for comfort. But he was also wrong about one vital matter: those gods, all of them shunted aside in the glare of science's advance, were not calmly returning to embrace their people again.

They were angry.

They hated.

Wes bolted from the booth and ran for his car. As he rounded the corner of the building, the supervisor slammed open the rear door and began shouting at him, cursing, then running to the exit and grabbing for the open-windowed door as Wes slowed for the narrow gate.

"Where the hell do you think you're going?"

"Iowa," Wes said, punching at the hand until it fell away.

"Fine! Then take this, and don't expect to be paid!"

Something flew from the supervisor's hand into Wes's lap, but he ignored it until he'd pulled onto the highway and was heading rapidly west. Then he freed a hand from the wheel and picked it up. It was his time card. He laughed, made to toss it out the window, then decided to hang on to it as a souvenir of his tenure in the booths. As his headlights turned the air grey in front of him, he leaned over and dropped the glove compartment lid, took his eyes from the road long enough to shove the card in . . . and saw the silvered coin.

"But I don't believe it!" he screamed to the steering wheel that refused to release him.

"I don't," he insisted when the light engulfed him and the car stalled and the slope to the river pulled him gently.

"Please," he whispered to the dogheaded man, "I don't believe in you."

"That," said the man with the head of a jackal, "is no longer *my* problem."

The Reach

Stephen King

The work of Stephen King is the culmination of the long tradition of horror fiction. A good example is "The Reach" (1981), a traditional tale of the supernatural with a distinctly modern tone. Like his predecessors, King blurs the boundaries between the worlds of the living and the dead, and leaves to speculation whether the story's ghosts are real or simply figments of a mind that has lost its ability to distinguish between memories and events of the moment. But King tempers the potentially frightening supernaturalism of his story with hope, and transforms his heroine's preoccupation with death into a celebration of life. "The Reach" is a paragon of how the modern tale of the supernatural reexamines and renovates the foundations laid by classic horror fiction.

"The Reach was wider in those days," Stella Flanders told her great-grandchildren in the last summer of her life, the summer before she began to see ghosts. The children looked at her with wide, silent eyes, and her son, Alden, turned from his seat on the porch where he was whittling. It was Sunday, and Alden wouldn't take his boat out on Sundays no matter how high the price of lobster was.

"What do you mean, Gram?" Tommy asked, but the old woman did not answer. She only sat in her rocker by the cold stove, her slippers bumping placidly on the floor.

Tommy asked his mother: *"What does she mean?"*

Lois only shook her head, smiled, and sent them out with pots to pick berries.

Stella thought: She's forgot. Or did she ever know?

The Reach had been wider in those days. If anyone knew it was so, that person was Stella Flanders. She had been born in 1884, she was the oldest resident of Goat Island, and she had never once in her life been to the mainland.

Do you love? This question had begun to plague her, and she did not even know what it meant.

Fall set in, a cold fall without the necessary rain to bring a really fine color to the trees, either on Goat or on Raccoon Head across the Reach. The wind blew long, cold notes that fall, and Stella felt each note resonate in her heart.

On November 19, when the first flurries came swirling down out of a sky the color of white chrome, Stella celebrated her birthday. Most of the village turned out. Hattie Stoddard came, whose mother had died of pleurisy in 1954 and whose father had been lost with the *Dancer* in 1941. Richard and Mary Dodge came, Richard moving slowly up the path on his cane, his arthritis riding him like an invisible passenger. Sarah Havelock came, of course; Sarah's mother Annabelle had been Stella's best friend. They had gone to the island school together, grades one to eight, and Annabelle had married Tommy Frane, who had pulled her hair in the fifth grade and made her cry, just as Stella had married Bill Flanders, who had once knocked all of her schoolbooks out of her arms and into the mud (but she had managed not to cry). Now both Annabelle and Tommy were gone and Sarah was the only one of their seven children still on the island. *Her* husband, George Havelock, who had been known to everyone as Big George, had died a nasty death over on the mainland in 1967, the year there was no fishing. An ax had slipped in Big George's hand, there had been blood—too much of it!—and an island funeral three days later. And when Sarah came in to Stella's party and cried, "Happy birthday, Gram!" Stella hugged her tight and closed her eyes

(do you do you love?)

but she did not cry.

There was a tremendous birthday cake. Hattie had made it with her best friend, Vera Spruce. The assembled company bellowed out "Happy Birthday to You" in a combined voice that was loud enough to drown out the wind . . . for a little while, anyway. Even Alden sang, who in the normal course of events would sing only "Onward, Christian Soldiers" and the doxology in church and would mouth the words of all the rest with his head hunched and his big old jug ears just as red as tomatoes. There were ninety-five candles on Stella's cake, and even over the singing she heard the wind, although her hearing was not what it once had been.

She thought the wind was calling her name.

"I was not the only one," she would have told Lois's children if she could. "In my day there were many that lived and died on the island. There was no mail boat in those days; Bull Symes used to bring the mail when there was mail. There was no ferry, either. If you had business on the Head, your man took you in the lobster boat. So far as I know, there wasn't a flushing toilet on the island until 1946. 'Twas Bull's boy Harold that put in the first one the year after the heart attack carried Bull off while he was out dragging traps. I remember seeing them bring Bull home. I remember that they brought him up wrapped in a tarpaulin, and how one of his green boots poked out. I remember . . .

And they would say: "What, Gram? What do you remember?"

How would she answer them? Was there more?

On the first day of winter, a month or so after the birthday party, Stella opened the back door to get stovewood and discovered a dead sparrow on the back stoop. She bent down carefully, picked it up by one foot, and looked at it.

"Frozen," she announced, and something inside her spoke another word. It had been forty years since she had seen a frozen bird—1938. The year the Reach had frozen.

Shuddering, pulling her coat closer, she threw the dead sparrow in the old rusty incinerator as she went by it. The day was cold. The sky was a clear, deep blue. On the night of her birthday four inches of snow had fallen, had melted, and no more had come since then. "Got to come soon," Larry Mc-Keen down at the Goat Island Store said sagely, as if daring winter to stay away.

Stella got to the woodpile, picked herself an armload and carried it back to the house. Her shadow, crisp and clean, followed her.

As she reached the back door, where the sparrow had fallen, Bill spoke to her—but the cancer had taken Bill twelve years before. "Stella," Bill said, and she saw his shadow fall beside her, longer but just as clear-cut, the shadow-bill of his shadow-cap twisted jauntily off to one side just as he had always worn it. Stella felt a scream lodged in her throat. It was too large to touch her lips.

"Stella," he said again, "when you comin across to the mainland? We'll get Norm Jolley's old Ford and go down to Bean's in Freeport just for a lark. What do you say?"

She wheeled, almost dropping her wood, and there was no one there. Just the dooryard sloping down to the hill, then the wild white grass, and beyond all, at the edge of everything, clear-cut and somehow magnified, the Reach . . . and the mainland beyond it.

"Gram, what's the Reach?" Lona might have asked . . . although she never had. And she would have given them the answer any fisherman knew by rote: a Reach is a body of water between two bodies of land, a body of water which is open at either end. The old lobsterman's joke went like this: know how to read y'compass when the fog comes, boys; between Jonesport and London there's a mighty long Reach.

"Reach is the water between the island and the mainland," she might have amplified, giving them molasses cookies and hot tea laced with sugar. "I know that much. I know it as well as my husband's name . . . and how he used to wear his hat."

"Gram?" Lona would say. "How come you never been across the Reach?"

"Honey," she would say, "I never saw any reason to go."

In January, two months after the birthday party, the Reach froze for the first time since 1938. The radio warned

islanders and mainlanders alike not to trust the ice, but
Stewie McClelland and Russell Bowie took Stewie's Bombar-
dier Skiddoo out anyway after a long afternoon spent drinking Apple Zapple wine, and sure enough, the skiddoo went
into the Reach. Stewie managed to crawl out (although he
lost one foot to frostbite). The Reach took Russell Bowie and
carried him away.

That January 25 there was a memorial service for Russell.
Stella went on her son Alden's arm, and he mouthed the
words to the hymns and boomed out the doxology in his great
tuneless voice before the benediction. Stella sat afterward
with Sarah Havelock and Hattie Stoddard and Vera Spruce
in the glow of the wood fire in the town-hall basement. A
going-away party for Russell was being held, complete with
Za-Rex punch and nice little cream-cheese sandwiches cut
into triangles. The men, of course, kept wandering out back
for a nip of something a bit stronger than Za-Rex. Russell
Bowie's new widow sat red-eyed and stunned beside Ewell
McCracken, the minister. She was seven months big with
child—it would be her fifth—and Stella, half-dozing in the
heat of the woodstove, thought: *She'll be crossing the Reach
soon enough, I guess. She'll move to Freeport or Lewiston and
go for a waitress, I guess.*

She looked around at Vera and Hattie, to see what the discussion was.

"No, I didn't hear," Hattie said. "What *did* Freddy say?"

They were talking about Freddy Dinsmore, the oldest man
on the island (two years younger'n me, though, Stella
thought with some satisfaction), who had sold out his store to
Larry McKeen in 1960 and now lived on his retirement.

"Said he'd never seen such a winter," Vera said, taking out
her knitting. "He says it is going to make people sick."

Sarah Havelock looked at Stella, and asked if Stella had
ever seen such a winter. There had been no snow since that
first little bit; the ground lay crisp and bare and brown. The
day before, Stella had walked thirty paces into the back field,
holding her right hand level at the height of her thigh, and
the grass there had snapped in a neat row with a sound like
breaking glass.

"No," Stella said. "The Reach froze in '38, but there was snow that year. Do you remember Bull Symes, Hattie?"

Hattie laughed. "I think I still have the black-and-blue he gave me on my sit-upon at the New Year's party in '53. He pinched me *that* hard. What about him?"

"Bull and my own man walked across to the mainland that year," Stella said. "That February of 1938. Strapped on snow-shoes, walked across to Dorrit's Tavern on the Head, had them each a shot of whiskey, and walked back. They asked me to come along. They were like two little boys off to the sliding with a toboggan between them."

They were looking at her, touched by the wonder of it. Even Vera was looking at her wide-eyed, and Vera had surely heard the tale before. If you believed the stories, Bull and Vera had once played some house together, although it was hard, looking at Vera now, to believe she had ever been so young.

"And you didn't go?" Sarah asked, perhaps seeing the reach of the Reach in her mind's eye, so white it was almost blue in the heatless winter sunshine, the sparkle of the snow crystals, the mainland drawing closer, walking across, yes, walking across the ocean just like Jesus-out-of-the-boat, leaving the island for the one and only time in your life on *foot*—

"No," Stella said. Suddenly she wished she had brought her own knitting. "I didn't go with them."

"Why *not?*" Hattie asked, almost indignantly.

"It was washday," Stella almost snapped, and then Missy Bowie, Russell's widow, broke into loud, braying sobs. Stella looked over and there sat Bill Flanders in his red-and-black-checked jacket, hat cocked to one side, smoking a Herbert Tareyton with another tucked behind his ear for later. She felt her heart leap into her chest and choke between beats.

She made a noise, but just then a knot popped like a rifle shot in the stove, and neither of the other ladies heard.

"Poor *thing,*" Sarah nearly cooed.

"Well shut of that good-for-nothing," Hattie grunted. She searched for the grim depth of the truth concerning the departed Russell Bowie and found it: "Little more than a tramp for pay, that man. She's well out of *that* two-hoss trace."

Stella barely heard these things. There sat Bill, close

enough to the Reverend McCracken to have tweaked his nose
if he so had a mind; he looked no more than forty, his eyes
barely marked by the crow's-feet that had later sunk so deep,
wearing his flannel pants and his gum-rubber boots with the
gray wool socks folded neatly down over the tops.

"We're waitin on you, Stel," he said. "You come on across
and see the mainland. You won't need no snowshoes this
year."

There he sat in the town-hall basement, big as Billy-be-
damned, and then another knot exploded in the stove and he
was gone. And the Reverend McCracken went on comforting
Missy Bowie as if nothing had happened.

That night Vera called up Annie Phillips on the phone, and
in the course of the conversation mentioned to Annie that
Stella Flanders didn't look well, not at all well.

"Alden would have a scratch of a job getting her off-island
if she took sick," Annie said. Annie liked Alden because her
own son Toby had told her Alden would take nothing
stronger than beer. Annie was strictly temperance, herself.

"Wouldn't get her off 'tall unless she was in a coma," Vera
said, pronouncing the word in the downeast fashion: *comer*.
"When Stella says 'Frog,' Alden jumps. Alden ain't but half-
bright, you know. Stella pretty much runs him."

"Oh, ayuh?" Annie said.

Just then there was a metallic crackling sound on the line.
Vera could hear Annie Phillips for a moment longer—not the
words, just the sound of her voice going on behind the crackling—and then there was nothing. The wind had gusted up
high and the phone lines had gone down, maybe into Godlin's
Pond or maybe down by Borrow's Cove, where they went into
the Reach sheathed in rubber. It was possible that they had
gone down on the other side, on the Head . . . and some
might even have said (only half-joking) that Russell Bowie
had reached up a cold hand to snap the cable, just for the hell
of it.

Not 700 feet away Stella Flanders lay under her puzzle-
quilt and listened to the dubious music of Alden's snores in
the other room. She listened to Alden so she wouldn't have to
listen to the wind . . . but she heard the wind anyway, oh

yes, coming across the frozen expanse of the Reach, a mile and a half of water that was now overplated with ice, ice with lobsters down below, and groupers, and perhaps the twisting, dancing body of Russell Bowie, who used to come each April with his old Rogers rototiller and turn her garden.

Who'll turn the earth this April? she wondered as she lay cold and curled under her puzzle-quilt. And as a dream in a dream, her voice answered her voice: *Do you love?* The wind gusted, rattling the storm window. It seemed that the storm window was talking to her, but she turned her face away from its words. And did not cry.

"But, Gram," Lona would press (she never gave up, not that one, she was like her mom, and her grandmother before her), "you still haven't told why you never went across."

"Why, child, I have always had everything I wanted right here on Goat."

"But it's so small. We live in Portland. There's buses, Gram!"

"I see enough of what goes on in cities on the TV. I guess I'll stay where I am."

Hal was younger, but somehow more intuitive; he would not press her as his sister might, but his question would go closer to the heart of things: "You never wanted to go across, Gram? Never?"

And she would lean toward him, and take his small hands, and tell him how her mother and father had come to the island shortly after they were married, and how Bull Symes's grandfather had taken Stella's father as a 'prentice on his boat. She would tell him how her mother had conceived four times but one of her babies had miscarried and another had died a week after birth—she would have left the island if they could have saved it at the mainland hospital, but of course it was over before that was even thought of.

She would tell them that Bill had delivered Jane, their grandmother, but not that when it was over he had gone into the bathroom and first puked and then wept like a hysterical woman who had her monthlies p'ticularly bad. Jane, of course, had left the island at fourteen to go to high school; girls didn't get married at fourteen anymore, and when Stella saw her go off in the boat with Bradley Maxwell, whose job it had been to ferry the kids back and forth that month, she knew in her heart that Jane was gone for good, although she would come back for a while. She would tell them that Alden had come along ten years later, after they had given up, and as if to make up for his tardiness, here was Alden still, a lifelong bachelor, and in some ways Stella was grateful for that because Alden was not terribly bright and there are plenty of women willing to take advantage of a man with a slow brain and a good heart (although she would not tell the children that last, either).

She would say: "Louis and Margaret Godlin begat Stella Godlin, who became Stella Flanders; Bill and Stella Flanders begat Jane and Alden Flanders and Jane Flanders became Jane Wakefield; Richard and Jane Wakefield begat Lois Wakefield, who became Lois Perrault; David and Lois Perrault begat Lona and Hal. Those are your names, children: you are Godlin-Flanders-Wakefield-Perrault. Your blood is in the stones of this island, and I stay here because the mainland is too far to reach. Yes, I love; I have loved, anyway, or at least tried to love, but memory is so wide and so deep, and I cannot cross. Godlin-Flanders-Wakefield-Perrault . . ."

That was the coldest February since the National Weather Service began keeping records, and by the middle of the month the ice covering the Reach was safe. Snowmobiles buzzed and whined and sometimes turned over when they climbed the ice-heaves wrong. Children tried to skate, found the ice too bumpy to be any fun, and went back to Godlin's Pond on the far side of the hill, but not before little Justin McCracken, the minister's son, caught his skate in a fissure and broke his ankle. They took him over to the hospital on the mainland where a doctor who owned a Corvette told him, "Son, it's going to be as good as new."

Freddy Dinsmore died very suddenly just three days after Justin McCracken broke his ankle. He caught the flu late in January, would not have the doctor, told everyone it was "Just a cold from goin out to get the mail without m'scarf," took to his bed, and died before anyone could take him across to the mainland and hook him up to all those machines they have waiting for guys like Freddy. His son George, a tosspot of the first water even at the advanced age (for tosspots, anyway) of sixty-eight, found Freddy with a copy of the *Bangor Daily News* in one hand and his Remington, unloaded, near the other. Apparently he had been thinking of cleaning it just before he died. George Dinsmore went on a three-week toot, said toot financed by someone who knew that George would have his old dad's insurance money coming. Hattie Stoddard went around telling anyone who would listen that old George Dinsmore was a sin and a disgrace, no better than a tramp for pay.

There was a lot of flu around. The school closed for two weeks that February instead of the usual one because so many pupils were out sick. "No snow breeds germs," Sarah Havelock said.

Near the end of the month, just as people were beginning to look forward to the false comfort of March, Alden Flanders caught the flu himself. He walked around with it for nearly a week and then took to his bed with a fever of a hundred and one. Like Freddy, he refused to have the doctor, and Stella stewed and fretted and worried. Alden was not as old as Freddy, but that May he would turn sixty.

The snow came at last. Six inches on Valentine's Day, another six on the twentieth, and a foot in a good old norther on the leap, February 29. The snow lay white and strange between the cove and the mainland, like a sheep's meadow where there had been only gray and surging water at this time of year since time out of mind. Several people walked across to the mainland and back. No snowshoes were necessary this year because the snow had frozen to a firm, glittery crust. They might take a knock of whiskey, too, Stella thought, but they would not take it at Dorrit's. Dorrit's had burned down in 1958.

And she saw Bill all four times. Once he told her: "Y'ought to come soon, Stella. We'll go steppin. What do you say?"

She could say nothing. Her fist was crammed deep into her mouth.

"Everything I ever wanted or needed was here," she would tell them. "We had the radio and now we have the television,

and that's all I want of the world beyond the Reach. I had my garden year in and year out. And lobster? Why, we always used to have a pot of lobster stew on the back of the stove and we used to take it off and put it behind the door in the pantry when the minister came calling so he wouldn't see we were eating 'poor man's soup.'

"I have seen good weather and bad, and if there were times when I wondered what it might be like to actually be in the Sears store instead of ordering from the catalogue, or to go into one of those Shaw's markets I see on TV instead of buying at the store here or sending Alden across for something special like a Christmas capon or an Easter ham . . . or if I ever wanted, just once, to stand on Congress Street in Portland and watch all the people in their cars and on the sidewalks, more people in a single look than there are on the whole island these days . . . if I ever wanted those things, then I wanted this more. I am not strange. I am not peculiar, or even very eccentric for a woman of my years. My mother sometimes used to say, 'All the difference in the world is between work and want,' and I believe that to my very soul. I believe it is better to plow deep than wide.

"This is my place, and I love it."

One day in middle March, with the sky as white and lowering as a loss of memory, Stella Flanders sat in her kitchen for the last time, laced up her boots over her skinny calves for the last time, and wrapped her bright red woolen scarf (a Christmas present from Hattie three Christmases past) around her neck for the last time. She wore a suit of Alden's long underwear under her dress. The waist of the drawers came up to just below the limp vestiges of her breasts, the shirt almost down to her knees.

Outside, the wind was picking up again, and the radio said there would be snow by afternoon. She put on her coat and her gloves. After a moment of debate, she put a pair of Alden's gloves on over her own. Alden had recovered from the flu, and this morning he and Harley Blood were over rehanging a storm door for Missy Bowie, who had had a girl. Stella had seen it, and the unfortunate little mite looked just like her father.

She stood at the window for a moment, looking out at the Reach, and Bill was there as she had suspected he might be, standing about halfway between the island and the Head, standing on the Reach just like Jesus-out-of-the-boat, beckoning to her, seeming to tell her by gesture that the time was late if she ever intended to step a foot on the mainland in this life.

"If it's what you want, Bill," she fretted in the silence. "God knows I don't."

But the wind spoke other words. She did want to. She wanted to have this adventure. It had been a painful winter for her—the arthritis which came and went irregularly was back with a vengeance, flaring the joints of her fingers and knees with red fire and blue ice. One of her eyes had gotten dim and blurry (and just the other day Sarah had mentioned —with some unease—that the firespot that had been there since Stella was sixty or so now seemed to be growing by leaps and bounds). Worst of all, the deep, gripping pain in her stomach had returned, and two mornings before she had gotten up at five o'clock, worked her way along the exquisitely cold floor into the bathroom, and had spat a great wad of bright red blood into the toilet bowl. This morning there had been some more of it, foul-tasting stuff, coppery and shuddersome.

The stomach pain had come and gone over the last five years, sometimes better, sometimes worse, and she had known almost from the beginning that it must be cancer. It had taken her mother and father and her mother's father as well. None of them had lived past seventy, and so she supposed she had beat the tables those insurance fellows kept by a carpenter's yard.

"You eat like a horse," Alden told her, grinning, not long after the pains had begun and she had first observed the blood in her morning stool. "Don't you know that old fogies like you are supposed to be peckish?"

"Get on or I'll swat ye!" Stella had answered, raising a hand to her gray-haired son, who ducked, mock-cringed, and cried: "Don't, Ma! I take it back!"

Yes, she had eaten hearty, not because she wanted to, but because she believed (as many of her generation did), that if you fed the cancer it would leave you alone. And perhaps it worked, at least for a while; the blood in her stools came and went, and there were long periods when it wasn't there at all. Alden got used to her taking second helpings (and thirds, when the pain was particularly bad), but she never gained a pound.

Now it seemed the cancer had finally gotten around to what the froggies called the *pièce de résistance*.

She started out the door and saw Alden's hat, the one with the fur-lined ear flaps, hanging on one of the pegs in the entry. She put it on—the bill came all the way down to her shaggy salt-and-pepper eyebrows—and then looked around one last time to see if she had forgotten anything. The stove was low, and Alden had left the draw open too much again— she told him and told him, but that was one thing he was just never going to get straight.

"Alden, you'll burn an extra quarter-cord a winter when I'm gone," she muttered, and opened the stove. She looked in and a tight, dismayed gasp escaped her. She slammed the door shut and adjusted the draw with trembling fingers. For a moment—just a moment—she had seen her old friend Annabelle Frane in the coals. It was her face to the life, even down to the mole on her cheek.

And had Annabelle winked at her?

She thought of leaving Alden a note to explain where she had gone, but she thought perhaps Alden would understand, in his own slow way.

Still writing notes in her head—*Since the first day of winter I have been seeing your father and he says dying isn't so bad; at least I think that's it*—Stella stepped out into the white day.

The wind shook her and she had to reset Alden's cap on her head before the wind could steal it for a joke and cartwheel it away. The cold seemed to find every chink in her clothing and twist into her; damp March cold with wet snow on its mind.

She set off down the hill toward the cove, being careful to walk on the cinders and clinkers that George Dinsmore had spread. Once George had gotten a job driving plow for the town of Raccoon Head, but during the big blow of '77 he had gotten smashed on rye whiskey and had driven the plow

smack through not one, not two, but three power poles. There
had been no lights over the Head for five days. Stella remembered now how strange it had been, looking across the Reach
and seeing only blackness. A body got used to seeing that
brave little nestle of lights. Now George worked on the island, and since there was no plow, he didn't get into much
hurt.

As she passed Russell Bowie's house, she saw Missy, pale as
milk, looking out at her. Stella waved. Missy waved back.

She would tell them this:
*"On the island we always watched out for our own. When
Gerd Henreid broke the blood vessel in his chest that time, we
had covered-dish suppers one whole summer to pay for his
operation in Boston—and Gerd came back alive, thank God.
When George Dinsmore ran down those power poles and the
Hydro slapped a lien on his home, it was seen to that the
Hydro had their money and George had enough of a job to
keep him in cigarettes and booze . . . why not? He was good
for nothing else when his workday was done, although when
he was on the clock he would work like a dray-horse. That one
time he got into trouble was because it was at night, and night
was always George's drinking time. His father kept him fed,
at least. Now Missy Bowie's alone with another baby. Maybe
she'll stay here and take her welfare and ADC money here,
and most likely it won't be enough, but she'll get the help she
needs. Probably she'll go, but if she stays she'll not starve . . .
and listen, Lona and Hal: if she stays, she may be able to keep
something of this small world with the little Reach on one
side and the big Reach on the other, something it would be too
easy to lose hustling hash in Lewiston or donuts in Portland
or drinks at the Nashville North in Bangor. And I am old
enough not to beat around the bush about what that something might be: a way of being and a way of living—a feeling."*

*They had watched out for their own in other ways as well,
but she would not tell them that. The children would not
understand, nor would Lois and David, although Jane had
known the truth. There was Norman and Ettie Wilson's baby
that was born a mongoloid, its poor dear little feet turned in,*

*its bald skull lumpy and cratered, its fingers webbed together
as if it had dreamed too long and too deep while swimming
that interior Reach; Reverend McCracken had come and bap-
tized the baby, and a day later Mary Dodge came, who even at
that time had midwived over a hundred babies, and Norman
took Ettie down the hill to see Frank Child's new boat and
although she could barely walk, Ettie went with no complaint, although she had stopped in the door to look back at
Mary Dodge, who was sitting calmly by the idiot baby's crib
and knitting. Mary had looked up at her and when their eyes
met, Ettie burst into tears. "Come on," Norman had said, upset. "Come on, Ettie, come on." And when they came back an
hour later the baby was dead, one of those crib-deaths, wasn't
it merciful he didn't suffer. And many years before that, before
the war, during the Depression, three little girls had been molested coming home from school, not badly molested, at least
not where you could see the scar of the hurt, and they all told
about a man who offered to show them a deck of cards he had
with a different kind of dog on each one. He would show them
this wonderful deck of cards, the man said, if the little girls
would come into the bushes with him, and once in the bushes
this man said, "But you have to touch this first." One of the
little girls was Gert Symes, who would go on to be voted
Maine's Teacher of the Year in 1978, for her work at Brunswick High. And Gert, then only five years old, told her father
that the man had some fingers gone on one hand. One of the
other little girls agreed that this was so. The third remembered nothing. Stella remembered Alden going out one thun-
dery day that summer without telling her where he was going,
although she asked. Watching from the window, she had seen
Alden meet Bull Symes at the bottom of the path, and then
Freddy Dinsmore had joined them and down at the cove she
saw her own husband, whom she had sent out that morning
just as usual, with his dinner pail under his arm. More men
joined them, and when they finally moved off she counted just
one under a dozen. The Reverend McCracken's predecessor
had been among them. And that evening a fellow named Daniels was found at the foot of Slyder's Point, where the rocks
poke out of the surf like the fangs of a dragon that drowned
with its mouth open. This Daniels was a fellow Big George*

Havelock had hired to help him put new sills under his house and a new engine in his Model A truck. From New Hampshire he was, and he was a sweet-talker who had found other odd jobs to do when the work at the Havelocks' was done . . . and in church, he could carry a tune! Apparently, they said, Daniels had been walking up on top of Slyder's Point and had slipped, tumbling all the way to the bottom. His neck was broken and his head was bashed in. As he had no people that anyone knew of, he was buried on the island, and the Reverend McCracken's predecessor gave the graveyard eulogy, saying as how this Daniels had been a hard worker and a good help even though he was two fingers shy on his right hand. Then he read the benediction and the graveside group had gone back to the town-hall basement where they drank Za-Rex punch and ate cream-cheese sandwiches, and Stella never asked her men where they had gone on the day Daniels fell from the top of Slyder's Point.

"Children," she would tell them, "we always watched out for our own. We had to, for the Reach was wider in those days and when the wind roared and the surf pounded and the dark came early, why, we felt very small—no more than dust motes in the mind of God. So it was natural for us to join hands, one with the other.

"We joined hands, children, and if there were times when we wondered what it was all for, or if there was ary such a thing as love at all, it was only because we had heard the wind and the waters on long winter nights, and we were afraid.

"No, I've never felt I needed to leave the island. My life was here. The Reach was wider in those days."

Stella reached the cove. She looked right and left, the wind blowing her dress out behind her like a flag. If anyone had been there she would have walked further down and taken her chance on the tumbled rocks, although they were glazed with ice. But no one was there and she walked out along the pier, past the old Symes boathouse. She reached the end and stood there for a moment, head held up, the wind blowing past the padded flaps of Alden's hat in a muffled flood.

Bill was out there, beckoning. Beyond him, beyond the

Reach, she could see the Congo Church over there on the Head, its spire almost invisible against the white sky.

Grunting, she sat down on the end of the pier and then stepped onto the snow crust below. Her boots sank a little; not much. She set Alden's cap again—how the wind wanted to tear it off!—and began to walk toward Bill. She thought once that she would look back, but she did not. She didn't believe her heart could stand that.

She walked, her boots crunching into the crust, and listened to the faint thud and give of the ice. There was Bill, further back now but still beckoning. She coughed, spat blood onto the white snow that covered the ice. Now the Reach spread wide on either side and she could, for the first time in her life, read the "Stanton's Bait and Boat" sign over there without Alden's binoculars. She could see the cars passing to and fro on the Head's main street and thought with real wonder: *They can go as far as they want . . . Portland . . . Boston . . . New York City. Imagine!* And she could almost do it, could almost imagine a road that simply rolled on and on, the boundaries of the world knocked wide.

A snowflake skirled past her eyes. Another. A third. Soon it was snowing lightly and she walked through a pleasant world of shifting bright white; she saw Raccoon Head through a gauzy curtain that sometimes almost cleared. She reached up to set Alden's cap again and snow puffed off the bill into her eyes. The wind twisted fresh snow up in filmy shapes, and in one of them she saw Carl Abersham, who had gone down with Hattie Stoddard's husband on the *Dancer*.

Soon, however, the brightness began to dull as the snow came harder. The Head's main street dimmed, dimmed, and at last was gone. For a time longer she could make out the cross atop the church, and then that faded out too, like a false dream. Last to go was that bright yellow-and-black sign reading "Stanton's Bait and Boat," where you could also get engine oil, flypaper, Italian sandwiches, and Budweiser to go.

Then Stella walked in a world that was totally without color, a gray-white dream of snow. *Just like Jesus-out-of-the-boat,* she thought, and at last she looked back but now the island was gone, too. She could see her tracks going back, losing definition until only the faint half-circles of her heels could be seen . . . and then nothing. Nothing at all.

She thought: *It's a whiteout. You got to be careful, Stella, or you'll never get to the mainland. You'll just walk around in a big circle until you're worn out and then you'll freeze to death out here.*

She remembered Bill telling her once that when you were lost in the woods, you had to pretend that the leg which was on the same side of your body as your smart hand was lame. Otherwise that smart leg would begin to lead you and you'd walk in a circle and not even realize it until you came around to your backtrail again. Stella didn't believe she could afford to have that happen to her. Snow today, tonight, and tomorrow, the radio had said, and in a whiteout such as this, she would not even know if she came around to her backtrail, for the wind and the fresh snow would erase it long before she could return to it.

Her hands were leaving her in spite of the two pairs of gloves she wore, and her feet had been gone for some time. In a way, this was almost a relief. The numbness at least shut the mouth of her clamoring arthritis.

Stella began to limp now, making her left leg work harder. The arthritis in her knees had not gone to sleep, and soon they were screaming at her. Her white hair flew out behind her. Her lips had drawn back from her teeth (she still had her own, all save four) and she looked straight ahead, waiting for that yellow-and-black sign to materialize out of the flying whiteness.

It did not happen.

Sometime later, she noticed that the day's bright whiteness had begun to dull to a more uniform gray. The snow fell heavier and thicker than ever. Her feet were still planted on the crust but now she was walking through five inches of fresh snow. She looked at her watch, but it had stopped. Stella realized she must have forgotten to wind it that morning for the first time in twenty or thirty years. Or had it just stopped for good? It had been her mother's and she had sent it with Alden twice to the Head, where Mr. Dostie had first marveled over it and then cleaned it. Her watch, at least, had been to the mainland.

She fell down for the first time some fifteen minutes after she began to notice the day's growing grayness. For a moment she remained on her hands and knees, thinking it would be so easy just to stay here, to curl up and listen to the wind, and then the determination that had brought her through so much reasserted itself and she got up, grimacing. She stood in the wind, looking straight ahead, willing her eyes to see . . . but they saw nothing.

Be dark soon.

Well, she had gone wrong. She had slipped off to one side or the other. Otherwise she would have reached the mainland by now. Yet she didn't believe she had gone so far wrong that she was walking parallel to the mainland or even back in the direction of Goat. An interior navigator in her head whispered that she had overcompensated and slipped off to the left. She believed she was still approaching the mainland but was now on a costly diagonal.

That navigator wanted her to turn right, but she would not do that. Instead, she moved straight on again, but stopped the artificial limp. A spasm of coughing shook her, and she spat bright red into the snow.

Ten minutes later (the gray was now deep indeed, and she found herself in the weird twilight of a heavy snowstorm) she fell again, tried to get up, failed at first, and finally managed to gain her feet. She stood swaying in the snow, barely able to remain upright in the wind, waves of faintness rushing through her head, making her feel alternately heavy and light.

Perhaps not all the roaring she heard in her ears was the wind, but it surely was the wind that finally succeeded in prying Alden's hat from her head. She made a grab for it, but the wind danced it easily out of her reach and she saw it only for a moment, flipping gaily over and over into the darkening gray, a bright spot of orange. It struck the snow, rolled, rose again, was gone. Now her hair flew around her head freely.

"It's all right, Stella," Bill said. "You can wear mine."

She gasped and looked around in the white. Her gloved hands had gone instinctively to her bosom, and she felt sharp fingernails scratch at her heart.

She saw nothing but shifting membranes of snow—and

then, moving out of that evening's gray throat, the wind screaming through it like the voice of a devil in a snowy tunnel, came her husband. He was at first only moving colors in the snow: red, black, dark green, lighter green; then these colors resolved themselves into a flannel jacket with a flapping collar, flannel pants, and green boots. He was holding his hat out to her in a gesture that appeared almost absurdly courtly, and his face was Bill's face, unmarked by the cancer that had taken him (had that been all she was afraid of? that a wasted shadow of her husband would come to her, a scrawny concentration-camp figure with the skin pulled taut and shiny over the cheekbones and the eyes sunken deep in the sockets?) and she felt a surge of relief.

"Bill? Is that really you?"

"Course."

"Bill," she said again, and took a glad step toward him. Her legs betrayed her and she thought she would fall, fall right through him—he was, after all, a ghost—but he caught her in arms as strong and as competent as those that had carried her over the threshold of the house that she had shared only with Alden in these latter years. He supported her, and a moment later she felt the cap pulled firmly onto her head.

"Is it really you?" she asked again, looking up into his face, at the crow's-feet around his eyes which hadn't sunk deep yet, at the spill of snow on the shoulders of his checked hunting jacket, at his lively brown hair.

"It's me," he said. "It's all of us."

He half-turned with her and she saw the others coming out of the snow that the wind drove across the Reach in the gathering darkness. A cry, half joy, half fear, came from her mouth as she saw Madeline Stoddard, Hattie's mother, in a blue dress that swung in the wind like a bell, and holding her hand was Hattie's dad, not a mouldering skeleton somewhere on the bottom with the *Dancer,* but whole and young. And there, behind those two—

"Annabelle!" she cried. "Annabelle Frane, is it you?"

It *was* Annabelle; even in this snowy gloom Stella recognized the yellow dress Annabelle had worn to Stella's own wedding, and as she struggled toward her dead friend, holding Bill's arm, she thought that she could smell roses.

"Annabelle!"

"We're almost there now, dear," Annabelle said, taking her other arm. The yellow dress, which had been considered Daring in its day (but, to Annabelle's credit and to everyone else's relief, not quite a Scandal), left her shoulders bare, but Annabelle did not seem to feel the cold. Her hair, a soft, dark auburn, blew long in the wind. "Only a little further."

She took Stella's other arm and they moved forward again. Other figures came out of the snowy night (for it *was* night now). Stella recognized many of them, but not all. Tommy Frane had joined Annabelle; Big George Havelock, who had died a dog's death in the woods, walked behind Bill; there was the fellow who had kept the lighthouse on the Head for most of twenty years and who used to come over to the island during the cribbage tournament Freddy Dinsmore held every February—Stella could almost but not quite remember his name. And there was Freddy himself! Walking off to one side of Freddy, by himself and looking bewildered, was Russell Bowie.

"Look, Stella," Bill said, and she saw black rising out of the gloom like the splintered prows of many ships. It was not ships, it was split and fissured rock. They had reached the Head. They had crossed the Reach.

She heard voices, but was not sure they actually spoke:

Take my hand, Stella—

(do you)

Take my hand, Bill—

(oh do you do you)

Annabelle . . . Freddy . . . Russell . . . John . . . Ettie . . . Frank . . . take my hand, take my hand . . . my hand . . .

(do you love)

"Will you take my hand, Stella?" a new voice asked.

She looked around and there was Bull Symes. He was smiling kindly at her and yet she felt a kind of terror in her at what was in his eyes and for a moment she drew away, clutching Bill's hand on her other side the tighter.

"Is it—"

"Time?" Bull asked. "Oh, ayuh, Stella, I guess so. But it don't hurt. At least, I never heard so. All that's before."

She burst into tears suddenly—all the tears she had never wept—and put her hand in Bull's hand. "Yes," she said, "yes I will, yes I did, yes I do."

They stood in a circle in the storm, the dead of Goat Island, and the wind screamed around them, driving its packet of snow, and some kind of song burst from her. It went up into the wind and the wind carried it away. They all sang then, as children will sing in their high, sweet voices as a summer evening draws down to summer night. They sang, and Stella felt herself going to them and with them, finally across the Reach. There was a bit of pain, but not much; losing her maidenhead had been worse. They stood in a circle in the night. The snow blew around them and they sang. They sang, and—

—and Alden could not tell David and Lois, but in the summer after Stella died, when the children came out for their annual two weeks, he told Lona and Hal. He told them that during the great storms of winter the wind seems to sing with almost human voices, and that sometimes it seemed to him he could almost make out the words: "Praise God from whom all blessings flow/Praise Him, ye creatures here below . . ."

But he did not tell them (imagine slow, unimaginative Alden Flanders saying such things aloud, even to the children!) that sometimes he would hear that sound and feel cold even by the stove; that he would put his whittling aside, or the trap he had meant to mend, thinking that the wind sang in all the voices of those who were dead and gone . . . that they stood somewhere out on the Reach and sang as children do. He seemed to hear their voices and on these nights he sometimes slept and dreamed that he was singing the doxology, unseen and unheard, at his own funeral.

There are things that can never be told, and there are things, not exactly secret, that are not discussed. They had found Stella frozen to death on the mainland a day after the storm had blown itself out. She was sitting on a natural chair of rock about one hundred yards south of the Raccoon Head town limits, frozen just as neat as you please. The doctor who owned the Corvette said that he was frankly amazed. It would have been a walk of over four miles, and the autopsy required by law in the case of an unattended, unusual death had shown an advanced cancerous condition—in truth, the old woman had been riddled with it. Was Alden to tell David and Lois that the cap on her head had not been his? Larry McKeen had recognized that cap. So had John Bensohn. He had seen it in their eyes, and he supposed they had seen it in his. He had not lived long enough to forget his dead father's cap, the look of its bill or the places where the visor had been broken.

"These are things made for thinking on slowly," he would have told the children if he had known how. "Things to be thought on at length, while the hands do their work and the coffee sits in a solid china mug nearby. They are questions of Reach, maybe: do the dead sing? And do they love the living?

On the nights after Lona and Hal had gone back with their parents to the mainland in Al Curry's boat, the children standing astern and waving good-bye, Alden considered that question, and others, and the matter of his father's cap.

Do the dead sing? Do they love?

On those long nights alone, with his mother Stella Flanders at long last in her grave, it often seemed to Alden that they did both.

Biographical Notes

Edgar Allan Poe
(1809–1849)

A list of Edgar Allan Poe's contributions to American letters would fill a book. Poe is credited with popularizing the short story as a literary form, creating the detective story, and introducing the psychological perspective into the tale of horror. His first story collection, *Tales of the Grotesque and Arabesque,* was published in 1840 and contained "The Fall of the House of Usher" and the classic doppelganger tale "William Wilson." It was followed five years later by the *The Raven and Other Poems,* a collection of some of the most exquisitely crafted poems in the English language. Poe was also an important literary critic and theoretician who published his essays and reviews in *Graham's, The Southern Literary Messenger,* and other prestigious magazines of his day. No collection of horror fiction would be complete without his stories "The Black Cat," "The Tell-Tale Heart," "The Facts in the Case of M. Valdemar," "The Masque of the Red Death," and "The Cask of Amontillado." Since his death in 1849, critical estimation of Poe's work has fluctuated wildly. The Library of America resolved this problem by bringing out *Edgar Allan Poe: Poetry and Tales* and *Edgar Allan Poe: Essays and Reviews* in its standard American authors series in 1984.

Joseph Sheridan Le Fanu
(1814–1873)

The grand-nephew of Restoration playwright Richard Brinsely Sheridan *(The School for Scandal),* Irish writer Joseph Sheridan Le Fanu is considered by many to be the single greatest author of ghost stories in the English language, as well as a pivotal figure in the evolution of the horror story from its Gothic crudeness to literary sophistication. Much of Le Fanu's reputation derives from his overthrow of Gothic conventions, which included toning down the volume of his horrors, eschewing didactic aims for his fiction, and creating malicious supernatural creatures whose motives are distinct from those of human beings. Several of his twenty-eight supernatural stories are undisputed horror classics, among them "Green Tea," "Schalken the Painter," and especially "Carmilla," a major influence on Bram Stoker's *Dracula*. Le Fanu was an important influence on M. R. James, and, through James, on the entire ghost story tradition. Definitive collections of his short fiction include *Through a Glass Darkly* (1872) and the posthumously published *Madame Crowl's Ghost and Other Tales of Mystery* (1923). His collected works fill fifty-two volumes.

Ambrose Bierce
(1842–?)

Like many American men born near the middle of the nineteenth century, Ambrose Bierce saw action in the American Civil War. His experiences at Chickamauga, Shiloh, and other battlefields profoundly colored his view of human nature and inspired more than a few of the bleak tales in his first story collection, *Tales of Soldiers and Civilians* (1891). Included in this volume was his classic "An Occurrence at Owl Creek Bridge," a story that broke down the boundaries between the horrors of war and supernatural experience. Though the tales gathered for his second collection *Can Such Things Be?* are slightly less gruesome, both books display Bierce's penchant for irony and sardonic humor. Bierce had a mordant wit appropriate for his grim subject matter, and it is probably best displayed in his masterpiece of comic cynicism, *The Devil's Dictionary* (1906). He spent a good portion of his life making enemies through the columns and articles he wrote for William Randolph Hearst's *San Francisco Examiner*. Bierce disappeared en route to South America in 1913, presumably in the turmoil of the Mexican Civil War. His possible fate has served as the subject for several works of fiction.

Robert W. Chambers
(1865–1933)

Like some of the most accomplished weird fiction writers, Robert W. Chambers backed into his calling. Although he initially aspired to be an artist (knowledge of which profession he obviously mined for the background of "The Yellow Sign"), he discovered he could make a better living as a writer. *The King in Yellow* (1895) demonstrated Chambers' familiarity with the fiction of Ambrose Bierce and is presumed to have inspired H. P. Lovecraft. The book was a popular success for Chambers that, unfortunately, tempted him to try his hand at historical and romance novels. The demand for these ephemera proved so great that Chambers produced only two other noteworthy books of supernatural fiction in his lifetime, *The Maker of Moons* (1896) and *The Slayer of Souls* (1920).

W. W. Jacobs
(1863–1943)

Most people become acquainted with W. W. Jacobs' horror masterpiece "The Monkey's Paw" when they are children. And very few learn anything about Jacobs beyond that age. In part, this is because Jacobs, a British journalist, was best known in his day as a writer of sea stories and humorous sketches. In all, he penned only about a half-dozen weird tales, which can be found interspersed with his more typical writing in the volumes *The Lady of the Barge* (1902), *Sailor's Knots* (1909), and *Night Watches* (1914).

Arthur Machen
(1863–1947)

Although Welsh-born Arthur Machen had a long and prolific writing career, the bulk of his best work appeared between 1890 and 1904. These years saw the publication of his oft-reprinted "The Great God Pan" and "The White People," the episodic novel *The Three Impostors* and his poignant autobiographical novel *The Hill of Dreams*. Machen subordinated the themes of his fiction to his belief that Man's rationality has blinded him to the "ecstasy" of existence, and that to attempt to pierce the veil that shields him from this ultra-reality is to invite madness. Coincident with this article of faith is the idea he explored most brilliantly in "The Novel of the Black Seal" and "The White People," that Man's perceptions of the natural world obscure its hideous and threatening truths. Criticized for dealing with objectionable subjects in his fiction, Machen spent most of his last 40 years in poverty, writing for newspapers or acting on the stage. Until relatively recently he was probably best known as the author of "The Bowmen," the tale of a heavenly host coming to the aid of soldiers at the Battle of Mons that many of his countrymen took to be true.

Algernon Blackwood
(1869–1951)

British writer Algernon Blackwood held a series of jobs including crime reporter, male model, and dairy farmer before a friend convinced him to submit a collection of his short fiction to a publisher. The result was *The Empty House and Other Ghost Stories* (1906), a collection of supernatural tales that were exceptional by any standard but particularly promising for a novice. This was followed the next year by *The Listener and Other Stories,* which contained Blackwood's landmark tale "The Willows." Nearly all of Blackwood's fiction is rooted in his mystical faith in the natural world, with "The Willows" and its companion piece, "The Wendigo," providing its fullest expression. Blackwood's first two story collections, along with *John Silence, Physician Extraordinary* (1908) and the novel *The Centaur* (1911) are the cornerstones of his vast literary output. Michael Ashley's *Algernon Blackwood: A Bio-Bibliography* (1987) is the definitive study of Blackwood to date.

M. R. James
(1862–1936)

M. R. James very much resembled the academic characters of his stories: he catalogued manuscript collections, wrote cathedral histories, and served as the provost of Eton College. So it was only natural that when he indulged his passion for writing ghost stories, he named his first two collections *Ghost Stories of an Antiquary* (1904) and *More Ghost Stories of an Antiquary* (1911). These two books, along with *A Thin Ghost* (1919) and *A Warning to the Curious* (1925), contain some of the most famous horror tales in the English language, among them "Count Magnus," "Canon Alberic's Scrapbook," "An Episode of Cathedral History," "The Stalls of Barchester Cathedral" and "Casting the Runes." Though James' fiction output was very small, he ranks with Poe and Lovecraft as one of the first writers to elucidate the principles of effective weird fiction writing. The term "Jamesian ghost story" is now a familiar designation in the critical canon of horror.

Henry Kuttner
(1915–1958)

Before Henry Kuttner married C. L. Moore and became one half of the most productive writing team in the history of science fiction, he was a protégé of H. P. Lovecraft. He contributed numerous horror stories thick with Lovecraft's influence to the pulp magazines *Weird Tales* and *Strange Stories* before departing for John W. Campbell's *Astounding* and *Unknown Worlds* and finding his own voice. One of the most prolific of all science fiction writers, Kuttner found it necessary to use a score of pseudonyms during the war years. With C. L. Moore, he wrote many classics of science fiction's Golden Age under the bylines Lawrence O'Donnell and

Lewis Padgett. Although a large percentage of his science fiction has been reprinted in *A Gnome There Was* (1950), *Ahead of Time* (1953), *Line to Tomorrow* (1954), *Bypass to Otherness* (1961), and *The Best of Henry Kuttner* (1975), to date, his weird fiction remains largely uncollected.

Robert E. Howard
(1906–1936)

Texan Robert E. Howard was the quintessential pulp writer, contributing a monthly volley of fiction to the horror, fantasy, adventure, detective, sports, and western pulps. Fortunately, Howard's specialty, the heroic warrior, proved easily adaptable to every pulp medium. Although Howard is best known for his sword-and-sorcery tales of Conan the Barbarian, he produced a handful of straight horror stories ranging from the Lovecraft pastiche "The Thing on the Roof" to strong regional tales of the South and Southwest, such as "Black Canaan," "The Dead Remember," and "Pigeons from Hell." Howard tended to mix his genres freely, and the horror element is especially strong in his saga of swashbuckling Puritan adventurer Solomon Kane and the sword-and-sorcery tour de force "Worms of the Earth," an outstanding fusion of fantasy and horror that was influenced by the tales of Arthur Machen. The two definitive collections of his stories are *Skull-Face and Others* (1946) and *The Dark Man* (1963).

Fritz Leiber
(1910—)

Fritz Leiber worked at a number of jobs before becoming a professional writer, including stage and film acting, preaching, and editing *Science Digest.* He is perhaps the only writer ever to have made significant contributions on so large a scale to the fantasy, science fiction, and horror genres. His characters Fafhrd and the Gray Mouser rival Howard's Conan as models of heroic fantasy, and his science fiction stories have garnered him a combined total of 10 Hugo and Nebula awards. Leiber's smallest output has been in the horror field, but his three novels and smattering of stories are important. *Conjure Wife* (1953) is perhaps the best novel ever written on witchcraft, while *You Are All Alone* (1950) is a masterpiece of urban paranoia. *Our Lady of Darkness* (1977), which won World Fantasy Award, is a direct response to issues he raised in his groundbreaking 1941 tale of urban horror, "Smoke Ghost." His stories "Belsen Express," "Gonna Roll the Bones," "Black Gondolier," and "The Girl with the Hungry Eyes" are essential reading for any student of modern horror fiction. Leiber was honored with the Life Achievement Award at the 1976 World Fantasy Convention.

Theodore Sturgeon
(1918–1985)

Like Fritz Leiber, Theodore Sturgeon distinguished himself in the fantasy, horror, and science fiction genres. Sturgeon's career began in the pulp magazines, where he brought a quirky, idiosyncratic humor to stories published in *Astounding* and *Unknown Worlds*. His award-winning novel *More Than Human* (1953) displays the affection for humanity that became the trademark of his science fiction tales. Nearly all of Sturgeon's horror fiction has been short-story length, with "It" his one genuine monster story. A handful of his tales deal with children who either recieve ("The Professor's Teddy Bear") or inflict ("Talent" and "Shadow, Shadow on the Wall") injury as a result of their extraordinary abilities. *Some of Your Blood* (1961), concerned with the vampiric uses of menstrual blood, was neglected at the time of its publication but warrants reconsideration in light of the horror genre's enduring fascination with vampire stories.

Robert Bloch
(1917—)

Robert Bloch was seventeen when he sold his first short story to *Weird Tales*. Though probably the most talented of Lovecraft's young correspondents, Bloch outgrew Lovecraft's strong influence and became a distinguished writer of horror, light fantasy, mystery, and science fiction. His interest in the psychopathology of evil, evident in early *Weird Tales* stories like "Slave of the Flames," "One Way to Mars," "Yours Truly, Jack the Ripper," and "Enoch," led eventually to the creation of such outstanding novels of psychological suspense as *The Scarf* (1947), *Psycho* (1959), and *Firebug* (1961). Bloch is usually thought of as horror's humorist for larding his fiction with malapropisms, puns, and endings that are horrific variations on figures of speech, but he is also one of the most outspoken critics on the explicitness of contemporary horror literature and film. He has written two sequels to his most famous novel, *Psycho II* (1982) and *Psycho House* (1990). An introduction to his vast short fiction output is the three-volume *Selected Stories of Robert Bloch* (1987). Bloch was awarded the Life Achievement Award at the First World Fantasy Convention in 1975.

Ray Bradbury
(1920—)

The bulk of Ray Bradbury's horror fiction appeared in *Weird Tales,* during the same years that he was trying to break into the science fiction market. The stories collected into his first book *Dark Carnival* (1947), which Stephen King has called *"The Dubliners* of American horror," represent a watershed in American horror fiction that separates the loud legacy of pulp horror from the quiet, intensified forebodings of modern horror fiction. Except for *Something Wicked This Way Comes* (1962), Bradbury all but gave up writing horror by 1950 to concentrate on his science fiction novels *Farenheit 451* (1951) and the elegiac *The Martian Chronicles* (1950). Occasional horror pieces can be found in his collections *Long After Midnight* (1976) and *The Toynbee Convector* (1988). Bradbury wrote the screenplay for John Huston's film adaptation of *Moby Dick* (1956) and, more recently, has concentrated on writing poetry. His latest novel, *A Graveyard for Lunatics* (1990), is the third installment of the autobiographical trilogy that includes *Dandelion Wine* (1957) and *Death is a Lonely Business* (1986).

Harlan Ellison
(1934—)

Harlan Ellison is science fiction's most decorated writer, a remarkable achievement when one considers that he does not write science fiction. Since the genre's New Wave movement of the 1960's, Ellison has mixed elements of science fiction, fantasy, and horror in his writing with the same postmodern abandon that marks *Dangerous Visions* (1967), his seminal anthology of experimental fiction by top fantasy and science fiction writers. A good example is his 1975 collection *Deathbird Stories,* which presents a frightening vision of the world we live in and the gods we extrapolate from it. Ellison's professional writing career began in 1956. Since then he also has distinguished himself as an editor, social critic, and screenwriter. His collections *I Have No Mouth and I Must Scream* (1967), *The Beast that Shouted Love at the Heart of the World* (1969), *Strange Wine* (1978), and the World Fantasy Award Winning *Angry Candy* (1988) contain some of the most potent imaginative fiction written in the last 30 years. Ellison also earned Bram Stoker Awards from the Horror Writers of America for his collections *The Essential Ellison* (1988) and *Harlan Ellison's Watching* (1989).

Ramsey Campbell
(1946—)

Just as it once used to be said that no one could compile a representative anthology of American horror fiction without including stories by H. P. Lovecraft or Edgar Allan Poe, now it can be said with the same certainty that any anthology of modern horror that lacks a story by British author Ramsey Campbell is flawed. Campbell published his first book, *The Inhabitant of the Lake and Less Welcome Tenants,* in 1964. His seminal collection *Demons by Daylight* (1973) marked his break with the influence of Lovecraft and announced one of the most original and profoundly disturbing voices in contemporary horror fiction. Campbell's atmospheric tales of modern horror have been collected into *The Height of the Scream* (1976), *Dark Companions* (1982), *Scared Stiff* (1987), and *Dark Feasts* (1987). He has also distinguished himself as one of the horror genre's most intelligent novelists, combining the principles of traditional horror literature with his unique contemporary perspective in *The Nameless* (1981), *Incarnate* (1983), *The Influence* (1987), and *Midnight Sun* (1990). Campbell is a two-time winner of the World Fantasy Award and a four-time winner of the British Fantasy Award.

Charles L. Grant
(1942—)

When discussing Charles Grant's legacy to modern horror it is difficult to decide which is greater, his contributions as an editor or a writer. Grant called his ten-year career as a science fiction writer quits in 1977, and since then has produced nearly twenty horror novels and story collections, including eight novels and three collections of novellas set in his fictional town of Oxrun Station. Grant also has written several novels of atmospheric horror set in the beach communities of his native New Jersey, including *The Pet* (1986), *For Fear of the Night* (1988), *In a Dark Dream* (1989), and *Stunts* (1990). Through his stories and novels, Grant chronicles the experiences of people whose efforts to adapt to social and personal change plunge them into a world of terrifying uncertainties. His intimate brand of subtle, deeply personalized horror has strongly influenced the ten critically acclaimed *Shadows* anthologies that he edited between 1978 and 1988, and which define the school of "dark fantasy" that has served as the dominant mode of literate horror fiction for the last decade. Grant is a three-time winner of the World Fantasy Award and writes humorous fantasy under the pseudonym Lionel Fenn.

Stephen King
(1947—)

Like Edgar Allan Poe, Stephen King is an American institution who needs no introduction. King's 1974 novel *Carrie* and its successful film adaptation two years later are in large part responsible for the modern horror boom. Under his own name, the pen name Richard Bachman, and in collaboration with Peter Straub, King has written nearly 20 novels, almost all of which have achieved bestseller status. Novels such as *The Shining* (1977), *The Stand* (1978), and *The Dead Zone* (1979) were a major factor in turning modern horror from a short story- to novel-oriented branch of fiction. In later novels such as *Pet Sematary* (1983), *It* (1986), and *Misery* (1987), King presents a view of the American landscape in which nothing in our lives—our homes, our schools, our pets, our families, our favorite diners—is immune from influence of horror. King has also written the Dark Tower trilogy, a series of stories set in a postapocalyptic world that includes *The Dark Tower* (1982), *The Drawing of the Three* (1987), and *The Wasteland* (1991). A generous sampling of his short fiction is available in *Night Shift* (1978), *Different Seasons* (1982), *Skeleton Crew* (1985), and *Four Past Midnight* (1990). His non-fiction book *Danse Macabre* (1981) is one of the best popular studies of horror's enduring appeal.